The Kushnameh

The publisher and the University of California Press Foundation gratefully acknowledge the generous support of the Joan Palevsky Endowment Fund in Literature in Translation.

The Kushnameh

The Persian Epic of Kush the Tusked

———

Iranshah ibn Abu'l-Khayr

Introduced by Kaveh L. Hemmat and Hee Soo Lee
Translated by Kaveh L. Hemmat
Edited by Hee Soo Lee

UNIVERSITY OF CALIFORNIA PRESS

University of California Press
Oakland, California

© 2022 by Hee Soo Lee

Library of Congress Cataloging-in-Publication Data

Names: Īrānshāh ibn Abī al-Khayr, active 11th century, author. |Hemmat,
    Kaveh L., translator. | Yi, Hŭi-su, editor.
Title: The Kushnameh : the Persian epic of Kush the Tusked / Iranshah ibn
    Abu'l-Khayr; introduced by Kaveh L. Hemmat and Hee Soo Lee ;
    translated by Kaveh L. Hemmat ; edited by Hee Soo Lee.
Other titles: Kūshnāmah. English
Description: [Oakland, California] : [University of California Press], [2022] |
    Includes bibliographical references and index.
Identifiers: LCCN 2021038164 (print) | LCCN 2021038165 (ebook) |
    ISBN 9780520385306 (paperback) | ISBN 9780520385313 (ebook)
Subjects: LCSH: Epic poetry, Persian—Translations into English.
Classification: LCC PK6477.I68 K8713 2022 (print) | LCC PK6477.I68 (ebook) |
    DDC 891/.5511—dc23/eng/20211122
LC record available at https://lccn.loc.gov/2021038164
LC ebook record available at https://lccn.loc.
gov/2021038165ClassifNumber   PubDate
DeweyNumber'—dc23   CatalogNumber

Manufactured in the United States of America
28   27   26   25   24   23   22
10   9   8   7   6   5   4   3   2   1

CONTENTS

Contents

ACKNOWLEDGMENTS

In the early 2000s, while working with Iranian scholars to locate material related to ancient and medieval Korea described in Persian manuscripts, I came across *The Kushnameh*, a Persian epic and part of a mythical history of Iran written by Iranshah b. Abu'l-Khayr between the years 1108 and 1111. Not only was the book not well known to Korean scholars, but I was surprised to learn that the land of "Besila" that appears in the book refers to the ancient Korean kingdom of Silla. As a scholar who has studied historical encounters between Korea and the Middle East, the Besila story in *The Kushnameh*, although in the form of an epic romance, was of extraordinary interest to me. I thus worked with Daryoosh Akbarzadeh to translate the parts of *The Kushnameh* set in Korea into Korean, using Jalāl Matīnī's edition of the text. As a result of this work, over the past decade, three international conferences on *The Kushnameh* were held in Seoul, Tehran, and Istanbul.

It was my great luck to meet Kaveh Hemmat, and I suggested he translate *The Kushnameh* into English in order to share it with a wider audience of researchers and readers. With the support of the Korean Studies Promotion Services, in 2017 Dr. Hemmat began this translation, based on the British Library manuscript, OR 2780. Thanks to his efforts, I hope that the scholarly world and ordinary readers with an interest in Persian literature and historical interactions between Korea and the Middle East will find this book useful.

In truth, our research on *The Kushnameh*, including this translation, would not have been possible without generous support from the government of Korea. This work was supported by the Laboratory Program for Korean Studies through the Ministry of Education of the Republic of Korea and by the Korean Studies Promotion Service of the Academy of Korean Studies (AKS 2015 LAB 1250001).

Finally, special words of appreciation go to Nam-Kyu Min and Kyoo Chul Moon, both of whom provided unwavering support and patient advice throughout the research process. I would also like to thank the University of California Press for their interest in the book, especially Eric Schmidt and the editorial staff for their professional advice and cooperation during all stages of production.

Hee Soo Lee
June 2021

The present work is only one of the more visible results of a long, collaborative endeavor, and I am grateful for the support of Hee Soo Lee and other members of the project for all their work. I would like to thank Cameron Cross and Austin O'Malley, much more knowledgeable scholars of Persian literature than myself, for their early feedback on the translation. My thinking about the text has benefited greatly from conversation with colleagues in the Great Lakes Adiban Society, including Alexandra Hoffmann, Rachel Schine, Sam Lasman, and Paul Losensky. Special thanks are due to editors Eric Schmidt and Cindy Fulton and copyeditor Caroline Knapp for their patience, diligence, and speed in helping to bring this volume to the public. I would also like to thank my father, Amrollah Hemmat, a far more accomplished translator than myself, for encouraging me to take on this project with the advice that one learns the art of translation from the many hours spent doing the work. I wish to express gratitude and appreciation to my young daughter, Veda, for her patience while I was at the computer even more than usual, and for her persistent curiosity, which brings me joy every day. Finally, and most of all, I would like to thank my partner, Özge Kocak Hemmat, the love of my life, for her encouragement, patience, and feedback, for being not only my closest and dearest companion, but a partner in reading and thinking.

Kaveh Hemmat
June 2021

NOTE ON THE TEXT

The present translation is based on the sole manuscript of the *Kushnameh,* held in the British Library, OR 2780. The line numbers follow Jalāl Matīnī's edition, and manuscript folio numbers are provided in brackets. The manuscript has a number of section headings, which appear in capitals; additional section headings added for this edition are marked with square brackets. The section headings in OR 2780 do not always appear consistently, except in the case of the letters written by characters in the story, which do, as a rule, have section headings. For the reader's convenience, the book has been divided into numbered chapters defined by major transition points. Unreadable passages and apparent lacunae in the manuscript are marked with ellipses.

Introduction

The Kushnameh, meaning *The Epic of Kush*, is an epic about a monstrous king with tusks and ears like an elephant. The story takes place across a vast geography that spans most of the Eastern Hemisphere, from China and Korea in the east to the Pyrenees and the Sahara in the west. Insofar as one can speak of medieval globalization—a process of encounter and increasing connectedness driven by the rise of diverse literate, urban societies across the Eastern Hemisphere, and an increasing consciousness of how large and how diverse the world was—*The Kushnameh* can be considered an epic of the global Middle Ages.

The Kushnameh not only reflects, but also *reflects on* the great size and diversity of the world and its peoples. As part of a deeply political literary tradition in which kingship is a core theme, *The Kushnameh* grapples with the intellectual and political challenges and opportunities these discoveries posed for the imperial traditions of Persia, Rome, and Islam. Building on the Sistani epic cycle—heroic stories that made up the most famous portions of great Persian *Epic of Kings (The Shahnameh)*—and on the example of Pseudo-Callisthenes's *Alexander Romance*, *The Kushnameh* enlarges both the geography and thematic depth of the epic tradition. However, it also does not represent a full-fledged transformation of the epic tradition into the erudite, cerebral, virtuosic works that would be undertaken by later poets such as

Nezami of Ganja and Amir Khosrow of Delhi. Instead, it stands somewhere in the middle: a heroic epic full of action and drama that ventures beyond the already rich example of *The Shahnameh* to explore both the most distant corners of the known world and the depths of evil concealed within the human psyche.

We know almost nothing about the probable author of *The Kushnameh,* Iranshan or Iranshah b. Abu'l-Khayr. There has been some disagreement about his name, which is only known from an anonymous historical work, *The Mojmal al-Tavarikh,* whose four manuscript copies spell the name in three different ways.[1] *The Kushnameh* is dedicated to the young Seljuq sultan Mohammad b. Malekshah, and the copyist's notes identify the author of *The Kushnameh* as "the Azeri sage" *(hakim-e azari),* which may mean he came from the region of Azerbaijan.[2] Iranshah was author of another epic, about the hero Bahman, which however may not be *The Bahmannameh* that survives.[3] The text of *The Kushnameh* contains evidence the author was a Shiʿi, or strongly sympathized with Shiʿism.[4] This is remarkable, given that the Seljuq sultans had a hostile relationship to their Shiʿi neighbors including the Fatimid state that ruled Egypt, and its offshoot, the Nizari Ismaʿilis (the so-called "Assassins") who had their redoubts in the Alborz mountains. Internal evidence allows us to date *The Kushnameh* to between 1108 and 1110 CE.[5]

The text survives in only one manuscript, which is held by the British Library, dated October 1397.[6] The copyist was Mohammad b. Saʿid

---

1. Īrānshān ibn Abī al-Khayr, *Kūshnāmah,* edited by Jalāl Matīnī (Tehran: Intishārāt-i ʿIlmī, 1377 [1998]), 25–30. In his introduction, Matīnī argues for reading the name Īrānshān. Mahmūd Umīdsālār makes the opposing case that Īrānshāh is the more likely reading. Mahmūd Umīdsālār, "Yāddāshtʿhā-yi Kūshʿnāmah," *ʿUlūm-i ijtimāʿī: Farhang-i Īrānzamīn* 30 (1384 [2006]): 313–20.

2. Īrānshān, *Kūshnāmah,* 26.

3. The extant *Bahmannameh,* contained in OR 2780, may not, in fact, be the same epic about Bahman that the author of *The Kushnameh* wrote. For discussion of this issue, see Marjolijn van Zutphen, *Faramarz, the Sistani Hero: Texts and Traditions of the Farāmarznāme and the Persian Epic Cycle,* Studies in Persian Cultural History, 6 (Leiden: Brill, 2014), 134–36.

4. Īrānshān, *Kūshnāmah,* 30–31.

5. The Persian text can be read in the critical edition edited by Jalāl Matīnī, Īrānshān, *Kūshnāmah.*

6. British Library, OR 2780. For an analysis of the manuscript, see Elaine Wright, "Firdausi and More: A Timurid Anthology of Epic Tales," in *Shahnama: The Visual Lan*

b. Abdollah al-Qadari. The codex also contains Asadi-ye Tusi's *Gar-shaspnameh*, a versified history of the Mongol conquests by Ahmad-e Tabrizi called *The Shahenshahnameh*, and *The Bahmannameh*; it originally also contained the text of Ferdowsi's *Shahnameh*. Each page consists of ninety-nine couplets divided into six columns. It contains two color illustrations, very generic depictions of armored warriors added at a later date.[7] There are thus no medieval illustrations specifically for *The Kushnameh*. The depictions of Yama and other fearsome deities in Central Asian Buddhist art, as well as Islamicate paintings of demons with elephant heads, offer us an idea of how audiences may have pictured Kush.

The fact that the text survives in only one manuscript indicates that it did not enjoy wide circulation, and did not have a very large presence in the intellectual life of the medieval Islamic world—although of course any text that survived in the manuscript tradition for more than nine hundred years can be deemed relatively important, and the fact of its survival in a unique manuscript is shared by texts that today enjoy much greater fame, such as *Beowulf*. Its scarce representation in the manuscript record can be considered the result of the text's own weirdness, rather than any literary shortcomings. It is unsurprising that such a work was not a frequent object of patronage by imperial courts, which produced the great number of copies of *The Shahnameh* and later epics and romances that populate the manuscript collections of libraries today. Those works were part of a literary canon that crystallized by the fifteenth century, and served the needs of the courts, which commissioned illustrated manuscripts of high quality.[8]

The Kushnameh is a strange book, a heroic epic in form, but with a certain spiritual kinship to *The Thousand and One Nights'* underworld of demons, concubines, eunuchs, and one-eyed dervishes, of sorcery, enslavement, and exile, and even to modern horror stories—which themselves owe no small debt to *The Nights*. Bearing in mind that it was

guage of the Persian Book of Kings, edited by Robert Hillenbrand, 65–84 (Burlington: Ashgate, 2004).

7. Wright, "Firdausi and More," 70.

8. Paul E. Losensky, *Welcoming Fighānī: Imitation and Poetic Individuality in the Safavid-Mughal Ghazal*, Bibliotheca Iranica, 5 (Costa Mesa, CA: Mazda Publishers, 1998): 145–53.

a courtly work, dedicated to and reproduced for kings and princes, not a work of popular literature like *The Thousand and One Nights*, we may still classify *The Kushnameh* along with the various versions of *The Nights* as part of a body of more experimental writing, a realm of literary production more inclined to produce a great variety of different stories in different configurations, than to produce many copies of a few canonical texts. To dismiss such works because they do not, individually, survive in many manuscript copies would be to dismiss precisely what was creative and experimental in medieval Islamic literary culture.

The Kushnameh in particular is a record of a time of discovery. Iranshah rewrote old stories upon a geographical stage that had rapidly and recently been enlarged by travel and scientific investigation, as well as by dramatic economic and social change across the hemisphere, especially in East Asia.[9] By the twelfth century, the circulation of Arabic geographies across the whole Islamic world made geographical knowledge widely available.[10] Readers of Arabic in Spain could learn of the existence of a state such as Korea at—almost—the other end of the hemisphere; people in Yemen who obtained copies of geographical works could read about the Subarctic.[11] Decades earlier, the Central Asian scholar and scientist al-Biruni (973–c. 1050) had completed a measurement of the earth's circumference and speculated that there might be people living on the opposite side of the world in unknown lands.[12]

9. While there is geographical content in texts like *The Bundahišn*, which enumerates mountains and other geographical features, and in texts like *The Šahrestānihā-i Erānšahr*, which enumerates Sassanian cities, geography as a distinct discipline was likely absent from Pahlavi literature. See Dan Shapira, "Was There Geographical Science in Sasanian Iran?" *Acta Orientalia Academiae Scientiarum Hungaricae* 54, no. 2/3 (2001): 319–38; Domenico Agostini and Samuel Thrope, trans., *The Bundahišn: The Zoroastrian Book of Creation* (New York: Oxford University Press, 2020).

10. Hyunhee Park, *Mapping the Chinese and Islamic Worlds: Cross-Cultural Exchange in Pre-Modern Asia* (Cambridge: Cambridge University Press, 2012).

11. Kei Won Chung and George F. Hourani, "Arab Geographers on Korea," *Journal of the American Oriental Society* 58, no. 4 (1938): 658–61; Abū Zayd Ḥasan ibn Yazīd Sīrāfī and Aḥmad ibn Faḍlān, *Two Arabic Travel Books*, edited by Tim Mackintosh-Smith and James E. Montgomery, Library of Arabic Literature (New York: New York University Press, 2014).

12. Hakim Muhammad Al-Biruni and Ansar Zahid Khan, *Al Biruni: His Times, Life, and Works* (Delhi: B. R. Publishing, 1990), 123–36. Cited in Frederick S. Starr, *Lost Enlightenment: Central Asia's Golden Age from the Arab Conquest to Tamerlane* (Princeton, NJ: Princeton University Press, 2013), 591n174.

The *Kushnameh*'s plot, themes, and setting draw on historical memory and up-to-date knowledge of regions and states that interacted with the Islamic world, whether through trade or war. These include the Korean kingdom of Silla (57 BCE–935 CE), which gives its name to Besila, one of the most important locales in the story, Jaca, a principality in the Pyrenees that would grow into the kingdom of Aragon, and Basque country.[13] Iranshah read his geographical sources carefully, perhaps with guidance from travelers. Had he been less deliberate and programmatic in his use of geography, he might have chosen any number of toponyms for regions in China or cities in the Iberian Peninsula. Instead, he identified precisely those independent states or regions that lay just beyond the frontiers of the Islamic world, the Roman Empire, and China.[14]

So, it is important to understand that the world of this epic was both an ancient world of myth and legend—the mythic past of epic heroes who traveled the breadth of the earth—and a modern world of learning, discovery, and geopolitical conflict. Not long after al-Biruni's scientific work came the Seljuq Turks' conquest of Southwest Asia and their defeat of the Byzantine Roman Empire at the Battle of Manzikert, which led to Turkic conquest and settlement of Anatolia, and a few decades later, the Crusades. Iranshah likely believed that history was cyclical, and that the present repeated the past. But that did not mean the present was the same as the past, and the names, places, and actions of the characters in the various parts of the main narrative and the double frame tale conspicuously belong to distinct period settings.

13. These terms may have been derived from Ibrāhīm ibn Muḥammad Iṣṭakhrī and M. J. de Goeje, *Kitāb masālik al-mamālik*, 3rd ed., photomechanice iterata (Leiden: Brill, 1967). On the name of Korea, see Mohammad Bagher Vosooghi, "Silla, Basilla, or Bosilla: New Findings Concerning Korea from Persian Manuscripts," in *Proceedings of the 1500 Years of Korean-Iranian Cultural Encounters Based on the Persian Epic Kush-Nāmeh*, 100–13 (Seoul: Hanyang University, 2013). On Jaca and Basque country, see Daniel König, *Arabic-Islamic Views of the Latin West: Tracing the Emergence of Medieval Europe* (Oxford: Oxford University Press, 2015), 301.

14. Northern Spain had been assumed until recently not to have seen settlement by Muslim populations; however discovery of Muslim burials shows substantial local populations in Tauste, north of Zaragoza. See Guede et al. "Isotope Analyses to Explore Diet and Mobility in a Medieval Muslim Population at Tauste (NE Spain)," *PLoS ONE* 12, no. 5 (2017): 1–27.

Knowledge of one era could enable greater understanding of other eras, the present, and even the future.

Was there a global Middle Ages, and did globalization begin around the year 1000 CE, as recent scholarly conversations and works have proposed?[15] What *The Kushnameh*, as a literary work, can tell us is that some people at the time *knew* they were living in a larger and more interconnected world than that of their ancestors. Both Korea and Spain, peninsulas at the far ends of the Afro-Eurasian landmass, appear in the story as island paradises (the Perso-Arabic term, *jazireh*, can mean either a peninsula or an island). Korea, in particular, is reached by the virtuous king, Abtin, through a set of plot twists reminiscent of the frame stories by which utopia is reached in More's *Utopia* and derivative works. *The Kushnameh* was completed about twenty years before the first appearance of the Prester John legend, the rumor of a powerful Christian king in Central Asia that circulated widely in Europe during and after the Crusades. The depiction of Prester John's kingdom in the fourteenth century text, *The Travels of Sir John of Mandeville,* has been interpreted as a medieval European utopia. The concept of an island paradise, which also anticipates Marco Polo's island of Cypangu, whose gold Columbus sought, certainly draws on travelers' tales, and may have been influenced by Daoist legends of Islands of the Eastern Sea.

Utopian rumors were fed by authentic travelers' lore. *The Kushnameh* was written in a time when China, under the Song Dynasty, had witnessed rapid technological change, and scarcely resembled the land of China portrayed in older Persian texts. Foundries there had begun to use coal for fuel, producing steel in unprecedented quantities, while improved shipbuilding techniques and the invention of the compass, gunpowder, and printing would soon begin to transform travel, warfare, and the circulation of knowledge worldwide. Porcelain supplanted silk as the iconic and inimitable product of Chinese craftspeople. The Islamic world was at least broadly aware of this technological transformation. China, with its large and prosperous population of Muslim merchants, was portrayed in Islamic literatures as a land of master

15. Valerie Hansen, *The Year 1000: When Explorers Connected the World—and Globalization Began* (New York: Scribner, 2020).

craftsmen and a font of knowledge.[16] Chinese civilization was under-stood by some Muslim thinkers to be the product of human invention, not prophetic revelation.[17] In Iranshah's epic vision, the *sources* of uto-pia—the island paradise of Korea—are both the journey and the act of invention, the operation of human reason across a vast, agreeable world.

THE MEDIEVAL PERSIAN EPICS AND THEIR HISTORICAL CONTEXT

To make sense of how and why *The Kushnameh* was written, and how it was read, we must look back to Ferdowsi's *Epic of Kings (The Shahnameh),* completed a century earlier in 1010 CE, and the earlier background of how Persian became the second most prevalent written language of the Islamic world. *The Shahnameh,* more than any other single text, represented the revival of the Persian imperial tradition after the Islamic conquests, and provided a foundation for later epics, ranging from the more light-hearted, heroic fare of the epic romances, to Nezami-ye Ganjavi and Amir Khosrow's didactic and philo-sophical Alexander epics, to elaborately crafted courtly romances. *The Shahnameh's* tale of Persian kings and heroes from the dawn of humanity to the Islamic conquests was the backdrop against which the strange tale of the monstrous Kush was written and read. *The Shahnameh* advanced a compelling vision of the political order, one which privileged aristocratic lineage *(nezhad)* and the exalted but problematic status of kings. Understanding this political vision is essential to understanding the significance of events and characters in *The Kushnameh.*

The Islamic conquests of the mid-seventh century seized the Roman Empire's most populous and wealthiest territories, Egypt, Palestine, and Syria, and completely eliminated the Sassanian Persian empire. Peroz, son of the last Sassanian ruler, Yazdegerd III, fled to China and

16. Francesco Calzolaio, "China, the Abode of Arts and Crafts: Emergence and Dif-fusion of a Persian Saying on China in Mongol Eurasia," *Ming Qing Yanjiu* 22 (2019): 136–54. The prophetic tradition *(hadith),* "Seek knowledge even unto China," consid-ered inauthentic by Muslim scholars, was nonetheless invoked in texts such as *The Kushnameh* (lines 45–50).

17. Tarif Khalidi, *Islamic Historiography: The Histories of Mas'ūdī* (Albany: State University of New York Press, 1975), 110–13.

he and his descendants were supported there for several decades.[18] The first dynasty of caliphs, the Umayyads, depended heavily on the administrative expertise of the Middle Persian-speaking Sassanian scribal class, now subjugated by the Arab conquerors in this new, Islamic political order. In 750 CE, a coalition of rebels overthrew the Umayyads and brought to power the Abbasid Caliphate. The revolutionaries included Persian-speaking converts as well as Shi'is, Muslims who believed that the caliphs elected after Muhammad's death by leaders of the Muslim community were not its rightful rulers, and that instead, Muhammad's son-in-law, 'Ali b. Abu Taleb, had been designated as his successor, and he and his descendants were the rightful rulers.

The Abbasid caliphs ultimately turned on the Shi'is, but their government incorporated Arab and Persian Muslims on essentially equal terms. Arabic was still the official, cosmopolitan language of the Abbasid Caliphate and became the host language for translations of a vast range of literature, from works of Greek philosophy to *The Fables of Bidpai*, a Middle Persian translation of the Sanskrit *Panchatantra* known in Arabic as *Kalilah wa Dimnah*. The Abbasid capital of Baghdad, founded in 760 not far from the site of the Sassanian administrative capital, Ctesiphon, became a cultural and commercial entrepôt. By the ninth century, Arabic geographies described regions spanning most of the Eastern Hemisphere.

The Abbasids lost effective political power in 942 CE, when the Buyids, a Shi'i dynasty from the forested Caspian coast, took over and made the Abbasid caliphs their puppets. The Islamic world would henceforth remain divided between rival kingdoms, many of which nonetheless, like the Buyids, recognized the Abbasid caliphs as the nominal sovereigns of all Muslims and ostensibly governed on their behalf. These successor kingdoms included the Fatimid Imamate, based in Cairo, a Shi'i state whose rulers denied the legitimacy of the caliphs and claimed that they were themselves descendants and successors to Muhammad, with absolute authority over matters doctrinal and legal, as well as the Samanid Dynasty, which had asserted inde-

18. Yingjun Liu, "Possible Connections Between Historical Events and the Plots of Iranian Princes Exiled in Chīn and B.Sīlā Depicted in Kūshnāma," *Acta Koreana* 21, no. 1 (2018): 37–63.

pendence from the Abbasids in Transoxiana and present-day Afghanistan but remained nominally loyal to them.

Samanid ideology was founded on a revival of Sassanian imperial traditions, including courtly poetry in an eastern dialect of Persian—written in the Arabic script and incorporating a large number of Arabic loan words—which modern scholars call New Persian to distinguish it from the Middle Persian (Pahlavi) of the Sassanian Empire, and the Old Persian spoken in the time of Cyrus the Great. The oldest surviving example of New Persian is in fact a document from the eighth century, written in Hebrew script by a Jew from Khotan, quite far east of the Samanid domains—evidence that Persian in Central Asia had been gradually transformed through the adoption of Arabic terms after the conquests.[19] The Persian turn of Samanid court culture was not a rejection of Islam or of Arabic literary culture. Instead, the Samanids advanced a process of converting the Sassanian imperial tradition, a byword of which was "kingship and religion are twins," into a religiously amphibious political tradition that offered formulations of kingship stripped of their Zoroastrian character and adaptable for use by both Muslim and non-Muslim rulers. Over the next seven hundred years, New Persian would become a cosmopolitan language: an increasingly important language of public affairs and religious instruction in a vast triangular region stretching from the Balkans to the Deccan in Southern India to the Gansu Corridor in northwestern China, as well as for Muslims throughout China.[20]

It was under Samanid patronage that Abu'l-Qasem Ferdowsi, a native of Tus (present-day Mashhad, Iran), began composing the *Epic of Kings (The Shahnameh),* which memorialized and codified the histories of Iranian kings and heroes related both in Middle Persian texts and in Arabic histories such as Tabari's *History of Kings and Prophets.*[21] The

19. British Library, OR 8212/166. Bo Utas, "The Jewish-Persian fragment from Dandan-Uiliq," *Orientalia Suecana* 17 (1968 [1969]): 123–36.

20. For an overview of the spread of Persian, see the essays in Nile Green, ed., *The Persianate World: The Frontiers of a Eurasian Lingua Franca* (Oakland: University of California Press, 2019).

21. Ṭabarī, General Introduction, *and,* From the Creation to the Flood, translated by Franz Rosenthal, vol. 1 of *The History of Al-Ṭabarī* (Albany: State University of New York Press, 1988).

home of these Iranian world-kings is called Iranzamin or Iranshahr. These toponyms are imprecise and correspond roughly to the territory of the Sassanian Empire, including Mesopotamia, the Iranian plateau, and present-day Afghanistan—distinct from the Roman Empire in the west, and Turan, which refers to lands in the east. Scholars have found it useful to divide *The Shahnameh* into "mythic," "heroic," and "historical" sections or eras, the first heavily rooted in the Avesta (the oldest body of Zoroastrian scripture), the latter two making up the great majority of the text. A cyclical view of history is essential to Zoroastrian cosmology, and there are many self-evident parallels between characters and events in different eras in the epic. The heroic section includes stories of epic heroes like Rostam, called the Sistani heroes, because they were associated with the province of Sistan located in the southeast of present-day Iran and southern Afghanistan. In the heroic section, Turan, which includes the lands of the Turks and China—the domain of Kush in *The Kushnameh*—is the principal enemy of the Iranian kings.

The heroic section is followed by a brief narrative of Alexander of Macedon based on the *Alexander Romance* of Pseudo-Callisthenes, followed immediately by a much longer narrative of the Sassanian rulers that ends with the Arab conquests. The Seleucid (312–63 BCE) and Parthian (247 BCE–224 CE) eras are essentially omitted. The historical sections tell of the wars and other interactions between the Sassanian kings and their rivals, including the Roman Empire (Rum) and Chin, a term which can refer to China, but in these texts often refers to Central Asia, reflecting the reality of nomadic Tabghach rule over China's heartland during the fifth century.

WORLDVIEWS OF *THE SHAHNAMEH* AND EPIC ROMANCES

The Shahnameh, along with the other epics and epic romances composed in the eleventh century and later, drew on a large common body of Middle Persian oral and textual sources, including a Sassanian-era work called *The Khwadaynamag (Book of Kings),* through which each epic expressed its own political and aesthetic vision.[22] *The Shahnameh* is

22. Dick Davis, "The Problem of Ferdowsi's Sources." *Journal of the American Oriental Society* 116, no. 1 (1996): 53–56; Zutphen, *Faramarz, the Sistani Hero,* 138–42.

often thought of as an Iranian national epic that glorified the ancient rulers of the Persian empire after centuries of Arab rule and thus kept alive an Iranian national identity during another eight centuries of rule by Turkic and Mongol dynasties. This reading has increasingly been challenged. Not only is interpreting a medieval epic through modern national identities anachronistic, but why would Mongol conquerors and later Turkic rulers promote an epic if one of its core messages was that they were foreign usurpers? In an Islamic context, *The Shahnameh* may be best understood as an imperial epic that put the legacy of the Persian empire at the disposal of dynasties from Oghuz Turkic, Mongol, or other lineages. Looking back to *The Shahnameh*'s sources in an older oral epic tradition and the Sassanian-era *Book of Kings*, its cosmopolitan imperial vision was based on the Sassanians' "vision of a global political order" based on Zoroastrian cosmology, which positioned the Iranian world-kings as "guarantors of the peace and prosperity of the entire world."[23] The *Book of Kings,* like the other sources that *The Shahnameh* and *The Kushnameh* were based on, articulated the cosmological functions of kingship by narrating kings' successes and failures.[24]

Social hierarchy was central to this cosmology. Aristocratic lineages were an essential, foundational component of the older political order. Establishing genealogies of living dynasts through legendary ancestors was an important part of the process by which Persians, Arabs, and other social groups were constructed and negotiated their membership within a common Islamic community.[25] The concept of *nezhad,* lineage, held central importance in the epic: an individual's lineage determined their character and, to a great extent, their actions and their destiny.[26]

23. Richard Payne, "Cosmology and the Expansion of the Iranian Empire, 502–628 CE." *Past and Present* 220 (August 2013): 3–33, 8.

24. Payne, "Cosmology and the Expansion of the Iranian Empire," 14.

25. On the process of identity-formation as a whole, see Sarah Bowen Savant, *The New Muslims of Post-Conquest Iran: Tradition, Memory, and Conversion,* Cambridge Studies in Islamic Civilization (New York: Cambridge University Press, 2013). See also Patricia Crone's analysis of accounts of Mazdak as an ancient communist in Patricia Crone, *The Iranian Reception of Islam: The Non-Traditionalist Strands: Collected Studies in Three Volumes.* Islamic History and Civilization, 130, vol. 2 (Leiden: Brill, 2016), 19.

26. See Edmund Hayes, "The Death of Kings: Group Identity and the Tragedy of Nezhād in Ferdowsi's Shahnameh," *Iranian Studies* 48, no. 3 (2015): 369–93, for in-depth discussion of this concept.

Although the Samanids, Ferdowsi's original patrons, were not Shiʻi, Shiʻi sympathies had long been entangled with Persian and even Zoroastrian revivalism, and the epic's strong emphasis on lineage dovetails with the core conviction of Shiʻis that the rightful leaders of the Muslim community were ʻAli's descendants.[27] There is also internal and external evidence that Ferdowsi was Shiʻi.[28]

Two major axes of conflict in *The Shahnameh* and related texts are the cosmic struggle between good and evil, and the conflicting moral imperatives of duty to one's ruler and individual moral integrity. The first axis of conflict does align with glorification of legendary Persian emperors, but this is the dominant theme only in the "mythic" sections of the epic. The theme of cosmic struggle between good and evil is certainly not absent from the much longer "heroic" and "historical" sections, but the second axis of conflict—between hierarchy and moral integrity—becomes more important.

From the beginning of *The Shahnameh* and through the earlier chapters, the cosmic principle of good is embodied in the lineage of world-kings, beginning with Gayomard, a being who gave rise to the first humans in Zoroastrian scriptures, and who in *The Shahnameh* is the first king. The later good kings are descendants of Gayomard, and this lineage *(nezhad)* is repeatedly invoked as a necessary qualification for kingship. The greatest world-king, Jamshid, presides over an Edenic era of perfect justice, in which death and disease are gone from the world. He then claims to be God, falls from grace, and is replaced by the tyrant Zahhak, who makes Jerusalem his capital. Ferdowsi's spelling of Zahhak is conspicuously Arabic (similar to how a name with umlauts would read as conspicuously German to English-speakers). The character of Zahhak, who has snakes growing from his shoulders, is based on the evil dragon king of the Avesta.

When Zahhak comes to power, Jamshid flees to the east and hides until he is caught and killed near the Sea of China. Eventually, Faridun, son of Abtin, who is a descendant of Jamshid's father, Tahmuras,

27. Sean W. Anthony, "Chiliastic Ideology and Nativist Rebellion in the Early ʻAbbāsid Period: Sunbādh and Jāmāsp-Nāma," *Journal of the American Oriental Society* 132, no. 4 (2012): 641–55.

28. Khaleghi-Motlagh, Djalal. "Ferdowsi, Abuʻl-Qasem: 1. Life," *Encyclopaedia Iranica*, 2012, https://www.iranicaonline.org/articles/ferdowsi-i. Accessed June 6, 2021.

emerges from the region of Mount Damavand near the Caspian coast. Faridun is based on the dragon-slaying king, Thraētaona, of the Avesta. His father having been killed by Zahhak's agents, his mother, Faranak, had him nursed by a cow, Barmayeh. Faridun rises up to overthrow Zahhak and restore the rule of good kings.[29] The Faridun cycle can be considered the legendary background for the main narrative of *The Kushnameh,* which begins with the story of Abtin.

The Shahnameh has a well-defined moral geography that identifies the lineage of good and evil kings with known places and events. Jerusalem, the capital of the Arab tyrant Zahhak, while of course a sacred city in Islam, was also closely identified with Christianity, the religion of the Roman Empire, the main rival of the Sassanians. Just as Jamshid flees east, the last members of the Sassanian dynasty took refuge in the Tang court in China. Just as Faridun returns after having been sheltered in the east, the Abbasid revolution that ended Umayyad rule began in the east, in Khorasan (corresponding roughly to present-day Afghanistan), and just as Faridun was traditionally said to be born and raised on Mount Damavand, the Buyids' takeover of the Abbasid caliphate in 942 also began near the Caspian coast. The cosmological association between great kings and the sun rising in the east—*ex oriente lux*—may also have influenced the story of Faridun and, later on, that of Siyavash (see below). The epic's sense of time is cyclical, and its moral geography invites interpretation of the "legendary" sections as allegories for relatively recent events, as well as templates for staging a future revolution.[30]

This brings us to a second major axis of conflict: the dilemmas faced by good heroes who serve highly flawed kings. *The Shahnameh* has been received as a pro-monarchical text that glorifies the legendary Persian emperors as biological or cultural ancestors of current rulers. Evidence from manuscript paintings confirms that even

29. Jalāl Matīnī, "Rivāyat'hā-yi mukhtalif dar bārah-i dawrān-i kūdakī va nawjavānī-yi Farīdūn," *Iran 'namah* 4, no. 1 (1364) [1986]: 78–132, 88–96.

30. For example, in the late fifteenth century, the Safavid state founder Shah Esma'il I was given refuge, as a child, in a fortress in the Caspian coastal region of Gilan, and his march out of Gilan was remembered as the triumphal beginning of his reign as Safavid Shah. Michel M. Mazzaoui, *The Origins of the Ṣafawids: Šī'ism, Ṣūfism, and the Ġulāt,* Freiburger Islamstudien, 3 (Wiesbaden: F. Steiner, 1972), 79–81.

unsympathetic kings in the epic were objects of reverence.[31] But its most important characters were not the kings but the warrior heroes *(pahlavan)*—noble Sistani paladins, such as Rostam. Many scholars have accepted Dick Davis's view that the epic places greater emphasis on the dilemmas misguided kings create for the heroes than on the kings' glory.[32]

Rostam and other Sistani heroes were the subject of other, often anonymous epic romances, written in the same heroic meter as *The Shahnameh,* that appeared starting later in the eleventh century.[33] These include *The Garshaspnameh, The Faramarznameh,* and *The Bahmannameh*—all, like *The Kushnameh,* named for their title characters. Such works do not attempt to recreate the cosmic scope of *The Shahnameh,* but instead tell the stories of individual heroes.[34] They often are more light-hearted in tone, and have distant settings, such as "India" (Hend) which includes both South Asia and the islands of the Indian Ocean, not unlike the European concept of "the Indies."[35] On a formal level, *The Kushnameh* belongs to this group of epic romances, however its tone and thematic content are more serious, and its chronology more properly epic in character.

A great part of the content of *The Shahnameh,* as well as of *The Kushnameh,* concerns politics, statecraft, and warfare, including battlefield tactics.[36] Part of this content, including *The Kushnameh'*s depiction of espionage, is similar to texts on statecraft such as *The Book of Government (Siyasatnameh),* written by the Seljuq grand minister

---

31. Francesca Leoni, "Picturing Evil: Images of Divs and the Reception of the *Shahnama,*" in *Shahnama Studies II: The Reception of Firdausi's Shahnama,* edited by C. P. Melville and Gabrielle Rachel Van den Berg, 101–18, Studies in Persian Cultural History, 2 (Leiden: Brill, 2012), 111.

32. Dick Davis, *Epic and Sedition: The Case of Ferdowsi's Shāhnāmeh* (Fayetteville: University of Arkansas Press, 1992).

33. For a detailed and ambitious study of these epics, see Zutphen, *Faramarz, the Sistani Hero,* 62–144.

34. Zutphen, *Faramarz, the Sistani Hero,* 65.

35. Saghi Gazerani, *The Sistani Cycle of Epics and Iran's National History: On the Margins of Historiography,* Studies in Persian Cultural History, 7 (Leiden: Brill, 2016), 55–61.

36. Matīnī catalogs these stratagems in the *Kushnameh.* Jalāl Matīnī, "Barkhī az nīranghā-yi kār-i zār dar Kūsh'nāmah (bih yād-i ustādam Zabīhullāh Safā)," *Iran'shinasi* 43, no. 11 (1378) [2000]: 649–67

Nezam al-Molk.[37] A reader or listener could thus expect to find many stories of political interactions, both violent and nonviolent, that could serve as instructive examples.[38] Other important themes, such as dynastic succession and royal lineages, are of a less practical, more theoretical nature, but still concern the foundations of kingship.

The Shahnameh and its offspring were thus a literary marriage of pen and sword that provided material for imperial ideology across the whole Balkans-Deccan-Gansu triangle, beginning with a core region including present-day Azerbaijan, Iran, Afghanistan, Turkmenistan, Uzbekistan, and Tajikistan, and establishing a wider reach over time. The political nation that the epic represented in the eleventh century and beyond included not only the Persian-speaking elite of the Iranian plateau and regions to the east, but also Turkic elites educated in Persian, and the Persian-speaking Muslim elite of South Asia.[39] Nor was this imperial culture confined to Islamic polities. Versions of the epic were produced in the Georgian and Armenian languages. The Mongol emperor Abaqa (r. 1265–82), son of Hulegu (r. 1256–65), who in his conquest of the Middle East pillaged Baghdad and had the last Abbasid caliph killed, built a palace at a former Sassanian site known as the Throne of Solomon (Takht-e Soleyman) during the 1270s, and decorated it with ceramic tiles that bore inscriptions from The Shahnameh alongside Chinese motifs such as dragons and phoenixes.[40] A tradition of making ceremonial visits and writing inscriptions on the ruins of Persepolis, which continued from the Sassanian period through the fifteenth century, and references by poets in the fourteenth and fifteenth centuries to the province of Fars, where the ruins were located, speak to how this institution of universal empire was

37. Niẓām al-Mulk. The Book of Government, or, Rules for Kings: The Siyar al-Muluk, or, Siyasat-Nama of Nizam al-Mulk, translated by Hubert Darke, 3rd ed. (London: Routledge, 2002).

38. Nasrin Askari, The Medieval Reception of the Shāhnāma as a Mirror for Princes, Studies in Persian Cultural History, 9 (Leiden: Brill, 2016).

39. Davis, Epic and Sedition.

40. Yuka Kadoi, Islamic Chinoiserie: The Art of Mongol Iran, Edinburgh Studies in Islamic Art (Edinburgh: Edinburgh University Press, 2009), 51–52; Assadullah Souren Melikian-Chirvani, "Le Livre des rois, miroir du destin. II—Takht-e Soleymān et la symbolique du Shāh-nāme," Studia Iranica 20, no. 1 (1991): 33–148

grounded in specific sites and lineages.[41] The process of making Persian a cosmopolitan language of power and authority required that the Persian imperial tradition's rootedness in local places and lineages be reconciled with growing awareness of the great size of the world. *The Kushnameh* represents an important stage in this process.

THE KUSHNAMEH AND ITS
POLITICAL CONTEXT

The following discussion of *The Kushnameh* will, as a rule, avoid revealing details of the plot, in order to preserve the dramatic quality of the narrative. Iranshah's epic contains plot twists and a sense of dramatic time that may be representative of a more novelistic approach to writing, surprising audiences not only with fresh wordplay, but with fresh characters and other narrative content. This "spoiler-free" approach should be understood as precautionary, rather than as dictating a particular reading of the text. A synopsis of the epic is available in the entry in *Encyclopaedia Iranica*.[42]

To understand the worldview represented in *The Kushnameh*, it should first be noted that the name and character of Kush are entirely absent from *The Shahnameh*, although the legends it was based on may have been known to Ferdowsi. *The Kushnameh* expands on episodes that take up only a handful of lines in *The Shahnameh*, and weaves the figure of Kush throughout much of *The Shahnameh*'s chronology.[43] The frame tale in which Alexander the Great discovers a statue of Kush corresponds to a passage in *The Shahnameh* where Alexander discovers a statue of a monstrous king in a crystalline dome. Other events of the epic, including virtually the whole second half, are extraneous to *The Shahnameh*. Iranshah claims that Kush was responsible for convincing King Kavus to undertake a foolish expedi-

41. Dominic Parviz Brookshaw, "Mytho-Political Remakings of Ferdowsi's Jamshid in the Lyric Poetry of Injuid and Mozaffarid Shiraz," *Iranian Studies* 48, no. 3 (2015): 463–87.

42. Matīnī, "Kuš-nāma," in *Encyclopaedia Iranica*, 2008, https://iranicaonline.org/articles/kus-nama-part-of-a-mythical-history-of-iran, accessed June 10, 2021; See also Zutphen, *Faramarz, the Sistani Hero*, 87–88.

43. See Matīnī, "Rivāyat'hā-yi mukhtalif dar bārah-i dawrān-i kūdakī va nawjavānī-yi Farīdūn," 88–104, for a comparison.

tion to Mazandaran—a very important section in *The Shahnameh* that includes the seven labors of Rostam. *The Shahnameh* does not mention Korea (Besila) at all, and its references to the Iberian Peninsula (Andalos) are significant, but confined to the section on Alexander. Iranshah signals his disagreement with certain fantastical or mythic elements in the legends narrated in *The Shahnameh*. He rationalizes these mythic elements, replacing the peacock-hued cow, Barmayeh, with the sage, Barmayon, who nourishes Faridun with knowledge (lines 4670–80), and the snakes that grow out of Zahhak's shoulders with cancerous growths, explained with reference to Galenic medical theory (lines 2920–30).

Iranshah tells us that he produced his epic by versifying a prose text he received from an elder sage. In the Middle Persian texts that Iranshah's work was based on, Kush represented the Kushan Empire, which ruled Bactria and other regions of Central Asia between the Iranian Plateau and the Indus Valley. The Sassanians subdued the Kushan kings and made them their vassals at the turn of the third century CE.[44] That "Kush" was a dynastic name is one explanation for why there are multiple characters named Kush, with no commentary on the repetition of the name. The frame tale and episodes involving Korea clearly were not part of this source material. With Korea and various cities in western Africa and Europe playing an important role as settings in the epic, *The Kushnameh* plays out over a modernized geography, conspicuously different from that of *The Shahnameh*, connecting the latter's legendary figures to the world of the present. Part of Iranshah's reimagining or modernizing of the epic's geography was his shifting of the main setting for the first half of the narrative from the domains of the Kushan Empire to China. References to places such as Kabul and Qandahar being within China are artifacts of that shift (lines 1810, 4889).[45]

On the other hand, while the text conveys the impression that Iranshah was modernizing and rewriting mythic narratives, we should not discount the possibility that in the twelfth century and earlier, *The Kushnameh*'s tale of Abtin—a central figure in *The Kushnameh*—was

---

44. Saghi Gazerani, "Kush-e Pildandān, the Anti-Hero: Polemics of Power in Late Antique Iran," *Iranian Studies* 52, no. 5–6 (2019): 859–901, 867–74.

45. Gazerani, "Kush-e Pildandān, the Anti-Hero," 872–74.

also an important part of the older epic tradition. The narratives Ferdowsi and Iranshah drew on had, over their millennia of history, been subject to repeated episodes of bifurcation into different regional variations and of reconciliation, as these regional variants were compiled into a master tradition. The figures of Faridun, Abtin, and Siyavash, which contain closely parallel mythic elements—an association with renewal, fertility, and restoration of justice, and for Siyavash and Abtin, magnificent horses and sacrifice—likely originated as divinities with similar roles in different regional traditions, sharing distant Indo-European roots and some Mesopotamian influences.[46] The compilers of the Avesta reconciled the parallels, or redundancies, of these figures by assigning them to different historical eras.[47] Where Ferdowsi greatly abridged the story of Abtin and emphasized Faridun, Iranshah—against the background of Ferdowsi's increasingly well-known epic—expanded on the story of Abtin. It is also possible that these competing redactions date back to the Sassanian period. In any case, given that *The Kushnameh*'s frame tale is self-evidently a work of historical fiction (see below), it appears that Iranshah and his readers were acutely aware that these epics were being put together out of many divergent historical traditions. Their attitude to their sources, and the larger epic tradition, was skeptical and critical. Moreover, myth and legend were not merely (unreliable) sources for Iranshah, but also his medium—he was writing a new myth, meant to be understood as such.

The Kushnameh has been classified as a "secondary epic" and as an "epic romance," as discussed above, and while this classification is justified by *The Kushnameh*'s organization around the story of a single character, the geography, chronology, and atmospherics of *The Kushnameh* all set it apart. Epic may be defined as the "maximal narrative of a particular society."[48] The epic romances do not aspire to the grand scope of Ferdowsi's text, which begins with Creation and ends

---

46. Prods Oktor Skaervo, "Eastern Iranian Epic Traditions I: Siyāvash and Kunāla," in *Mir Curad: Studies in Honor of Calvert Watkins*, edited by Jay Jasanoff, Craig Melchert, and Lisi Oliver, 645–58 (Innsbruck: Institut für Sprachwissenschaft, 1998).

47. Yaroslav Vassilkov, "An Iranian Myth in Eastern India: Gayōmart and the Mythology of Gayā," *Orientalia Suecana* 47 (1998): 131–49, 132.

48. Dan Ben-Amos, "Introduction," *Research in African Literatures* 14, no. 3 (1983): 277–82, 279.

with the Arab conquests. This definition is, however, applicable to the Alexander epics of Nezami-ye Ganjavi (d. 1209), which aspire to greater geographical universality and depth—and to a more cosmopolitan vision of kingship, which seeks to transcend that of Ferdowsi.[49] But while the Alexander epics define kingship in positive terms, with reason, wisdom, cunning, and inquisitiveness being combined with military leadership in the person of Alexander, *The Kushnameh* is an exploration of the limits of geography, morality, and humanity.

There is evidence of a number of other, later Persian stories of an evil king named Kush, which are different from *The Kushnameh* of Iranshah.[50] *The Kushnameh* is unusual within the Persian epic tradition, and probably also different from these other stories, because of its focus on characters whose ontological status lies somewhere between human and monster. Monstrosity in the epic represents not only cultural and moral difference, but also anxieties about lineage *(nezhad)* that are expressed less grotesquely elsewhere in the epic tradition, for example in the mixed ancestry of heroes like Rostam.[51] As an antihero, Kush is not simply a demonic foil for heroes, but both a monster we revile and a hero whose feats of strength and courage drive the plot. As a focal character in much of the epic, Kush does not simply function as an enemy or obstacle.

What preoccupied Iranshah was not only the ugliness of forbidden behaviors, but also how ugly character and physical forms are, or are not, rooted in nature *(seresht, gohar)* or lineage, and the processes of organic transformation through which natures or essences become fully realized—or transformed. The bizarre and forbidden are thus joined to the familiar and intimate. Graphic depictions of battlefield violence, such as blood flowing in rivers, or bodies crushed and dismembered, are common in the Persian epic tradition and by no means

49. On the Alexander epic, see Owen Cornwall, "Alexander and the Persian Cosmopolis, 1000–1500," PhD diss., Columbia University, 2016.

50. Fātemeh Şādeqi Naqd Ali ʿAwliyā and ʿAliAsghar Bashiri, "Bar-rasi va muqāyisah-yi dāstān-i 'Kush-i pil-dandān' dar Kush-nāmah va Ṭumārhā-yi Naqqāli," *Do māh-nāmeh-ye farhang o adabiyāt-e ʿāmmeh* 6, no. 24, 1397 [2018]: 69–90.

51. For an analysis of these themes in *The Kushnameh*, see Alexandra Hoffmann, "Visual Alterity, Monstrous Sexuality, and a Transformation: Kush, the Elephant-Eared," paper presented at Geography and Identity in Islamicate Culture Workshop, April 18, 2021.

absent from *The Kushnameh*. But what is more unusual, and remarkable, in Iranshah's writing, are portrayals of trauma and violence away
from the battlefield. Such violence is often gendered, and psychologi-
cally vivid. This vividness does not derive from elaborately developed
interiority, but from the visible motivations of his characters' betrayal
of fundamental covenants, such as that between parent and child. The
grotesqueness of *The Kushnameh*'s subject-matter, a possible motive
for its exclusion from Ferdowsi's *Shahnameh*, evokes horror rather
than humor.

The Kushnameh's preoccupation with the (sometimes monstrous)
growth of bodies and souls, with characters who are fugitives or monsters, venturing beyond the Islamic world and even beyond the frontiers of the ancient empires of Rome and China, breaks the "round[ed]
totality" or wholeness that inheres in epics as maximal narratives.[52]
While Jamshid and Alexander represent *every* king because they epit-
omize kingship, and even Rostam as the ultimate hero is reflected to a
small degree in every reader (like Odysseus, or "Nobody," as he first
identifies himself to the cyclops he has just blinded, to conceal his
identity and avoid retaliation), this simply cannot be said of Kush,
though we may certainly identify with him in particular ways at particular moments. Moreover, the pivotal events narrated in *The
Shahnameh*, such as Jamshid's death or Faridun's overthrow of Zahhak, are positioned as a narrative background for events involving
Kush and other primary characters. They are never witnessed directly;
the reader and the primary characters learn about them from letters or
second-hand reports, frames that remove the events of the narrative
from their epic backdrop.

This is not to say that Kush or Abtin are characters fully realized
with unique individual features, in the manner of modern novels.
Rather, they may be said to represent maximal narratives of evil and
cosmic forces of fertility and generation. But by telling a story that

---

52. Here I refer to Lukács's theory of epics in *Theory of the Novel*. While his theory
of the epic was mainly designed as a foil for his definition of the novel, his observations
are still useful, and the same trajectory from psychological homogeneity to interiority
and individuality that novels seek to achieve can also be found between examples of the
epic, epic romance, and novel forms. György Lukács, *The Theory of the Novel: A Historico-Philosophical Essay on the Forms of Great Epic Literature*, translated by Anna Bostock (Cambridge, MA: MIT Press, 1971).

centers monsters and fugitives, Iranshah initiates the kind of rupture between the *selves* and the *worlds* of its protagonists that, for Lukács, was essential to the novel. Kush, Abtin, and other characters of the epic live in different, mutually incompatible meaning-worlds. The debased, grotesque world of fugitives and monsters is elevated to heroic status through encounters and transformations.

The geography of the epic is also imbued with moral qualities, both monstrous and human. This moral geography makes the epic an important source for understanding the history of anti-Black racism. Alexander in the second layer of the frame tale encounters dog-headed and horse-headed peoples in a remote eastern region. In the main narrative, southern Africa is the origin of the "armies" or "Blacks" from Nubia and Beja. Some discussion of codicology is necessary here. The manuscript's orthography is inconsistent: the first and most common term used is *sepahan,* meaning "armies," however this is replaced midway through with *siyahan,* meaning Black people. The inconsistency is almost certainly the result of copyist's error—the Y has two dots whereas the P has one dot. Ferdowsi uses the term *siyahan* for similar invaders. Thus, given that "Blacks" gradually replaces "armies," it appears that the original term was "armies" *(sepahan),* and the copyist lapsed into the more common term. Given that the "armies" in question are from Beja and Nubia in Sub-Saharan Africa, even the nonracializing term here conveys the sense of a monstrous invading force. These "Black Hordes" are simply referred to collectively and, except in one instance, with no mention of their kings or leaders, who are given names for every other army in the epic. So, the difference between *sepahan* and *siyahan* is small, but worth mentioning given the importance of the themes of geography, lineage, and most of all, physical appearance. This translation uses the phrase "Black Hordes" to convey the orthographic ambiguity and the similar contextual meaning of the terms. The racial difference of the Hordes is amplified by Iranshah's imagery, which paints Black bodies as a void, without even the kind of worldly political ambition exhibited by Kush. They invade but do not rule, becoming drunk on the spoils of their conquests.

At the other end of the geographical hierarchy are Korea and Spain, that is, Besila, a corruption of Silla, a dynastic name used for Korea in Arabic and Persian geographies, and Andalos, a term indicating roughly the southern two thirds of the Iberian Peninsula. These two peninsulas at the far ends of the known world are portrayed as virtual paradises and associated with civilization and beauty. East Asia more generally is significant here as the domain of Jamshid's descendant Abtin, and thus the origin of Faridun, the messianic world-conqueror. The notion of Jamshid siring children while on the run from Zahhak occurs in *The Garshaspnameh* as well, which has Garshasp, ancestor of the Sistani heroes, descended from Jamshid and a princess of Zabolestan.[53] In a Zoroastrian context, giving the Sistani warrior heroes Jamshidian ancestry imbued them with kingly charisma (Jamshid being a scriptural figure, rather than the protagonist of entertaining tales); Iranshah extends this kingly charisma and its implied political meaning further.[54]

The rather perplexing two-layered frame tale highlights the epic's preoccupation with strangeness and novelty in a different way as well. It begins in medias res, with a character named Kush, a king ruling in Baghdad (a name used for the Sassanian capital, Ctesiphon, as well as the Abbasid capital) who must be different from the title character, dictating a fake prophecy that he will use to deceive the Roman emperor, Manush. Intriguingly, the name Manush seems to refer to the same emperor defeated by the Seljuqs at the Battle of Manzikert in 1071, Romanus IV Diogenes.[55] This story includes mosques, placing it in the Islamic era, but there was no Kush ruling Baghdad in the Islamic period, so it is impossible to pin the story to any particular time—this Kush is clearly a cipher. In his edition of the text, Matīnī assumes that the in medias res beginning was the result of a copyist's error in which

---

53. Zabolestan is a medieval name for the region between Qandahar and Ghazni, near the modern border between Afghanistan and Pakistan.

54. Gazerani, *The Sistani Cycle of Epics and Iran's National History*, 44–69.

55. Romanus IV's name is spelled Armanus in near-contemporary Arabic chronicles: see ʿIzz al-Dīn ibn al-Athīr, *Al-Kāmil fī al-tārīkh*, edited by Carolus Johannes Tornberg, vol. 10, Al-Ṭabʿah, 6 (Báyrūt: Dar Ṣādir, 1965), 65; and Ṣadr al-Dīn ʿAlī ibn Nāṣir Ḥusaynī, *The History of the Seljuq State: A Translation with Commentary of the* Akhbār al-Dawla al-Saljūqiyya, translated by Clifford Edmund Bosworth, Routledge Studies in the History of Iran and Turkey (Milton Park: Routledge, 2011), 36, 38. The name Romanus would have been awkward to pronounce in Arabic and Persian. We may infer that the name was read as a compound of *Rum-* and *-Manush*, the first syllable being read as "Rome" and omitted, yielding *Manush*. The terminal *sh* is more common than *s* in Persian names.

some verses were omitted. While this is entirely possible, such an abrupt opening to the narrative is also very much in line with the frame tales' gesture towards the unreliability and fragmentary nature of textual knowledge. Although Kush the Tusked is identified in lines 4810–20 as the grandfather of Nimrod, corresponding loosely to Genesis 10:8 ("Cush begat Nimrod")—and as a great hunter and conqueror, his character is similar to that of Nimrod—virtually nothing about any of the Kushes of the epic corresponds to other Persian or Arabic epics or histories. Iranshah is inviting us to recognize his epic as invented and fictitious, without subjecting himself to the indignity of admitting to telling tall tales.

The parallel between Kush of the frame tale and the Seljuqs is even more peculiar given the geopolitical context of the epic's composition. A major axis of conflict at the turn of the twelfth century was between the Shi'i Fatimid state, which envisioned a world united under the rule of the imams, as rightful successors and descendants of Muhammad, and the Seljuqs, who acknowledged the nominal authority of the Abbasid caliphs.[56] The two decades before the epic was written saw the First Crusade and the capture of Jerusalem—a historic defeat that would prove less consequential in the long run than Manzikert, but that must have loomed large in the minds of Iranshah and his contemporaries and contributed to a sense that the Fatimid cause was failing. The epic praises the patron and dedicatee's recent conquest of the Nizari Isma'ili (Shi'i) fortress of Shahdez. The Seljuqs dominated the Persian-speaking world, so while Shi'ism had found considerable traction among Persian-speakers, and Shi'i beliefs had been closely connected with various messianic movements that invoked the memory of the Sassanian Empire, it is not at all surprising that a Persian epic like *The Kushnameh* would be dedicated to a Seljuq ruler, even though the epic contains Shi'i mytho-political themes.

With the exception of the Fatimids, no Shi'i state had ever attained great power, and Shi'ism tended to function as a kind of umbrella for a variety of revolutionary causes. The Abbasids persecuted the Shi'i imams, so while different Shi'i groups differed on the identity and exact lineage of the true imams, one of the most important notions for

56. Those loyal to the caliphs are now often thought of as Sunnis, however "Sunni" did not exist as a confessional identity at this time.

Shi'is was that the imam, as rightful ruler of the Islamic world, remained in a state of concealment *(satr)* until his return as the *imam-mahdi* or *qa'em*. Shi'ism, both as a form of political opposition to the ruling class and as a messianic belief system, was associated with social protest and rebellion, as in the case of the Zanj Rebellion in southern Iraq, which included enslaved East Africans, and the Qarmatians of the Arabian Peninsula.[57] Even in the case of the Fatimids, who became a powerful empire, a treatise of Islamic-Aristotelian political theory representing the dynasty's political ideology instructed the ruler to champion and protect the common people, contrary to virtually all other works of this genre, which called on rulers to preserve class hierarchy.[58]

The theme of the exiled true world-king—defined both by lineage and adherence to the good religion—hiding from the currently reigning tyrants until the appointed time of his return, the plot of the Faridun cycle in *The Shahnameh* and earlier Zoroastrian scripture, and also the first half of *The Kushnameh,* was a narrative that was central to Shi'i beliefs. Furthermore, the notion that the true king would hide not simply in the wilderness but in the geographically distant margins of the known world corresponded closely to the actual history of the rise and survival of Shi'i states in the ninth through eleventh centuries. The Qarmatian Shi'i state survived in a remote part of the Arabian Peninsula, whereas the Zanj movement in Iraq was quickly conquered. The Fatimid dynasty rose to power through preaching among the non-Muslim or recently converted Imazighen in distant corners of North Africa—they established their first capital, Mahdiyah (i.e., city of the *mahdi,* an Islamic messianic figure—a reenactment of the Prophet's establishment of his new community in Medina) in Tunisia before conquering Egypt. Other Shi'i dynasties or communities existed in South Asia and Central Asia, and a rumor of 'Alids hiding

---

57. On these Shi'i revolutionary movements, see Michael Brett, *The Rise of the Fatimids: The World of the Mediterranean and the Middle East in the Fourth Century of the Hijra, Tenth Century CE* (Leiden: Brill, 2001). On the connection between Shi'i and pro-Zoroastrian or Sassanian revolutionary movements, see Patricia Crone, *The Nativist Prophets of Early Islamic Iran: Rural Revolt and Local Zoroastrianism* (New York: Cambridge University Press, 2012) and Crone, *The Iranian Reception of Islam*, vol. 2.

58. Wadād Al-Qāḍī, "An Early Fāṭimid Political Document," *Studia Islamica*, no. 48 (1978): 71–108; cited in Brett, *The Rise of the Fatimids*, 137.

in China was attested in a number of texts.[59] The whole narrative arc of *The Kushnameh,* especially the Faridun cycle, reproduces not only the master-plot of Shi'i messianism, but also a geographical imaginary based on actual Shi'i revolutionary strategies deployed over generations in the Maghreb, the Arabian Peninsula, and elsewhere.

This connection between messianic redemption and the world's geographical margins is suggested particularly in one of the few asides by the narrator, which describes inhabited places across the ocean reached by Siyavash (2400–10). This direct address to the reader resembles a corresponding passage in *The Shahnameh.* In *The Shahnameh,* Siyavash is exiled to Turan in the east. He founds a city called Kangdez, greatly resembling Besila, somewhere beyond the sea. Ferdowsi describes Kangdez in a direct address to the reader that seems to place it outside of narrative time and space. In Zoroastrian traditions, Kangdez is associated with messianic deliverance.[60] The story of Siyavash is also considered to be closely analogous to that of Imam Hussein, the most important Shi'i martyr.

The Kushnameh may be connected with those rumors about 'Alids hiding in the distant east. About two centuries after the epic was written, the geographer al-Dimashqi and the encyclopedist al-Nuwayri, writing in Mamluk Cairo, shifted the 'Alids' eastern refuge from China to Korea.[61] Whereas Iranshah follows earlier geographies in depicting Korea as an idyllic place Muslim travelers cannot bear to leave, these texts depict Korea as a desolate place lacking water. The messianic role of Korea in the epic strongly connects it to the Shi'i legend of a paradisical Green Island ruled by the imam during the period of occultation, a legend which reconfigures themes in early Shi'i literature, including arcane cities called Jabolqa and Jabolsa inhabited by archetypal believers at the extreme eastern and western corners of the world; it also links it to the legend of Prester John, as

59. Francesco Calzolaio, "'Alidi lungo la via per la Cina: Le prime comunità musulmane cinesi riflesse in una leggenda del medioevo persiano," in *Armenia, Caucaso e Asia Centrale: Ricerche 2019,* edited by Giorgio Comai et al., 163–83 (Venice: Edizioni Ca' Foscari, 2019).

60. Pavel Lurje, "Kangdez," in *Encyclopaedia Iranica,* 2010, https://iranicaonline.org/articles/kangdez-fortress-of-kang, accessed August 17, 2021.

61. Hee Soo Lee, *The Advent of Islam in Korea* (Istanbul: Research Centre for Islamic History, Art and Culture, 1997), 50–51.

noted above.[62] It is perhaps surprising that an epic dedicated to a Seljuq sultan should center a ruler in hiding, Abtin, as its most sympathetic character. It may be relevant that the epic's geography, in which Abtin appears in the east, aligns him with the Seljuqs, whereas the Fatimids arose from the far west, where Kush will eventually rule.

So, it can be said that *The Kushnameh*'s relationship to its political context, and its engagement with questions of geography, lineage, race, and politics, are complicated. In *The Kushnameh*, Black Africans are the only human group implicitly associated with demons (lines 9580–600). Other medieval texts racialized Turks, emphasizing their facial features and associating them with the peoples of Gog and Magog.[63] There is no indication in the *The Kushnameh* that the peoples of the east are generally monstrous—quite the contrary, the people of Besila are described as beautiful. However, the Kush of the frame tale, who is analogous to the Seljuq sultans as discussed above, is described as having "eyes like the sky, a face like boiling blood," a description evocative of racialized depictions of Turks. Was Iranshah calling his own patron a monster? It seems that the question of how people from distant regions of the earth could not only be part of the social order of the Islamic world, but even become its rulers, was a troubling one that engendered deep reflection. The epic that would become the most iconic for the Persian cosmopolis, written well after *The Kushnameh*, in the late twelfth century, centered the most blatantly foreign of the Iranian world-kings: Alexander of Macedon.[64]

NOTES ON METHOD OF TRANSLATION

Because of the characteristics of the text described above, and because Iranshah's style of writing emphasizes dramatic development, rather than making rhetorical devices and wordplay themselves the center of

---

62. Omid Ghaemmaghami, "To the Abode of the Hidden One: The Green Isle in Shīʿī, Early Shaykhī, and Bābī-Bahāʾī Sacred Topography," in *Unity in Diversity: Mysticism, Messianism and the Construction of Religious Authority in Islam*, edited by Orkhan Mir-Kasimov, 137–73 (Leiden: Brill, 2014), 139–41.

63. Yehoshua Frenkel, "The Turks of the Eurasian Steppes in Medieval Arabic Writing," in *Mongols, Turks, and Others: Eurasian Nomads and the Sedentary World*, edited by Reuven Amitai and Michal Biran, 201–41 (Leiden: Brill, 2005), 222–25.

64. Cornwall, "Alexander and the Persian Cosmopolis."

attention, I have translated the epic into unrhymed verse and converted this into prose. Since Iranshah's word-play is relatively minimal, I have been able to follow a strategy of hewing to the author's literal wording rather closely, without straying too far outside the bounds of idiomatic English. Following this method, two main discrepancies emerge between the author's meaning and a literal translation. First, there are redundant words and phrases that were needed to maintain the metrical scheme. These have generally been omitted. Uses of hendiadys (using two synonyms together for emphasis or aesthetic effect—e.g., "a bulky and massive elephant") are likewise often rendered as a single word. Second, in the original text, pronouns are used in place of proper names, to the point that it is often difficult to follow the dialog and sequence of actions. Proper names are typically omitted even across multiple changes of voice or subject ("He said . . . He asked . . . He responded . . . He drew his sword . . ."). So, for the sake of clarity, many pronouns have been replaced with proper names.

Images and idioms that are unconventional in English have also been preserved, so long as they are not too awkward and are intelligible in context. For example, when Kush receives good news and "his face bloom[s] like a rose," it is perfectly clear that he is very happy. Likewise, when a rider travels "swift as smoke," and when "the commander of Iran confronted us, and we raised dust over his soul" after both sides disengaged and retreated to their respective camps, directly stating the meaning of the expression in English would add little information not already apparent from a literal translation. (What translator of Homer would replace the wine-dark sea with a blue one?) My intent is that the present text can serve as a scholarly translation while also keeping its main literary qualities—not, of course, its lyricality, but its pacing, building of suspense, foreshadowing, and imagery, which are how Iranshah seems to have most exerted his energies as an author.

To convey the pronunciation of names, places, and terms as clearly as possible without using diacritical marks, I have used a system of transliteration based on the system of the *International Journal of Middle East Studies*, with diacritical marks omitted and a few other modifications: *o* replaces *u* for the short *u* sound, *e* replaces *i* for the short *i* sound, and in Persian words, names, and toponyms, the suffix *-a* is replaced by *-eh* to conform to the most common modern Persian pronunciation. The abbreviation "*b.*" is used for the Arabic patronymic prefix normally written *ibn*. For names and places with common English spellings, such as Isfahan and Yemen, the common spelling has generally been used.

The following is a brief explanation of how to pronounce Persian names using this system. The few Arabic toponyms in the text may also be pronounced in the same manner. All single consonants are simply pronounced as in English, except that *t* is always aspirated, *h* is never dropped, *r* is always rolled, as in Spanish, and *q* is pronounced the same as the double consonant *gh*. The double consonants *gh*, *kh*, and *zh* are used for sounds that do not exist or do not have single-letter equivalents in English. *Gh* is a voiced velar fricative. This is similar but not identical to the French *r*. *Kh* is a voiceless uvular fricative, pronounced like the *ch* in the German name Bach. For Anglophone readers especially challenged by the pronunciation of foreign sounds, the least-worst approximation of *q/gh*, and *kh* will be to simply pronounce these sounds as a hard *g* and *k*, respectively. Qaren is pronounced somewhat like "Gahren" and not at all like "Qua-ren" or Karen. *Zh* is pronounced like the *s* in *usually*. 'Ayn (') and hamza (') (similar in appearance to left- and right-facing apostrophes) are pronounced as a glottal stop, as in Hawai'i.

Vowels are pronounced as follows: *u* is a long *u* sound, as in *fruit; i* is a long *i* sound, as in *eat; o* is somewhere between the vowel sounds in *board* and *hood; e* is somewhere between a short *e* and short *i* sound, as in *pin* and *pen* (these phonemes are undifferentiated in Persian, as in southern dialects of American English); and *a* is pronounced like the *a* in *spa*. To most closely replicate the stress patterns of Persian, stress and enunciate each syllable equally. Syllables with long vowels are in fact enunciated and drawn out a bit more than short vowels, but they are not stressed.

Persian-speakers will note that this system elides the very important distinction between short and long *a* sounds, which have a roughly equal distribution. The pronunciation of the short *a* is closer to the *a* in *bat*, whereas the Persian long *a*, especially in the recitation of poetry or other formal speech, tends to be drawn-out and strongly enunciated, as in "Ahaaaaa!" The inability to distinguish between long and short *a*'s without diacritical marks is somewhat of an embarrassment for all of the more common transliteration systems. For the benefit of those who aspire to correct pronunciation, the following are the text's common names and toponyms with the short *a* represented by *ae* and the long *a* by *aa*: Rostaem, Gaershaasb, Faeraamaerz, Baehmaen, Siyaavaesh, Maanush, Daarnush, Maehaanesh, Jaemshid, Zaehhaak, Nunaek, Faaraek, Mehraaj, Maahaeng, Aabtin, Nivaasb, Behmaerd, Behaek, Taeyhur, Aazorgoshaesb, Faeraaraeng, Negaarin, Aenushin, Faeridun, Saelkot, Kaamdaad, Baermaayon, Nushaan, Kaenʿaan, Naerimaan, Taelimaan, Kaarem, Naestuh, Qobaad, Qaaren, Qaeraa, Korukhaan, Maerdaan Khurreh, Faaruq, Iraej, Saelm, Maenuchehr, Aerzhaeng, Saenjaeh, Ghaendi, Faeraesb, Baasuz, Maachin, Besilaa, Maekraan, Aamol, Daemaavaend, Maazaendaeraan, Jaabolq, Haevaareh, Maaruq, Aershuy.

REFERENCES

Agostini, Domenico, and Samuel Thrope, trans. *The Bundahišn: The Zoroastrian Book of Creation.* New York: Oxford University Press, 2020.

Al-Biruni, Hakim Muhammad Said, and Ansar Zahid Khan. *Al Biruni: His Times, Life, and Works.* Delhi: B. R. Publishing, 1990.

Al-Qāḍī, Wadād. "An Early Fāṭimid Political Document." *Studia Islamica* 48 (1978): 71–108.

Anthony, Sean W. "Chiliastic Ideology and Nativist Rebellion in the Early ʿAbbāsid Period: Sunbādh and Jāmāsp-Nāma." *Journal of the American Oriental Society* 132, no. 4 (2012): 641–55.

Antrim, Zayde. *Routes and Realms: The Power of Place in the Early Islamic World.* New York: Oxford University Press, 2012.

Askari, Nasrin. *The Medieval Reception of the* Shāhnāma *as a Mirror for Princes.* Studies in Persian Cultural History, 9. Leiden: Brill, 2016.

ʿAwliyā, Fātimah Ṣādiqī Naqd Alī, and ʿAlī Asghar Bashīrī. "Bar-risī va muqāyisah-yi dāstān-i ʿKūsh-i pīl-dandānʾ dar Kūsh-nāmah va ṭūmārhā-yi naqqāli." *Du māh-nāmah-yi farhang u adabīyāt-i ʿāmmah* 6, no. 24, 1397 [2018]: 69–90.

Ben-Amos, Dan. "Introduction." *Research in African Literatures* 14, no. 3 (1983): 277–82.

Brett, Michael. *The Rise of the Fatimids: The World of the Mediterranean and the Middle East in the Fourth Century of the Hijra, Tenth Century CE.* Leiden: Brill, 2001.

Brookshaw, Dominic Parviz. "Mytho-Political Remakings of Ferdowsi's Jamshid in the Lyric Poetry of Injuid and Mozaffarid Shiraz." *Iranian Studies* 48, no. 3 (2015): 463–87. https://doi.org/10.1080/00210862.2014.1000617.

Calzolaio, Francesco. "ʿAlidi lungo la via per la Cina: Le prime comunità musulmane cinesi riflesse in una leggenda del medioevo persiano." In

Armenia, Caucaso e Asia Centrale: Ricerche 2019, edited by Giorgio Comai et al., 163–83 (Venice: Edizioni Ca' Foscari, 2019).

———. "China, the Abode of Arts and Crafts: Emergence and Diffusion of a Persian Saying on China in Mongol Eurasia." *Ming Qing Yanjiu* 22 (2019): 136–54.

Chung, Kei Won, and George F. Hourani. "Arab Geographers on Korea." *Journal of the American Oriental Society* 58, no. 4 (1938): 658–61.

Cornwall, Owen. "Alexander and the Persian Cosmopolis, 1000–1500." PhD diss., Columbia University, 2016.

Crone, Patricia. *The Iranian Reception of Islam: The Non-Traditionalist Strands: Collected Studies in Three Volumes.* Islamic History and Civilization, 130. Leiden: Brill, 2016.

———. *The Nativist Prophets of Early Islamic Iran: Rural Revolt and Local Zoroastrianism.* New York: Cambridge University Press, 2012.

Daryaee, Touraj. *Shahristan'ha-yi Iranshahr: Navishtah'i bih zaban-i Farsi-i Miyanah darbarah-i tarikh, hamasah va jughrafiya-yi bastani-i Iran.* Tehran: Intisharat-i Tus, 2009.

Davis, Dick. *Epic and Sedition: The Case of Ferdowsi's Shāhnāmeh.* Fayetteville: University of Arkansas Press, 1992.

———. "The Problem of Ferdowsi's Sources." *Journal of the American Oriental Society* 116, no. 1 (1996): 48–57.

Firdawsī, Abu'l-Qasim. *Shāhnāmah.* Edited by Djalal Khaleghi-Motlagh. New York: Bibliotheca Persica, 1987.

Frenkel, Yehoshua. "The Turks of the Eurasian Steppes in Medieval Arabic Writing." In *Mongols, Turks, and Others: Eurasian Nomads and the Sedentary World*, edited by Reuven Amitai and Michal Biran, 201–41. Leiden: Brill, 2005.

Gabbay, Alyssa. "'The Earth My Throne, The Heavens My Crown': Siyāvash as Supranational Hero in Ferdowsi's *Shāhnāma.*" *Journal of Persianate Studies* 14 (forthcoming).

Gazerani, Saghi. "Kush-e Pildandān, the Anti-Hero: Polemics of Power in Late Antique Iran." *Iranian Studies* 52, no. 5–6 (2019): 859–901.

———. *The Sistani Cycle of Epics and Iran's National History: On the Margins of Historiography.* Studies in Persian Cultural History, 7. Leiden: Brill, 2016.

Ghaemmaghami, Omid. "To the Abode of the Hidden One: The Green Isle in Shī'ī, Early Shaykhī, and Bābī-Bahā'ī Sacred Topography." In *Unity in Diversity: Mysticism, Messianism and the Construction of Religious Authority in Islam*, edited by Orkhan Mir-Kasimov, 137–73. Leiden: Brill, 2014.

Green, Nile, ed. *The Persianate World: The Frontiers of a Eurasian Lingua Franca*. Oakland: University of California Press, 2019.

Guede, Iranzu, Luis Angel Ortega, Maria Cruz Zuluaga, Ainhoa Alonso-Olazabal, Xabier Murelaga, Miriam Pina, Francisco Javier Gutierrez, and Paola Iacumin. "Isotope Analyses to Explore Diet and Mobility in a Medieval Muslim Population at Tauste (NE Spain)." *PLoS ONE* 12, no. 5 (2017): 1–27.

Hansen, Valerie. *The Year 1000: When Explorers Connected the World—and Globalization Began*. New York: Scribner, 2020.

Hayes, Edmund. "The Death of Kings: Group Identity and the Tragedy of Nezhād in Ferdowsi's Shahnameh." *Iranian Studies* 48, no. 3 (2015): 369–93.

Hemmat, Kaveh L. "Completing the Persianate Turn." *Iranian Studies* 54, no. 3–4 (2021): 633–46.

———. "Mountain Kingdoms, Travel, and Royal Charisma." In *Proceedings of the International Congress on Korea and the Muslim World: Historical and Cultural Encounters, April 2018, Istanbul*, edited by Halit Eren, 33–61. Sources and Studies on the History of Islamic Civilisation, 41. Istanbul: IRCICA, 2019.

Hoffmann, Alexandra. "Visual Alterity, Monstrous Sexuality, and a Transformation: Kush, the Elephant-Eared." Paper presented at Geography and Identity in Islamicate Culture Workshop, April 18, 2021.

Hudūd al-Ālam. Preface by V. V. Barthold, translated by V. Minorsky. London, 1937. Reprint, Frankfurt am Main: Institute for the History of Arabic-Islamic Science at Johann Wolfgang Goethe University, 1993.

Ḥusaynī, Ṣadr al-Dīn ʿAlī ibn Nāṣir. *The History of the Seljuq State: A Translation with Commentary of the* "Akhbār al-Dawla al-Saljūqiyya. Translated by Clifford Edmund Bosworth. Routledge Studies in the History of Iran and Turkey. Milton Park: Routledge, 2011.

Ibn al-Athīr, ʿIzz al-Dīn. *Al-Kāmil fī al-tārīkh*. Edited by Carolus Johannes Tornberg. Al-Ṭabʿah, 6. Báyrūt: Dar Ṣādir, 1965.

Īrānshān ibn Abī al-Khayr. *Kūshnāmah*. Edited by Jalāl Matīnī. Tehran: Intishārāt-i ʿIlmī, 1377 [1998].

Iṣṭakhrī, Ibrāhīm ibn Muḥammad, and M. J. de Goeje. *Kitāb masālik al-mamālik*. 3rd ed., photomechanice iterata. Leiden: Brill, 1967.

Kadoi, Yuka. *Islamic Chinoiserie: The Art of Mongol Iran*. Edinburgh Studies in Islamic Art. Edinburgh: Edinburgh University Press, 2009.

Khaleghi-Motlagh, Djalal. "Ferdowsi, Abuʾl-Qasem: 1. Life," *Encyclopaedia Iranica*, 2012, https://www.iranicaonline.org/articles/ferdowsi-i. Accessed June 6, 2021.

Khalidi, Tarif. *Islamic Historiography: The Histories of Masʿūdī*. Albany: State University of New York Press, 1975.

Kim, Jong Wee. "The Muslim Image of Korea in the Early Arabic and Persian Literature." *Annals of Japan Association for Middle East Studies* 8 (1993): 373–96.

König, Daniel. *Arabic-Islamic Views of the Latin West: Tracing the Emergence of Medieval Europe.* Oxford: Oxford University Press, 2015.

Lee, Hee Soo. *The Advent of Islam in Korea.* Istanbul: Research Centre for Islamic History, Art and Culture (IRCICA), 1997.

———. "A Preliminary Study on *Kush-Nāmeh,* an Ancient Persian Epic, and Its Description on Silla." In *Proceedings of the 1500 Years of Korean-Iranian Cultural Encounters Based on the Persian Epic* Kush-Nāmeh, 100–13. Seoul: Hanyang University, 2010.

Leoni, Francesca. "Picturing Evil: Images of Divs and the Reception of the Shahnama." In *Shahnama Studies II: The Reception of Firdausi's Shahnama,* edited by C. P. Melville and Gabrielle Rachel Van den Berg, 101–18. Studies in Persian Cultural History, 2. Leiden: Brill, 2012.

Liu, Yingjun. "Possible Connections Between Historical Events and the Plots of Iranian Princes Exiled in Chīn and B.Sīlā Depicted in *Kūshnāma.*" *Acta Koreana* 21, no. 1 (2018): 37–63.

Losensky, Paul E. *Welcoming Fighānī: Imitation and Poetic Individuality in the Safavid-Mughal Ghazal.* Bibliotheca Iranica, 5. Costa Mesa, CA: Mazda Publishers, 1998.

Lukács, György. *The Theory of the Novel: A Historico-Philosophical Essay on the Forms of Great Epic Literature.* Translated by Anna Bostock. Cambridge, MA: MIT Press, 1971.

Lurje, Pavel. "Kangdez." In *Encyclopaedia Iranica,* 2010, https://iranicaonline.org/articles/kangdez-fortress-of-kang. Accessed August 17, 2021.

Matīnī, Jalāl. "Another Verse Translation of Part of Buzurgmihr's *Book of Advice.*" *Iran Nameh* 5, no. 1 (1986): 115–42.

———. "Barkhī az nīranghā-yi kār-i zār dar Kūsh'nāmah (bih yād-i ustādam Zabīhullāh Safā)." *Iran 'shinasi* 43, no. 11 (1378) [2000]: 649–67.

———. "Kuš-nāma." In *Encyclopaedia Iranica,* 2008, https://iranicaonline.org/articles/kus-nama-part-of-a-mythical-history-of-iran. Accessed June 10, 2021.

———. "Rivāyat 'hā-yi mukhtalif dar bārah-i dawrān-i kūdakī va nawjavānī-yi Farīdūn." *Iran 'namah* 4, no. 1 (1364) [1986]: 78–132.

Mazzaoui, Michel M. *The Origins of the Ṣafawids: Šī'ism, Ṣūfism, and the Ġulāt.* Freiburger Islamstudien, 3. Wiesbaden: F. Steiner, 1972.

Melikian-Chirvani, Assadullah Souren. "Le Livre des Rois, miroir du destin: II—Takht-e Soleymān et la symbolique du Shāh-nāme." *Studia Iranica* 20, no. 1 (1991): 33–148.

Minorsky, Vlademir. *Sharaf al-zamān Tāhir Marvazi on China, the Turk and India*. London: Royal Asiatic Society, 1924.

Niẓām al-Mulk. *The Book of Government, or, Rules for Kings: The Siyar al-Muluk, or, Siyasat-Nama of Nizam al-Mulk*. Translated by Hubert Darke. 3rd ed. London: Routledge, 2002.

Park, Hyunhee. *Mapping the Chinese and Islamic Worlds: Cross-Cultural Exchange in Pre-Modern Asia*. Cambridge: Cambridge University Press, 2012.

Payne, Richard. "Cosmology and the Expansion of the Iranian Empire, 502–628 CE." *Past and Present* 220 (August 2013): 3–33.

Pollock, Sheldon I. *The Language of the Gods in the World of Men: Sanskrit, Culture, and Power in Premodern India*. Berkeley: University of California Press, 2006.

Savant, Sarah Bowen. *The New Muslims of Post-Conquest Iran: Tradition, Memory, and Conversion*. Cambridge Studies in Islamic Civilization. New York: Cambridge University Press, 2013.

Shapira, Dan. "Was There Geographical Science in Sasanian Iran?" *Acta Orientalia Academiae Scientiarum Hungaricae* 54, no. 2/3 (2001): 319–38.

Sīrāfī, Abū Zayd Ḥasan ibn Yazīd, and Aḥmad Ibn Faḍlān. *Two Arabic Travel Books*. Edited by Tim Mackintosh-Smith and James E. Montgomery. Library of Arabic Literature. New York: New York University Press, 2014.

Skaervo, Prods Oktor. "Eastern Iranian Epic Traditions I: Siyāvash and Kunāla." In *Mir Curad: Studies in Honor of Calvert Watkins*, edited by Jay Jasanoff, Craig Melchert, and Lisi Oliver, 645–58. Innsbruck: Institut für Sprachwissenschaft, 1998.

Starr, Frederick S. *Lost Enlightenment: Central Asia's Golden Age from the Arab Conquest to Tamerlane*. Princeton, NJ: Princeton University Press, 2013.

Ṭabarī. General Introduction *and* From the Creation to the Flood. Translated by Franz Rosenthal. Vol. 1 of *The History of Al-Ṭabarī*. Albany: State University of New York Press, 1988.

Umidsālār, Mahmud. "Yāddāsht'hā-yi Kūsh'nāmah." *'Ulum-i ijtim'ī: Farhang-i Īranzamīn* 30 (1384 [2006]): 312–36.

Utas, Bo. "The Jewish-Persian Fragment from Dandan-Uiliq." *Orientalia Suecana* 17 (1968 [1969]): 123–36.

Vassilkov, Yaroslav. "An Iranian Myth in Eastern India: Gayōmart and the Mythology of Gayā." *Orientalia Suecana* 47 (1998): 131–49.

Vosooghi, Mohammad Bagher. "Silla, Bassila, or Bosilla: New Findings Concerning Korea from Persian Manuscripts." In *Proceedings of the 1500 Years of Korean-Iranian Cultural Encounters Based on the Persian Epic Kush-Nāmeh*. Seoul: Hanyang University, 2013.

Wright, Elaine. "Firdausi and More: A Timurid Anthology of Epic Tales." In *Shahnama: The Visual Language of the Persian Book of Kings,* edited by Robert Hillenbrand, 65–84. Burlington: Ashgate, 2004.

Zutphen, Marjolijn van. *Farāmarz, the Sistāni Hero: Texts and Traditions of the Farāmarznāme and the Persian Epic Cycle.* Studies in Persian Cultural History, 6. Leiden: Brill, 2014.

The Epic of Kush

Iranshah ibn Abu'l-Khayr

Invocation

O thou wise one, thy spirit is illumined—thus did God make your tongue fluent! He gave wisdom, life, and intellect pure, an enlightened heart, seeing eyes, and ears, that you may praise him purely, supplicate him night and day, and teach those who are unaware, those who do not know the path to this royal court. For while you see many a heart that is enlightened, many a heart is chained to Ahriman.

The horse knows its own master, so why be blind of eye and heart? The author of the moon, sun, and firmament, consider him more manifest than sun and moon! He is greater than whatever you may believe of him, is other than whatever may be apparent to you. Whatever is, is a sign of his being, whether the eye sees it or the hand grasps it: 10 wind and rain, spring clouds, smiling rose, and well-watered tulip, whatever can be seen was created, and none can see the creator.

This sublime world, ever-expanding, he created from the B and E of "Be."[1] None is his partner in creating, in this act of creation there is no toil for him. No moment spent is a moment without him—that maker of places, placeless himself! See the rose and rose petals: dry twigs have blossomed and musk issued from the deer's navel! He did not create us in jest, the throne was not created to seat us! A world created

---

1. That is, "be," the command by which God calls creation into existence. The Arabic letters are *kaf* and *nun*.

he, who needs not a thing in the world. Tis not for fear of enemy the hidden one remains hidden! He is one, yet both seen and unseen, bright day and dark night his signs.

He makes bright day of dark nights, and rain makes the face of the dust a garden. 20 The spring seasons come up well-watered roses, the autumns encase each mountain in snow. He generates from each grain ten bunches, each bursting with a hundred grains. From rocks he generates fire, like water from clouds. He takes water out of stones and snow out of clouds. From the rain, he makes shells full of jewels, just as he makes sugar of green cane. He makes the rocks fruitful and the scrub verdant, to one giving color, to the other, scent. Here, a rock takes the name of garnet or ruby, there, a stick takes the name raw aloeswood.

Neither the astronomer nor the naturalist offer due thanks to the Lord, for what does a substance know of good and bad? The star knows nothing of spirit or wisdom. What would become of a Venus or a Saturn? Pisces would be underwater and Aries out to pasture! Philosophy has drawn you toward exile in damnation, into the maws of lions and tigers! 30 Don't scratch the dragon's neck, for if it breathes you'll find no escape. It never was that God was not. It could not be that he is not, that he should not be praised. What would you want with why and how? Do not war with your creator! [188b]

A songbird like the *tayhu* flies higher than a falcon, but has not been endowed with talons. The raven can puff its chest bigger than the nightingale, but knows not how to sing like the nightingale. For, what good is the pure-white color of the mountain ewe when hunted by the lion and tiger?

You, artless one, have country and army, while I, artful, have been given much less. Thus did the world-creator create—this wonder has appeared since the beginning! It's all over in just five days, when we look at it, both ease and hardship pass us by, and one who travels lightly in both houses is better off. One who travels lightly is more acceptable to God. 40

Thus, acquire knowledge as best you can, for there is nothing that will come to your aid like knowledge. By knowledge you can reach your creator, who has created nothing else like it. Knowledge is a tree crowned with the Pleiades. Its branches and fruits are all good deeds. Man's wealth is knowledge, a knowing heart is full of joy. From knowledge Satan flees, and the community is illuminated.

If I knew knowledge only by my own power, I'd be able to reach the heavens. The clever, the wise, the teacher, could these three reach the creator? Thus did Sendbad say to his pupil: "Be a pupil, that you may become a master."[2] Did not the Prophet of pure creed say to seek knowledge even if it be in China?

If knowledge does not travel alongside wisdom, you will achieve nothing—neither good nor bad. 50 Thus should the heart be washed through to its secrets, that the divine secret may reach it. Wisdom has struck roots far beneath it and branched out like spring shoots. Wisdom is the guide, awareness and calm accompany it, beneficent teachers.

Estranged from him are passion, anger, and hatred. Who have you ever seen with such a heart? Whoever hasn't a trace of wisdom, you would not entrust your treasure to him. Let your words lead the army of wisdom, for speech increases it day by day. Wisdom appears in speech, know that speech is wisdom's key. Speech based on knowledge, like a contented person, is always proliferating. Wisdom is the gift of the creator. Tell me, what could be better? Wisdom is a mail coat for a man's body, it is the remedy for all pains. 60 Wisdom holds at bay the works of demons, shuts down the demon's bustling market. Wisdom judges between the everlasting spirit and ephemeral breath.

ON THE IMPERMANENCE OF LIFE

It seems that the world is but a breath, be it in happiness or grief. In but a single breath, you will become nothing. Better that all your breaths be taken in goodness. You spend your days lording it over a palace. Where, then, would your spirit walk beside you? [189a] When dear life is freed from its narrow straits, your palace won't remain long. Be content with slim pickings from the world, don't tie your heart to a fleeting abode. What good are spreading wealth and treasure? Life is short, and the world steals it. Why should I multiply my enemies by burning up spirits for the sake of one thing or another? If I had even a little wisdom, I'd expend none of my lifetime on the world. 70

We have seen many kings who passed and took nothing with them. Good man, cut the throat of greed with the sword of contentment—

2. Sendbad is a sage, title character of *The Sendbadnameh (Book of Sendbad)*, a work of wisdom literature translated into Middle Persian from Sanskrit.

don't go near it! Wrap the benighted body in a felt shroud, for the beggar's bowl of fearlessness is better than any drink. Our Lord never commanded that you bury treasures in the ground and leave them there. While you try to bury what you covet, your betters meet their doom.

When fortune favors someone and the world is all in order for them, it sprouts whole trees for them as if they were spring shoots, bearing twigs and blossoms, bearing the rose of felicity. So verdant are its branches and leaves, spring itself smiles at their fragrance and color, and everything it bears is scarlet and yellow, breaching the sapphire dome. Should one obtain its fruits, his name will remain upon the earth. And should one be thus deprived, no lofty name will he leave behind. 80 That same cold wind and winter would drop those leaves and fruit like scattered coins—empty-handed, without leaf or fruit, forever given over to plunder.

When he returns to the other realm, headache and trouble increase. When he returns from this fleeting abode, to where he once was, he is left ashamed. When you've obtained food and clothing, no more can be gained from this palace. Do not hoard pains of the heart and the fruits of the body, no, give away and eat—listen to what I say! You are not more glorious than the glorious [vulture-like] huma, and what fare has God provided it with? Don't waste precious honor before great and small over just anything. Accept whatever God has wrought, and even if you don't want it, know that he did. 90 Whether you accept it or not, you have no way around what he has wrought.

IN PRAISE OF THE PROPHET

The pinnacle of justice, the Prophet of pure faith, if he wanted the treasures of the earth, they came to him, surely—gold rained down on him from the sky! Whoever has set foot upon his canopy, his station is higher than the arc of the sky. Gabriel drew him ahead, he saw paradise, and wine from the fountain of paradise. Wolf and lion smile to see his face, the brave dragon quivers in the dust before him. With the sword, he makes religion manifest. The angels gaze upon his face. The clouds appear and break on his command. The lion and tiger supplicate before him. In one night he sees two worlds entire, his ear hears greetings from the divine. With his finger he makes two halves of the moon, so why should silver and gold be dear to him? 100 He wished to live on earth, hungry, for he knew the earth to be a place of calamities. From the beginning, when God created a man, it was the first sign of Muhammad's name, Mu-h-mm-d. Shaped like a man, the *Mu-* like a head above the two hands of the *-ha-*, with his torso as a *mim* and two feet like the *-ad*.[3]

You have heard that when his Lord called for him to appear before him, no gold was left him, no silver. Then, his daughter complained to him that her hands were swollen from hard work. You, if you're a man, cut short your greed, cut a path to your Prophet. Whatever you earn, give away what you do not need, don't restrain your generosity. This is our praise for such a man: more abundant than the raindrops and the leaves of the trees!

[REGARDING THE REASONS FOR COMPOSING THE *EPIC OF KUSH*]

I told a story before just as I had heard it, relating all the virtues of the kingship of Bahman. 110 I adorned it in verse like a treasure, ordered its design like a garden. I dedicated it to the great king of exalted lineage, his father and grandfather crowned kings. I put it in the hands of a confidant and sent it to the king's threshold. Fearing ill-wishers, I sent it in secret, in the hands of a person of good intent. When they took hold of it before the lofty throne, they read it and deemed it acceptable. The king bestowed upon me a regal robe and sent me garments and gold. My abode was verdant with brocades, my works adorned with coins like a beauty. When the people became aware of my secret, of my words and the king's deeds, of that glory, of that regal palace, of those ranks I was honored with before the army, and of his splendor and generosity and justice, of his grace and munificent heart, 120 in his name, I rose in dark of night to pray to the divine for his majesty's satisfaction! I made a prediction that this crown and station would not be lost to him for a long time.

And so did my prediction come true. Now that I am more than forty years old, his talent, faith, and peace have spread his name far and wide. May there be no one like him in the world, may no other king command an army. The king's beneficence burnt away my need,

---

3. The name Muhammad, written in Arabic, resembles the human form: محمد.

my heart lit up again like a fire. My poetic muse became ebullient like a sea struck by the wind, effortlessly bringing verses to my mind.

Since fortune favored me, my heart wished for a new saga. I knew a noble man in the city, endowed with learning and civility, a youth whom anyone that encountered him would whisper God's name in awe. 130 Tall as a cypress, strong of stature, face like milk and wine together, his head like the family of Ya Sin and the house of 'Aba, a son of 'Ali—'Ali the chosen—said to me, "If you are interested, I have a story of the king of China. Anyone who reads it attentively would learn much from the deeds of Kush."[4]

I looked at this useful document, full of knowledge, thoughtful ideas, and advice; a garden, but deprived of rain; a beauty, but afflicted with troubles. Would that I receive more than this from the maker of the world, a little more time upon the earth, that I may benefit from this learning and render the epic in my own verses—so that I may adorn it like a spring garden and polish it clean of verdigris.

IN PRAISE OF THE EMPEROR OF ISLAM

In the name of the world-conquering emperor, a Faridun in knowledge, an Alexander in intellect, 140 a Gayomard in honor, of Manuchehr's grandeur, with the vision of Siyavash and glory of Hushang![5] With a neck like Faramarz, locks like Fariborz, Zal-statured and colossal of heart, with the frame of Sam![6] Like a priest in piety, like Kesra in

---

4. The phrase "son of 'Ali the chosen" refers to Hasan, the son of 'Ali *mojtaba* (the chosen); the more common epithet *Hasan-e mojtaba* is an abbreviation of this title. The "family of Ya Sin" and the "house of 'Aba" refer to Muhammad's family.

5. "The emperor of Islam" refers to the dedicatee of the epic, the Seljuq ruler Ghiyas al-Din Mohammad b. Malekshah, aka Mohammad I Tapar (r. 1105–18 CE); see introduction. Faridun is the messianic king in *The Shahnameh* who arises to overthrow Zahhak and restore the rule of Jamshid's descendants; see introduction. Gayomard is the first king in *The Shahnameh,* and the protoplast of the first human in Zoroastrian scripture. Manuchehr is a hero of *The Shahnameh,* famous for his role as a lover. Siyavash is a very virtuous hero in *The Shahnameh.* Hushang is a virtuous world-king in the mythic section of *The Shahnameh* and an ancestor of Jamshid.

6. Faramarz is a Sistani hero in *The Shahnameh;* see introduction. Fariborz is a prince in *The Shahnameh.* Zal was a king of Sistan in *The Shahnameh,* son of Sam. Abandoned in the wilderness by his father because he was born with white hair, he was raised by the *simorgh,* a mythical bird, until he and his father reconciled; father of Rostam.

justice, of the seed of Pashang, with the character of Qobad![7] An elephant in might, a tiger in ferocity, driven like an ocean, generous like a raincloud! With his intellect seeing all that could be, like Kaykhosrow with the world-seeing chalice![8] He could stitch up a lion with a single arrow, as Bahram's arrow made an onager into a deer.[9] The host of stars, his nobles, a meteor the sword of his Turks! From the time of Gayomard to our own time, no one was higher than our emperor!

How much will you speak to me of the brazen-bodied Esfandiyar?[10] Those words have grown old. A devotee of his majesty's throne would exceed Esfandiyar in manliness! 150 For who destroyed Shahdez, such an awesome fortress and mountain?[11] Its towers soared above the mountaintop, as if it shared a secret with the stars, [189b] reaching so high it could hardly be called a castle. A bloodthirsty man within, with an army like the accursed demon, the world in fear of the glint of their blades—at night Isfahan dared not sleep, soldiers and civilians alike. The king waged war for a year, with no success against the demonic mountain. When the bloodthirsty man rolled boulders down from the mountain, he wrecked armies.

Then, by the power of the Lord, the commanding king destroyed that terrifying place. The malicious lord was caught, and in time, stripped. Of those fools, not one was left—hurrah for the lion-hearted king who answered the cry! 160 The world won security from the deeds of that army, their treasure was lost beneath the dust. Isfahan swelled with pride for his glory, that the king should make his residence there.

7. The name Kesra is a cognate of Khosrow, used as both a name and a title; it is most often translated in this text as "sovereign." The palace of Ctesiphon was known as the palace of Kesra. In *The Shahnameh*, Pashang is king of Turan, a nation which is frequently at war with Iran; he is father of the Turanian king Afrasiyab, who features in many stories in the *Shahnameh's* heroic section (see introduction). Qobad is a hero of *The Shahnameh*.

8. Kaykhosrow is the most virtuous king in the heroic section of *The Shahnameh*.

9. Bahram was a Sassanian emperor famous for feats of hunting, among them shooting arrows into the head of an onager, a type of wild ass, so that they looked like a gazelle's antlers.

10. Esfandiyar is a prince and a supporter of Zoroaster in *The Shahnameh*.

11. Shahdez was a Nizari Isma'ili fortress held by the Bateni Shi'i leader Ahmad b. 'Abd al-Malek 'Attash; see introduction.

May he be happy in body and soul, may the only fruit of his sword be justice! Though the scent of milk is still on his lips, his every word is a learned discourse. What will he be like when he comes of age? The heavens under his foot like a plain! No, he does not rely too heavily on his ministers, nor do his decisions only benefit his close companions. For fear of him, the lion of war tears his own heart and by his justice, the crocodile dares not harm the fish. For some time the kings of the earth drew up ranks before the seekers of enmity.

These few years the life of the king continue, and never for one day having seen his army defeated, Malekshah's eyes would brighten to see the young king clad in mail, 170 his heart and soul alike would fill with pride at the field where the king charges on his horse.[12] In celebration, he's an orbiting moon, in battle a foe-slaying king. The world is illumined with the richness of his fortunes, the earth secured at the foot of his throne.

Have you heard what harm befell the army of the Arabs at the hand of the king?[13] Were I to tell it all, it would be another volume, but I have something else in mind. When the infidel's time ended, that rebel of wicked creed fled, and a company was sent after him from Iran, to chase him stealthily.

The king of the Arabs took him in and said, "I am your ally, with my life and my property. If the king wants to get you from me, I am as a shield before you."

That worthless one had no idea what kind of harm those words would bring! 180 He had no idea how a drunkard flees from the high sun. When the king became aware, he supplicated the Arab king, but his advice was not heeded. He turned his head from good advice, not listening to anyone. He did not know that the one who stretches his neck out in rebellion has wrapped himself in a bloody shroud.

The king of the Arabs said, "He is under my protection, the king's army is my prey."

12. Malekshah is the former Seljuq sultan and father of the dedicatee, Mohammad b. Malekshah.

13. This army was that of a noble (amir), Sayf al-Dowlah b. Sadaqah b. Mansur b. Dabis b. Mazid al-Asadi. Following the defeat of the Bateni Shi'is of Shahdez, the governor of Saveh, Abu Dolaf Sorkhab Kaykhosrow Daylami, fled, and he and others were given shelter by Sayf al-Dowlah. See Īrānshān ibn Abī al-Khayr, *Kūshnāmah*, edited by Jalāl Matīnī (Tehran: Intishārāt-i 'Ilmī, 1377 [1998]), 155n3.

The drums roared from the royal gate, "King, bring ruin unto the enemy!"

The kettle-drum proclaimed, "For the faith, brandish the heavy mace of enmity at their throats!"

Those brave heroes of regal stature girded themselves to fight the Arabs. A black cloud rose up over the heavens, the king striking a path like a racing dragon.

When the Arab king learned that the high-born emperor was coming, 190 Arabs boiled forth like ants and locusts, and plain, mighty river, and mountain turned black. Their spears turned the earth into a reed-bed, each rider's heart taking notice. The Arabs struck like judgment day, on fleet-footed steeds like fluttering crows, huffing and puffing over seas and plains. Each one congratulated himself, none aware what secret the day held. You'd have said they did not consider them manly—the king's riders hunted them.

The aspiring world-conqueror bared his head and came to the prayer-place seeking justice. He said, "O God most high and exalted, you are the creator and the guide! You know that for the sake of the faith, year after year I have drawn my sword. You have given me kingship and throne. May you now ease this difficult labor!" 200

As soon as the words left his mouth, a dragon appeared from the sky—a dragon, like a black mountain! The king and army were terrified of it. From the sky, it turned its face to the king, and the commanding sovereign was worried.

At that moment, it revealed to him a secret, "I'll take the life of your foe." Then it turned towards the enemy as the two armies watched it. You'd have said Deneb was joined with Mars—a day that went down in history.

Shortly after, a sturdy champion brought the head of the enemy to the king. There was a great thundering sound and a black cloud arose, the Arabs' hearts filled with pain. The Arab riders were routed, like leaves falling from a branch. The whole field filled with dead and wounded, as if their horses' legs were bound. 210 Arrows rained behind them and water was in front of them, the fish racing to eat their guts. In that field, for years after, lions and wolves sated their hunger from those Arabs.

Whoever is an enemy of this king, the dragon's venom is their enemy. No one else comes close, he is the commander of the age and the lord of the conjunction. Whoever opposes him will, like the Arab king, have his head severed from his body. I am first among the nobles in praising the world's king. I have told this story of the past, in the name of the world-keeper, pure of creed. It has been scattered around the world, but only great men are worthy of hearing it.

Read and praise the king, supplicate God for his sake! This very epic I owe to him, for the revolving heavens turn in his favor. 220 An epic that praises the king has won me praise, and now another story will be a memento from me for noble men, until the world's end. You are an ocean, o king, and I a pearl-seeker with his face turned hopefully to the sea. Should I take a pearl from there, it would not do the ocean any harm. Show me the generosity that kings show to wise men and noblemen. For I am your servant and beneficiary, praising your station and crown, my lips beseeching God on your behalf day and night, and cursing your enemies.

Frame Tale

Now look deep within this story, it calls you to heed its guidance. See, now, what Kush did upon the earth, leader of steel-clad heroes, two eyes like the sky and a face like boiling blood, his visage worse than an elephant's.[1] 230

"Three hundred and some years after today, from Iran, a man will come like no other. Every king who follows his command will hold onto his crown and his life. If he leads an army to Rome, my descendants will no longer rule there. Ruin will befall anyone who goes to war with him. Give him whatever treasure he wants, so that he leaves without causing injury or hardship."

Once Kush had recorded this message, he rolled it up and placed his seal on it. That very clever king drew the face of Darnush upon that seal, gave the writer a sum of dinars, and bound his tongue with an oath so that no man or woman would learn the secret from him no matter how he was asked.

Right then, he quickly brought a jug, inside which he placed the smoky deer-hide on which the message was written. 240 He secured its mouth with tin and covered it with a coin, like a seal. The confident king had a gold pitcher from the treasures of Syria brought in. He had it stamped with the seal and made it part of the treasure, and did not concern himself with it further.

---

1. See introduction for a discussion of this in medias res opening of the frame tale.

The king summoned one honored man from among the merchants, who had eaten and drunk with him, one of his confidants. He spoke to him at length and then advised him, asked him to swear oaths, "Do not tell anyone my secret, only you and God know it!"

Then he gave him the pitcher and the jug and said, "You, honorable hero, should go to Rome, to the city where Manush resides, that malevolent Christian—a city full of people, food and song, long ago the realm of Darnush.[2] Stay there for a while. [190a] 250 When your caravan disembarks at the city gate, dismount in a muddy spot. Rest one night outside the city, and then discuss your business with a small group of people and dig a pit like Bizhan's prison.[3] Dig down ten yards and throw this treasure into it. Place the jug down in this hole, then put in the pitcher, so it's above.

"Cover over the hole with the dirt and mud, then get that small group of people drunk with wine. Put poison in the wine to end their lives and throw them in the ocean so that the fish feast on them. When night turns to day, enter the city, set up shop and spend your time there. When the secret of the pit becomes known, pack up and leave. 260 Keep traveling, day and night, and inform me right away, and when you return to this place, I'll give you a high rank in the army. I'll reward you generously and in perpetuity."

The merchant acclaimed him and pressed his face to the floor in gratitude. He said, "O brave king, may the days never tire of you! Your name will surpass the heavens. I'll satisfy your demand, I'm at your command."

He gave him a robe of honor, and the merchant left Baghdad for Rome. He arranged it so that, on the pretext of performing an extra prayer by the gate of Manush's city, he dismounted near the gate where there were trees in front and behind, and a running river.

Whoever was there to do business little by little came to him from the city. 270 They said, "Get up and come into the city tonight, you couldn't stand toe-to-toe with crooked bandits."

2. The name Manush appears to refer to the Roman emperor, Romanus IV Diogenes, defeated by the Seljuqs in the Battle of Manzikert. See introduction.

3. In *The Shahnameh*, Bizhan was an Iranian hero who fell in love with Manizheh, a princess of Turan. The king of Turan disapproved and Bizhan was imprisoned in a pit, from which he was eventually rescued by Rostam.

He answered, "Tomorrow at dawn I'll observe a sign from a star pointing out my path. Then when day breaks I'll enter the city and try to turn a profit with what little I have."

The day's heart lit up just as night broke, and diggers struck shovels into the heart of the soil. They dug the pit and threw in the treasure, and five diggers were thrown into the ocean. When the day had buried the night, the savvy man entered the city. Apart from the king, no one in the world knew his secret. He brought many gems before Manush, dazzling enough to make one pass out. He stayed two years in that verdant land. A little wealth turned into a lot.

Meanwhile, a laboring man dug away at that grime, until he dug the dirt out of the hole. 280 Little by little, he reached the pitcher, he saw it and ran to the caesar's court. "I saw a treasure outside the city! Would that the king would let me have a little of it?"

The king's minister took over the excavation.[4] They drew the jug out and took it to the king. When the caesar looked at it and saw the seal, and saw the figure of Darnush, he was filled with joy. He said to his minister, "This is my ancestor, the treasure he hid is mine."

They poured out the coins before the caesar and everyone crowded around to have a look. When his minister opened the seal of the jug, a deerskin came out of it. Manush laughed and said, "What is this? An inventory of the treasure?"

When he opened the skin and saw that visage, he took fright, biting his lip. 290 He quietly pondered this for a while, thinking, "What is this devilish thing? Surely it's a talisman for the city to protect it from those who wished us harm."

When his minister read out the letter, the king became frightened and anxious. He said to the minister, "Lowly man, who would dare encroach on these lands? Since when would anyone rebel? How long is left of the time indicated on the letter?"

4. Throughout *The Kushnameh,* the term minister *(dastur)* means an adviser to the king or a government minister—someone responsible for managing finances, written correspondence, and other bureaucratic duties—not a clergyman with exclusively religious duties, although the ministers are also responsible for knowledge of religion. A comparison may be made to the priests of ancient Egypt and Mesopotamia, who were a literate professional class with knowledge of the law and a range of worldly responsibilities.

He answered, "It says three centuries, now the heavens' wheel has turned three hundred and seven times. It would seem that that time, o king, has come to pass in this day."

All the land became informed of that secret just as the merchant returned. He approached the king and gave him the news, which pleased him.

Immediately, he summoned his forces from across the realm, so that there was not a knight left in Iran. 300 A measureless army gathered before him, more than three hundred thousand altogether: all of Gilan and Daylam, company after company, all joined in purpose like a mountain, all thirsty for brave enemies' blood, warlike as a roaring lion.

On the first day of the month at the cock's crow, the sound of the drum issued from the gate. The sun shouted and the moon wept from the noise of the drum, from the army's dust. So many mail-coats, blades, and javelins painted the earth and sky the same color. The army was a deluge pressing down on desert and mountain. When the leader arose from his abode, he took his place as their heroic king.

They immediately advanced to Tartus and turned everything upside down with their plundering. He commanded, and they stretched out their hands, flattening the country all around. 310 A cry arose in Rome: "It is happening exactly as Darnush said!"

KUSH WRITES A LETTER TO MANUSH

The great king sent a letter to Manush. The scribe picked up the slender reed-pen, and began: "From the roving and vengeful king of the Arabs and Iran: Do not confront me, the world-conquering king whom the mountains cannot hold back. To Manush, the king of Rome, of the knights of that land, praise be to the lord of the sun and Saturn, who bestowed strength, glory, and victory! We will extirpate evildoers from the land, cast the bodies of idolaters into the dust. We will crush all the idols under our feet, treading the path of God. Now that the Black Hordes have been stopped, driven bloodily back to Nubia and Zanj, we have rescued the world from malice, and struck a blow against those Arabs.[5] 320 Now it is shown in the stars that we must

5. Zanj, or Zangi, is a Perso-Arabic term for Black Africans.

oppose the Romans. Now I have informed you of my plans, if you do not appear before me you will face the consequences."

When that king finished the letter, he sealed it with his ring. He chose a soft-spoken emissary whom he knew spoke the language of the Romans. His swift horse raced over plains and mountains without tiring.

KUSH'S LETTER IS RECEIVED BY MANUSH, AND MANUSH WRITES BACK TO KUSH

He went until he reached Manush's gate, forgetting all the weariness of the road. When Manush read the king's words, his face turned the color of straw. He said to the envoy, "Though this new king is a warlike champion, do not think I am like his defeated enemies, the Zangi and Arabs. If I go to that court, it will be with an army numerous as the sands of the desert." 330

He said, "Take in the envoy, give him wine, rest, and music." His heart grew heavy with worry and he chose a pure-hearted fellow from his assembly. He said, "Go to the envoy and get him talking. Get him to tell you what the king's face looks like, and tell me what he says."

The envoy went and inquired, and what he found corresponded exactly to the deerskin. When Manush was certain about this matter, he quickly brought his minister and said, "It is he the ancient kings spoke of, and none other. This same furious, warlike king has come who was foretold by Darnush. You must now go without an army and pay a visit to this king. His appearance, frame, face, and manner, his comportment, his creed, 340 all these you should observe, and the condition and number of his army. If it is clear I cannot face him, I will give him what he wants from me and do as he says, except that I will not go and appear before him. Otherwise, tell him he may ask anything he wants."

He gave generous gifts to the envoy, plenty of dirhams and dinars. He ordered a response written quickly, in which he expressed much kindness. He said, "O warlike king, God has not commanded us to seek enmity. [190b] He did not command us to plunder or spill blood, to raise turmoil on the earth. Otherwise, I would not hesitate to use my treasure and men-at-arms. I would not shy away from war. For even one of my troops to die would be worse than that my lands be laid waste. If my words do not trouble you, then accept your treasure and be content. 350 We will pass on just as our predecessors passed on. What did they take with them that we could take? Let us eschew oppression and seek honor. Be satisfied with the land of Iran. I have now sent an experienced envoy without an army to your court, to understand your intentions. He will give you what you wish without delay. The world is not worth war and strife—life is too short to waste on that." When the scribe had written the letter, he ordered the minister to mount his horse.

News of the emissary came to the king and he sent his forces to receive him. He had the warden bring a few men out of the prison. He had them thrown before soldiers at the gate, to be injured by them. Each soldier then tore into one of them, a frightening scene for the minister! 360

The minister shook like a tree, lost his senses, and went up to the throne in that condition. When his eyes fell upon that throne and crown, he besought God under his breath. His tongue shriveled and blackened. His spirit was agitated with worry. He was too full of fear to acclaim the king or prostrate himself. The attendant seated him before the throne. The king of Iran did not meet his eye until the envoy collected himself, and then he praised Darnush.

The king said to him, "My good man, why has the caesar troubled you?"

He responded, "O king, may the passing days bring you satisfaction. I have come to this court for an audience with the king, to see what the king, of noble character, wants from Rome. 370 Since I have seen the throne and crown of the king, my tongue has frozen in my mouth."

He said to him, "Without doubt, Manush's days will come to an end. Why has he not come, and sent you instead? Does he think his blade will be victorious? My fist would land harder upon his face than anything has before. If he does not come, I will go to meet him and seize him by his neck and his body."

The minister said to him, "O sovereign king, brave, glorious, and fortunate, if you come to Rome, it will be ruined, and glory extinguished in that land. This would hardly be appropriate for the world's king, that harm should come to innocents. The Romans have never caused any harm, nor is Manush foolhardy enough to interfere with his majesty. If the king makes his demands known, then war and conflict can be avoided. 380 He will deliver to the king whatever he has, whatever treasure he has hidden." The minister pleaded with him until the king was satisfied.

He said to him, "This time, for your sake, I will spare this king and your city, but he must pay tribute for two years, as in the time of the proud Kesra, the greatest man to wear a crown, Anushirvan, shelter of heroes, crown of the kings. He must pay a tribute of three hundred thousand golden eggs to this court, each one more than forty grams, such that the sun would be ashamed struggling to outshine it. And thirty men of the nobles of Rome, notables of the city, knights of the land, must be sent as collateral to this court.

"I want his oldest brother as a hostage, whose orders hold sway throughout Rome. 390 And, the believers' mosque in that capital where Manush abides must be improved, for from what I have heard, he has ruined it. He must use gold and other materials that will not wear out. He must guarantee that no one persecute any Muslim in his lands, or else every monastery in the lands of Iran and Rome will be crushed—I will bring all my wrath down on them. On these conditions, I will turn back, otherwise, I will march my forces on Rome."

The minister said, "I shall do as you say and carry out all the orders you give. Since I obey his majesty's orders, by his benevolence, his name will remain everlasting. If his majesty allows it, I will send notice to Manush." 400

The king thus gave him his hand and swore an oath. "As soon as the king is satisfied, he will not bring his armies here again. He will return to the land of Iran, satisfied, and never thus return to Syria." He gave him three months.

The minister forthwith launched a speedy messenger, "The world-king is satisfied with this tribute, do what is required. I entreated him at length and sought agreement from everyone. If you want to see the face of the ruler of the earth, look at that deerskin. This king is glorious and wise, just as Darnush had written. A thousand praises for the king's wisdom, knowledge, and authority! If he had not handled this matter wisely, the whole realm would have become deserted. 410 This place is garrisoned from mountain to mountain, the east wind loses its way in that thicket of spears."

That messenger reached Rome in a week. When Manush unsealed the letter, he read it and put his hand on the ground, then rested his forehead on his sleeve. He said, "O creator of the heavens, you have radiated kindness into the king's heart. You have appeased him with the offer of tribute, else happiness would have been driven from the land."

After that, when his minister arrived, he told him everything he said and heard. The king ordered his minister to prepare to collect the tribute within one month. He added to it slaves and horses, as he was told. He chose thirty men from the heroes of the city, men of great account[, and the oldest of his brothers, Sarkesh].[6] He sent them on their way, telling them to go straight to the king. 420

When Sarkesh appeared before the king of Iran, he offered his acclamation to him in the Roman language. He presented what was demanded before the king, the slaves and caparisoned horses.

The triumphant king was pleased with this. Right then, he withdrew from Tartus. Having taken his tribute by means of this ruse, the devious king returned to Baghdad. Satisfied, the great king sat upon the throne, let go his worries and opened up the wine. Other kings became anxious about what he had done, but were unaware of how he did it. Each one became afraid of the king in his heart, and each one of them became his subordinate.

As the great king little by little became aware of that noble young man Sarkesh's learning, he was pleased by his manners, happy at the sight of him, and was impatient to visit him. A savvy and sun-like youth, eloquent and pleasing to the eye, 430 he observed the world-king to see what would please his heart and his eyes. That youth observed that nothing seemed dearer to the sovereign than the tales of kings. Day and night, a book was his companion and learning his labor.

He sent a letter to his brother: "O excellent, honorable king, the king holds me dear to himself, and favors me above the great warriors. I am beside him day and night, whether with a book before him or wine in his hand, Day by day I become more important to him, I have no chance to leave him. When you send gifts, send knowledge, for the world-king is devoted to learning."

---

6. It appears that some lines were omitted by the copyist, since the name Sarkesh appears in line 420 without explanation.

MANUSH SENDS NINE VOLUMES TO KUSH

Manush was pleased with the conduct of the king, and said so to his minister. He sent the king nine volumes, each of them revealing a path to knowledge, 440 all of them oceans of knowledge, each one greater than the last. Of those nine, two were books of medicine, the likes of which existed nowhere else. [191a] One of those was called the Sixteenth Book of Galen, reading it would satisfy a learned man. Another contained the science of Hippocrates in chapters, which one does not tire of reading.[7] The fourth contained knowledge of the causes of things, recorded nowhere else. Apollonius is its author, perusing his discourse brings life to the reader.

He also sent five books reporting the deeds of kings, telling of what they endured: histories of the kings of Rome and their deeds in that land. One was about the reign of Efriqos, with good advice for all kings—his father was Abraha, a well-born king.[8] To speak of his far-reaching dominion, 450 all the west was under his command, and demons fled his slicing blade. He built a city in the west, which his minister called Efriqiyeh. His commands were obeyed for two hundred years as if there were no other king in the world.

In the companion volume were the deeds and works of Decius, and those dear companions, the seven sleepers of the cave, and Raqim.[9] There is a mountain reaching to the clouds, with lions, leopards, and tigers everywhere, rising near Tartus like a wall connected to the sky. There is a place like a cellar up in the mountain wilderness, the sight of which would frighten a demon: a dark cave, uninviting, where day and night are one. The way from there to daylight is a ladder of polished black stone 460 climbing more than eighty steps—countless even, beyond description. If you go up and enter the cave, you'll come upon a delightful palace.

7. *The Aphorisms* of Hippocrates. The third book's author and title appear to have been omitted.

8. Efriqos was a king of Ethiopia who took over southern Arabia in the sixth century CE and, according to Islamic tradition, attempted to invade Mecca with elephants in his army in 570–71 CE. This year, which was also the year of Muhammad's birth, became known as the Year of the Elephant.

9. Raqim is the name of the dog who accompanies the sleepers; he is mentioned again below.

There are thirteen of them there and a dog, and not a vein moves on those thirteen.[10] Their spirit left and their bodies remained—so amazing are God's works! Of those thirteen, there were seven, and the dog, that fled the city. One of them was a pleasant-faced youth who had just reached the fullness of manhood. Fleeing Decius and Rome, they avoided disaster. When they went into the cave, transcendent God removed the pure spirit from their limbs. When the religion of Jesus was manifest in Rome, six more fled Rome and joined the seven. They were from among the worshippers of God and the pure of faith, who were followers of the Christ. 470 When he had gathered them into the cave, one by one, he medicated them, which prevented their organs from decaying—such is the cave and its story.

Then comes the story of the Pilate in Rome, shamed to the core for the shedding of Christ's blood. I will give an account of his deeds, he was a caesar among rebels! At the time Christ appeared, a group of Jews agitated against him. Everyone insulted him publicly, and he went into hiding from them. Judas revealed him to them, for he was a companion of the precious Christ. When what happened to Jesus came to pass, God hastened him to heaven.

There remained on earth twelve fierce warriors faithful to that pure-bodied one, who are called the apostles, their pursuits guided by Simon.[11] 480 Driven to avenge Christ, armed men joined him from every direction. Twelve thousand Jews he killed, and departed this world.

Ten of his companions remained—his close followers, his intimates. Of them, two went to Rome and arrived in that land in stealth. One was that excellent fellow named Andreas, a wise youth in full manhood. And if you ask me the name of the other, it is Matthew, and the two of them agreed that they must not be discovered.

Matthew hid and Andreas went to the Pilate, strutting confidently towards him, presenting himself as a doctor, and spoke of medicine. The Pilate now had his henchman hold court. 490 The nobles of the city were gathered, altogether more than sixty men. When Andreas spoke of medicine, the whole gathering was astonished, disconcerted,

---

10. This story is commonly referred to as the Seven Sleepers of Ephesus, with the number of people in the cave usually being seven.

11. The Simon meant here is Simon the Canaanite, also known as Simon the Zealot.

and dumbstruck. They all called him a magician. Andreas grew closer and closer to the king—his position kept improving.

The nobles took umbrage at Andreas. One by one they went to the king saying, "Andreas spoke some stimulating words, but he knows nothing of medicine, neither drugs nor remedies, nor diseases, o king, don't be taken in by his tricks!"

Andreas said to him, "A great king would ignore the words of those mighty ignoramuses. Instead, have me cure a subject's ailment, whether of vapors or of blood. Send me whoever is deaf and blind, lame, with paroxysms in their limbs. 500 Even if the illness has been established for ten years, let them come from city and countryside, if I can cure them in one month, then my own body is spared. And if not, who could escape the caesar? Spill Andreas's blood right away!"

A crier went out, around the city, "Whoever is afflicted with an ailment, bring them immediately before the king, bring them to this worthy man of the court. Andreas will fix all of them, we will wash away their pains with his cures. He does not require that anyone provide medicines, he looks only to the man of God."

In one week, an army of sick people came to the king's court. By the month's end he had dispatched that army of the sick, and not one was further afflicted. Andreas made all of Rome well, his name was glorified to the Pilate. 510

Knowing Andreas had taken great pains in this, he rewarded him with robes of honor, coin, and treasure. He became the Pilate's physician and companion, this man of faith and that idolater, together. Concord brings you what you wish—a life of ease for whoever is known for concord!

And so it went on, for a time, until a youth who was dear to the king, part of his family, his companion (he showed him more kindness than his own children), died suddenly one day of an aneurism. The Pilate sunk into distress and sorrow, and tore up all his caesar's garments, scattered like dust over his crown and throne.

When he heard this, Matthew went to the court, and when he arrived as a stranger before the king, he said to Andreas, "You scoundrel! The king grieves because of you. You lost a youth like this! For were it not for you, his heart would not have known death! 520 If you have no knowledge, cure, or diagnosis, don't go round the doors of kings."

Andreas replied, "Don't talk nonsense! Don't go strutting along the path of injustice, for no one who lives is immortal, everyone who is born dies, surely."

Matthew said to him, "Ignorant one! God has decreed a time for old age. The body decays because of how one sleeps and eats. By means of knowledge we can preserve people. Since your knowledge was incomplete, you let him succumb through incompetence. If you don't acquire knowledge, surely you will kill healthy people. The prophet, the Messiah, taught me this—but you denied his prophethood. 'When you profess your faith then I will guide you.' I will bring this one to life in God's name, now, I will lift him from the dust. In a week, I will bring him before the king." 530

Andreas said to him, "I share your goal, and will follow your path to it. If you bring the dead to life, then it is fitting that we be your followers. I will be the first king who accepts the religion. Then the minister and these lords I pledge to you, from this border to the distant frontier."

The warlords said, as did the caesar, "Now there is no excuse left. [191b] If you raise this man from the dead, then we will all convert and follow the path you tread."

They made their pact and Matthew took that corpse from their midst. By the palace, he washed that dead body. He applied his cures to him for a week. On the eighth day he came running to the caesar, the youth with him, color returned to his face. They all pledged to him and converted, taking up his creed and his path. 540 All of Rome joined the Christian faith, woman and man took up the path of the bishops. When God wants something to happen, it will be done even with only the slightest effort. The faith of Mary's child grew, until the Jews were confounded. This was another story sent to the just king.

DISCOURSE ON KING STALINAS

There was a king by the name of Stalinas who had all he needed of both learning and treasure. In a city called Constantine, he founded a monastery beside the Euphrates. How much gold and how many jewels he sunk into that monastery, no one knows. That sovereign king raised another column three hundred spans into the air. Upon it was a square, like a marble banquet table—the tomb of that noble king. King Stalinas was placed in there, to protect him from the air.[12] 550

A talisman was placed above the grave: a horse and saddle of precious gold. One of his hands holds the reins, the other is raised towards the city, as if calling the people forth, and they all know him to be king. Everyone who has seen this and knows about it will attest that I have told the truth.

The monarch kept with him the best of the stories of past kings. In them, all learning, wisdom, culture, and authority, every trick, deceit, and stratagem. Reading them would increase your cleverness and wisdom, your face would show astonishment. I found this written in Greek and Pahlavi, if you'd hear it from me:[13]

12. The intention seems to have been to protect his body from exposure and corruption.

13. The implication here is that now we will read a story contained in the fifth book given to Kush, which was about the histories of kings. This is the second layer of the frame tale. It is not clear if the claim "I found this written in Greek and Pahlavi" indicates that the author compiled different sources from each language, or refers to the fact that the Pseudo-Callisthenes *Alexander Romance*, written originally in Greek, could also be read in a Pahlavi translation—in other words, that it was a widely known tale.

A Story [of Alexander's Travels in the East]

When the world was under Alexander's rule, he wanted to tour the earth. From Darius of Iran to Porus of India, the world was delivered unto his gleaming sword.[1] 560 The world-seeking king came to the east, with an army that could block the wind. He went on until he reached the sea that conceals the sun.

At the edge of the deep sea were a group of terrifying men. Naked head to toe and black of hide, like the heart of a vengeful man, mouths and teeth like dogs and faster than dogs in the chase. Their weapons were javelins, and they tore apart and ate each other. They soon saw Alexander's army. Each one seized a man from the saddle. They ate many of the troops, and many were slain by the javelins. They tore them apart like dogs, leaving behind neither flesh, sinew, skin, nor veins.

Alexander turned his face to the heavens, he said, "O recourse for those who seek recourse! 570 You are the creator of good and evil, you are the cultivator of tame and savage beast! Relieve my heart from this enemy, free my army from evil!"

And then, he ordered that they rain death from their arrowheads like hail. When his forces reached into their quivers, they seized the ground from the Black Hordes. They killed so many that the sea turned red like blood, dark night came near. The army of the Black Hordes was routed and Alexander departed that place.

1. Darius and Porus were kings defeated by Alexander in the Pseudo-Callisthenes Alexander romance.

He traveled with his forces one day and one night, and they reached a black stone. The honorable king saw an idol made of marble atop the black stone and approached it. He saw written upon its hand:

> This is a statue of Kush, of twisted character, the elephant-tusked king and commander of China, possessed of imperium, crown, and royal seal, 580 who saw pleasures none of the mighty would know, and who vanquished what no other could, then died and left all he had behind. He departed and all was wind in his hands. He was wrecked and the world flourished. If you look on my works, my command, my power, my wisdom, my manliness, treasure, and vast armies, my fighting and feasting, my crown and throne, you would not set your heart on this world, which appears sweet without but is poison within. Three times five hundred years I walked the earth, its kings all humbled by my blade. All that I ruined was made right again. Gold bloomed from the dust of my horse's hooves. By my javelin piercing an anvil, I breathed the sweet scent of satisfaction. Now my organs have rotted: the fate of all men. 590

Alexander wept profusely, and said "The world is a fairy tale and a dream! Whether we last a hundred years or a hundred thousand, this is how it ends! If only someone would tell me the truth of this matter. I wish to know the works and ways of Kush, whose likeness we have seen in stone."

He left that place vexed, and carried on day and night for another month. At the start of the month, he reached a group of people the likes of which no one ever saw, with heads of horses and voices like small birds. Alexander's heart was entranced. He took great pains to understand their language, to no avail. They could find no translator in the vicinity and the king of the Romans grew despondent.

When the night grew dark he supplicated God. "O judge who shows us the way, 600 it would be fit if you taught me their song, that I could know their secrets. Do not conceal their speech from me, your servant. Would that I could learn the works of Kush!"

When the sun spread its glory out across the plain, the whole earth turned the color of gold. Alexander came out to pay them a visit, and now could understand their speech. He knew that God had uncovered the secret, he dismounted and bowed in prayer. He said, "O pure deliverer, none could open the locked door for me, but you."

He asked them about how they obtained food, what they get and how they grow it.

One of them replied as follows: "For food we eat these fish, and seeds of plants and fruits. These three things are all we eat."

He asked, "Is there one of you who is a keeper of wisdom, 610 and who could tell auspicious days from bad, could calculate the influence of the stars, an old and wise one, crowned with glory, aware of the deeds of past kings?"

They responded, "You will find no one here who has much knowledge, but if you travel for a day, you will find one who has the appearance of a king, an old, learned fellow named Mahanesh. This is what your majesty seeks. He has made himself a home upon the crest of a mountain, having chosen seclusion and remoteness. The treasure he needs is whatever he finds there, everything is to his satisfaction. Whatever may be, he describes it just as it is. No one is more learned than he. At every new year, all of us together make our way to the crest of the mountain, offer our praises to that wise old man, and supplicate him. 620 Whatever will occur in the coming year, the old one reveals entirely. He shows us health from sickness and good from bad, abundance and scarcity, so that we understand."

ARRIVAL AT THE SKIRT OF THE MOUNTAIN

Alexander sent two men ahead of the group, and had them go near the mountain. It was mountainous desert there, and he ordered that they dismount. [192a] When the mountain's slopes became crowded, he and a few others ascended it. He saw a place there fit for kings with fruiting trees and flowing water. A sturdy stone house stood on the peak, as if resting upon the clouds, above the sky.

The sage turned and looked behind him, and he saw a crowd of man-faced men. He came down and welcomed them, his complexion now ruddy with joyous excitement. 630 He hailed each of them, asked about their health, and kissed the hand of the aspiring world-conqueror. He took him and sat the king down under a tree, praising him strongly.

Alexander bade him be seated, telling him, "The purpose of our visit was to see you."

He said, "O king, your highness, o commander, it behooves me not to sit in your presence. I am aware of your fame, your reputation. To sit in your presence would be absurd."

Alexander was struck by his words, swearing to God under his breath. He said to him, "O pure elder, what do you know of my lineage, my name?"

The answer, without hesitation, was, "Surely, you are the king, Alexander, the one king in the world who knows God, with whom the ungrateful cannot contend. God has shown the signs of your glory, which weakens the necks of the rebellious. 640 Three hundred years before your arrival, o reputable one, a painter painted your face."

The learned man went into his house and retrieved a yellowed deerskin. He unfolded it and showed it to them: it was the image of Alexander, just as he was. All his deeds, his career, all that would later become known, all was written within—and it had been three hundred years since it was written!

Alexander looked at his companions and said, "Whoever saw such a thing?!"

"You, o wise elder, sit before us then and satisfy me with your presence." The king was persuasive and insistent with his request, and Mahanesh sat there before them. Everyone sought his knowledge, and his answers were comprehensive. They found him very learned, for God had hidden nothing from him. 650

Alexander praised him and said, "May wisdom ever accompany your pure soul, I know no one like you in all the world, out of all the knowledgeable and well-informed men."

He replied to the king, "O you elder king of guests, you must eat something!"

Alexander replied, "You must first eat some of this simple, ripe fruit."

The wise man said to him, "O peerless one, it has been one hundred sixty years that I have not broken fast except at night, and I have taken a vow of silence, except for one day of the year, on which almighty God has ordained for me a feast. On that day my body receives nourishment and my life is sustained by these fruits."

"Which is it," he said, "that precious day that these delightful signs appear to you?"

He said, "The third day of Ordibehesht is what God, in his generosity, ordained. 660 On that day Adam departed this abode, God sent his soul to paradise."

"How do you know," he said to him, "that it was this day, this same fortunate month and day? If you were to find documentation of this, you'd be wiping mud off of solid brick. No writing remained after the Deluge that anyone could read."

The learned man laughed at the king's words, and said to him, "O lofty, glorious king! It is beneath you to make such a hasty judgment. Though the whole world was taken by the water, it did not destroy everything such that if Enoch found writing about it, it disappeared when he read it.[2] I'd be surprised to hear these words from an ignoramus, much less from the world-king at the head of his company! Though water overcame the world, those who worship God remained unharmed, 670 for such creation was for those who did not know the creator.

"Those who were on Mount Rahvan were very, very numerous.[3] I heard that there were five thousand who worshiped God in those days. They all spoke of God and recited Adam's book. When Adam descended from the sky, he descended on Rahvan. The two footprints of our dear father are visible there upon that mountain. In the land of Sri Lanka, the Indians visit that mountain every year.

"When the ark reached Mount Rahvan, its messenger, Noah, saw those people. He was glad to see them and said, 'O good people, I feared that the creator of Babel had made the world devoid of people. 680 I give thanks to God that I have seen you here.' Then, he entrusted to them those bones of Adam that he kept, saying, 'These should go with you now. The creator will ask this of you, that you bury them away from water, and do not let the sun shine on them.' And the ship sailed on from that place, it reached Jowdi and remained there. It is a small mountain in Mafareqin, others have said much about it.[4] If the king wants me to tell his majesty, he has a path to all knowledge."

Then, Mahanesh spoke more to him, whatever wisdom he could give. The world-king praised him and said, "I have never heard such things!" And then he asked him, "My good man, who showed you the way here? 690 How did you come to this mountain without an army, such that no harm befell you on the way? How do you live here among these sorry people? I have been on the road three months, and such

2. Enoch here is Hermes Trismegistus.

3. Mount Rahvan is a mountain in Sri Lanka where, according to legend, Adam left a footprint.

4. Mafareqin is near modern-day Diyarbekir, Turkey.

evil my army has seen on this wicked road! We saw no one who worships God, only you here on this mountain."

He replied, "O king, listen to the answer, give it its due and don't
react badly to the truth. You have been drawn here by greed and ambition, the path of greed cannot be tread without pain. You seek fame
and comfort in the world, I flee from both. I worship God, you worship the world. See, now, who has triumphed? Thus have I roamed so
far from every people, and chosen a mountaintop as my home. And as
for this mountain and my nourishment, I am content with the food
and shelter I find here. 700 For a day will come when I leave this
abode, and I do not wish my spirit to suffer. If my body was dirtied on
the road, then I would be held back from what I wish. If my limbs and
organs subjected me to interrogation, it would be a drawn-out affair, o
proud king."

He replied, "God has shown you the path to faith and to learning.
If people learn from you, you will bring faith to many of the faithless.
When your knowledge was fruitless, it was like a treasure buried in the
ground."

The just man answered him, "How can we give what God did not?
The one God has chosen is far greater in knowledge and faith than I
am, o acclaimed king, and if that one has not been endowed with these
two things, how then could we bestow them?"

Alexander said to him, "Oh, good fellow, tell me more about your
lineage and origins. 710 Tell me how you came upon this mountain.
How did you leave your homeland?"

He answered, "Transcendent God brought me here where I have no
fear. I am from the line of Jamshid, o born-of-kings. No one is left of
that lineage but me. In those days when the turning of the heavenly
sphere cut Jamshid off from its favor, the world fell under the command of the demon Zahhak, and screams of the terror of his demons
were heard from every direction.[5] The presence of those who worship
God was weakened by fear of that sorcerer. The face of Jamshid's fortune paled, and every avenue was cut off to him. His own wife and two
sons he sent with his relatives and their allies to a place called Arghun

5. Jamshid is the greatest of all world-kings in *The Shahnameh*. During his reign
there was no sickness or death. Because of this, he claimed to be God. His subjects
rebelled, and the evil Zahhak became the new world-king. See introduction.

in China, where the whole land is covered in forest so dense that an eagle could not escape it.[6] 720 His wife was the daughter of the king of China, and he gave him treasures of all kinds.

"When it was time to leave he said to his army, 'Keep this secret completely hidden. When they saw my two children, they were satisfied by their learning and manliness. [192b] But no king will arise from the line of Farak who could seek vengeance. From Nunak's line a king will appear to take revenge against the demon-faced.[7] He will avenge me against the sorcerer, Zahhak, and the world will be set aright by my faith. Revere him, in all the world, for the heavens keep many secrets.'

"When Farak heard these words from Jamshid, he offered him a sound suggestion: 'O king of the world, if this is how it will be, then kingship shall never be mine—this, the turning heavens revealed. 730 Show me the way to worship God, since I am a pauper in this fleeting abode. When Nunak gains the throne, let the other world not be lost to me.'

"When Jamshid heard these words from Farak, his weary world brightened. The lofty king gave him three volumes filled with science and wisdom, with all the pages of the messengers of God, written in the pure-hearted king's hand. He said to him, 'Heed them, if you want to keep harm at bay. If you devote yourself for a time to these three books, that will deliver you unto God without a doubt.'

"He then sent them to Arghun, so that no one would find them. Jamshid marshaled his army there and went to battle with Mehraj.[8] When a man's fortunes have been crushed, what recourse does anyone

6. Curiously, while there is no Arghun in Central Asia or China, this is the Arabic rendering of Aragon, the Spanish kingdom.

7. Accounts of the line of descent from Jamshid to Faridun vary among *The Shahnameh*, the Avesta, and Tabari's history. In the latter two, the names of Faridun's ancestors are all portmanteaus of the Persian word for cow (*gav*) indicating that they had many, or good, cows. An anonymous twelfth-century Persian history, the *Mojmal al-Tavarikh va'l-Qesas*, gives names for Jamshid's sons similar to those in *The Kushnameh*. The *Kushnameh* disagrees with *The Mojmal* about the name Farak; however its spelling is consistent, and has thus been retained. The name of the other son is written inconsistently—however all variants are orthographically close to "Nunak," the spelling given in *The Mojmal*, which has thus been used here. See Īrānshān ibn Abī al-Khayr, *Kūshnāmah*, edited by Jalāl Matīnī (Tehran: Intishārāt-i ʿIlmī, 1377 [1998]), 187n5.

8. Mehraj is the king of India in *The Shahnameh*.

have to improve them? 740 He remained in Zahhak's prison fifty years, and that chosen king was without rival. Look at how he ended up, and what the executioner did: sawed him in half![9]

"Word reached Nunak in Arghun that the face of the earth was emptied of kings. He sent a messenger to his grandfather, saying, 'What has befallen us? The world-king was caught in his war and that put us in dire straits. We do not know where to turn. We are waiting for the king's orders. Do we come? Do we go? What is the solution? I will do whatever you order.'

"When Mahang, the king of China, learned of this evil, he was bowled over by the news. He was frightened for Jamshid's family, lest Zahhak learn the secret, and doom find him from that serpentine man; his throne and crown would be lost. 750 The king sent a message to his daughter, 'Do not try to send anyone to me. It is better that you hide in the forest than that you die by Zahhak's hand. I want no one to see you. The secret must be kept. Stay where you are for one week, I will send you whatever is necessary.'

"In that forest, those men fled day and night, their hearts pounding and mouths dry. They stayed there until the king of China turned to battle Mehraj with all ferocity. The Mehrajians suffered defeat, not one of those famous horsemen remained. Mehraj's son was killed on that battlefield, and his rule was shaken. He fell ill for a time from that injury and appeared weak to his nobles. His mind fell to reflecting on how he could drench his dagger with Mahang's blood. 760

"One of his agents said, 'His daughter is the wife of Jamshid. He has two children by her, like the moon, all three are hidden under the king's roof. The three of them never see the light of day, and they never sleep for fear of Zahhak.'

"When Mehraj heard this, he quickly arose, and rewarded the one who gave him this information with much clothing, and silver and gold, as well as a caparisoned horse, helmet and girdle. He said to him, 'Now I am better.' He requested food, musicians, and wine. He sent a letter to the sorcerer Zahhak, composed of falsehoods. Even if the lie was worthy of reproach, he would be happy that it saved him. Lies must never be heard, blessed is he who repeats even less than he heard.

9. In the *Shahnameh*, Jamshid flees to the east. He is eventually found by Zahhak and sawed in half.

[MEHRAJ] SENDS A MESSENGER WITH
A LETTER [TO ZAHHAK]

"The letter began,

To his majesty, who is like the sun and master unto the world, 770 who has the turning heavens under his command. All wants are cured by his remedies. If the mighty king does not turn his ear to the words of this servant, then this unfortunate one will come to ruin. I am beholden to his majesty. When the king's decree reached this servant, that Jamshid had vanished from the earth and I should search that land to find him, I set myself to searching this region. To the Sea of China I came with a great army, and that ill-fated man was found. When I found out, I marched on him, doubtful I would prevail. I knew not who would be the victor, who fate would favor. When his day ended he was captured, humbled by such a lowly servant as myself. I sent him to the king's threshold and considered the situation carefully. 780 I was terrified by the secret I uncovered, a sin committed by Mahang of China. He had covertly sent him troops and given him his daughter in marriage. She has two children from that demon-faced one, to whom Mahang has shown much kindness. When the investigators found out, they hurried back to me with this news.

I sent him a messenger with wise and worthy counsel, "You are a loyal servant of the king, why would you shelter his enemies? If my hand were an enemy to the king I would cut it off, and not call it my own. If you have any love for the king, do not shelter his enemies. When you befriend his enemy, you yourself become his enemy. A wise Brahman gave good advice: 'Do not expect to remain a friend of one whose enemy you befriended.' 790 The two descendants of Jamshid are with you, though they are your own flesh and blood. Since they have grievance and want vengeance against the king, they must not be seen upon the earth. They must be sent to me and I will send them together with some of my own men to the world-king, lest he become aware of what is going on. Things would turn out badly for you and me both, so do not seek even the slightest pretext to delay. I say all this in kindness: I would not want the land of China to be ruined. If you delay in handling this, you will be putting yourself in dire straits. If you deviate from the king's commands in this way, you will be considered a criminal."

When the messenger reached the environs of China, I knew he was aware of this. He did not read my letter to the end, but sent off the envoy like a stray dog. 800 He spoke ill of me and of your majesty, words unbecoming to friend or foe. All the things that malicious man said should not be repeated, except this one. Stating he has no fear of Zahhak, he said, "I consider him no higher than the dust, and I consider no one higher than myself, to issue commands over me and my domains."

I was appalled at this message, and by his unworthy opposition and enmity. Right then, I marshaled a strong army on which I spent my whole treasury. I put in command my eldest son and sent him to do battle with that king. They killed so many on that field of strife, the Sea of China turned red with their blood. Just as they reached the moment of victory, the winds turned in favor of the Chinese. This worthy army was defeated and my dear son was entombed in the earth. 810 My heart burned a long time from his death and my mind was on fire. A scarce few of that worthy army returned to India—one in a hundred. Every house weeps and mourns. Instead of wine and celebration, sorrow. Now I have heard that that malicious man has gathered a limitless army, which prepares to march on me. You are the king and the refuge of the helpless! If you sent me reinforcements from your army, you would make your rule impervious. God forbid that that mighty one march a great army against this land. All color and life would be gone from India, the gleaming axes would turn its streams red. A thousand praises for the king, may he make the hands of the malicious recoil.

"He sent a year's tribute along with the letter to the court of proud Zahhak. [193a] 820 They traveled a year's journey in six months to the king in Jerusalem.

"When the letter arrived, Zahhak read it at once and summoned his forces from wherever they were. He summoned a great army to his court and chose five hundred thousand men. He sent them to King Mehraj, and when Mehraj saw that elite army, he equipped them well and led them towards China, nursing his vengeance against Mahang. Between the two armies there was much fighting, distraught minds deprived of rest and victuals. Zahhak's army passed Kabul and Zabol and arrived to bolster King Mehraj's forces.[10] The king of China could not withstand the attack, and he killed him to avenge his son's blood. 'When you have killed one who is your equal, know that they will kill you too, o foolish one!' He cleaned out Mahang's treasury, and ground that verdant land into the dust. 830 His wives, children, treasure, and whatever else he had, he sent it all to Zahhak.

10. Zabol is a city in present-day Iran, in Sistan province.

"He returned to his own land, as the days now favored him. This is what the world is like, its ways and works: sometimes an enemy, sometimes an ally, sometimes it's with you and sometimes it's not, sometimes kind, sometimes malicious. When Nunak and Farak became aware of what had happened, they departed that land. They traveled for a month. The army followed them, but it saw no one and turned back.

"The world's ways changed even more when Zahhak learned that the ruler of China and Machin had been killed.[11] He called on his brother, Kush, to appear before him, and told him what had transpired. He said, 'Go to that place where you can see the sun rise over the water, 840 and whoever you find from the seed of Jamshid, cut him in two.'

"Kush went and seized China and Machin; the whole region came under his command. He went to the source of the sun, his armies moving with haste. No one could stand against him in battle, and when he returned, he took up residence in Khandan [Chang'an].[12] He ordered that the city be renovated, so that you'd think it was a piece of heaven. Whoever saw any trace of the Jamshidians told Kush where they were, and he sought them there. But wherever Kush and his

11. In most Arabic and Persian geographical writing, the phrase "China and Machin" can be taken to mean "China and neighboring states." Machin is almost never mentioned in Persian except in the pair "China and Machin" *(chin o machin)*. *Chin* corresponds roughly to the modern concept of China, though of course not to its modern borders, and is described in Arabic and Persian geographies in detail, including information about culture, governance, agriculture, and the names and locations of several major cities. Accounts of Machin, on the other hand, are very brief and vague.

12. Chang'an, (adjacent to present-day Xi'an) was the location of the imperial capital of ancient China from unification by the Qin emperor until 9 CE; it became the capital again when China was unified by the Sui dynasty in 582 CE and remained so under the Tang dynasty (618–907 CE). Hence, Chang'an was described in Arabic and Persian geographical writing as the imperial capital of China, even in twelfth-century texts. Modern scholarship generally assumes the Perso-Arabic rendering of the name to be Khomdan, however renderings such as Chandan/Jandan (orthographically identical) and Khandan, which are closer to the Early Middle Chinese pronunciation, appear in tenth- to thirteenth-century New Persian texts, including in *The Bahmannameh*, possibly also written by Iranshah. The orthography in the *Kushnameh* manuscript is inconsistent, but the appearance of spellings such as Jandan and Khandan here and in other texts suggests that these alternatives should not be dismissed as copyists' errors. See Īrānshān, *Kushnameh*, 195n2.

armies went, they found not one child of the Jamshidians. When God, the exalted, is with them, what have they to fear from Zahhak or Kush?

"Farak said to Nunak, 'Why should I bother? I will never be king, so why should I live in fear of the enemy? 850 Why not remain hidden and make some corner of the world my own? The source of all this pain is fear and nothing else, no one has seen anything worse than this fear. All ailments dissolve the body, except fear, which destroys the mind. I should go where they will not find me, where I will live happier than if I had wealth and kingship.'

"His words troubled Nunak, who said, 'O king of noble character, I wish you would not say such things, why do you want to flee and leave me behind? You bring new distress to my heart. If you abandon me, I will abandon my life. If you remain hidden from me, who else do I have in the world? If heavens bring down misfortune, whether here or on a high mountaintop, you will not escape from God's will, you cannot force the heavens' turning wheel.' 860

"Having spoken at length, Farak cried hard, not looking at his brother, and got dressed. He took the road to Rome and reached his destination, hidden from Kush and the shameful Zahhak. Nunak taught his son to avoid everything, and the same to the rest of his family. He told them, 'My companions, God ends our suffering. Security and comfort in a strange city is better than kingship with treasure and fear. Be content, be safe, do not consider my counsel lowly and weak. Tell no one who we are, or what we are about in these lands. We must worship God Almighty every day, for this is our way. You will depart from this world, so it is unwise to grieve for its loss. Whoever wanted wife and child, and then was happy when his wife was miserable? 870 When a child comes, a man must remain by his wife's side. We remove difficulties better by knowledge than by longing, it is hard to assess trouble in time of need. One who succeeds in pursuing worldly things will not succeed, God will throw their affairs into disarray. This is better than for the world to get the better of him and conceal him under the dust. He will not remain here forever, nor will this gain him entry into heaven.' He continued to give such advice, until years had gone by.

"The world-king departed this world, his seed scattered over the earth. I am of his seed, living upon this mountaintop—the best kind of contentment, your majesty.[13] The glorious Faridun is my ancestor, and now my place is upon gravel and thorns. Thus, God is more pleased with me than all the kings sitting on their thrones. 880 More than one hundred and eighty years it is that I have been apart from my family. I went from Rome to the land of Yemen in this state that you see me, unaccompanied. Then I came from there to these mountains, and made a home of bare stone, feasting on hardship until this sapling bore fruit. I worshiped both during the day, and when the world-illumining sun went down, I ate plants and roots, a diet which gradually weakened my body. Now the tree bears fruit, the creator has given me to eat from it. I am grateful to God, for he has shown me the way, He is my protector, your majesty."

The king and his grandees ate the fruit. Alexander said to the others, "See here, this fruit is not dry, it tastes sweet and smells like musk!" 890 He then said to him, "O you who are the essence of gravity and intelligence, do you know anything about Kush? When I came here with my army, I saw a black stone along the way. A hideous form stood upon it, and a wayfarer had written upon its hand that this was the statue of Kush, world-king, to whom all hidden things were known. He surpassed the kings of the earth, living more than three times five hundred years. No one in the world would ever see what he saw, and who knows how to reach the places he reached? It is my wish to know his story, o essence of the righteous, if you have any knowledge of his story, please take the trouble to repeat it to me."

Mahanesh heard and lowered his head, his heart wounded by worry. Then he looked up at the sky. He said, "O creator of the world, 900 it would not do for you to fail in this, and so embolden the rebellious. World-conquering king, you must not set your heart on this fleeting abode. Whether we live ten years or ten thousand, whether we are a slave or royalty, the coming of death makes all those days vanish, for slave and king alike.

"This Kush was raised by Abtin, who found him in the forests of China. The events of his life are all known to me, even though he is not of my blood. I will give the king his story, and many other books of ancient times. For I wish that the creator would bring my days to an

---

13. The hermit, Mahanesh, thus reveals that he is descended from Jamshid's son Farak.

end, as I have tired of life upon this mountain, and I will not see another person after you leave. It is my hope that this one wish be granted by your command, o benevolent one: 910 now that God has brought my time to an end, hide me away in this house."

He said this and performed his ablutions, then knelt before God. He prostrated himself twice, face to the ground, and prayed until he gave up his life. Alexander was astonished by what he'd said, and tears streamed down his cheeks. They washed his body and prayed over it, and opened the door of that narrow house. They made that house into his tomb and buried him in the earth there. The world will do this to everyone: this is the place of the meek and the mighty. He removed a number of books and looked over each one. He found a book of deerskin parchment, and the king's minister immediately began to read it. [193b]

The Story of Kush the Tusked

Chapter 1

The story begins with praise of God, who erected the turning heavens. 920 He illumined the world with sun and moon, distinguishing day from black night. In this way, he created the world in six days, he who hid fire inside stone and created spring after the month of January. Sugar appeared within the canes at his command! The world's place is not beside his, and no one is privy to his secret, for why would he enthrone one like Kush and crown the head of the Tusked?[1]

Everyone who knows the secret of this story knows that to set your heart on the world is foolishness. Kush gained satisfaction from the world that no one could match. No one ever endured upon the earth like him. Who has seen five times three hundred years, every year in comfort and wealth? And yet, he bit the dust—this is the way of the world. When you learn his secret, you will be astonished. A wise person would learn from it. 930

The experienced sage told me the following:[2]

1. "*Kush-e pil-dandan*" can be literally translated as "Kush the elephant-toothed"; for the sake of brevity, this epithet will henceforth be translated as "the Tusked."

2. The reference to the sage here marks the beginning of the main story, and the preceding lines have the standard form of the preface to a book—Iranshah is describing the book he has, ostensibly, translated into New Persian verse. Here and a few other times in the main text of the epic, Iranshah refers to the person from whom he learned the story of Kush as "the experienced sage." It is possible that this is merely a narrative device. Given the probable Sassanian-era origins of the story, it seems that Iranshah intended to draw attention to his and his readers' need to rely on archaic, possibly

"What I heard is that when Zahhak called on Kush he sent him to China from the west, and gave him rule over the east. He said to him:

"'Wherever you find any sign of Jamshid's descendants, those fools, destroy them, for they are wicked and malevolent. At the time that I killed him, he said, in front of the troops, "A king will arise and avenge me." You must ensure that there is no one left from the seed of the wayward ones. Do not let even an infant escape, for even the dragon starts out as a snake! If you underestimate your enemy, he will cause you great suffering. No kindness will come to you from an enemy even if he is of your own skin and blood. 940 He may deceive you with his tongue at first, but you'll soon find out his true nature. A sweet, oily tongue, and a heart full of enmity are a trap set by a devil. If he gets you, he'll kill you, and though you plead with him, he will not let you go.'"

When Kush and his army arrived in China, he looked all over for them. In every forest, mountain, and sea, he looked, but saw no sign of them.

Fearing the malevolent Kush, they were in flight year after year over fields and mountains, fleeing sometimes like leopards into the mountains, sometimes like whales into the sea. They endured this hardship, lamenting bitterly the whole time. When six hundred years had passed, Nunak died. His son predeceased him, and destiny had left his throne empty. 950 His son's name was Maharu, and he and his other relatives loved him dearly. Maharu's wife bore a child near the time he died, who was given to the wet-nurse. When Nunak saw him, he named him Abtin. He brought joy to man and woman. Since he valued him dearly, he was so attentive to his needs at all times that even his relatives could scarcely tell that it was not his own son but his grandchild.

When Nunak fell ill, he summoned people to him, and spoke at length about Abtin. He said, "This year, this month will be my last. Abtin is now your king. Devote yourselves to Abtin just as you were

---

unreliable texts for knowledge of the distant past. These asides by the author of course raise the question of where the frame tales we have just read came from. Most likely, both frame tales were largely Iranshah's own inventions, the first having clear parallels to events of the eleventh century, the second inserting the epic's title character into more widely familiar, accepted narratives about Alexander. See introduction for further discussion.

devoted to me, with your property and life. For from him comes the king who will bring ruin upon the serpentine one. He will empty the world of demons and sorcery, and place upon his head the kingly crown. 960 He will adorn the world with justice and faith, and hasten to take revenge on the vile Zahhak." The troops showed their devotion to Abtin and remained in that forest.

When Kush saw no enemy from any direction, he led his army against the elephant-eared people. He killed and captured many of them, and distributed the captives among his men. He found a girl from among them, so bright of spirit and pure of mind, her coquettish glances were Babylonian magic, her face a blooming Zabolian rose. Her stature was like a cypress crowned by the moon, her presence put camphor and ben oil to shame. That moon made the king's heart bubble over, his every wish and thought was of her. After a year, she bore a child the like of which the creator never created: two boar tusks, two elephant ears, a red face and hair, and two eyes blue-black as the Nile. 970 Between his shoulder blades there was a mark, black like the bodies of sinners.

He saw him and was very afraid, and said to his wife, "Low-born, ill-omened woman! People give birth to people—men and women. How is it that you have borne a devil-child?"

His heart was so filled with anger that he cut off her head with his sword. Such is the way of the world, which hides many secrets. Secrets emerge every day from the fog, and what did the king get? A warthog!

Secretly, then, he took that child down the road to the forests of China. He threw him away there and returned, and kept the secret. An unaccomplished deed remains unknown, but one accomplished becomes known to the world. Every secret, even one between two people, someday becomes public. 980

The next day when Abtin and his troops were out hunting, they came to that spot. He heard the cries of a child from the thicket. He hurried towards the voice and saw him, and was astonished by the sight. His spirit was troubled by what he saw. He said to himself, again and again, "This can be nothing other than a devil-child."

He ordered his servant to pick him up and returned to the camp. He threw him before a dog, and the ravenous beast fled from him. He threw him before a lion, but the lion did not eat him, and Abtin's face turned yellow with fear. They threw him into the fire, and it did not burn him. Everyone's jaw dropped. Whoever God, the just, protects, will not be destroyed by sword or fire. He ordered that the baby be thrown out the door, or else his head be removed from his body. 990

His wife said, "Noble king, do not commit rank injustice before the creator! There must be a secret behind this phenomenon—he will surely be someone of great importance. Give him to me and I will care for him like my own soul, I will bring him a caring wet-nurse."

He said to her, "Raising him would not benefit us, do you not see how his head and neck are like a boar?"

Because of how his wife entreated him, he gave him to her, and she turned her attention to rearing him. She sometimes called him "Tusked One" and sometimes "Ears," these being the only two names that described him.[3]

She sent him to a tutor when he was seven—he was already growing up strong. Two years passed and he had learned nothing, being more disposed toward the bow and arrow. He was a brute who took gargantuan satisfaction in beating up the other children with his fists. Everyone called him a demon. The teacher complained about him, 1000 and went to Abtin and wailed about all the trouble he caused.

Abtin said to him, "My good man, get a hold of yourself, and keep your distance from him. He is demon-born, an ill-tempered brute, the demon's heart is blind to culture. Wait and see how he turns out, and we can find him work befitting his appearance. He is hard-hearted, bad-natured, and ugly. Know that his character was forged in hell!"

When the child passed ten years of age, he took his bow and arrows out to the plain, hunting and trapping whatever beasts he saw. He could chase them and catch them on foot, he could grab their legs and pull them to the ground. Abtin was amazed by what he could do. His game was lions and leopards—he could catch a leopard as easily as if it were a fox.

When he reached fifteen, he was as strong and as tall as a tree. 1010 His bravery was so great that none of the soldiers dared face him. Fly-

3. Because the letters K and G were not differentiated in medieval Persian, ear (*gush*) was orthographically identical to Kush, so while there are legendary precedents for the name Kush, it is also possible Gush was the intended pronunciation. For readers of the text, as opposed to those hearing it recited, the ambiguity may have been significant in its own right.

ing birds could not escape his arrow, no dragon could escape his blade. Thus did heaven's great wheel turn: Kush never tired of bow or lasso. He rode with great endurance as his age passed thirty-five. [194a]

One day, the commander of China made a surprise attack on Abtin. They encountered him when he was outside the forest, and suddenly a melee broke out. There were more than ten thousand of the Chinese, and of the Iranians, only three hundred riders. The battle was joined and before long a number of the Iranians were wounded.

When Abtin saw his forces' situation, he ordered them to take flight into the forest. He threw on his armor and sprang onto his horse. 1020 He roared, "You honorable warriors must survive the day! If you show the slightest weakness, you'll find no quarter from the enemy! And as you stand and face them, never lose trust in God. From him alone are all victory and strength, and not from any army. These men are sinful and corrupt by nature, under the command of Zahhak the sorcerer. Many times, a great host has fled suddenly from battle with a small force."

He spoke these words, and with all the speed of his fast horse he turned on the enemy army. Wherever he struck with his mace he laid low a man, and where he struck with his blade, he severed heads and limbs.

When Kush saw King Abtin in this situation, he let out a mighty roar. He had a bow and ten arrows, and no other weapon in his hand. 1030 With ten arrows, he took down ten great, brave Chinese warriors. He looked sadly at his quiver when his arrows finished, and called out to a proud man of his army. He took his armor, his helmet, and donned them the way a weed sprouts leaves, planted his feet in the stirrups and, roaring, he routed the enemy forces with a single charge. He was like a raging elephant. The whole field was filled with arms, legs, and heads.

When the Iran-army saw Kush's coup against the enemy, his energetic, ferocious action, they all rallied and attacked and pushed that army across the river. His blade left a creek of blood along the ground, enemy heads were like polo balls to his horse. Whoever his mace landed on, their souls departed their bodies. His arrows drove all life from the air and the ground turned deep red from his sport. 1040 Whoever he came upon by surprise, and they saw him, their hearts beat rapidly like madmen. Fleeing, they prayed to God. Their hearts would not be the same for many months.

They killed more than five hundred brave men in that attack, and Abtin gained the upper hand. The Chinese commander was saddened with shame, his spirit within him turned its back.

He said, "You famous warriors, you have brought shame on yourselves, what have you to fear from foes so few that you could kill them even if you were unarmed? It has been a full three hundred years that the king has searched for these foes! And you're going to just turn around, now that you found them? We have hurried here from China for this very task, what will you say tomorrow before the king, if you retreat from the Iran army?"

His words roused his forces, their drums raised a clamor, 1050 they unsheathed the blades of ferocity from their scabbards—no time for delay or debate! The air filled with cries of deadly vengeance, blood flowed in rivers. Men of the Iran-army were killed, and they lost some ground with each casualty. The fighting went on until nightfall, and then the two armies disengaged. The Chinese commander dismounted there.

Abtin went into his tent. He sent for Kush, kissed him, and bade him sit beside him. He said, "Good child of mine, dearer to me than my own family and relations. What you did to my enemies truly brought joy to my body and spirit." He gave him generous gifts, with which Kush was nicely adorned: horses, a sword and shield, a helmet and cloak and a royal girdle. 1060

Abtin said to his men, "Tonight, the Chinese commander is troubled. Tonight we must go to the forest, where we will be hidden from the enemy. We must not allow them to disgrace us when they fight us tomorrow."

Kush said, "There is another way. When they see we have abandoned our position, they will be encouraged and come after us, and both army and king will be lost. If the king would entrust me with command of some troops, his best riders from this company, I will make a nighttime raid on them, fill field and valley with their blood. For their army will all be fast asleep, none of them is afraid of us now." Abtin was encouraged by what he said and praised Kush profusely.

That night, he gave command of his forces to Kush, and they quickly departed. 1070 When half the night had passed, Kush blew the battle horn. A cry rose up. The brave warriors drew their swords, the Chinese were half-drunk in their deep sleep. One came charging towards the wood, another was too weak to move a muscle, one had not put his armor on all the way when a deadly spear pierced him. Another, not having mounted his warhorse, took a slicing blade to his torso.

It was a night full of terror and battle, as the flame of war never waned. When it turned to day, the Chinese commander looked and saw the whole field covered in dead and wounded. He was frightened and could not immediately take command of his forces, and Kush was coming at him. He returned to the main Chinese camp and gathered reinforcements.

Kush took all of the booty and distributed it, and Abtin praised him. 1080 He kissed both his cheeks warmly, exclaiming that skill was more befitting a brave man than a pretty face. He gave him many garments, much gold and silver, horses and beasts of burden, a helmet and girdle. He gave him command over those few soldiers, and appeased them with booty. That same day Abtin and his men collected equipment, and then rode into the forest like the wind. Having raced toward the forest for two days, he arrived there with his troops in good spirits. Abtin sent several scouts to climb up the trees so that if the enemy sent an army, they would see them coming and warn the king.

When that army returned to China, Kush the king of China was filled with rage.[4] The commander complained, pleaded that the enemy had slipped right through their fingers. He explained how, since they were unsuccessful in fighting, that night they feasted and slept, 1090 and when the enemy saw their weakness in battle, they launched a nighttime raid.

Kush was upset by the commander's words.[5] His heart boiled over at the Chinese army. He banished them from his throne room, accusing them of being weak and having bad intentions.

Of his own army that he had brought, which Zahhak had sent out with him, he selected thirty thousand swordsmen, fierce riders brave

4. China and other names of inhabited places can refer to either the land as a whole or its main city. Thus, we are told the forest of Arghun is in China, but we may infer that it is outside its main cities and inhabited areas.

5. This Kush is Zahhak's brother, Abtin's enemy. Note that we have now seen three characters named Kush: the character in the frame story, Kush the brother of Zahhak sent to rule China, and his abandoned monstrous son raised by Abtin.

in battle. He gave this great army to Nivasb, who was his son and crown prince, a youth the like of whose handsomeness had not been seen as long as the heavens turned. Though young and fresh as a violet, his stature would make a young cypress bend over in amazement.

Nivasb reached the forest, searching day and night. Looking over all the forest, plain, sea and mountain, they searched until they were exhausted. 1100

A day later, the watchman saw them from the trees and shouted, "O fortunate king! the forest is filled with enemy forces from a different army."

The Iranians heard this call and donned their armor, ready for the fight. Having won the first battle, they rushed into this fight like fierce lions, [194b] like a falcon upon a dove, a lion upon a ram, they now went straight towards the enemy, their heads battle-hungry and hearts warlike.

Then they reached a gushing river with rapids like quaking mountains, roaring and foaming like the sea. The steel-coated riders were like ships, like crocodiles lurking in its depths, like serpents. On the river's banks were lions and tigers and their prey.

Abtin said to his army, "O noble, vengeful warriors, 1110 we must not cross this river, no one should dismount." They drew up ranks right there, lances, swords, and javelins in hand.

When Nivasb reached that spot, the riverbank could scarcely be seen through the crowd of enemy troops. He shouted, "You warriors, fleeing day and night out of fear of the king, like wild beasts of the fields, deserts, and mountains, hiding away from human company, even if you become boulders by the sea or stars in the sky, no one can hide from the sun, and sun-like is the world-king![6] All of you, look at your situation now! Prepare to reap the reward for your deeds."

From Nivasb's words and from all the roaring, both Abtin and Kush grew anxious. They all strung their bows, fingers knotting the strings. 1120 At once, they let loose such a rain of arrows that blood turned the riverbank to grime.

---

6. Note the irony here: the sun does outshine the stars, but the heavens turn and the sun always sets.

Nivasb was so stunned by the Iranians that, raging, he spurred his horse straight into the fray. His army followed him and threw themselves into the water with the speed of a bird. Hoping to gain the upper hand, they put themselves in dire straits.

When half the army had emerged from the water, they rushed to engage them. The Iran-army put up such a fight, the king on one side, Kush on the other. They threw themselves at the enemy, here striking a head and there a flank. With that attack, they unhorsed a thousand of that estimable army.

The clanging of swords and the roar of hoof-beats would have made a roaring lion lose its nerve. The heroes' maces became splitters of skulls. The quiver of arrows knitted steel. 1130 Men's hearts were crushed by beasts, with lance-heads seizing brave men's livers. The two armies collided with such ferocity that no one knew the way out. The wounds inflicted by the charging riders and the fear of their charge threw many men into the water. Some were cleft by blades and others vanished underwater.

Nivasb tried a hundred ways, and at last made the crossing. Crying out, he circled around the field. He saw no more than half his army left and lost hope, the wind sucked out of his liver.

The two armies camped in the forest near the river. The riders of both armies, day and night, remained thirsty, their lips dry. No one dared go down to the river or take their horse there to drink. They faced off for a month, hearts clouded by pain and bodies exhausted by wounds. 1140 When Nivasb saw such hesitation from the enemy, he looked for every possible way out of the fight.

Abtin held the crossing, but he began to worry about the Chinese general. He said to Kush and to his army, "Our situation has changed. Once they have built a great fleet of ships, a new army will come from China and take us by surprise. Our food is running out and we cannot delay any longer. We must disappear tonight, leave and cover our tracks."

As the world unfurled its black tresses, the Iran-army packed its bags. Two hundred select veterans remained with Kush and Abtin. They set fire to the camp fortifications and spilled out into the woods again. 1150 When half the night had passed, the king hurried after his army.

When day came and the mountainsides were gilded, the land cloaked in a golden shawl, Nivasb gradually realized that the face of the forest was wiped clean of the enemy. He smiled and swore, "So, they've done it again! In dark of night they took off from the riverside. They must be hiding. Once I begin crossing the river with my army, they will ambush us."

So he sent several men to search the forest, and they found no one. When it was certain that the enemy had departed, they crossed the river, Nivasb in the lead. His army emerged from the water behind him in hasty pursuit of the enemy. Three thousand elite mounted swordsmen hurried along with him. 1160 They caught up with them near a mountain, the Iranian scout spotting them from far away.

The scout charged toward Abtin, reporting that the forest was full of Chinese knights. Abtin responded, "May the exalted one bring ruin upon them in this battle!"

He examined the state of the turning heavens, seeing how the moon and sun would pass, and saw a great victory in the stars—each of his warriors would become a fierce lion. He was beside himself with joy, and said, "O one, fair-dealing Lord, you set the righteous on the straight path and protect the fortunate. I give you thanks for this blessing, for you are ever my shelter and support."

He bound himself tightly with the royal girdle and hurried to fight the enemy. He chose two hundred from his army, capable, battle-hardened veterans. 1170 He dispatched them together with Kush, and they charged ahead.

As Kush approached the Chinese, he saw some of his vanguard killed by the enemy. Angered, he attacked the Chinese, raising a cry and stirring up dust. Like a berserk lion, like a drunk elephant, he laid heroes low with blows of his mace.

When Nivasb saw what Kush did, he roared like a vicious lion. He fought his way to the Tusked, laying several men level with the earth.

When the Iran-army saw his lethal blows, the brave men all made way for him. Those fierce riders collapsed, as blood blossomed over the ground like tulips. Kush became angry with his knights and said to his chosen men, "This lion-hearted man stands alone, he is not so brave, nor is he an elephant in armor. 1180 Are you all not ashamed, that no one dares face him?"

Having said this, he spurred his horse, charging like the fire of Azorgoshasb towards Nivasb.[7] They engaged for a long time, mixing dust and blood into grime. When Nivasb saw this bravery from him, he drew a steel javelin. He stood up in his saddle, putting his full weight in the stirrups. With great force, Nivasb threw the javelin at Kush with a shout. The lance missed his head, for the turning heavens yet withheld secrets.[8]

Kush brought his mace down upon Nivasb's helmet and his brains spilled from the wound. He fell to the dust, having lost his wits. His army then circled around Kush, setting upon him in vengeance, and it seemed the earth held fast his horses' hooves. They killed his horse between his legs, but not one blow touched his body. 1190

The brave men of Iran raced towards him, fiercely brandishing their lances. They killed several of the stout men of China, their blood turning the dust red. Kush struggled free and escaped the killing field, recovered, and mounted a fresh horse. In a rage, he cast off his helmet and removed his heavy mace from his belt.

When he showed his unmasked face to the enemy, everyone who saw it was terrified of him. His ugliness made them all believe he was a demon, their bows and arrows dropped from their hands.

They all said, "He can be nothing other than a demon! Riders and footmen are all the same to him! He has the head of a boar, the body of a demon, his two ears and tusks like those of elephants!" [195a] That lion-hearted army turned in flight from that lethal, elephantine apparition and his men. Kush and his troops charged after them, slaying many with their swords. 1200

---

7. Azorgoshasb, also written Azargoshasb, is a Zoroastrian sacred fire, founded during the late Achaemenid or Parthian period. Its name meant "stallion fire." See Mary Boyce, "Ādur Gušnasp," *Encyclopædia Iranica*, I/5, pp. 475–76; an updated version is available online at http://www.iranicaonline.org/articles/adur-gusnasp-an-atas-bahram-see-atas-that-is-a-zoroastrian-sacred-fire-of-the-highest-grade-held-to-be-one-of-, accessed November 5, 2021.

8. Some text may be missing here. There is no ambiguity about the sequence of actions, however it is conventional for descriptions of battle in Persian epics to describe the warriors advancing to close the distance before engaging in hand-to-hand combat. Such omissions are common in this manuscript, and may have been a feature of Iranshah's style, but may also be a result of the copyist losing interest in these scenes.

THE VICTORY OF KUSH THE TUSKED OVER
THE CHINESE ARMY

Three thousand of those brave riders survived the battle and group of the wounded reached the army camp at suppertime. A hue and cry arose from the Chinese army's camp, they were all astonished. The night was full of apocalyptic terror, none of them knowing how to escape. Hail fell from the sky and a wind rose up, infantry and riders falling all over each other in panic, footmen and Arabian horses stampeding in the commotion, amid the shouts and cries.

Some of the fleeing men were pierced from the front by arrowheads, others from behind. Whoever got close to the river was pushed in by the charging enemy. In that stampede, riders and footmen alike threw themselves into the water. The river carried away ten thousand mounted Chinese swordsmen. 1210 At nightfall, the fearsome crocodiles did not sleep, pulling men down two by two.

At that time, Abtin learned of Nivasb's fate and that of the Chinese knights. The other troops followed in Kush's wake, their wind-footed steeds raising a gale. By the time they reached the Chinese camp, they saw no one there. They saw shelters, tents, and equipment, those same clothes and blankets laid out.

Abtin held his face to the ground, and praised the creator. He said, "O, higher than sun and moon, you turned the heavens to bring my heart's desire. You are the almighty, we are incapable, heaven's wheel turns at your command! What could the Iranians say to thank you, who made a hero grow from a sorcerer's seed? . . . My heart wanted a bit of vengeance against Zahhak, and you took away a bit of my grief for Jamshid." 1220

He sent a rider, swift as smoke, to bring whatever supplies there were. He said, "This place is most fortunate, we ought to make camp here." He then distributed booty to the troops and one by one, their faces radiated joy, and they turned to their wine and revelry, all drunk and joyous, along with Kush. He gave Kush whatever had belonged to Nivasb—crown, throne, and horses.

When the army reached China, they all lowered their heads to the floor before the king, saying, "Your majesty, a demon has escaped from hell, he came and killed our officers. Any one of us that saw him, his heart beat right out of his chest. His face is a soul-killing terror that made everyone's limbs weak with fear. No cutting blades affected him, nor arrows, nor razor-sharp javelins." 1230

The king of China became sullen at their words, the neighborhoods of the city were also in turmoil. A cry arose from the streets, from the market, and a host assembled at the Chinese king's court. The proud monarch asked them, "What does this demon from hell look like?"

They thus described that demon, "It was as if he had taken an elephant's ears, and spread them over his great broad face. A camel gave him its lips, a boar its tusks. His two front teeth are like an elephant's tusks, dark cheeks and eyes blue-black as the Nile. Nivasb charged at him, like a mountain, and was never seen again."

When the commander of China heard this, he rose up and tumbled from his throne. He tore the royal robe from his shoulders, took his crown and threw it on the ground. He poured ash over his head and smote it with his fists, in pain. 1240 Wailing and moaning day and night, he sat and spoke to no one for two weeks.

The women of his harem filled the world with weeping, from the fish beneath the earth to the moon. Like a rose blossoming from a hazelnut, red cinnabar inscribing ivory, they scratched at their faces. Like a stalk casting off its hyacinths they tore out their hair, and all the musk of Tibet filled the palace. Pearl-tears tortured the narcissus-eye, plucked from their shells by sorrow.

Shut away inside his royal court pavilion, his attendants hung rings black as pitch. A horse's tail and mane were painted black for the mourning of Nivasb. The king of China became delusional, not resting or laying down his head in his agony. Such is the deepest pain of the heart, and why the wise call their sons their heart. But pain of the heart will pass, the world will bring sorrows to an end. 1250 Whoever has suffered the loss of a child thinks it better to never have had any.

There was a wise man, the king's minister, whose father had died by Jamshid's hand. The minister's name was Behmard. His heart ached to avenge his father's blood, and he said, "Renowned king, it would not do for you to bring yourself to ruin! The enemy could do no worse to you than what you are doing to yourself. You must go with your proud men and search everywhere for signs of Nivasb. If he lives, take him again, and if not, prepare for war to avenge him. Life is temporary, and crying does a man no good."

The king heard the minister's words, and he ate and rested for a while. He summoned armies from China and Machin and all but emptied the land of horsemen. 1260 Such an army he summoned, it covered the hills and plains—a landscape of mounted men, the sky lit by the galaxy of spearheads. He selected seventy thousand brave swordsmen and opened the doors of the armory and treasury and gave them supplies and salaries. The stout trumpet blew at dawn, a bellow to terrify demons. Stowing their baggage and supplies, they hurried toward the forest of Tar'aneh.

He declared, "By the life and crown of King Zahhak, they'll never see us at rest until I take revenge against Abtin for my dear son. Or, if he lives, and they give him to us, we'll hold no grudge against Abtin."

ABTIN IS ALERTED TO THE ARMY'S APPROACH

From across the river, beyond the battlefield, Abtin had sent ten riders. 1270 They were all positioned in tall trees to prevent an ambush. As they saw the army approach, they took off, one by one, for Abtin.

"The sky was red, yellow, and violet with the twisting streamers of their banners filling the air, and the earth groaned under their weight. It seems the king of China has come, with all of China and Machin riding for vengeance." They occupied the river's edge and blocked the way, their eyes watching carefully.

When the king of China and his forces reached there, he found Abtin prepared for him. From atop his midnight steed he cried out, "O wicked, ill-bred devil, you can stay a while in this forest, but what good will it do you in the end? 1280 The snake races out of its hole onto the road when it faces its doom. When my eyes find Abtin, I'll drive his eyes out of his head! By the soul of my brother, my king, my support and shelter in all matters, I shall not leave any of Jamshid's kin alive who gird themselves for battle with me. I will hang all of you people caught up with this wretch from tree branches! I will kill them all in groups, sending each nobleman's head to a different city."

Abtin restrained his troops from responding, lest they rush into the water. "Haste is the devil's work! When a group of the army reaches this side we will block their way, for their horses are all tired out, having marched day and night from China. 1290 May the Lord, exalted creator, bring destruction upon them once again."

The king of China was surprised when he received no reply, and hurried to cross over. Someone said to him, "Your majesty, at this point our numbers are small. A hundred men cannot be defeated all at once, we must wait for others to reach the field. To delay for one night is better than that your name be disgraced. The enemy is well prepared, they will escape into the night. We can cross the river early in the morning, and not dismount on the other side. [195b] We'll advance like an arrow from the bow, and surely gain the upper hand. As soon as Abtin is captured, we'll stitch up the rear of their force with arrows. If we are prevented from crossing the water, we can use ships to take us into battle." 1300

When the king heard that counsel, he set up camp in that same spot.

When the dark night had leveled the earth, Abtin and his army vanished swift as smoke. He made camp near a mountain and called Kush over. When he sat down with him, they spoke openly of the mighty force approaching them. "What do you think I can do now to avoid the wrath of this army? With such materiel, men, and horses against me, I fear my name will be disgraced."

Kush said to him, "Proud king, don't worry about that endless army: we will set our backs against the mountain and bring that whole horde to ruin. No army in the whole world, if it came here, could gain access to that mountain—unless the heavens have reversed our good fortune. 1310 When the decree has been revealed by the heavens, mountain and moon alike meet their end. Likewise, our breaths are numbered, we cannot breathe one more or one less."

Abtin's heart was filled with joy by the words of his lion-hearted, inspiring companion. He praised him abundantly and dismissed him, and they all returned to their tents. Abtin had been anxious for years on account of Jamshid's testament, in which he secretly warned his descendants to avoid the enemy: "You must remain so well hidden that they believe you have disappeared. When fortune turns its face to you again, it will place my descendant upon the throne. None of Zahhak's offspring will remain ascendant, for God will grant you kingship."

The king of China figured out what was going on the next day and hurried after Abtin. 1320 He marched his forces close to Abtin and sent a rider across the river. The troops would carry the baggage there, where the commander would be ready with a detachment. From the other side, the king sent an advance guard of three thousand brave men.

They drew near the Iranians, a brave fellow from the middle of the group yelling out, "You utter fools, you'd best want nothing but mercy from this king! You should beg for mercy! His magnanimity is greater than to put at risk the blood of young men. Not one of you will survive this battle, submission is your only hope. Quickly send the one who killed Nivasb in chains to the king. When the blood of the killer is spilled in revenge, he'll leave Abtin alone. Otherwise, wash your hands of your own lives—good luck to whoever thinks they can escape this mountain!" 1330

A stout warrior shouted in response, "You insolent companions of Satan! No one gives up hope of justice, for the creator is the only true recourse! If we are killed to a man, that's fine! Death comes to every animal's body, better for a man to die in battle than to seek refuge with the enemy!"

The detachment stood there when, from afar, Kush advanced like a ferocious lion. He threw a black garment over his coat of mail, charging as if Mount Qavar were in motion.

He said to the Iranians, "Why get so upset over the nonsense they say? We fight our enemies with the sword, we don't get upset over words like women do."

This he said, and attacked the Chinese, killing whomever he struck with his mace. Soon he had struck down thirty men—Iranians, Persians, and Chinese.[9] 1340 When his mace had crushed many helmets and brains, he reached for his sword and slew many foes without stopping, as if his hand had dried up around its handle.

One by one, shouts were heard from this side and that, "This can only be the devil that killed Nivasb and his brave men, for he strikes like a twisted demon!"

The detachment was frightened and turned their backs, Kush and his mighty blows following them. With a single attack he scattered them back to the Chinese camp. When the army and king of China learned of this, the fierce heroes all mounted up.

9. The Iranians *(irani)* and Persians *(parsi)* here refer to men from the army that Zahhak had sent to China.

A battle was joined like the heavens had never witnessed, as the ground saw nothing but streams of heroes' blood. The bodies of brave men piled up to the turning heavens, as if for to share their secrets with the stars. The sun and moon were obscured by the army's dust, as if the sky were raining death. 1350 Blood's tulip color flowed to the fish and the dust they raised blackened the sky. The Chinese army's dead covered hills and fields, and some of the Iranians lay dead, too. The world covered its eyes no sooner than it had opened them. The two sides broke away from each other, one towards the river, the other towards the mountain.

The king of China remonstrated with his forces, asking where this weakness and cowardice of theirs came from. "How can you be afraid of so few men? You could kill these dogs with nothing but dirt!"

His army responded, "Your majesty, what frightens us is this demon-faced knight. No fire burns like he does, no chaos in the world is as destructive as him. Truly, he is a foul demon! He killed each of our knights with a single blow! If he were not with the Iran-army, they would be destroyed in a single attack." 1360

The king said, "By the time the shining sun rises again, I will leave neither his army nor that demon-face alive."

When the Tusked came before Abtin, he told him what he had done to the heroes of China. "I killed more than a thousand of their swordsmen, but that army is a black morass a ship would capsize in. When daylight returns to the earth and sky we will attack more fiercely, for they will come for us at dawn. There will be such a huge battle, then. You, o king, should guard our rear."

Abtin said to him, "How kind you are, may the heavens decree your satisfaction. You are my child, and always thinking of my well-being. You are the backbone and shelter of my army. My army depends on you who are more dear to me than my eyes to my face! 1370 Since I have no fitting recompense for your great labor, seek it from God. If the passing of days brings me kingship, then I shall make you prosper. Kingship and great wealth would be mine and I would delegate to you command of the army and the royal seal and treasury."

Kush's heart was pleased by these words, he kissed the ground, and went to sleep. When the dawn's light shone over the mountain peaks, silvering over the world's pitch-blackness, the two armies rose up and came to the field and raised dust to blacken the earth and sky. The sound of drumbeats battered the mountain, deafening both sides' ears, and pipes howled from the earth as if to threaten the stars. When the lines of the two armies were formed up, each man looked at his enemies.

The king of China wanted the other group to come down from the mountain to the field. 1380 Abtin did not give up the high ground, but instead held fast to the mountain's armor. When the king of China saw his move, he set his forces upon him. Heavy maces thudded and sent officers' heads falling to the dust. The mountain cried out, the plain howled, and the roar of pandemonium overtook the sky. The world turned dark as blackest night and death drew near to men's bodies. Weak men's hearts fluttered and brave men's souls boiled away.

When Abtin and Kush looked out from the center of their position at the vigor of the Chinese army, threatening to deal their forces a sudden defeat, they immediately reached for their maces. They swung them at the fleet-footed foe and forced that army back, attacking the center of the king of China's army, striking ahead and to the sides. 1390

Five hundred of the Chinese were killed, and their advance was reaching closer and closer to the king. Astounded, he spurred his horse away in anger, racing away like the fire of Azorgoshasb. He engaged with Abtin's forces, striking several men down with his lance. Everyone who came face-to-face with him fled, the enemy army driven back in a panic.

When the Chinese king returned to his lines, both sides raised a cry, but again those forces were driven back to their king, fleeing the Tusked warrior's attack. [196a]

Angered, the king spoke to his army, "Woe and pain be with you! I drive all the foe towards the mountain, and then as I approach their lines you flee the foe like flocks of sheep, dissolving into a mob around me. With so little courage and gall for battle, how will you avenge Nivasb for me? 1400 You should all have stayed at home with your beloveds. The women of the harem are better than you—such a tale they'd tell about you!"

The officers said, "Your majesty, don't be so sharp with your words. If our opponent were human, who among us would have met any difficulty in this battle? When that demon of hell shouts, even the devil's seven organs tremble! It's as if each of his fingers were a tree trunk, his ugly face could tear one's heart. When we see him on the field of battle, our blades and javelins fall from our hands. No horse can keep up with his horse, their spirits startle when he roars."

"Show him to me," the king said. "Point out the sign on his armor and helmet, and when I see him from afar, I'll make him a feast for the vultures." 1410

One of them said, "That one who, at the head of the army, cut down and slew a rider, his breastplate tulip colored with blood, his lips and mouth like Leviathan's maw. You'd think the field on which he charges his horse was a polo ground. Battle is a trifling matter in his eyes, it's like a game to him!"

When the king saw him from afar, he charged forward until he was close to him. He looked at his face, teeth, and limbs, and his spirit quavered. His heart trembled in his body as if he had been dead and had just then come to life. He was ashamed, afraid to charge at him, but saw there was no going back. The king now reluctantly engaged him and both sides paused to watch the spectacle. They clashed—now with spear, now with sword—occasionally pausing to catch their breath. 1420 Now and then the father would strike the son with his spear, or the son strike his father with his blade.

The work of fate is strange sometimes. It cuts off father and son from each other's kindness. The one was not aware of the situation of his son, nor the other of his father and his station. When the world darkened in slumber and sunlight was extinguished in everyone's eyes, they both drew back, for their strength had waned.

Kush returned from that battle to Abtin, and said, "O wise and glorious king, I was joined in battle with a warrior who fought better than any crocodile in the sea. I struggled with him amidst our forces, hoping to defeat him, but my blows could not affect him, my spear could not penetrate his armor. Now I hope that tomorrow the creator grants me the victory I deserve, 1430 that the point of my blade will send him to the dust, tumbling into calamity's trap."

Abtin praised him and said, "May great virtue accompany good men."

On the other side, the king of China retreated to his tent, his brave retainers seated before him. His body was so tired from fighting so hard that even his shirt felt heavy on his torso. He said, "This demon-faced rider who engaged me in combat has the heart of a lion and the body of a raging elephant, his war cry so fierce it was as if it bound my hands. I remonstrated with my army in sharp words, 'How can we flee from such a meager army?' I've now seen the proof of their courage. If they can all fight like this, they'll defeat us in this battle. We would not last long, then, who knows what the creator wills!" 1440

The men around the king replied, "These two are the lions of the Iran-army, one demon-faced, the other was never at rest in the battle. Their horses' sudden bursts of speed make our bodies tremble. Aside from these two, our forces face no threat from them."

People spoke of all things, but the king of China stayed awake worrying about this one thing. His mind remained occupied with thoughts of the child he had abandoned in the wood. His heart told him he was correct, but still he besought the heavens for this secret. He thought, "This demon-faced one is my issue, he who I said was Satan's spawn. This is none other than the one I abandoned with such grief, in the woods, hoping for his death. Since I was unsatisfied with the creator's justice, now he brings ruin upon me." 1450

All night long he contorted like a snake, sometimes in wonder, sometimes thoughtful. "When was it that that child appeared, that he should now be such a robust youth? It has not been forty years but he looks like the rock of Bisotun."[10]

When the sun showed its face over the mountains, the moon was hidden from the glow of its warmth. He summoned the grandees and ministers, and spoke much about this matter. "An astonishing matter has come to light about that Tusked one, of twisted character. Know that that year I led the army from China to where the elephant-eared ones dwell. I plundered and killed aplenty, and found a sweet-faced girl. The sun and moon were ashamed before her face, sugar could scarcely answer her sweetness. First they trained her to serve, then my heart sought union with her. 1460

"A year later a child was born, and when I saw him I was enraged. His head and ears were like those of an elephant, his eyes deep blue-black as the Nile, his two teeth like an elephant's tusks, my heart was wounded by his face and appearance. I secretly took him away from his keepers before the night had passed. I took him towards the forest and cast him away so that man-eating beasts would tear him up. I cut his mother's head off with a blade—alas, she was so beautiful!

10. Bisotun is a mountainous rock formation in Kermanshah province, Iran, with an inscription by Darius I.

"Now that I think back to those days, this demon-faced rider is none other than he. The Lord creator kept him safe, and returned him to me like this, that the world might know, once again, that there are hidden secrets in God's works. Savage and tame beasts', fishes' and birds' natures are to care for their young when they're born. 1470 When I believed my child to be an enemy, I cast him aside with contempt.

"The creator was offended by my deed and now he gives me my just desserts. He has grown now, and my dear son was killed at his hand. I have no quarrel with the Lord, this was my reward for sin. He also had a mark on his right shoulder, nobody knows it's there but me. It's a sign like a black seal-stamp, no one has seen this mark. I have never revealed this secret to anyone, no one has ever heard these words from me.

"I need an honorable volunteer from this court, to whom I can give my breastplate and horse. He must know Persian [Parsi] and Pahlavi, and not be ill-tempered. The volunteer must advance from our lines, approach him, and invite him to my camp. 1480 He should delay him there when he comes, use cunning and sweet words to lure him, in order to investigate him, and if he shows the sign of being this noble child, the envoy should dismount and convey my greetings.

"Tell him, 'You are my offspring, dearer to me than all my family. When I inflicted injustice on you, injustice visited me in return. When I looked at you and your face, in a rage, I hastily washed my heart of any affection for you. Ashamed of you before the nobles, I took you, cast you aside in the field, left you there. I became a sinner before the creator. Much shame my sin brought me. Had I not abandoned you, I would not be mourning the loss of Nivasb. Now, the creator has given me my recompense: Nivasb was killed in battle. 1490 I still grieve over his death, my eyes run with tears of blood. I have not eaten or slept properly for a long time. I am like a bird caught in a trap. Alas, courageous prince, pillar of the army, of noble lineage! Now his days have come to an end, my back is bent in mourning. For every moment until my time ends, this grief is my destiny. [196b]

"'I have no offspring left but you, please come to my side in good will. The moment my foot slips off the throne, none besides you will take my place. When you come, when you arrive at the court, I will entrust to you my throne and crown. I swear this oath, before God, by the moon and sun and throne and justice, that I will not disregard your pleasure or will. To you I entrust my lands and armies. 1500

"'Why should you serve someone who truly ought to be serving you? When you are seated on the throne of China, you'll have thousands of servants better than Abtin. You live like a wolf or leopard, not resting in inhabited places. You've crossed deserts, fields, and mountains the sight of which would terrify a demon. When you see rose-gardens, verdant retreats, wine, running streams, and peaceful places of rest arrayed with comfortable beds and beauties with faces like the clear full moon, you'll be drawn to them, drunk and gleeful, to gardens and leafy pavilions. See just a bit of your great city, and taste a bit of what you are meant to have, you'll despair of this life you've led in the wood, living like a slave, like the wolf, sometimes hungry, sometimes full, like the birds, sometimes in the air, sometimes on the ground.' 1510

"He should say all kinds of kind words to him, to soften his heart. A clever man uses sweet words to draw a snake out of its hole. If he comes before us, he'll be drawn apart from the Iran-army, their back will be broken, not a rider among them will have the courage to gird himself for battle. We'll chain them up one by one, send them to the lord of the world."

When the minister heard the king's words, he stood up from his place and acclaimed him. He said, "This plan is the height of the king's wisdom, it's perfect, and no other plan will do! This will be quite a tale to tell! How the heavens' wheel has turned for the king of China. Now I, in the name of the glorious world-seeking king, will bring him to this court."

The other nobles and ministers were delighted and each one expressed their praise for him. 1520 The king gave Behmard his horse and armor fit for battle, and his heavy weapons. He put them on and mounted up, charging ahead and roaring, spear in hand. As he approached their watchmen he let out a roar like a savage lion, saying to them, "That Tusked one, crooked man, tell him to come out to the field of battle. He will not get away today like he did yesterday, he'll be seized in the fierce dragon's jaws."

So a rider, released from the detachment like the wind, brought word to Kush. Surprised, he put on his armor and sought his bow, sword, mace, and lasso. He went from his army straight for the man, and roared when he approached him, "You wrested yesterday from my hands, but today will be your death."

He replied, softly, "O courageous rider, I have no appetite for battle with you. 1530 The king of the East has sent me here to learn a thing or two about you. I seek a sign from you, first, and if I see the correct sign, this matter will be resolved quickly—we are all your servants and you our lord. Things will go our way, you will be master of the world."

When Kush heard Behmard's words, his reins grew heavy in his hands and he gave him his ear. He confronted him, saying, "What sign do you want from me? Speak!"

The minister replied, "Don't be harsh with a man who has kind words for you. I have the same manhood and power as you, the same mace and club. You were not born greater than me, your essence is no more than human. Is there no other marking on you besides the form in which you were created? 1540 Or do you know a mark you have carried from your mother, a mark you were created with? Then speak, for that mark is a sign. And if you do not have it then alas, a battle is in order!"

He answered, "Upon my right shoulder there is a mark that neither grows nor diminishes, like the black stamp of a signet ring. That is the only mark you'll find."[11]

Behmard was pleased by those words and quickly dismounted. The minister kissed the ground in front of him profusely and said, "O king of Iran and China, you are son of the king, and we, obedient. We act now on your orders alone! None of us knew your secret, only your father and God! When that bereaved king faced you in battle yesterday, he laid eyes on your face, and affection for you grew in his heart. 1550

"He said to me, 'Go, seek a sign from him, a sign which only I have seen. If he gives you the correct sign, then immediately give him my warm welcome. Tell him, 'Everyone who struggles against the creator will meet a bad fate. Whoever does not accept God's will will suffer pain, sorrow, and torment. Because you suffered injustice, it was fair that you caused suffering as well. We committed no sin by casting you out, no one can blame you either—there was no choice. This was the work of destiny, be it justice or injustice, cruelty or kindness. God created you with this

---

11. After Rostam unwittingly fights and kills his son, Sohrab, in *The Shahnameh*, he recognizes him because of a similar birthmark.

face; the demon, Varun, drew me along this path, in which the reins many times grew heavy in my hands. I could not make it through the night, ashamed before the nobles, for the sake of my honor, I left you in the forest for the leopards. 1560 God was watching out for me as well, by letting you grow into manhood. The retribution for what you suffered was my grief for the glorious Nivasb. When I quarreled with God, look what my reward from him was! Now all this pain is behind me. Good and bad pass like dust in the wind. When I saw you, my heart felt joy.'

"O proud young man, don't turn away! If kingship over the east is yours, why should you eat and sleep in the woods? Come now, take the throne as befits a fortunate man. Your father is the king of China and your father's brother king of everything upon the earth! But like a wild beast in the field, you feed off what you hunt, having submitted yourself to someone who displeases God. 1570 He is bad to the core, an enemy of the king, his ancestry is Satanic. God gave Jamshid the whole world and command over the greatest of men. He reigned for thousands of years. In those days was no death, no sickness. Then he developed evil thoughts in his heart: 'I have driven away people's sorrows, the world over. Since it was I who drove them away, who was it that brought sorrow, toil, difficulty—pain and death?' When he attributed God's works to himself, his kingdom collapsed. He was captured by the world-king. His sinful body was destroyed. What hard times for his people, to whom God did not give any protection! They were scattered all over the earth, year after year, hidden in mountains and woods. When they found you, they rushed to turn your heroic strength against the king. 1580

"You'll see, when you disentangle yourself from them, what will happen to the Iranians. Better to rule, yourself, than to be a companion of the wicked. Better that you stay in a great palace than in woods and mountains. Better that you enter gardens filled with wine and sweet aromas, narcissus and jasmine beneath your feet and above your head, the evergreen boughs of China, the handsome palace boys before you, behind you lutes and sweet-sounding songs. Left and right, beauties adorned in treasures, all aglow. The wise man would never give up his throne for a rock, or for the burning fire of war. And now there is no quarrel between you and your father. There is not even a mile between you and the king! Come, that you may see what fortune will bring you tomorrow: command of an army and greatness and kingship and a throne! 1590 Why remain together with evil-doers, hiding in the woods and mountains?"

Kush heard the words of Behmard, whose heart was overflowing with affection. Since his words were sweet, buttery, and warm, they could turn a granite heart to soft wax. When gentle words are spoken, snakes are drawn out of their holes. [197a] Thus did the wise priest say, "Buttered words draw the snake out of its hole."

One by one, the youth gulped down those sweet, hopeful words. Then Kush said to the king's minister, "Do not keep the king's secret from me. I am not safe from the king's vengeance, for my brother was slain by my hand. I fear he remembers and decides to take my life. 1600 He could kill me in revenge—no one knows what's in the king's heart."

Behmard replied to him, "O prince, don't let your heart be troubled by such thoughts. He committed the first fault at the moment when God created you. Such a creation was unacceptable to him, he took you and cast you away in the forests of China. Then he sent a number of armies to destroy you—you, who were innocent. You never knew Nivasb, you were not charging at his horse in particular. Had he gained the upper hand over you, he would have spilled your blood. When two people gird themselves to wrestle, surely one of them bites the dust. When two worthies are joined in battle, surely one of them will be buried. You have nothing to fear, for Zahhak has no other offspring, 1610 he has no son but you, and is afraid, lest the Kayanid crown fall into the hands of the enemy after his death—this is why he sent me.[12] If the king of China were to harm you, he'd be handing his lofty throne and crown to the enemy! Who have you ever heard of that would ruin his own kingship? The great king has not gone so mad as to drive a wolf out of the mountains right into his flock! You are the very eyes of the lofty monarch! No one would pluck their own eye out with their finger.

"When you command it, I will return whence I came, I will hold the king to his oath, that he never concern himself with your deeds, that he never confront you with your past. Bound by this oath, the

---

12. In *The Shahnameh* and other texts, "Kayanid" refers to group of Iranian world-kings whose rule begins after the reign of Manuchehr, Faridun's son. In *The Kushnameh*, it refers more generally to the Iranian world-kings descended from Jamshid.

king must come to terms with the death of his son. Since a man's oath is a heavy chain, a wise man does not bind himself with a vain oath. 1620 You, proud son of Kush, try a little to win the king's heart. Perhaps those knights, descendants of Jamshid, should be short one snake? The king's heart would be pleased and at ease with you, he would never think of Nivasb again!"

Kush said back to him, "O chief of righteous men, I've heard all you said, I'll consider all of what you said and crush Abtin's head with my foot. But you must keep this promise—that you must hide nothing from me! Tell the king exactly what you told me, bind him to this oath in soul and body."

That experienced fellow swore to him, "Upon the sun's rays, upon the azure dome, upon the sun, moon, souls, divine messengers, if King Kush has any ill will towards you, I'll have no part in it, rather, I'll send you a warning! 1630 I'll make him swear on his life, bind him in an oath of allegiance with you."

As Kush's heart was put at ease by the noble man, he prepared to return, satisfied. The noble man said, "You, man of good will, stay where you are for a while, then attack me with great ferocity, that I might turn and flee from you, lest your forces suspect that we have just come to an agreement."

They drew their sharp blades on each other, attacking and retreating. When the sun descended from the sky to the level plain, dark night was drawn over the enemy's mountain. Behmard said, "O raging-fierce lion, I am tired of fighting with you, I'll return now to the king, and bind him in this oath. Then I'll return here with a mighty army. 1640 I'll tie a candle from my long spear, this will be our secret. When you see it, it means I've come with my army: make your arrangements to come to the meeting-place. The baggage train, all the supplies and things there—let them be, you'll have plenty of that. You must reach us hale and whole, the body of the malicious enemy weakened."

When Kush returned from the battleground, he went straight to Abtin and bowed to him. Abtin stood up immediately, he called him over, and had him seated on his right. He said, "What did you do with the Chinese, mighty elephantine warrior?"

He answered, "That lion-hearted man who had fought me one-on-one came again to the battlefield, calling me out from this vast army. I engaged with him the whole day long, sweat, blood, and dust all mixed together! 1650 I could not defeat him, I could not turn back that warrior. He has the body of an elephant, the heart of a lion, practically overflowing with skill! He shouted at me, 'You, rider! Prepare yourself for battle tomorrow!' When tomorrow comes, I'll come at him like a savage lion. We'll see who will be ruined!"

Abtin praised him and said, "May sorrow befall your enemy! You are my support, shelter of the army, pillar of bravery and the sun of our days! My eyes and heart are set on you, my hope rests on your blade in its sheath. For today's toil you have my endless thanks. Whatever enemy falls under your heel, you'll be rewarded by me and by God."

In the other camp, Behmard said to the king, "All is well, then. 1660 He is your descendant, this brave ambitious man. Put aside any thoughts of injustice against him. He wants a strong oath from you, that you renounce all spite against him. He asked that I swear that a just agreement be made with the king."

Then Behmard took the commander of China's hand, bearing witness before earth and sky. "As long as I live, we will never harm him, never wish him ill, never give an order that he be harmed. I will protect him like my own dear life, day and night, in cheer and happiness, I will entrust him with my arms and treasure, and never confront him for his sins."

The minister's heart grew joyful, he came outside and went on his way. He brought such an army with him that the ground was wearied by the hooves of their horses. He arrived at the meeting-place with his forces, then tethered his horse there. 1670 The troops found a position in the mountains, and he placed a candle at the end of his spear. It was as if Canopus, the star, had come from Yemen, landed in China, and lit up the earth.

All night, the Tusked was restless, his eyes and ears set on the agreed-upon spot. When his eyes settled on that light, happiness returned to his heart. He told his servant, "Arise, quickly, a light shines through the dark smoke. I will go over to the king of China's side. Abtin wishes us ill."

They equipped themselves and drove ahead, abandoning the stranger and seeking others like themselves. Carrying spear and sword in hand, he galloped ahead like a raging elephant. He hurried ahead along the right side, leaving a bit of clothing and equipment behind.

When Abtin realized what he was up to, he ordered that they saddle their horses, 1680 and mount up, their steeds racing like the north wind. When he came near Kush he cried out, "You, wicked, base, and demon-born! What is your excuse for turning on me like this and joining the enemy? What harm did you ever see from me, that you are so quick to break your covenant?" He went on, but no answer came from Kush, and Abtin's heart surged faster.

Abtin had a son like a tall cypress, brave and wise and enlightened, bright like the moon and wise like a divine messenger. Kush used to call him his brother. A brave rider, his name Sovar, he was never one to ride away from the fight. Little by little he gained on Kush, entreating him, swearing oaths upon his own life and the soul of his grandfather.

"Get that alchemy out of your head! 1690 Turn around, go back the way you came and come beside me, I cannot stand for you to leave! You should listen to me and turn around, do not disappoint the king of Iran! Come, I want to know what this is about, show me who has wronged you!" [197b]

Kush did not answer or even turn his face. He drove his night-shade horse ahead, swift as smoke.

Sovar, now far away from the troops and his father, drove his own night-shade horse ahead until it tired. He had not the troops before him or their banners behind him, no vest on his shoulders or shoes on his feet. Only a shirt, he rode on in sadness, his heart immune to hardships. When Kush found him far from his army, he charged at him like the wind. Roaring, he struck his blade into his thigh, severing it. Sovar tumbled upside-down, and Kush sat upon him like a lion. 1700 He cut his head off and then mounted up, tying it to his saddle.

When he had ridden for a mile, his father's army came out to meet him. Behmard dismounted and showered him with abundant praises. He bowed and kissed the ground before the army, and everyone looked at his face. He gave Behmard the head to send to the exalted king. He said, "This is that dear head that is loftier than the heavens to Abtin. I severed it as retribution for my brother, that the king might be pleased with me."

When the riders approached the king, announcing to him that his descendant had arrived, he received him with a mighty entourage, the great men of China and other brave warriors.

When they approached Kush, they all but lost their senses. 1710 They all asked, "What is this demon? Should we not weep for our land? He is not human, but surely of Ahriman! His face is satanic, his body elephantine. If this monstrous demon becomes our king, the army must be careful. For nothing but evil could come of this face, it has no trace of divine glory!"

When the commanding Kush saw his father, he dismounted and showered him with praise. He lowered his face to the dirt for a moment, entreating him. The commander of China then pulled him up from the dust, kissed him and embraced him tightly. The king was most affectionate and solicitous, seating Kush upon his own horse. He rode alongside him for a while, asking questions of all kinds. Kush replied, giving answers of all kinds to his father, with wisdom and gentleness. 1720 When they entered the royal tent, having followed that rough road, the king placed him on the throne. Then the cooks set out a banquet worthy of the two kings. After finishing the banquet and enjoying the feast, they called a council.

The king ordered his commander to bring the severed head of the son of the king of the Iran-army before them. He saw it and put his two hands on his heart, and said, "We are cheered by our fortune, the vengeance of our dear son has been wiped away by the hand of this brave lad."[13] He showered much praise on Kush and said, "May success ever be with your body and actions."

LETTER FROM KUSH TO ZAHHAK

Right then, he summoned the scribe and had him record an account of what had transpired. When the reed-pen had transcribed the address and entreaties of the letter, it cast forth the good news: "May the world-king rule the earth as long as it lasts, may the hands of the malicious be cut short of reaching him. 1730 May he remain ever safe and secure, and ever victorious over his enemies.

"Know, your majesty, that in recent days, numerous astounding things have come to pass. A dear son of mine was lost and my heart was wearied by his absence. I bit my thumb in astonishment, for he

---

13. "Brave" here is literally "of Niv-aspect"—a pun on Nivasb's name—hinting that Kush the Tusked will take the place of Kush's deceased son.

defeated my army. He charged at his enemies like a huma, routing my whole force. He killed my honorable son with a steel javelin and a great blow. Then, a short time ago, the situation was illumined, and fate revealed him as my son. Fate thus returned him to me. Destiny satisfied the world-ruler. He turned to take revenge on all those ingrates, and severed the head of the king's enemy. I have sent it, now, before your majesty, the severed head of the renowned Sovar. 1740

"Abtin and his group are incapacitated, they will never make it out of those mountains. They have no way out, and no other army will come to their aid. Thus, by the grace of the world's overlord, I will turn that mountain upside down. I will send him as a prisoner into the hands of this dear and courageous lion-seizing king." He chose a hundred men from his forces, distinguished for bravery in battle. He gave them a year's provisions and sent them off on their long journey.

That same night, Kush arranged a feast. There was clamor from the musical instruments. He raised a toast to his son, feeling such joy to see him face to face. No matter how foul it may be, a son's face is like the gardens of paradise to his father. When the stout men had got good and drunk on the wine, he said to his child, "Tell me, o hero, 1750 what stratagem should we deploy against Abtin? The world-king is troubled by him."

He answered, "My king, do not trouble yourself with such sorry matters, I am devoted to the king, I'll bring ruin to those ingrates. They are stuck there, above those foothills. They have no way out. The only way is over a mountain's crest that even a demon would be terrified of crossing. That long and difficult road leads to Machin, their army will find no recourse there.[14] If the world-king gives me the order, let him provide me with an army and I will cross the mountain peak on foot and advance towards them, lest they find their way to Machin. I will bring my army down over their heads and kill him with my sword. You'll see heads, arms, and legs all over the mountains!" 1760

The king of China was pleased by this, as if his heart had just escaped the enemy. He said, "May your judgment be ever bountiful, and the enemy's hearts screaming in terror." Then he said to Behmard,

14. While Machin in Arabic and Persian geographical knowledge is defined only vaguely as a reference to East Asian states other than China, in this narrative it clearly has a distinct, specific identity.

"Give him one half of the materiel, treasure, and troops, of the horses and palace page boys, tents, pavilions, and animals, of whatever great treasure I have brought from China that I took from their nobles. Upon my descendant bestow one half of all these things, for he is now commander of China and Machin. I give him command over my army, as well as over my house, my treasure, my realm."

The great men and nobles arose and acclaimed him again. They bowed their heads to the ground before Kush and the steel-clad commander. That same night, Behmard divided his possessions in half. 1770 To the awe-inspiring Kush it was all granted, he now the shepherd, the nobles his flock. That same night, the king sent ten riders racing like the wind toward China, summoning whatever footmen and riders were there to come to him.

Among the people waiting on them was a pure-hearted child, one of the Iranians, before whose bright face the sun would be embarrassed. He had been placed in Kush's care along with other children. He became aware of their scheming, enmity arose in his heart, and all affection for Kush left him. This child of great foresight asked about his companions who had been part of Abtin's army. He stayed put and watched until Kush was drunk and fast asleep.

The pure-hearted child fled, racing all night through water and mud. 1780 When he finally reached King Abtin, he lowered his face into the black earth. The king was so stricken in his mourning for Sovar, he was unaware of what had happened. Of Kush's departure, or where he had gone to, he had not been informed by anyone. The child let Abtin in on the secret, as if opening a door before him.

"Kush was the descendant of the viceregent of China—hear me o king of Iran! When the king of China became aware of Kush's feats, he marshaled an army against you. When he realized defeat was upon him, he planned a stratagem to deceive Kush. The song he sang for the simple-minded Kush was that he should kill the king's son with a mighty blow, to avenge his brother. [198a] The cruel, demon-faced Kush said to the evil king last night that 1790 the mountain the Iran-army occupies is too steep to cross on horseback, too exhausting for the horses. It is better to fight here on foot. He has called for forces from China, renown footmen and elite cavalry. He told him, 'I'll cut the path to Machin off from him, and take my revenge on him!' When I heard this I raced to you, having parted ways with that evil-natured one. Now do whatever you know you must, o king, and don't think twice.'"

Abtin asked about the infantry force. "When will they reach this forest?"

He answered, "O king, they will reach the forest but three days from now."

Right then, he ordered that of those assembled, a hundred should ascend the crest of the mountain. They guarded the enemy's route of approach, their shouts rising beyond the heavens. 1800 That same night, the king ordered a trench dug, and they brought out their shovels and picks. They made a deep pit of imposing depth, width, and breadth across the path and drew their baggage train up the mountain, leaving behind only tents.

They found the mountainside covered in fruit, springs, and meadows. They brought the good news to Abtin, returning from the sky to the ground, "This mountain is entirely covered in freshwater and greenery, where in the world could this be?"

He replied, "Though Kush cut us loose last night and went over to Kush, the creator did not abandon us—we have no complaint with him. He never shut a door on someone without opening other doors for them. Who could conquer a place like this? We are unlikely to suffer ill fortune here." 1810

At the new moon, they drew up ranks on the mountainside. Kush marshaled six thousand warriors, fearless and mighty swordsmen. He circled the mountain to see what he could do, and perhaps launch a surprise attack on Abtin. Upon arriving from Kabul, he came face to face with the trench, and when he saw its depth his heart leapt.[15] He was astonished by what King Abtin had done, he spurred his black horse and went to the edge.

He said, "O unfortunate king, the blade has reached your heart and your situation is dire. What good are this trench and this high mountain when the heavens will soon bring your destruction? When you

15. The reference to Kabul here reflects the geography of the story in the original source used by Iranshah, which referred to Sassanian wars with the Kushan Empire that ruled the region of Central Asia between Iran and the Indus Valley. See Saghi Gazerani, "Kush-e Pildandān, the Anti-Hero: Polemics of Power in Late Antique Iran," *Iranian Studies* 52, no. 5–6 (November 2, 2019): 872–73.

are about to be killed, what good are brocaded pillows? What good will sweet drinks do when your lives are about to be taken? You have at most three days left, o king, so raise your head. 1820 When my infantry arrive, we'll make a hundred paths across this trench. We'll fill it with dirt and rocks and my blade will turn the mountain to ruby. With the blood of your riders, o king, I will paint all these mountains the color of garnet. I'll not rest as long as any of you remains in one piece, and you I'll cut down first."

When Abtin heard Kush's words, he grinned and raised his voice in response.

ABTIN REPLIES TO KUSH

He said, "You, with the face and temper of a demon, have you not heard the tale of the crocodile? A crocodile came out of the sea, was stranded, and a camel-driver came upon it. It was dried out, its lips shut from the cold, stuck there the whole month of January. He loaded it onto a camel and covered it to keep it warm, fed and tended to it. This went on until they reached the sea, and the irascible crocodile woke up. 1830 When it saw the sea, it recovered. It confronted the camel-driver, saying, 'You have two choices, each one worse than the other. I want no more than what you wanted of me. Either a strong young camel or your own body. One of these two is all I will take, one cannot eat more than what one has in one's stores.'

"The gentleman said to him, 'O distinguished crocodile, restrain your teeth and claws a moment. Were you not fallen by the roadside, shriveled up, did I not pick you up out of the black dirt? Did I not feed you until you regained your strength and keep you protected from the cold?'

"The cruel crocodile said, 'Young man, don't ask of me what I cannot do, you have your work and I have mine, I've given you the choice. Can you really expect humanity from me, as if you were the crocodile and I were the human?' 1840

"The camel-driver responded to him, 'Eat the camel, then,' and escaped his doom. When the camel-driver was departing on foot, he saw the camel in the teeth and claws of the crocodile. And he said, 'Anyone who treats a wicked person humanely only makes him stronger.'

"This is what happened between us, would that it had never happened to anyone! Now see what this one, whom you call 'father,' did to his son! That same night you were born, o drunkard, he took you and abandoned you in the forests of China. He left you as a meal for ferocious lions, but it was fated that I give you life. I saw you and took you in, held you dearer than any son. When you were grown up, I gave you more than I gave any of the Iranians. I gave you shelter, horse and pack animals, named you commander and leader. 1850 I had great expectations for you, and you became a great among the greats. I gave you a portion of whatever I had, not pleasing to God, nor troubling to the Jew.[16]

"Whatever hope I had of kingship, I gave you tidings of victory. Without seeing any injustice from me or from the nobles of this company, you have suddenly turned away and abandoned me. You killed my son with your sword—oh, that poor, dear brave man! Like a brother, he begged you to come back, sacrificing himself to keep you with us! He had no weapons, no troops. How could you kill a brave man like that? You did exactly what we should have expected of you! The world-creator has created no evil like yourself! It is as if you were nursed by dogs or raised among swine, 1860 and so you are not ashamed before me. Have you no memory of how I treated you, that you brandish the blade of vengeance, having shed kindness and affection from your heart?

"Alas, elephant-tusked, demon-faced! May the heavens cut you off from their kindness at once! You may have cast me aside, ingrate, but God has not, and he knows what is good! He is my hope and my shelter, not a trench, not Kush, and not the Iran-army. He does whatever he wills, however he wills it—from him remedies, from him pain. Now I doubt that the creator will let these days stretch out too long, he gives kingship to this lineage, and he will give you grief and mourning."

Kush said to him, "You man of little account, don't entertain any thoughts of kingship. Were it not for me, like a crippled fox you would have no shelter, day or night. 1870 You spent every day in fear, never sleeping twice in the same place, nothing to eat for months, for years,

16. The second half of the sentence in the original has awkward syntax. The text may be corrupted. *The Shahnameh* and other medieval Persian poetry contain occasional derogatory references to Jews, so it is possible that is what was intended here.

but game you hunted, eating and sleeping in forest and mountain. What does it matter if you raised me and gave me status when you live off the forest like a wolf? When I grew strong, you became the rival of the king of China! When you could come from the forest to the plain or river, you faced the king of China. Twice, I defeated my father's army! I enriched you with silver and gold! You lacked nothing, I even killed my brother for your sake! Now that I've found out about my father, I prefer my father to a crooked stepfather! You were my guardian and my protector—kind, but not like the king. Now you want a reward for your guardianship, now that you've gone from poverty to wealth. 1880 I killed Nivasb in this war. Sovar was surely not his better!"

Abtin said to him, "You hot-headed fellow, your words perplex me. When you were out of luck, lonely and miserable in the forest, if I had just left you there in the black dirt, you'd be gone. You wouldn't be his son now, you wouldn't have his name now. [198b] You killed Nivasb because he tried to kill you first. You need not be so thankful to me, but be just to yourself. If you had not killed him in battle, he would have killed you without a second thought. But my dear boy was raised together with you, his heart full of love for you. He was coming after you like a brother. Everyone will blame you for killing him. 1890 You destroyed him, for nothing, and that sin will come back to you from every side."

"Since your heart has been wounded and taken many darts, let us walk about and play for a while, and charge our horses across this battlefield. Let us see how the battle turns out, who ends up in the dust. Perhaps you will avenge your son, or I may slay my enemy, and it will be clear from this battle whether you or the king of China is the victor."

Abtin said to him, "You have made your judgment, there's nothing more to say here. Have your army withdraw and, by God, I will test my strength against you."

The king ordered the army to stay back and then went back with them. He put on his coat of mail and dressed for battle, and the army's heart was sore for him. 1900

His men were clinging to his reins, and they cried out from the bottom of their hearts, "O king, do not treat your army this way, stay here and let others fight for you! For if something were to happen to you, we would be helpless and bewildered. Great and small, we're all doomed, not one will make it out alive."

The brave lion responded, "A lion is never afraid of a wolf, do not worry, I have faced many a warrior in battle. I'll do as I can, I have the heart of a lion and the stature of kings. By God's grace, may I destroy this demon-faced man in this battle."

This he said, and approached Kush. He attacked him with a lion's ferocity. The two were so entangled that their horses spilled blood and sweat. 1910 Now this one hit that one, then that one hit this one, one out of rage, the other vengeance. The two combatants shouted and landed blows, sometimes on the head, sometimes on the shield. Their spears broke and they drew their swords, now attacking and then retreating. Kush did not think Abtin could equal his strength in battle. Abtin was like a raging lion in the saddle, blade in one hand, his waist girded.

Kush saw the Kayanid glory and the strength of champions, and witnessed the martial skill of that essence of kings. He strove to fight more skillfully and made an attack swift as smoke. He rained down eight sword blows and held up his shield. Swinging his sword, Kush knocked off his helmet.

Abtin then attacked him, drawing his sword whose edge gleamed like a diamond, landed a mighty blow from above, and in one stroke, killed Kush's horse. 1920 That single stroke cut through its mail coat and severed its head, and his troops were astounded.

Abtin came for Kush with his sharp blade, and he turned to flee. He ran towards his army, his footsteps sinking into the black mud. The riders of China received him and saved his life from Abtin's attack. He mounted another horse and came back wielding a bow. He rained arrows on Abtin and made fear loom over his army.

When Abtin saw such courage from Kush, he rose up like a raging thundercloud. Abtin then took hold of his arrows, a master displaying his skills. The first arrow to be released by his thumb struck the forehead of the horse, which reared up and cast Kush to the ground. Abtin struck again. 1930 Kush suffered a fearsome wound to his arm and turned back, spent.

Fleeing towards his troops and fearing for his life, he ran towards the royal horse. The army once again rushed to him and found him wounded. They put him on a horse quickly and brought him back—such an army retreating from Abtin!

They bound his wounds, and cheered for his good luck. "Such wounds you've inflicted on the enemy! Even if they were birds they'd be unable to escape. Trapped by a towering mountain, in constant fear of death, why put your life in danger? Wait until your father's army arrives. When the army comes, we will crush them in a single battle. This vile enemy fights using everything he's got, don't put yourself in his path. 1940 We'll see what's what this very night, when reinforcements from China will reach your majesty. Not one of the Iran-army will be left alive, you will please the king."

Abtin returned to his camp, and spent the night awake and lost in thought.

Likewise, Kush went back to his father, and related to him what had happened. He grew melancholy and said, "Abtin is a sorcerer, impure and unworthy. You must not try to face him in battle, that will bring nothing but misfortune. Wait until the army from China arrives; when it comes, the enemy will be wrecked." Night fell and they dispersed, and Kush slept, and rested, and awoke.

When the stars disappeared from the sky and the dawn's quicksilver ranks advanced, a loud cry arose from the mountainside. "O king! Ruin is upon us! 1950 An army of infantry has come from China, their thicket of blades obscures the forest."

The king asked the watchman, "Why do you prattle on like this? Why do you not tell me their condition and numbers, their location and what they are doing?"

He answered, "Your majesty, they number more than fifty thousand. The air is filled with lances and swords, that army fills up the plains and forests. They have reached a meeting point, and the army of the king of China has welcomed them."

The king spoke pained words to the Iranians. "Now that the heavens have turned against us, we must devise a way to avoid the enemy's attack. They are not preparing for a battle tomorrow, but for a victory feast!"

He ordered that whatever baggage they had be immediately brought up the mountainside. 1960 Then, those brave men extracted thirty boulders from the slopes, and several men hid behind them, courageous warriors all. They kept watch up there, and called out to the brave men of the army.

Abtin said to them, "Proud warriors of Iranzamin, I have done this so that when the China-army comes, they see no trace of me on the face of the earth. They'll be completely sure that I and the others have fled over the mountain. When Kush comes looking to do battle with us, we'll let loose thirty boulders. My hope is that the Chinese will be turned back. Then our infantry can retreat and riders make their escape."

They were pleased with this plan. 1970 They arranged a code for the watchmen and conveyed the lord's instructions. "When they see the mountain turn purple from the color of the waving banners, they should give this code to the troops: 'The Chinese army loses splendor.' When the warriors hear this phrase, they'll tip over the stones."

When the solar host ascended the mountainsides, the army made its way toward the mountaineers. The steel of their blades turned the earth the color of the sky, and their dust was like a fog over the mountains that dimmed the sun's face. The sound of their footsteps reached the moon. When the soldiers reached the foot of the mountain, they saw not a single one of the Iranians. Kush galloped out from among the troops and raced toward the mountain. The base of the mountain they found deserted, only a few old tents there. 1980

Kush said to his army, "The enemy has turned their backs and fled. [199a] Those rebels must not find a place to hide, or we'll have lost them! They'll harass our forces. Let the king's heart not be troubled again."

When Kush spurred his horse up the mountain, they all were prepared to advance in his wake. On each side, an army took off marching toward the heavens like an arrow shot from a bow. More than thirty thousand footmen and cavalry were ascending the mountain. The fearsome leopard was not to be found as the warriors hoped. A number of their camels and horses were thwarted by the terrain and ran back down. The warriors became so eager for the fight that the mountainside was like a gentle rolling meadow to them.

When they had halfway traversed the mountain, a cry rose up from the Iran-army. 1990 "Victory! Long live Abtin! May he trouble the heart of the king of China for many years!"

Their roar reached the ears of the brave men, you'd think it had mauled the hearts of the malicious. Abtin executed his plan. Everyone let loose their boulders. The rocks tumbled down from up high, killing malicious and noble men alike. Death rained on the Chinese troops, the rolling stones giving no escape or quarter. Riders galloped for miles from the terror and clamor of the raining rocks. Of that peerless army, shouting and crying out, there remained scarcely five hundred and Kush. Not a worthy warrior was left on the mountain, not a rider at its foot.

When that small force returned to the king, they grieved yet again. One out of a hundred soldiers was alive, all wounded and exhausted. 2000

He said, "What kind of catastrophe is this? Who can know God's secret will? By the life of the worthy king, by the blood of his honorable rider, Niv[asb], I will wait a whole year if I have to, to have Abtin in my hand. I will exact vengeance against him for my son, a vengeance befitting the brave men and heroes of old."

He remained there by the mountain for a month, hoping to wear down Abtin so that he would be forced to come down from the mountain's crest onto the plain, so he would eventually obtain satisfaction and water the ground with the blood of his men.

Abtin had no such intentions. He set up tents on the mountain, planted upon it as if they had always been there. They came down, sometimes in the day, sometimes at night, and looted the bodies. 2010 It was not very long before the hearts of both armies were tired of fighting.

One day, a very large caravan crossed over the great mountain from Machin. The caravaneer drove them close to Abtin, and the king inquired from the merchants, "How can we get to Machin from here? How far is it, what is the road like? Who is king there? What are you carrying on these animals? How has your business been?"

One of them said to the king, "It's more than ten days from here. There is a wise and glorious king in Machin, generous as the clouds and good as an angel. The king's name is Behak, and the city is so beautiful you'd think it was the other side of heaven. The king is so just that a lion under his rule would not dare touch a deer. He undertakes such labor doing God's work that the learned are astonished at his learning. 2020 These animals are all bearing edible goods, no clothing or rugs. We are taking them to China to trade; we take this route to China every year. We return by the same route every year, obtaining clothes and carpets and tools. We double our investment, that is no exaggeration."

Abtin said to them, "Good knowledgeable fellow, what can you tell me of this long, difficult road? If I make your work easier, if I double your wealth and treasure, what could I get from you, if I shorten the route to China for you?"

The spokesman said, "O beneficent one, free your heart of any concern of reward from this servant. Look to God for a reward for this good news, for it is he who gives blessings and guidance."

He ordered that they remove some of the baggage and set it before the world-conquering king. 2030 Then whatever goods were brought down, they paid twice the price for them.

That experienced merchant lowered his face into the black earth before the king. He said, "O beneficent king, may time's ravages stay far from you. If only I had the means to please you."

And so the decision of the God-fearing king was that he should not stay put. "When January makes the mountaintop whiten with age, the mountain will be impassable. If you don't labor in the spring, you won't have two grains of wheat to rub together in February. If you don't strive for anything in your youth, you'll be just as poor, and helpless in old age. If you don't think of tomorrow today, tomorrow will be a dark, piercing wind between your fingers. When the month of February comes, that rainy fog will march on the mountain 2040 and drive out my army. We need a solution."

ABTIN'S LETTER TO BEHAK,
KING OF MACHIN

The king summoned his wise secretary and spoke at length to him, and ordered a letter written to Machin, to Behak, the beneficent king. "In the name of our Lord guardian, may he give us strength and many days. The omnipotent does whatsoever he wills, brings old age and youth to the world. He turns black night to day, and after midwinter, he enlivens the world. He sometimes gives me sorrow, sometimes happiness. Thus has he laid the world's foundations.

"O lofty king, you do not know what the turning heavens have inflicted on us. These days have drawn out and driven me through their depths and heights, sometimes like a wolf running around the forest, sometimes like a leopard leaping over the mountains, 2050 years and months in flight from the Zahhakians, sometimes fleeing, sometimes fighting. By the orders of Jamshid of pure creed, I must thus remain in hiding, because he saw in the stars that his time had passed, that his reign had worn out, and that that unfortunate one would be caught and destroyed by Zahhak.

"He summoned my grandfather, who was his son, and advised him that however much he wandered in fields and deserts, even if he were imprisoned under the sea, 'Let no Zahhakian see you, and deceive you. Give your children the same counsel, make them swear to follow this advice. Tell them to remain hidden from those of evil race—let their lineage vanish from the earth. When Zahhak's days near their end, a king will appear from among us 2060 who will take him and imprison him, and bring ruin to the Zahhakians. Kingship will then be yours, as it was before, this dark smoke will give way to splendor.'

"Following the words of he of pure faith, I have thus remained hidden, on the run. Until I am ready to wage war, I do not want to disgrace myself. However much we strive for our honor, time holds destiny's reins. I still survive, in spite of war and plots. The turning heavens have brought me low. You are my only hope, I call on you as refuge of my body and soul.

"Of Jamshid's testament, his advice, this is what his son passed on to me: 'If the world closes in on you, then pack up and go to Machin, for there is a king there, just and God-fearing. Zahhak cannot lay a hand on him. 2070 He fears no one but God, and by God, you can find shelter only from him. He can watch over you. Take shelter with him and with God. Now it has been countless years that we have been worn and wounded by the passing days. The heavenly wheel has cut us and our ancestors off from its kindness, o king. We have never troubled you, never entered your territory. Now things have gotten out of hand and we have no other recourse. [199b] Behind us are the mountaintop and our enemy, you are now the only one who can bring us down from here. We salute you, o splendid king."

When he had pressed his seal on the letter, he appointed someone to go with the caravan. He gave many things to the merchants, dinars and Arabian horses. 2080 They went with the letter and the king's man to the beneficent king, Behak.

When Behak learned of the letter and the man, he fully understood his trouble. He looked inward and struggled in his heart, crafting a wise judgment there. He hosted the emissary for three days, and on the fourth, when the world-illumining sun lit up the earth, he ordered his scribe approach him, a wise and sharp youth.

He ordered a letter of response to the king be drafted. "In the name of the Lord over sun and moon, who illumines the dark night with the moon, and by the sun's light makes the earth ebullient, who draws spring from the heart of the cold and adorns the world with "B" and "E, I have received and understood your words, o essence of the righteous. I was saddened by your fate, by the persecution of your dynasty 2090 that has such faith in the turning wheel—how could such a dynasty be abandoned like this? But no one is apprised of its secret, we have no way to know its works. Finally, all must be set right, and the body of the king of Iran must regain strength, the turning wheel must show him kindness and bring ruin to the body of that demon-faced one. As you have sought shelter with me, may the moon's creator be your shelter. I am endowed with lands and armies, treasure and a home filled with the choicest things. I support you. I would not say otherwise—for this house and your house are as one. Of Arabian horses, mail, and blades you would not be wanting, your majesty.

"However, in my precarious position here, I am too exposed to the constant ravages of the Zahhakians. The king of China threatens me day and night. 2100 When he becomes aware that you are with me, he will bring ruin upon all my armies. He would bring to Machin an army whose black dust would block out the sun. I cannot face that army, nor can I protect you from it. I fear for my life from Kush's blade.

"If you want to avoid distress, listen well. Chivalry is of the same essence as righteousness, abundant lies are all calamity. Upon righteousness the light shines, rectitude heralds probity. If you are righteous and upright, know that both worlds are yours. But I will show you a secret path, in line with the advice of Jamshid, world-king.

"There are two Machins upon the earth. You must first reach my Machin. Then, you must travel in haste: one month's journey by ship across the water. 2110 At the month's end you will see a mountain. Its depth, height, and great expanse are imposing, its bulk sprouting like a reed, by God's command, from the sea into the sky. Its breadth is two hundred leagues and its length the same. Upon that mountain are eighty choice cities, each of them better than Machin and China, and those cities have four thousand villages, all with verdant gardens. There is a king upon the mountain and country endowed with all the perfections in the world. He is a wise king by the name of Tayhur, and most fortunate. He is such a God-fearing king that it is as if he had never sinned. There is one and only one way into the mountain, two people cannot traverse it at the same time. There is a strong gate, like a deep pit, snowed-in all year. 2120 If all the armies in the world turned on that meritorious king, his men would guard the mountain unafraid and they would not be able to overcome them.

"And so it is: a better country than this one, its armies more numerous than the stones of the desert. Its ruler always calls me a brother, a worthy and good-hearted king. If you wish to meet that king, I can arrange everything. I will send ships to the seashore, so make for the sea, your majesty. When you have reached the sea, at that time my army will reach you. I will send several men with you and a letter to King Tayhur. I will inform him of your situation and make him fear God and hell. Once you reach that place, you will suffer no harm, whether from sorcerous Zahhak or raging demon. 2130 Even if the elephant-eared one were to become a flying bird or a messenger angel, he would not come within miles of the entrance to that mountain. Know this, o proud king! A doctor, regardless if he knows damp humors from dry, still knows the disease no better than the patient."

He gave the envoy many things, so that Abtin would lack nothing. He sent someone along with the envoy to bring back word of Abtin's decision, and to persuade him to go in case he had any misgivings about taking to the sea. They would prepare whatever would be needed and have it sent to the seaside.

The emissaries went on their way, ten days to reach the king. The answer brought joy to Abtin's heart, and he generously rewarded the emissary. He said to him, "Go, tell your king, "We will do just as you said. 2140 Prepare ships and whatever else you need, send it by sea, o lofty king. For now I come with my army, I'll reach the seashore in no more than two weeks.' The envoy returned and they set out on the road, while the king, untroubled, remained on the mountain. He ordered no attacks, he threw no rocks, and the enemy waited there the whole time.

When a whole month had passed like this, the commander of China was vexed by that mountain. One day, Behmard the minister said, "Praise the king's soul! What good does it do us to tarry here? Whoever learned how to fight a mountain? Perhaps the enemy is too afraid to come down, but are you not fed up with this forest? You have cleared the land of the enemy today, he has succumbed to the cold on that mountain. Is the king not informed of his situation? There is no passage from there but to Machin. 2150 If he hurries to Machin, with one letter I'll have him in my grasp. Behak will send him to the king, and if not, we'll send him an army that will bring Behak and the Iranians in chains before the lofty king. A satisfying fate, with those scoundrels under your heel and your honor vaunted over them!"

Thus did the commander of China answer him: "I have sworn an oath before faith and justice: I will not turn away from fighting Abtin until I have him in my grasp! I want revenge on him for the brave Nivasb!"

The wise minister did not take his oath lightly. Who would swear an oath, but someone wounded by time's darts? There is no shame worse than swearing an oath, nothing as vicious as a merciless oath.

Behmard said to him, "Your majesty, listen now to what this servant has to say. 2160 You avenged Nivasb when you killed your enemy's son. Even if you turn back from here, your thoughts will still be on the enemy. You can go after the enemy again, you are still young and have your throne. With the enemy in the mountains and us on the ground, what could be done to him, o king of China? But the son of the world-king has desires he has not spoken: he wants the throne himself, wants his heart to be nourished by the king's grace."

The commander of China knew it was just as that reliable minister said. He ordered that they pack up and return to China.

Abtin was delighted by his departure, it was as if his sorrows ended. He sent a few riders out, they searched the forest and found no one. 2170 He waited another week on the mountain as though still not weary of that bare rock. As the eighth night ended, he had the gear loaded up, descended from the mountain, and set off. [200a] He proceeded until he was by the seaside, where he set up camp beside a stream.

He saw Behak's troops, ships, and materiel arriving from Machin at just that moment. All sorts of gifts were brought, to eat and to wear, and to hand out. Of those who knew the way by sea, ten were sent to accompany the king. Behak wrote a letter to King Tayhur, in a proud, confident hand. Abtin took it with great pleasure and praised that worthy one. It took a week on the seashore for them to arrange everything.

On the eighth day they happily boarded ships, which were set in motion by the wind. 2180 Day and night they sat contented on board, the old mariner driving them over the sea. When the moon revealed its face through Scorpio, land appeared and the king beheld it. The ship set anchor at a distance from shore and the people on board were astonished, amazed at the sight of the sea and that mountain. They all looked on in contemplation.

At once Abtin said, "O creator! Wise and powerful protector! You have raised such a mountain out of the water and keep fire hidden within stones. All of your works are wondrous, the whole world in awe at your deeds." The king appointed an emissary. He had a letter he had written when he was with Behak. He handed it to him, and he raced like the wind towards the king of Machin. 2190 He straightaway explained his situation to him, the injuries he had suffered at the hands of the malicious.

Chapter 2

They reached the frontier garrison happily and the watchman called out, "Who and what are these worthies who approach us, on what business have they come to us?"

Behak's emissary answered, "O great, worthy, and noble one, we are emissaries from Machin, to the king. Let us through, if you would."

The man immediately sent a rider to Tayhur to inform him. Tayhur sent a man of rank to the frontier garrison, with a hundred mighty riders. They were thus given entry and taken all the way to the king's court. When the emissaries were in sight of the throne, they praised them most graciously. They gave both letters to him, and Tayhur presented them to his translator. 2200 He ordered the letters be read out, and they spoke of many things.

When he heard the contents of Abtin's letter, it was as if his feet were nailed to the floor, his two eyes like glistening pearls shedding even more pearls down his cheeks.

He spoke, a gale issuing from his lips, "See what destiny has done to good men. Alas, that the pious have departed, and the corrupt have appeared! That pure seed was cut off from the world, the earth fallen into the hands of demons. The noble are routed, too—what worse thing could befall the world?" He called forth Abtin's envoy, bid him be seated before him, and asked, "Tell me what is the situation? Why have you come here from your king?"

"From a day's journey to this gate the king sent me to appear before your majesty." 2210

He ordered his minister to compose a letter crowned with all manner of courtesies. "May the world's king be happy and upright. He seeks a route to my abode. I submit all my treasure to your service, and would easily lay down my life. Now that you are here, you have nothing to fear. Before you, there is nothing lower than Zahhak. My kingdom is at your service, my heart and soul the salve for your wound. Your command shall be effective over my army, and I, like my army, will not transgress your command. Be at ease, do as you will. Day or night, feast joyously until the world is cleansed of Zahhak and his ravenous demons, as Jamshid foretold. When you have achieved what you want, leave here and go to your kingdom in good cheer."

He bestowed gold on the emissaries, and horses, robes, helmets, and girdles too. 2220 The emissaries acclaimed Behak, launched their ships and sailed a good distance. After that, he summoned his two sons. He placed them at the head of two detachments, sent them to receive the king, the troops traveling towards him like an ocean wave.

When the emissary reached the king, he was given a letter, addressed with courtesies. His heart was cheered by this graciousness, though he was ashamed by the extent of Tayhur's generosity.

When the monarch passed from the sea to dry land, he found the whole coast occupied by soldiers. Tayhur's two sons were at the head of the troops. They dismounted, and altogether they acclaimed the king. The king and the two sons embraced each other, then mounted their spirited steeds. When the king had passed through the gate, they cheered loudly. They traveled for a day, toiling over the rough black stone road. 2230 He gave generous gifts to the frontier garrisons, silver and gold coins and embroidered cloth. When the road had all but used up the king's fortitude, King Tayhur appeared in the distance. They approached each other, dismounted, walking across the cobblestones. Tayhur, his lips brimming with praise, addressed Abtin, saying, "Happy this day when we have seen your face, your majesty! You have come to this table bringing joy. May the malicious heart meet a fate that pleases you."

Abtin said to him, "O worthy one, my heart is overjoyed at the sight of you. I have asked God for this for many years and my heart's wish has been granted."

They traveled several days, the whole path blooming with blissful tulips. At each fortified stopping-place they received victuals, clothing, and gifts. 2240 The whole way, musicians, beautiful young women, and wine were presented to the aspiring world-king.

On the fifth day he reached the city of Besila. No one has seen anything upon the earth like Besila. Two leagues wide and just as long and filled with gardens, the gardens filled with jasmine. It was the throne of Tayhur, not a city but a heaven filled with houris. Every lane had fountains and running streams lined with cypresses. Its streets and markets were adorned, its walls built of stones laid one upon the other so neatly, nothing could fit in the cracks. Its height was so great that a hawk could not reach the top in a day. The moat encircling the city wall was so great that the Red Sea possessed but a portion of it. 2250 Water flowed through it, and ships—more than a hundred.

When the city's gatekeeper opened the gate, it was as if heaven had sent a portion of itself. Such a fragrance wafted from that city that one's heart and mind would be lost. The steeds strutted spiritedly ahead and they cast gems before Abtin. Every lane and district filled with delights, decked with Chinese embroideries. A sweet-sounding musician played on every rooftop, the whole city crying out in songs and tunes. This was how the fortunate king brought Abtin to his throne.

In the older son's soaring palace, the crowned king Abtin alighted. They decorated that heavenly abode as God adorns heaven: everywhere was gold upon lapis lazuli, the seats encrusted with rubies and yellow garnets. 2260 Its paintings were all beautiful like a young bride from China, as if placed there from heaven's heights. With its gardens, cypresses, and flowing water, the residence was truly regal. The rose garden was filled with nightingales, carpeted in flowerbeds, blooming with bouquets of narcissus, and filled with partridges, peacocks, and doves like idols in the women's hands. Tayhur sent him provisions of all kinds, and they wanted for nothing. The king took care of his every need, whatever was befitting a king. His two sons came twice a day to ask the king if he needed anything. Every time the minister came to see him, he brought gifts.

When ten days had passed, King Tayhur came to see Abtin. Abtin was delighted by his visit. They sat and exchanged stories 2270 of bygone days. Abtin told of all that had happened to him. [200b] Tayhur was saddened by all the king told him and said, "Your majesty, you are distressed by these events. If you have any desire to hunt in the fields, we should spend tomorrow on such entertainments."

Abtin was delighted by his words, he smiled and praised the king. The next day, Tayhur and his soldiers mounted their horses and set out. Abtin mounted his horse as well, and was joined by his riders and brave swordsmen. They went with cheetahs, falcons, and hawks, and fleet-footed hunting dogs. When they reached the field and the soldiers, they realized that Tayhur had no dogs, cheetahs, or hawks, and the proud king was astonished. 2280 This was strange to them, and they wondered if the hunting animals had been sent out ahead of the hunters.

When they approached the hunting-grounds, hunting commenced all around. The men were excited to hunt, but there was not a deer, mountain sheep, or wild ass in sight. The brave men of Iran unleashed dogs and cheetahs from their horses, and they hunted. But they saw no game in the great round hunting field, and they returned embarrassed and exhausted.

Not much later, King Tayhur came up from behind the troops, strutting like a boar, two of which were strapped to each of his riders' horses—some slain, some wounded by arrows. The king was embarrassed and when he saw this sight he looked more closely at their horses. They were two hands and two feet taller than his own steeds, their necks as broad as a camel's.

Tayhur understood that that lion-hearted fellow was ashamed before the feats of the Turanian hunters. 2290 He said, "Wise and stalwart king, look here, do not be upset. Today, the game escaped from you, another day it will be in your grasp. Our steeds have the character of wind, their stock is of horses from the sea. Tis no dishonor on your part, no weakness or shame, for they catch prey without delay. The game can never outrace them. Cheetahs and dogs are no use to us."

He asked, "How do you pull that off? Bringing horses out of the sea?"

Tayhur said to him, "In the springtime I send many horses to the sea. Fleet-footed Arabian horses with bodies like rhinos and the speed of storm-winds are each tied up in front of a man, who keeps watch over them. In the dark night a horse comes out, snorting and prancing like the sacred fire of Azorgoshasb. 2300 When he catches the scent of the mares' bodies, he races to them like the wind. He impregnates them and then becomes ashamed, and returns to the sea.

"He then comes back to kill the mares, and so the watchman lights a fire. When the horse sees the fire, he stops, then flees back to where he came from, turning back from the fire to the ocean-world. Just one glimpse of evil and he disappears. He so fears the fire, that steed, as would people who are blinded by daylight. How strangely hard-hearted are humans, that we have no fear of fire? Every year, the spring's gateway opens and these two worlds are put into contact. The next spring, a colt appears from that horse. At ten years of age we saddle him, and this is how we get steeds from the sea. 2310 At swimming under the water like a fish, climbing mountains like a running leopard, neither rhino nor lion nor man can compare to them."

Abtin was astounded, he said, "That is amazing!"

Right then, King Tayhur ordered that his troops take whatever they had hunted and distributed it to the Iranians, and they celebrated.

That night passed and dawn broke, and the king had a feast prepared. He sent for King Abtin and had him seated on a golden throne. The nobles of Iran and the house of Tayhur were assembled and prepared. The king's two sons were standing with golden helmets and Chinese robes. When the cooks were done, they laid out the banquet cloth and set it. 2320 That banquet imbued the whole world with color and scent, and the sound of their harps echoed from the heavens. Such cuisine appeared on the table as had never been seen nor heard of by the kings of Iran. Straightaway they reached their hands into the food and relished whatever they ate. There were more than a hundred dishes—how happy, whoever fed on such fare! They finished and washed their hands before returning to sit on their thrones. [201a]

The servants set the banquet cloth again, decked out with creations of all kinds. All of the dishes were jewels shining upon gold, as if the peacock of China had again spread its feathers. The whole banquet-setting was a golden treasure hoard adorned with gems, beauty upon beauty, and upon that, flowers, a hundred kinds, making the king's wounded heart bloom. And by the donkey-load, mounds of citrus and quince were heaped before the royal throne. 2330 So much incense of ambergris and musk was burned that everyone became sleepy. Such was the crying of the harp and the song of the flute that Venus leapt to its feet to dance. When they poured wine and began to drink, it took hold of the brave men's minds. Headstrong men's heads grew heavy from its scent, its color shone in their faces.

Kush's voice rung in Abtin's ears and wit took flight from his sober heart. The armies of wisdom are routed by wine and the veils of shame were lifted from the royal visage. Abtin spoke to Tayhur over the commotion. "Some of the Iranians and I have come to this most worthy court seeking asylum. Do for my sake what befits your station, for meanness is unbecoming for a king."

In response, Tayhur said, "O clear-thinking one, now that you have spoken, listen to me. 2340 By God, who is my creator, my companion in hardship, I will never seek to do you harm, and if I must forsake my life for you, I will strive to be faithful to you and never let you be persecuted. I will not turn you over to the enemy. Have no suspicions of me. Our ancestors, the ancient kings, did not consider any king greater than themselves.[1] My dominion is an island and a separate, isolated region, and I have no authority over other lands. There is no way across this mountain but the one you saw, by way of the sea that encircles the world and is greater than the other elements. On two sides are uncrossable ocean, impassable to large ships and small boats alike. 2350 Another side faces the route to Machin and China.

"Iranian ships come from the fourth direction. They must brave the fearsome sea for a year and a half. Then the seashore appears: Mount Qaf, blanketed in meadows. The wearied men emerge from the sea, worn down by its ravages. There are several cities there, their people worn, lean, and hungry. Gog and Magog are near them, day and night breathing down their necks. From there, they must pass Qaf. The foundation of the world is no tall tale! From Qaf, they reach the land of the Slavs and Rome, where signs of habitation appear again. And from those cities beyond the mountains come countless merchants. They come every twenty years, bringing every kind of thing from those lands. 2360

"Consider my home to be your home, consider me your father, your family. During the day, hunt, and at night, put on comfortable clothes, take moon-faced idols in your embrace. Know, o wise king, that it has been more than a thousand years since we have founded this city, and thus have we gotten the better of fate. My ancestor laid its foundations. May he ever rest in glory! He named this city after himself, that we always remember his name. No one has ever invaded this mountain, and he never sought to attack anyone."

Abtin praised him and said, "May wisdom forever be with the king's soul. All of what you said here is right and in accordance with Jamshid's counsels. For you are kind and God-fearing, I could not find

1. The text here is obscure and may also read "never feared Chin and Machin."

any better shelter than your protection." 2370 He ordered his minister right then to bring the testament of Jamshid. The minister brought it in and had the translator read it for Tayhur.

When he heard what was written by that far-sighted one, he praised his knowledge, kissed him and wept, asking, "Who on earth could have such wisdom? Alas, such kingly knowledge was lost because of that ill-born man." Then he kissed Abtin's face and said, "O king of the earth, may the world's creator be pleased with you, and Kush and Zahhak suffer. Now that you have come here, concern yourselves with nothing but wine and winecup, mirth, and tranquility. For I have sworn an oath before moon and sun, by the life dearest to me and the sun-like face, [201b] that so long as you are here, I will cause you no harm, and hold you dear.[2] 2380 I will not let any foe even see your face, nor answer you with unkind words. My life and my wealth, and this mighty army, are all at your service."

He ordered thirty moon-like slave-girls be brought to the king, all of them dancing, harp-strumming, heart-stealing, and delightful. Covering their faces were Zabolian roses, their glances cast Babylonian spells, their heads swaying like cypresses, their cheeks of rose and burgundy, their eyebrows like recurved bows of pure musk erupting like springs, like knotted lassos of ambergris. They indulged in play and relaxation, such as would rouse a drunk man from his stupor. That flock of idols, light on their feet, were all presented to Abtin.

Two excellent horses he gave as well, and gold-embroidered brocades and all manner of things, 2390 and a regal throne and crown adorned with garnet and turquoise. When Abtin was all but senseless amidst such splendor, he returned to his dwelling. He spent all night rejoicing in the visit, giving revelry and joy their due, smiling sweetly as each one sang her song. He was struck by the moon and lost his wits again each time he opened his eyes. Each was more beautiful than the one before, and the one before more beautiful than the one before her. Men and women of that city had cheeks like the sun and faces like the moon, their eyes like fairies, of stunning stature, their visages like blood upon snow. Sweet-voiced, delicate, and upright—who would not seek marriage with people like them?

---

2. "The life dearest to me and the sun-like face" may refer to his sons.

The worldly-wise say that there are two places in the world, both concealed by the sea, 2400 whose quality is unmatched anywhere— no garden is so beautiful! One is this island we have described, endowed with the pleasantness of Eram. The other can only be reached by a seven-month journey by ship across the ocean, after which the seafarer is bent over by the turbulence of the sea. You'll reach a sea you'd call chainmail, wave after wave crashing down like ringlets.

When Siyavash crossed that frontier . . . gave him this advice about it . . .[3] "You will see a mountain as high as the clouds with no lion, wolf, or tiger living upon it. It is covered with gardens upon gardens, blooming meadows and fields of grain, its slopes carpeted in tulips and fenugreek. Those cities are decked with pleasant-faced men and women, as if the vault had cast down its stars."

But such a life passes quickly, and days and nights are spent in weeping, then death. 2410 If we ask who it was that made these two places prosper, and why, mean and lowly people would not believe it, and we cannot rid ourselves of them. People believe that when Adam descended from heaven, the world was a ruin, there was no human there. Learn whatever can be known, if you're truly human.

ABOUT THE KING [OF CHINA]'S ARRIVAL IN CHANG'AN AND HIS BEAUTIFICATION [OF THE CITY]

I now return to the tale of Kush. Listen to this pious *dehqan!*[4] When the commander of China led his forces towards the city of Chang'an, all the cities along the way awaited the king and his minister. The cities were all decked out in brocades, and the people came out to honor the king. He traveled in all that splendor to Chang'an. Coins were sprinkled over every alleyway, saffron sifted over his head. 2420 Chinese silk brocade lined the walls, the bazaars full of cheer and bustle. They stayed in one of the palaces of Chang'an, decorating and adorning its interior. An ivory throne was placed there, a crown suspended over it.

3. The text of this line is unclear.

4. *Dehqans* were a class of Persian gentry that existed in the Sassanian period and into the early centuries of the Islamic era. They were important bearers of Persian culture, including the oral literature on which Ferdowsi based *The Shahnameh*.

Kush was joyously seated, they called him the great king of China and Makran.[5] His father sent him a hundred slaves, a hundred choice horses with gold-adorned saddles, and a hundred and ten beautiful Khallokhi [Qarluq] handmaidens, and all manner of treasure.

The commander of China found out that three months earlier, Abtin had gone to Behak. He had a letter sent to Behak that complained impotently, "Your secret has become known to me, that the wicked Abtin is with you. If you are a true servant of the king, why did you give quarter to the enemy? [202a] 2430 A hundred tricks he played to escape my son, my army, and my followers. He escaped from the forests of China into the mountains, and from the mountains, to you. Now, if you don't want to come to ruin, bind all those wretches one by one. Wait until I send an army, and send them to this court. If you do not follow these instructions, you'll bring raging fire on yourself."

The messenger reached Machin like the wind, came before the king, and presented him the letter. When the king became aware of its content, he praised the king of China profusely. He rewarded the envoy too, giving him brocades and coins and such.

Right then, he drafted a letter of response, "Woe and pain unto the enemies of the king! These words are true before the king, that this bondsman has, since time of old, 2440 been friendly with your dynasty, and praised its glorious kings. If news had come that the Iranians passed through my lands, I would not eat or sleep until I had taken his head and sent it before the ruler of China. I would have spread my fame across the earth! But that ignoble one flew by night. At the beginning of the week when I became aware of this, I sent an army to attack him. They reached the sea, but found no one, and returned. The army had taken to the sea, their baggage train with them. They reached the island of Besila. He went to Tayhur, or so I heard. If the king is convinced I saw Abtin with my own eyes, 2450 I would not complain of the king's retribution, I would accept whatever he wills."

So it was sent, telling the king of China that Abtin had fled in the night and escaped. The king of China was naive and unaware, and

5. Makran was a large region in the southeast of present-day Iran, bordering Pakistan.

ashamed to receive that king's letter. And he said to the envoy, "When the enemy is so hopeless, it's better for him to have died than to be humiliated like this."

The news reached the Tusked that China and Machin were emptied of Abtin, that he had crossed the sea to the mountain of Besila. Then, how would they handle Besila?

He was angered and went before his father and said, "O crown-wearer, a wise man is not safe from his enemy until his body is clothed in dirt. As long as there is Abtin in the world, neither Zahhak nor the ruler of China is safe. Give me an army so I can attack him before he takes control of the sea routes. [202b] 2460 If Besila is higher than the heavens, and if the sea and mountain are filled with soldiers, I will make that mountain level with the plain and dye the sea red. I will send the heads of Tayhur and Abtin to the king of China."

The king smiled at his words, and said, "O proud, headstrong fame-seeker, if you set out across the ocean, what will you do about the sky? Zahhak with his divine glory, with his priestly insight and knowledge, knew of no way to deal with the Tayhurians in the mountain. There is one way, and no other, and that is to send an army to blockade the sea routes, so not one person can get from China and Machin to Abtin. When merchants cannot reach the mountain, the men and women will suffer from hunger. 2470 When the blockade has lasted a year, they will seek quarter from us. They will send Tayhur to me in chains, without making the army suffer, or any harm coming to you."

He said, "O guiding king! No sage could have offered a better solution. But this is my war to wage, for rage and vengeance are my lot! From this moment, I shall put an army to sea and bar the way to even birds and fishes. They will not be able to last a year like this, and Abtin will come to you in chains."

The king said to him, "O dear brave one, I have not had my fill of seeing you, at least remain with me longer, for my soldiers outnumber the stars. I will put an army upon the waters of the sea more numerous than the kings ever dreamed of!"

He replied to the king of China, "Until I have taken Abtin, 2480 I will have no rest or peace of mind. As long as my heart is full of worry, you can let me relax as much as I want, but it will be pointless. My heart must be free of sorrow and grief, far from worry and empty of trouble. Otherwise, who could enjoy drinking and relaxation, even if their winecup overflows? Such a soul could not be found in all the world. Be sober if you wish, or drunk. Though wine is a remedy for my pain, it's a joy followed by suffering. Turn your back on pleasant wine, lest your head suffer the hangover. As long as I'm alive, the enemy secure upon the earth, why should I relax with you together? When I have destroyed the enemy—that is the time for winecup and celebration! When the king is safe from the enemy, then I'll have settled my account with fate. 2490 As long as the seed of the Jamshidians exists, how can I avoid being at war with them?"

The king of China was delighted by his words, and acclaimed his wisdom. Right then, he opened up the treasury and prepared a year's provisions for the army. He selected fifty thousand of his troops, battle-riders, brave fighters. He assigned that army to the commanding Kush, equipped them well, and they set out. That mighty warrior reached the ocean, which is called "Great." They settled in and blockaded the route tightly, a group of soldiers in every position.

When Behak was informed of his approach, he asked about their plans and went to them. He provided them provisions of all kinds, horses and gifts. Then Kush had a ship rigged up, manned by a stout crew. 2500 He sent them off to Besila with many instructions.

He wrote to Tayhur while on his way, "You must take one piece of advice from me, you have no place in the world to go but that mountain, and the world-ruling king has no equal. Don't stick your feet too far out of your cloak, the cold will get you! When a black snake nears its end, it always comes out of its hole. All the world are the king's servants, while some are smaller than you, some are greater. They're not uncouth before the king, they do not speak to him as if they were kings. Would you have the gall to do that, you fool, when the world's king can exact vengeance on you? Why did you not imprison the king's enemy when he came to you, as you should have? After that wicked one escaped, nobody gave him shelter. 2510 You're his shelter upon the earth, and like him, you have made an enemy of the king. If you are quick to understand this matter, then you will chain up that degenerate. You'll escape from the anger and grief of the king, and have no need to fear my anger. And if you struggle against my command, I'll make your heart struggle from my punishment. When I mount up for war, you'll have a hard time changing my heart. By the life and soul of the king of warriors, by the soul and life of the king of the eastern lands, I will not forget this injury, I'll double the sea's volume with blood."

The envoy arrived, and they looked down at him from the mountain's gate. The citadel commander asked him, "What business do you have with sea and mountain?"

The envoy said, "O sweet-voiced man, don't be so quick to anger. 2520 We did not come here to ambush you, we are envoys sent by the king of China. We crossed the sea for one month. We have a letter to bring before the king."

When the gatekeeper heard those words he sent a rider along the road who rushed to the city of Besila. He informed the king about them. The king sent a man with a hundred riders who brought the envoy to him from the gate. When they saw those mountains and that narrow path, they thought to themselves that Kush lacks courage, wisdom, and awareness. What recourse does anyone have from the sky, even if he could make himself one of the stars? He and his army would wind up begging for mercy if he attacked this mountain fastness.

When they came before King Tayhur, they placed the letter before him. 2530 After he read out those importunate words, he said, "The demon-born is not blessed with wisdom."

The king was astonished, and summoned the executioner to kill both the envoys for the insult. When Abtin found out, he sent someone before the great throne. "The proud king is better than this. The messenger's blood is not permissible to shed. The kings of the world see no honor in harming messengers. For they are bondsmen and servants, they take orders, they do not give them."

He ordered a letter of response that would wound the Tusked's heart, and sent it to Abtin. It said, "This is what Kush sent us. These wretches deserve nothing but ruin, I wholly agree with your judgment. I grant you leave to avenge yourself against these nobodies, you may respond to them on my behalf." 2540

When Abtin heard the king's response he drafted a letter to the commander of China: "I read your ill-conceived letter—just what an ill-born wretch would write! I'm amazed by your stupidity, you certainly have not learned anything from the priest. Has no one made you fully aware of our situation, of this mountain and our good fortune? Ask, if you are not aware—you have reached a new level of ignorance. I recognize no one on earth, seen or unseen, above me. Who of my ancestors was anyone's vassal? They were all kings, and God-fear-ing. Do you consider me like Behak and the others—a lesser king than yourself? If the whole world turns on me, by God I will not leave my palace for the street. With one man and a stone from the black moun-tain, I'll turn back this raging army. 2550 Think on this matter more soberly, and do not doubt what I say." When the letter was finished he had it quickly sent before Tayhur.

He read it and praised it and said, "May wisdom always be with your pure soul." He paid the envoy and told him, "You have escaped the headsman's blade! If he sends anyone else, have no doubt that he'll not return, I'll have him thrown into the water to feed the fish." The envoys set off on their way, very worried. They both looked to the left and right, to find a way across that mountain. They saw none, which left them astonished, and they passed through the gate in fear. [203a] They boarded the ship and a wind like a sweet draught delivered them to Kush in a month's time. 2560

They placed that response before Kush and told him everything they'd seen. When he read out the letter, he wet his lips with rage. He ordered a ship prepared and provisioned, to take the battle to Besila. The envoy said, "O courageous one, have you now grown tired of your army? Have you heard none of our advice? Do not inflict disaster on them. If you became wind and your army clouds, if you were a lion and your men tigers, you'd make no headway on the mountain of Besila. If you go there, you'll be disgraced."

When he heard the words of those advisers, he furrowed his brow. He set many ships upon the sea, equipping them with whatever was needed. That brave one rode in his ship, twelve thousand elite warriors with him. 2570 They turned toward the mountain of Besila muttering curses, looking for a fight.

When Kush's envoy had left the mountain, people were talking about Kush all over the island. Abtin sent a message to Tayhur for that king to consider. "A few men sent to support the gatekeepers would not hurt. That foul demon-spawn is crafty, he knows many tricks and stratagems. He is so devilish, spiteful, and ill-natured that he's a wor-thy army all by himself. If the gatekeepers have reinforcements, we'll be protected from that villain's tricks."

When Tayhur heard his message, he laughed and turned his face to his minister, "You would think this Iranian is scared, afraid of Kush, and that good sense and wisdom have fled his soul. He does not know that if Kush were to come like the wind, he still could not set foot on this mountain." 2580 Several days passed and the world-illumining king grew worried.

Finally, he accepted Abtin's suggestion and he sent a number of his troops to support the gatekeepers. He advised them, "Be alert day and night, watchmen of the gate and citadel. I will send another force to the moat, and you should fall back quickly if needed. We must manage our forces so well that the enemy gives up and goes back to China. When they depart from the coast, we will no longer be troubled by them."

That force that the king sent to guard the frontier outpost was no more than three hundred men. They had not yet reached the outpost when ill fortune found them. Kush came out of the sea in the dark of night and had his companions armored in steel. 2590 They came down on the frontier outpost in secret, heads full of rage and hearts full of fury. Those gatekeepers were all asleep and drunk, so they drew their blades and set upon them, killing each one where he sat, their heads and feet never moving from their bodies. Such is the work of wit-stealing wine—if you're wise, don't drink it! I've never seen a key to evil as great as wine. Drink is a key to hell!

Kush informed his army, "I have cleared the frontier outpost of enemies! Let us rally from the sea! Make for the citadel and occupy it!"

When they'd gone half the distance, a force of the Tayhurians met them. They saw that the gatehouse was full of troops, if not from Kush, from a different foe. They immediately prepared to turn them back, and the roar of battle was heard. 2600

A rider raced back to the king, telling him, "Kush and his army have taken the frontier outpost! They have killed every one of the gate-keepers. You are our refuge, otherwise we are ruined!"

In front of him was a narrow and treacherous part of the road, and he stood there with his troops behind him. Rolling boulders cascaded down the mountain. The battle went on like this for two days and nights, boulders from above, arrows from below, and the demon's heart grew decrepit from the fighting. Brave men's heads were suddenly smeared and their waists blossomed with blood like tulips. The army was decimated by the rocks, and Kush's heart was troubled. He saw a number of his companions killed, blood pouring out of the mountain down to the ocean. Another detachment joined the Tayhurians, girded for battle. A number of brave men were killed by rocks, and the passage through the gate became crowded with bodies. 2610 Tayhur's brave men took courage and drove the enemy army below the gate.

When Kush saw them, he turned his face and ran back to the sea. Of this massive force of thousands, only seven hundred remained. They boarded their ships and took flight, barely escaping with their lives. When Tayhur was informed of this, he went with his forces and Abtin to the frontier outpost. The good news reached him while he was on his way, that that evil heathen was turned back with no more than a thousand troops left. The enemy were all killed or grievously wounded.

Tayhur was delighted by that news and went to Abtin. He kissed his head and eyes one by one, and held his dear friend in a tight embrace. He said to him, "What you said turned out to be right! Who on earth has such insight?" 2620

He became aware of his own imprudence and was pleased by that one piece of Abtin's advice. Right then, he ordered one of his officers to rebuild the gatehouse. They raised a wall over its gate and raised its top over the mountain. They erected a great iron gate, making it secure against the mighty Kush.

And thus, Kush, with that army, crossed the sea and took to the road. They carried their things from the ships to the land and struggled along. He sent a horseman to his father to tell him what fate the heavens had had in store.

"I was in such dire straits, trying to take that whole island in my grasp, because fortune was not with me. I had no army fit for battle. When they saw that mountainside and those rolling boulders, they turned their backs and did not fight. 2630 The lot of them were killed or wounded, only seven hundred brave warriors got away. I am now at the seashore. I do not want to show weakness in this task."

The king of China was astonished when he learned this. He grew mournful and threw his crown to the floor. He said to himself, "This stubborn man has now twice wasted an army!"

He said to the envoy, "Whoever does not listen to his father's advice brings evil on himself. Though sons be wise and enlightened, the young do not equal the old in knowledge. Even if your father misguides you, take his guidance anyway, for he wishes you the best. Even if the father is of evil nature, he would never wish harm on his son.

"I told you not to sail your ships across the sea with your army, for the world-conqueror's stratagems, despite all his wisdom, will not work on that mountain. 2640 You ignored my command and threw my army into the maw of death. Twice now this has happened to you, the turning heavens have spilled your blood. Have you ever heard of a wise man being bitten by a snake twice from the same hole? Being foolish has nothing to do with manliness, whoever benefited from haughtiness? Good men avoid haste, haste puts wisdom to sleep. The Lord has protected you, but the army is weaker now with you at its head. It is best if you stay where you are, don't attack the mountain again. When Tayhur begins to suffer, he'll submit to your demands without a fuss. He will send your enemies to you and make your allies happy. I will send you treasure, equipment, and more troops, I will send you whatever you need." 2650

When the envoy returned with his reply, that demonic force said to his troops, "If the king had not schemed as he did, I would have taken the island by now. When I broke through the gatehouse I gave battle to the Tayhurians. There was scarcely a mile left to go, but what good does manliness do for what the Lord does not want?" He went to the seashore with his forces, cutting off the sea routes to even the birds and the wind. Until the next year, he kept up the blockade so no ship could reach the island. But it suffered no deprivation, no one complained of lacking food or clothing.

NEWS REACHES KUSH OF THE DEATH
OF HIS FATHER

Kush was informed: "The lord of the east has passed on to another abode, [203b] and left his flock shepherdless and his throne empty. His viceregency and kingship are now yours."

He now feared the foe and packed up, taking his forces back to the throne. 2660 He poured the dust of mourning on his father's crown and tore his clothing in grief. A whole week he spent in grief and sorrow, and on the eighth day his heart was free of sadness. Such is the constitution and behavior of sons, their affection never matches that of their fathers. When three days have passed since the father's death, affection is spent from their minds and hearts. Wise was the learned *dehqan* who said, "Whoever you shut your eyes to, your heart is even farther from them." On the eighth day he ascended his throne, his forces assembled before him in his court. They cast jewels upon his crown, acclaiming him as king of the east.

When the sea was cleansed of Kush and his army, Behak was no longer afraid of anyone. He sent this good news to Tayhur: that the world was free of China's ruler, that Kush and his forces together had left the sea, with hearts full of grief. 2670

Tayhur was delighted by this and Abtin and his forces even more so. The envoy was given horses, brocades, coins, and other things upon his arrival. They told Behak's envoy to tell him, "Good news has turned its face to us. So long we have waited to hear good news about Zahhak and Kush. What we received today was the happiest of all. Two armies are in tears. We thank you for this good news, o beneficent and well-intentioned king!" The messenger returned to Machin swift as smoke and delivered the message.

Kush turned his attention to China and set things in order there. There was a beneficent man, honorable and fortunate, by the name of Nushan, son of Behmard. Behmard, minister of the miserable Kush, had no other sons. 2680 When both fathers departed this world, the one son took the other as his minister. He commanded Nushan to present himself before the threshold of the world-king. "Write a letter for the world-king, explain everything that has happened. See what it is he intends for us, I would not want to be disgraced before him."

Nushan kissed the ground before him and said, "I obey your command, king of China."

KUSH WRITES A LETTER TO ZAHHAK

Right then, he called for the scribe and spoke with him a while. He ordered a letter written for Zahhak, brimming with praise. "May the reign of the king of the world be eternal, may skill and fortune be ever with him. May his crown be verdant and the heavens aligned for him, his crown a lofty star, his army like the stars. Word of my father's passing has reached the lofty throne. 2690 Eternal be the reign of the great king, the world in servitude to his mighty threshold! This affectionate servant is girded to labor day and night in his service. May I bring low the enemies of the king and fill their palaces with mourning!

"After we were at war for ten years, in mountains and forests, with blades and boulders, when fate left the enemy no recourse, he turned and fled to the mountain of Besila. Four years he has remained there, and I have blockaded that mountain and sea. If I stay another year, I will have him in my grasp. I now await your orders. What would you have me do, clear-sighted king? Shall I come and pay my respects before the king or keep my watch on this mountain? When the king's orders reach me, I will give my life in service of his command." 2700

He then opened the doors of his treasury and had all manner of gifts prepared. Ten camels were loaded up with gold and jewels, ten camels loaded with cloth of gold garments. Qarluq slaves, maidservants from China, each one like roses and jasmine. He selected horses like raging torrents, blades of Indian steel, and mail coats. He selected two thousand of his men and with two horses each, he put them under command of his minister and counseled him, "Ride like wind-blown dust. Do not tarry anywhere on the way to the royal court."

The Chinese minister traversed two stages a day until he reached the court of the world-king. Zahhak became aware that his brother had died. 2710 Kush now sat on the throne in his place, the renowned and fierce knight. He was informed by Nushan who traveled there, and he ordered a welcome for him. He chose a verdant place for them, settling them in a garden. He sent them victuals and provisions to comfort them after their long journey. For a week they recovered from the hardships of the road and on the eighth day appeared in the king's court. The minister of China, when he saw Zahhak, lowered his face to the dusty ground.

The eloquent minister of China said, "Long live the world's king!" He then placed the letter before the king, and likewise had the gifts delivered to him. Zahhak accepted them and was pleased, and the translator had the letter read out to him.

When the ferocious king learned what it said, he asked, 2720 "What else has the king said?"[6]

"That servant of the king says, 'I know you are aware of what has come to pass. For more than sixty years now, I have not released

6. Some text is likely missing here.

Indian steel from my grasp. Night and day in battle with the king's enemies, sometimes in the wood, other times on stony mountains. I have beheaded Abtin's right hand, a warrior unrivaled in all the world. I sent his head to the threshold of the king, his armies ruined by my hand. They were scattered across the world and hopeless, crossing the sea in the dark of night. He found refuge with Tayhur, so I have now blockaded that mountain and sea. If death had not done to my dear father what it does to all, high and low, I would have crossed the sea again 2730 and brought those enemies down from the mountain to send them all in chains to the king.

"'Now I am occupied with mourning, and also with the business of the army. I have set the affairs of China in order so as to please the king of the world. My eyes are set on the king's command, I will observe and follow his orders. If the king says I should come to him, I will not disobey his command. My eyes and head will be given to the road, and I will come pay my respects to the king. And if I extend my siege over the sea, I will come with the enemy's head in my hand.'"

When Zahhak heard Kush's message, he thought to himself carefully and said, "He is devoted to us, how similar is he to my son?"

Nushan said, "Your majesty, none in the world is his equal. 2740 In battle, he is a mail-clad elephant, when he is angered it is as if he were on fire. Before him, an army is like a single soldier and a dragon is a mere snake. In his hands, a lion is lowlier than a fox, his arrows bring down birds in flight. He can take down a rider by the leg of his horse and turn him upside-down, that worthy brave man. He sprints faster than Arabian horses and tears apart an elephant's foot with his hands. If he had faced the enemy for two more years, all the men of China would have been felled by his blade. When he turned his back on the enemy and returned to us, that same day he killed Abtin's son. They have been driven out of the forests and mountains, we have taken the fight to them in Besila. But it cannot be denied that he has a hideous visage, two front teeth like tree trunks, his two ears like the ears of an elephant in length and breadth, and his eyes blue-black as the Nile. 2750 He is a little bit selfish, malevolent and short-tempered—his temper would cripple a lion's heart. [204a] When he rages he is like a fire, brave, proud, and headstrong."

The king said to him, "You are a fool! A talented rebel is rebellious. A king's heart is like a fire: it is either reduced to ash, or it is rebellious.

How great is a fire that burns high! If a lion is harmless, he's no more than a dog. When the ocean has waves, it is fearsome, and one is grateful to see it without waves. If Kush is hot-tempered and headstrong, this is pleasing to me. Men must be skilled and rebellious, whereas women are best reined in." This he said and went out to the hunting-grounds, and the night darkened over Nushan.

KUSH THE TUSKED'S RESPONSE
TO ZAHHAK

When the color of turmeric tinted the earth and pitch was washed from face of the sun, 2760 he called forth the scribe and ordered him to write a letter of response. He said, "O dear son of mine, dearer to me than any of my relations. Your letter arrived and I am informed that you have weakened the enemy. I am pleased with all that you have done, dearer it is to me than my eyes. No one has a higher place before me than you do, o benevolent one. I grant you kingship, counting you as my eldest son. Nushan's words have made me wish to meet you. When you read this letter, do not remain long, move quickly and show us your face. We will send you back in such a state as to melt the heart of the enemy."

When he told that tale in his letter, he called forth the minister of China. 2770 He gave it to him and said, "Tell him I said, 'Come to me at once. Were I not worried that the land of China be ruined by over-running its mountains, valleys, and plains with soldiers from all the seven lands, I would have come to visit you myself, to see your face with my own eyes. But if I leave my place, my army will trample your lands under their feet. Although it causes you trouble and headache, it is much better that you be the one to visit me.'"

He bestowed many things on Nushan and invested him with robes of honor, too. He left the court and set out for China, rejoicing and hurrying all the way. From ten stages away, he sent ten riders to take the news to the king of China.

When King Kush got word of Nushan, he called for a clever priest. 2780 He brought his army ahead one station. Kush was ready to receive him a mile ahead. When his eyes saw Nushan in the distance, he kissed the ground and rushed to him. He kissed his feet and stirrups and expressed much praise for him. Kush then ordered that he be seated, taking him by the hand. The king asked many questions about

Zahhak, about his customs, ceremony, and palace, and about his army, crown, throne, treasury, war elephants, and lands.

Nushan said to him, "King Zahhak is higher than the sun and moon. Light shines from his crown and the tree of justice springs from his glory. The stars are his army, his throne the heavenly sphere, upon it the world's king radiating warmth. He terrifies like a brave dragon; he's seized the hearts of the demons and the teeth of the lions. 2790 The world is made safe by his labor, the earth is entirely his treasure, under his name." So it went, until the king entered his court, Nushan speaking to him like this the whole way.

The brave king sat on his throne, and a golden chair was placed below it. The worthy Nushan took his seat upon it and put his hands in his sleeve. When he took out the letter and put it before him, he began to speak.

When he heard the message and read the letter, he smiled with joy and was excited. He said to him, "Now go and prepare, open my father's treasury." He sent a letter to every region, to every worthy and noble. He called the whole army to his court, so that there was not a rider left in China. He selected forty thousand of that army, honored riders, veterans. 2800 He put them under the command of Dayhim, one of good heart, faithful to the king.

He said to him, "Hurry to the sea and hold the sea routes. Make it so that flying birds in the air cannot reach that island. If those enemies know of my absence, our struggle with them will become more difficult. Request whatever you need from Machin, Behak will put his men at your service."

He also ordered a letter sent to Behak, with all entreaties, courtesies, and flourishes. "I will go with a group of nobles in haste to the court of the world's king. I will see him and size him up, o faithful, of good character, doer of good.[7] Year after year, you were loyal to us, a friend to our king with your whole heart. I sent a leader with an army to guard the sea routes. 2810 Do not begrudge him whatever he needs, of ships and instruments of war, of clothing, of gifts, beasts of burden, and victuals. Do this, for I will return from my visit to the king. It is best you deal with me nobly." He sent the envoy and took his army. Dayhim and his army headed for the sea.

7. The text here is obscure.

KUSH THE TUSKED GOES TO ZAHHAK

When the army went, he got everything in order, spending three months and some days on the task. He opened the doors of his father's treasury, and that great treasure delighted his heart. He selected worthy gifts for Zahhak: five hundred turquoises, twice three hundred rubies, whose radiance would illumine the dark night, a throne, each plank a hundred *maund*s of gold, set with all manner of jewels—a thousand men had sat upon it, yet now it was empty and cast aside— 2820 a thousand sturdy horses with golden bridles, a thousand handmaids and thousands of servants, with robes, hats, and belts all of gold, two thousand boards of Chinese brocade and countless elephant tusks, a thousand musk glands, and thousands of coats of mail the likes of which would perplex King David. Those who went to the king were worthies such as the minister and the great king's son. He had many gifts made for everyone—Kush went to such lengths! He chose seventy times a thousand men from his forces—brave swordsmen. He went magnificently to the imperial court in Jerusalem. When he was within three days' journey, he sent a greeting to the king. The king ordered that troops be sent to receive his younger relative and the minister. 2830

In that time there were few troops there, no more than seven hundred thousand. When that wave rose up from Jerusalem, they entered, rank upon rank. They all dismounted before Kush and lost their wits from fear of him. When Kush saw that army and its equipment, he saw his own heart grasped in a hawk's talons. Compared to that force, his army was like a pile of straw in the desert. When he saw Zahhak's son, he quickly dismounted, bowed, and praised him. Zahhak's son dismounted and went down the dark road, kissed him and embraced him tightly.

The king's son was astonished at the sight of him and looked him over for a long time. He said, "Such a child, born to the king of China! Such a thing is scarcely seen from the turning heavens—such suffering destiny brings us!" 2840 The youth was not so pleased with Kush, his ugly face, teeth, and ears. He rode alongside him, onlookers all looking at his face.

When they approached Jerusalem, Zahhak rode out one mile to meet them. Everywhere he looked, Kush saw more troops and arms, more brave men. [204b] He felt like a straw among them, his forces were lost in that army. When he saw Zahhak in his glorious magnificence, he was like a wingless, headless bird before him. Dismounting with the swiftness of Azorgoshasb's fire, he kissed Zahhak's horse, his stirrups, neck and haunches, making a scene before his troops. He took that great king in his embrace. He bade him mount his horse again, and they went on ahead. They were given a place to camp near the city, with many admirers paying them respects. 2850

The palace was decked out like spring, an apparition of gold upon lapis lazuli. Chinese brocades upon green carpets of grass, a garden full of roses and jasmine, nightingales and cypresses, bursting with cries of lovely pheasants. Peacocks' tails hung over the garden like a thousand lanterns, red rose petals were scattered about like the inside of a love letter. His army settled there on the field, and that same day, called for wine and music. The next day he made a request before Zahhak's threshold. Zahhak said, "This good man has embarrassed us with these gifts, as if he gathered up whatever was in China and in the treasury, things like no one has ever seen, and brought it all here."

All who saw them were amazed. 2860 He had so many dishes prepared for the king that they crowded the garden. He hosted him more than a month, along with his army officers and everyone else who came. The king tested his skills in fighting and feasting, polo and hunting. Kush did better than the king expected, there was no one in the great army like him. When the soldiers picked up his bow, they put it right back down, for they could not draw it even halfway, they all were embarrassed at their weakness. When the Arab went hunting on horseback, he could take down two deer with a single arrow. With his sword, he could cut a wild ass in two. With his spear, he could skewer a lion's heart. He lay low charging riders . . .[8] So much game was felled on the plain that the scavengers gave up eating it. 2870

I've heard told that Zahhak ate so much that his shoulder blades began to ache. His physician diagnosed him with cancer, a cold disease, and dry.[9] If you attack a disease's essence, if you undo it . . .[10]

---

8. The text here is obscure.

9. This refers to Galenic medicine, in which qualities, including wetness and dryness, cold and heat, must be balanced in the body.

10. The text here is obscure.

It was no doubt because of the game they had hunted that what looked like two snakes sprang from his shoulder blades.[11] When this happened to him, he shouted in pain and began to bleed. He called the wise physicians, but they were all stumped trying to find a remedy. A group of magicians from Babylon came before that headstrong king. No one could produce a cure, and that pain knocked the king over. He tied a blindfold over his eyes, but could not sleep, eat, or enjoy himself. Magic-wielding physicians remained stumped by God's work. 2880

An Indian man came to the court of the king, the dust of the road clinging to him. "I was told to travel to the king and show him my work." Everyone asked, "Who are you? What are you looking for in the court of the king?" He answered, "I am a physician, I know all manner of wet and dry conditions. I am ready here at this court for I know the remedy for the king's pain."

The doctors raised their fists and rained blows upon him, the Indian was beaten like a passed-out drunk. So did they humiliate an innocent, and he said, "Importunate men! I will pay back the harm you did me by presenting you with a remedy. It will require you to sacrifice every day a dear slave-girl and two honorable men."

Everyone laughed at his pointless boasts. 2890 At night, when court was empty, he entered, saying, "I am a doctor, let me through, let me through to see the king."

The attendant brought him to the king, and the world-ruler invited him to sit near him. The learned man went in and expressed profuse praise of the king. Then, he said, "I have been sent by the Indians in order to remedy this illness. God will relieve you of this pain."

Zahhak was pleased by these words and gave him many gifts.

He said, "Your majesty, you must order that two wicked men be taken from the prison and killed. When they bring me the heads from the two bodies, I will concoct the remedy."

He did as that corrupt man said, removing the brains from each head. 2900 When the remedy was applied to those wounds, he was at

---

11. In *The Shahnameh*'s more familiar version of this story, two snakes grow out of Zahhak's shoulders—a straightforwardly supernatural occurrence for which no scientific explanation is offered. Iranshah has rationalized the story, eliminating the magical and supernatural elements. See also lines 4670–80, where he expresses an equally critical view of Ferdowsi's story of the cow Barmayeh.

ease and forgot about the pain. The snake-shouldered king fell asleep and he slept the whole night. The next day, when the Indian came to the court, he filled his pockets with gold and gems.

The filthy man now lacked for nothing, for no one had seen anything on earth like this medicine. He said to Zahhak, "This is the remedy for your illness. Continue applying it and do not relent. Do not eat any more game, it is bad for this illness."

He applied this medicine and disappeared, and Zahhak's pain was thus eased. When the day broke before the king's eyes, he had two men of the city executed.

They made the rounds of the bazaars and streets, and the city filled with mourning and rumors. Men and women alike told the same tale: "That wasn't a Hindu, but Ahriman! 2910 He invited the king to spill blood, otherwise he would not be so willing to do this. Now it is clear he is not sick, those are two serpents that devour men!"

Many tales are told about this marvel that reveal the caliber of those who tell them.[12] And so, Zahhak remained beside Kush day and night, with drink, song, and food.

Meanwhile, elsewhere, Dayhim advanced his forces, deploying them at sea. The sea became so crowded that all paths were blocked as if by mountains.

King Behak, when he read the letter, said, "Woe unto Kush and Zahhak! He now has such army and arms, but I have some of my own!" He sent ten thousand men to join him, knights ready for war. They brought whatever they could, both food and property. 2920 Two months passed like this, and Behak was having difficulty providing for them. There were no cows left or sheep, they ate everything in sight. Such scarcity befell Machin as no elder or youth had ever heard of. There was such devastation, nothing was left. He had no means or access to find more, and could not support them.

The army had no provisions, and Dayhim advanced to Behak's court. "Now there is no food from Machin, nothing to sustain the army. Tell us how to resolve this, if you want to stay here."

That warrior said to his army, "We have no intention to retreating, find food wherever you can, it is up to you to obtain it." 2930

---

12. Here he refers to the common version of the story.

When the army heard that, they busied themselves with plundering. Behak did find one remedy, for God never leaves anyone completely without recourse.

BEHAK WRITES A LETTER TO TAYHUR

When he saw how they had ruined Machin, he wrote a letter to King Tayhur. He also sent a letter to Abtin. "O proud and noble kings, you have turned your attention to feasting, you have no intention of fighting like men. It is three months now that Kush has been gone from China and taken his steel-clad riders. [205a] He has sent an army, scattered and bare, toward the sea. If you'd launch a surprise attack, you'd fill the sea's water with blood. I have told my own forces, and not revealed the secret to anyone: when an army emerges from the sea, do not stand your ground, do not attack. 2940 When my army turns its back on them, they'll have nothing but the wind in their hands. When that army is out of your way, march into China immediately. It has been two years since the army has been seen there, you will be the only ones in the land of China. By the new year, he will become aware of this and that year march on China. In these two glorious years, the both of them will come to ruin." When he finished the letter he looked at his pure and upright minister. "You must go and do this, the secret is with you."

The minister had a boat readied, launched it, and set out on his trip. None of the army of China was traveling that way and none of them knew his secret. When he emerged from the sea onto land, he hurriedly told the gatekeeper, 2950 "Let me through to your king, or if not, race to him and let him know."

The rider immediately went to the king, and Tayhur was informed about the minister. He sent forth one of the sturdy riders who brought the minister before him. When he saw King Tayhur, he bestowed suitable praises. They set up a small throne for him and seated that sage before the king. He kissed the ground and gave the letter, repeating the whole secret and the message.

When the translator read out the letter to him, he immediately called in Abtin. He informed him about that letter and its secret, and opened the way in his heart for vengeance. He said, "Think on this matter and make a wise decision. If you exact your vengeance, you'll cause the enemy great pain." 2960

Abtin said to him, "O proud one, we can fight if we have men and materiel. If you support me, then I have no fear, the Chinese may as well be a handful of dust. If that wicked one is not with them, not one rider will find his way home. If they are thirty thousand or a hundred thousand, I'll put them all to the sword."

Tayhur replied, "The army and treasury are at your disposal, since army and treasure are the medicine for your wound." He ordered the minister to give him whatever he wanted, and the army was paid and equipped.

The world-seeker wanted eighty ships. Elite troops from among the warriors of the mountain boarded them, twenty thousand all with weapons of war. Their women, children, and treasure remained behind on the day that royal army set out. He gave many gifts to the minister of Machin, dinars and Arabian horses. 2970 He sent him from his court back to the king, bringing news that the army was coming.

ABTIN CROSSES THE SEA AT NIGHT

And so, Abtin and his army launched their ships onto the sea and its whirlpools. They emerged from the sea in the dark of night, leaving their ships anchored. It was a night like ebony. The sounding pipes and roaring drums rose like a black cloud from the sea. Abtin and his riders drew their blades. The army raised a shout to the heavens, and Kush's general awoke.

His forces, like a shepherdless flock, had no advance guard keeping watch. Everyone's heads groggy from sleep, they started awake and rushed out. They mounted horses bareback, no helmets on their heads or armor on their bodies. Brave men were put to flight. It was a night of terror crossed by blades. 2980 Sparks flying from swords and spears robbed the night of its color. The prey of those brave men was heads and livers—swords taking heads and javelins piercing livers. Gleaming like diamonds, blades and spearheads spilled blood into the sea.

Dayhim donned his armor, his head heavy from sleep, still affected by wine. They had no room to plan or communicate and the swords of vengeance were unsheathed. They held their ground and advanced into the fray, mixing the blood of brave men into the grime.

When gold flowed like water over the ground, Abtin saw the commander of China. The army gathered ten thousand strong around him, brave veteran riders. The two sides engaged and many men were cut down before him.

Abtin took off his helmet and announced his name, so they all knew who he was. 2990 He drew his heavy mace from his mountainous saddle, and they all cleared away from him. A gleaming sharp javelin in hand, bursting with rage like a drunk elephant, he charged at the commander, who turned to face him.

Foul curses poured from the commander's mouth, and, raising his head, he hurled his own javelin at Abtin. The javelin penetrated his shield, but no harm came to the crowned king. The world-seeker scored a blow to the head, and head and helmet hit the ground together.

When the troops saw their commander killed, his body stirred into the dust, they turned and fled, those brave men, one and all, like a flock fleeing a wolf. The world-seeker spurred his horse onwards, he and his allies breathing like Azorgoshasb's sacred fire. He killed so many, like locusts and ants, the ground was iced with the blood of brave men. 3000 Their horses charged like the wind, the Chinese horses fleeing before them like donkeys. The only ones to escape their swords were those who dismounted and surrendered. The escape routes were lost, as men's eyes were blinded by blades.

That night, when Abtin returned, he went to the enemy camp. He sat upon the throne of the commander of China, placing both hands upon it, his heart delighted. He said, "I have avenged my dear Sovar, taken back what fate owed me."

He summoned the Tayhurian nobles, calmly seating them before him. He held a victory celebration which put those proud men at ease. The next day he called for all the booty to be gathered before him. Whatever was worthy of the king and could be transported, 3010 he set aside, and gave away everything else, lighting up the troops' faces with that booty. He loaded up the eighty ships, forty with dirhams and dinars, forty filled with brocades and embroidered silks, and sent them with the Iranians to Tayhur, saying "This is for you, if it be worthy of your city."

ABTIN'S LETTER TO KING TAYHUR

He ordered the scribe to write a letter, saying, "May good men always have skill. O king, take comfort in this letter, for the ancient turning heavens have turned our way. The enemy is all scattered across the field. At the deep sea's shore are severed heads. Kush's commander made an attack that scared the wits out of the nobles. He struck his burning javelin against my armor, but God protected my body from his evil. I landed a blow on his head with my mace and at once shortened his stature. 3020 Now fortune has turned its back on Dayhim, his troops scattered like fallen leaves, routed before our charge. Not even a hundred of them escaped. All were killed in the battle, or else grievously wounded or captured. The army captured so much that every one of them has no more need for booty. With these bounteous treasures, baggage, and provisions, everyone is now wealthy like a commander. I have sent a portion of everything to the king's court and headed for China by sea, to explore that territory. I am preparing the brave men for war to see who would dare stand in my way."

When the ship set sail, he led his force toward China. [205b] He ordered an advance guard to drive everyone they saw one stage ahead of the king. 3030 Whoever did not obey the command immediately found his fortune changed. Dust was raised from that city and country as it was completely plundered. The people of China all feared him, and what recourse did a shepherdless flock have? None of the border guard put up resistance, men all feared for their lives. They carried on like that in every direction for a year, finding new treasure everywhere.

The army obtained such abundance, so much treasure, that the animals could scarcely haul it. Whoever had abandoned Zahhak's side and was in hiding from him, when they became aware of this, saw an opportunity, and many people from Iran joined him. His army soon numbered more than fifty thousand mounted knights with their lances. He went on until he reached the city of Chang'an, facing no resistance. 3040 In Chang'an a great wailing cry went up.

When Nushan, Kush's minister, saw this, he called the nobles of the city and army to him, and spoke to them, saying, "Do not worry too much about this business, these worthless ones have little time. Whenever news comes of Kush's return, he will turn this sorrow to happiness. Three months have passed since he left the king's court. When they become aware of the enemy's approach they will not remain in this land. The enemy will flee from him, or else be destroyed. Hold out for a few months, defend the city gate. Provisions are not scarce in our city, we must strive against shame, for our honor. Victory is not out of men's reach. This is that same Abtin, not the emperor of China. 3050 He fled through the forest of China ten times, his army dumping their helmets and armor."

The army took heart and their faces shone, and they manned the gates that day. He sent to each gate three thousand chosen riders ready for war. Upon the walls, various flags were flown, a display of red, black, and purple. Abtin reached the city and the ground became covered with tents, all of brocade and Chinese embroidery, with Abtin's banner in the middle. A shout rose from the city as they approached the front gates. Drums roared and pipes wailed, an army like the sea rose up from its place. So many troops came from the city that you'd think even the wind could not pass through them.

When Abtin saw that force he was astonished, and called for his officers. 3060 "This is not a city but a whole country, such armies are contained within it!" He ordered his troops to hold their ground, and they reached for their spears and blades.

There was a great melee, spearshafts groaned and arrows rained down. The clanging of sharp swords made Saturn take flight. Such a cloud of dust rose from the army that the sky and full moon were obscured. The blood of brave men ran in streams along the ground, and proud men's heads became polo-balls upon the field. The darkness made mountain level with plain. Abtin's army was terrified by the force from Chang'an, and bent like a branch in a gale.

When Abtin saw that terror, he sprung up, drew his sword, and mounted his horse. He charged into the fray, engaging with the warriors of Chang'an. 3070 He threw the Chinese army back with such force that you'd say its arms and legs were bound.

When his blade was sullied with gore, the army was turned back to the city gate. That attack left more than two thousand casualties, a stampede of horses and riders. They flung themselves into the city, taking their share of sorrow and pain in the battle. No one else came out of the city after that, the army held the walls and gates. Abtin besieged Chang'an, holding the road and blocking any passage. The city's inhabitants were at war day and night, raining darts and stones from the walls.

When Nushan saw that things were getting difficult, he secretly sent out several riders. He explained everything in his letter, "Long life and happiness to the lord of China! May the body of the world-king's

enemy be in chains, his heart aching and his spirit sorrowful! 3080
When the enemy saw that the lord of China had left, he marshaled his
army for vengeance. Behak had informed him that the forest of China
was emptied of lions. Abtin came out of the sea at night, swords rained
down all of a sudden. Dayhim fought hard but what good is struggle
when destiny has other plans? Behak's army fled quickly, they did not
stay long, for he had told his army, in secret, that when they saw the
army coming, they should retreat, that no one should fight, and if
Abtin attacked at night, not to remain.

"When those ill-born ones turned their backs, the brave commander, Dayhim, was killed. Of Dayhim's men, not one worthy
escaped, and none of the ill-born Behak's men was hurt. Now the city
of Chang'an is full of soldiers, and Abtin is camped at the gate. 3090
We battled outside the city, venomous darts rained on our troops.
Abtin threw himself at the army and killed them in a rage. Now the
city is besieged and battle rages twice a day. You'll find no house without mourning, sorrow has replaced all happiness. If the king does not
attend to this matter quickly, this city will go up in smoke." The envoys
wound along the road, all racing like birds.

Abtin continued besieging the city, at times waiting, at times doing
battle. In three months the city reached the point of scarcity, and word
of this reached Nushan. A cry rose up from the bazaars and streets,
"Kush has turned on you!" Women, men, and children were shouting,
all of them coming to Nushan's gate. 3100 "We're in great danger! You
are the king's minister, find a solution! If this goes on another month,
we will have no one left who can fight. No one in the city is left whole,
men's bodies are weak from not eating. Nothing sweet or salty is left in
the city, no strength left in the men of arms or men of the bazaar.
Abtin may be the king's enemy, but he has no quarrel with us. The spite
of Zahhak and the Jamshidians will bring an end to the people. They
have split some with their blades, others succumbed to famine.
Nobody has any access to food, or strength, no one has any recourse."

Nushan was frightened of such talk, so he faced those people,
answering them delicately. "O great men, do not be heavy-hearted
from these travails. 3110 I have no doubt that the king and his army are
more than halfway here. As soon as I heard about Dayhim, I set to
work to prepare for this. I sent swift couriers to inform the lofty king
of this matter. The world-ruler, Zahhak, will hurl his crown at the

ground when he hears about this. He will not rest as long as the enemy has any strength, it is an affront to his majesty. He would immediately endow our king with an army to chase away the enemy. Where would you fire an arrow with no head, but into the water? . . . is lacking, otherwise it lacks . . . A fire, though it be fearsome, can always be put out with dust. The moon is bright only as long as the shining sun hides its face. For every arm, there is an arm stronger than it, for every army there is another that is greater. 3120 And if you believe otherwise, then perhaps I can find another solution. I will send a rider to Abtin, to see if he is aligned with goodness or rage. I will offer him a year's worth of taxes if he turns back now." The crowd was soothed by his speech and the men and women applauded him.

The next day Nushan appointed someone who was well spoken and perceptive. [206a] He said to him, "Walk outside the city, and take this message to the men on Abtin's side. 'The city and the army all say that you are the king and commander. This siege is not wise, for the city will not be taken. Our food will last no less than ten years, for the king's storehouse nourishes us. The king has more than a thousand storehouses, all full of fresh food. 3130 If the king fights on for ten years, if he holds out a long time, our condition will be just as happy, he will gain nothing from time and delay.

"'Within China there are other cities with weaker fortifications than this one. Since you would not be stalled, you can take them by attacking. If you are ashamed to retreat, we will give you a year's taxes, though the world's king and the ruler of China would blame us. But it is good if you think on this, for peace is better than war.

"'And then, the ruler of China draws near with his army. Sooner or later he will arrive, and if the king has turned away, it would be better for you. These words are our advice for the king. May he be satisfied by it.'" 3140

When he heard this message, he added his reply, "These words will do no good for the city, Kush's womenfolk, children, and treasure too must be given to me, and nothing else will do. Why bother raising an army and besieging a city, only to let the enemy's palace bring ruin upon me?"

When the envoy returned to the city, the alleys and streets clamored, "We are all frightened by this response!" and began to talk among themselves.

"Would he do this, and when would he try? What will we say on the morrow to the ruler of China?"

They fought on for another month, with rocks, javelins, and arrows. Many from Chang'an and China were killed, the city's ramparts were drenched in blood.

THE KING OF MACHIN SENDS
A LETTER TO ABTIN

At the beginning of the month a letter to Abtin arrived from Machin. "What is the point of this? Why are you stalling at Chang'an when you know you cannot take it by force? 3150 Forget that city at once, hurry and turn your eyes to other cities. China has many armies, equipment, and treasure. Why do you trouble yourself with Chang'an? The cities and forts are full of Kush's treasure. You can take it without a fight. Be aware that your enemies grow weak when you have their treasure in your hands. When you have fermented milk in hand, the flies increase every moment. Silver straightens a bent back, and whoever loses it is bent. It will trouble his overflowing army and he'll turn his face from Iran to the treasure." When the king read that letter in secret, he regretted not having taken the tribute.

Again, a clamor arose from the city, for the men had all seen their share of suffering. They gave that man another message to deliver to Abtin. "O proud king, 3160 You know that we are obedient to you, we of the bazaar are well bred. We are all innocent of the king's cruelty, but here Kush's army outnumbers us. Take two years' taxes from us and other tribute, and trouble us no more. The whole city is filled with soldiers and armor, from the king's portico to the streets. We have no recourse, for the king threatens us with his army continually. There is a well-known saying, 'Everyone is king over his own property.'"

When Abtin heard what they had said he accepted their words, but was disappointed. So he took all that was demanded and took a detour for Efriqeh and Qasrayn.[13] Kush's treasury was in those cities, and the

13. The names Efriqeh and Qasrayn appear to be out of place here; they are more suggestive of the Maghreb than China, and recall Efriqos, mentioned in lines 449 and 10122. Arghun, the forest in China (line 719), is identical to the Arabic rendering of Aragon. It is possible Iranshah lacked detailed knowledge of Chinese cities and substituted names of places in the far west instead.

troops there put up resistance. They conquered both cities by the sword and the king took his share of their treasure. 3170 They remained in that land two and a half years, the army became rich with gold and silver. They exacted tribute from all over for two years, and at once adorned the turning heavens with a crown. All this booty was loaded onto the animals and sent immediately to the sea. He filled a hundred and twenty ships with cargo, full of Chinese garments and dinars. He sent it all to the island, they were left astonished by all of it. If you were to throw that gold into the ocean, you'd raise a gold mountain. And if you unfurled all of those Chinese silks, they would blot out the sky's color. If you spread out all the brocades, they would cover everything from the ground to the sky. Tayhur was pleased by all that booty, and praised the lion-hearted king.

When Nushan's riders raced to Jerusalem, they got word 3180 that the king of the world had gone west, and Kush was with them. They raced from there westwards, all but melting from travail, distraught. Hurrying, they reached Kush, men and horses alike exhausted. When he heard the letter's message read out, he was astonished and was too upset to sleep that night. When the black night's color was wiped away, he brought that letter before Zahhak. He announced the envoys to the king, and they repeated the contents of the letter. Zahhak was astonished and said to Kush, "You must ride like the wind."

He gave him five hundred thousand soldiers, war-riders and brave warriors. He issued a royal decree giving him command over the whole east. He generously bestowed all manner of things on him, dinars, a crown, and a throne too, 3190 a banner and royal crown, horses, equipment, heavy arms. He told him, "The enemy has gained strength by having control of China for two years. Go in such a way that you take him unawares, extirpate your enemy." He kissed the ground before the king and took his army on the road.

KUSH'S RETURN TO CHINA

When Kush had crossed half the distance, he selected a steel-clad fighting force. His troops numbered a hundred thousand, all battle-ready. He ordered them to hurry towards China, to take Abtin by surprise. The army raced to the gates of Chang'an, but found no enemy. They paused for a day at the gate of that city, and when night fell they decided on a new plan. They got word of Abtin, that he had gone to the Sea of China. 3200 When Kush's commander was struggling, his army foamed up like the sea. They had no choice but to go, and carried their supplies . . .

When the advance guard saw the army's dust in the distance, they sent word to the king. Kush commanded that the army stand its ground, they reached for their spears and blades. The brave warriors made such an attack that the sun's face lost its color. By heavy maces and javelins' steel, field and meadow filled with waves of blood. Now the Chinese retreated, now their enemies were driven back.

When the fighting was wrapped up and Abtin saw how the brave men of China grew bold, he charged his black horse ahead, abstaining from the blood of those who were retreating. A group of brave men behind his back, one of them brandishing a sword in his hand, 3210 he crushed that army so that the enemy could not tell their reins from their stirrups. Many riders were killed in that attack, the blood running like a brook.

When night fell, they relented from their slaughter, the commander of China retreated and made camp. Abtin was pleased by that battle, and he had wine and garments brought for the nobles. He gave generously in his feast, just as he had shown youthful vigor in combat. [206b]

He said, "Today we have exacted justice, and we take joy in this victory. If a hundred armies like this come before me, without Kush, I pay them no mind. However we believe that sooner or later, that demon-faced one will march on us with a great army, bringing many riders from Iran. Who knows when this battle will happen, and who will emerge victorious? 3220 Even though one is a fierce leopard in battle, he will not always emerge victorious from war. Though terra-cotta looks just like rock, it breaks when it hits a rock in the brook. It is better if we take our booty into the sea, hands full and victorious. We have more than two hundred ships, there is no reason to stay in this land."

The nobles were satisfied with this view, and they praised God. That night they loaded the ships and went to sea with their king. The two hundred ships sailing that way, you'd think there was not space enough in the sea.

When the sun advanced its host across the sky, Kush's advance guard could see no one. He informed the troops of their departure, and the travail of those proud men was cut short. When the army charged toward the sea, a cry rose up reaching higher than the heaven's turning wheel. 3230 Of the booty they took, some was left behind, and the Chinese soldiers took their share. On the tenth day, the world-conquering Kush together with his army reached the vanguard. They all wrung their hands in sorrow, for Abtin had escaped them. His army set up camp there, recovering for a day from the hardships of the road.

Then next day his minister arrived bringing victuals for the sovereign. He kissed the ground and praised him, asking him about the difficulties of the long journey. He said to him, "You have not spoken about what happened in your battle with Abtin."

Eloquent Nushan opened his mouth, and told him everything that happened. He repeated all the complaints he had about Behak, "He betrayed us and Dayhim. He collaborated with the king's enemy, this is why none of our riders escaped. 3240 No rider of theirs was struck or killed, for they immediately turned tail. Behak guided him to Chang'an, and he marched on Qasrayn by his advice. His guidance brought ruin to the land, and the ignoble enemy fled. Did he write a letter? Well, I wrote one too, which turned Abtin away from the city. Otherwise he would have plunged all China into chaos, he would not have left before taking that city. When the enemy returned here on his orders, they were not two parties but one—collaborators."

Kush then said to him, "Keep this a secret and tell no one what you know."

KUSH WRITES A LETTER TO BEHAK

He then ordered a letter written. "In the name of the peerless, unique creator, who gave me so much treasure and troops that enemies flee from the dust my armies raise. I heard how you suffered because of the impudent Iranians. 3250 I will make sure you are made whole, and I will closely consider your situation that you may live long, and if not I, then God protect you from harm. When I reached the seaside, I looked forward to a fight. What good does it do to flee if the enemy runs off with his prey like a wolf? When you read out this letter, I suggest that you equip your army, and do not rest. We will tour the land, and we cannot depart until you arrive. When you arrive, I will entrust to you China and the coast, so that you prosper. I'll swear an oath to defend you against the enemy. Commit your body and soul to me and I will take good care of your troops. If you bind your hands with this oath, you'll have freed my heart from the grief of the enemy." 3260

When Behak knew they were coming, he hid everything he had underground. When he saw the letter and heard its words, he was upset, but feigned happiness. He gave the envoy a horse and pack animals, had food brought to him and a winecup.

Right then, he had a response drafted. "May the lord of China be without pain and travail. I am very pleased by this visit, it is as if the turning wheel of the heavens gave me its reins. I give thanks to God that that threat has gone far from the borders of China. The enemy fled the king's sword, now the king has returned and all has been set right."

He spoke about the hardships he had suffered. "When the king arrived, those hardships vanished like the wind. The king must remain in good health, and God remove all pain from your heart. All the humiliation and difficulty that we suffered departed like a blowing wind. 3270 All of our troubles were caused by Dayhim, who showed weakness in judgment and battle. He scattered his forces far from the sea and cut them loose to plunder for themselves. He had no concern or fear of the enemy, he threw the army into a ruinous snare. His thoughts were only of himself, and he gave that treasure and army over to the wind. When a wise man is safe from the enemy, know that his blood still boils. He avoids the enemy whose brain is made of lesser stuff. As the ruler of China then summons me again, I will come and kiss the ground before his feet. However my forces are dispersed, I will call them back before I go. I will do whatever I am ordered to, and if that means offering my life too, so be it."

The clever envoy made haste from Machin and came before Kush. 3280 He repeated what Behak had said, and that he rejoiced at receiving Kush's letter, and that the whole army would be marshaled and summoned before the victorious sovereign, in all pomp and circumstance, to see the king.

Behak was suspicious of Kush's invitation and considered the matter carefully. Whatever womenfolk and children he had, he sent them all to a fortress. He gathered his forces and set off for Kimak, wiped clean from the borders of China and Machin. When one cannot remain at ease, the Lord has created a vast world.

When Kush found out his secret, he turned to make haste after him ... Beating the drums of war, he mobilized his army with the wind under his feet. Three hundred thousand crossed the sea, veteran riders. 3290 Whoever saw that army on the march, he killed, as though the world turned against the king of Machin. That violent king went from Machin to Kimak, and the people feared Kush's ravages.

He sent a message to the governor of Kimak, "Why have you given comfort to the enemy? If you are unconditionally a loyal subject of the king, imprison that spiteful one immediately. And if you reject my authority, you'll get your due." He sent the messenger and hurried ahead, trying to finish the job at once.

When the message reached Kimak, the provocation shredded his heart with fear. He secretly sent an agent to Behak, "Take to the road if you wish to spare your life! When Kush and his army arrive, I do not want to see you anymore. We cannot face Kush's army, spare your head tonight, don't delay." 3300

Behak forsook the city at nightfall, he and his army grieved. Kush learned of his departure and charged ahead, his troops brandishing their lances. He caught up with his enemy near Tibet. They trembled when they saw his army. His forces fled their positions, leaving Behak alone on the field. Left hanging there, he was stuck, his blood-shedding sword worn out. His blood turned Chinese silk to coral, then he was cut in two and cast into the dust. A hundred and twenty men of his army's leaders were captured by the king. He returned from that frontier and arrived in China with that army he had brought from Iran. [207a] He sent a good number of them back to Iran with valuable gifts.

KUSH WRITES A LETTER TO ZAHHAK
GIVING NEWS OF BEHAK'S DEATH

The king sent a letter to Zahhak, "When I marched my army from here, 3310 by the glory of the lord of the world, I saw not one of the enemy's riders. The same fate befell the governor of Machin that he inflicted on our forces. He had secretly consorted with the enemy, letting them cross the sea under cover like women. When this got back to us, I first sent him a polite letter. I summoned him before me and he did not come, so I sent armies over the sea. He fled, his forces with him, going to Tibet via Kimak. I caught up to him near Tibet and made flowing streams of his warriors' blood. I cast him into the dust in two halves, his body crushed under my horse's hooves. And so, too, all enemies of the king! May the land prosper in his glory! I stationed an army by the sea that would not let even a bird pass. 3320 If the enemy seeks asylum to end his deprivation . . ."

From there, he headed toward Chang'an, choosing an army of a hundred thousand brave men. He gave command to a man by the name of Shavar, brave and prudent, insightful and skilled, and sent them to the sea, instructing him and naming him commander of that frontier.

Now that he was secure from the enemy, his days and nights were filled with rest and delight. The whole year was spent in his portico, orchards, and gardens, in the company of fawning attendants who sang to him, accompanied with wine and flutes. The turning heavens now favored him. From the kings of Turan, Makran, Rome, and India, from the east, and every land, came envoys, tribute, and rich treasure from all places. They all bared their necks in obedience.

Kush was transformed by this new situation. 3330 He spurned the path of law, religion, and justice, and became oppressive in word and deed. He ceased being kind and took whatever he wanted from the people. He became oppressive, bloodthirsty, and shameless, his heart and hand purged of goodness.

During the day he asked about a beautiful woman, when night fell, he took her from her husband. He picked up sweet children from along the road, boys and girls alike, for his pleasure. The ministers were unable to dissuade him and the passing of years did nothing to lessen his harm. The whole of China faced ruination from the tyranny of the twisted Kush. Neither wife nor bride was safe, he was openly diabolical. No fear in his heart or shame in his eyes, no remorse for his people or kindness in his speech. When the heart knows no fear and the eyes no shame, you can do anything you please. 3340 Make your heart afraid if you consider yourself kind, examine yourself lest others take you. When heart and tongue are aligned and righteous, you have reached perfection, both worlds are yours.

People fell into hardship because of Kush, and no complaint about him could escape their lips. His army, those same men under his command, had it even worse. Suppliants turned their eyes toward the dust before God, the exalted. "Justice is yours, creator! Spare us from the evil of twisted Kush."

Meanwhile, Besila cried out with songs of joy when Abtin returned. They decked every alleyway and market with adornments of Chinese brocade. The worldly-wise Tayhur and his troops hurried all the way to the gate. He embraced Abtin warmly and said to him, "Fortunate king, 3350 I am overjoyed at the sight of you, you have exacted your justice on the enemy."

Abtin said to him, "Your majesty, I sought to stay by the seashore, wait some months longer, and fight Kush when he arrived. But I considered the matter more, and thought the king would be troubled if his men were lost."

Tayhur said to him, "O honor-seeker, don't be so ambitious. God has only given you so much. No mourning is heard from inside a palace. You have returned to the city in celebration and alighted at the palace in a shower of roses." He rained gems from his stores upon his head and his army gave silver coins to the beggars. Everyone was thankful to God that that God-fearing king had returned.

He seemed such a friend to the king that, to a stranger, they seemed of the same skin and flesh. 3360 The king passed the days in conversation with him, and was upset if he arrived late. He distributed the booty to the Tayhurians and his affairs were in splendid order. Men and women had such affection for him that there was always a crowd around his door and his balcony.

Even Fara', who was his translator, was given things of all kinds: valuable horses, saddles and fittings, dinars and royal Chinese brocade. Day and night they passed the time together, in both joy and sorrow. Abtin's kindness was as remarkable as his quickness on the battlefield. Now anytime he left the palace, the crowd was so thick there was no room for the spectators. Men and women came to pay him their respects, their bodies pressed together.

The king saw the women of Besila, like cypresses in stature, with faces like the moon. 3370 One day, while drunk, he said to Fara', "I want you to keep a secret for me. Of all the women I have seen in the world, I am most pleased by the women of Besila. They are idols, as if made of pure camphor, rosewater dripping from their fingertips. They are more flawless than the bright sun and more pleasant than a ravishing garden."

When Fara' heard these words from Abtin, he laughed and said, "O pious king, if the sight of these ordinary women is more pleasing than that of other women, then if you see the king's womenfolk, you will be moonstruck."

Abtin said to him, "My guide, will you not tell me something about them?"

He answered, "They are thirty daughters, each one brighter than the sun. Their stature is more lofty than a cypress and no one has seen anyone like them. 3380 However, there is one daughter among them who is more special than the rest. The world is brightened by the radiance of her face, she makes the palace and bedchamber into a rose garden. She is a beautiful ornament to the eyes, her glance is the very essence of sorcery. When she walks proudly through the palace, her tresses descend to her feet. When she lets down her hair, her locks land beneath her footsteps.

"They call her Fararang, and the king jumps out of bed to see her. If you have one look at her face you'll never be able to take your eyes off her loveliness. She scarcely laughs, and if she does so flirtatiously, the stars pray to her lips. Her wisdom is even greater than her elegance, and that elegance befits her wisdom. Her two eyes carry the weight of great wisdom, and she keeps them turned to the ground out of modesty. 3390 Women have skill, abstemiousness, and modesty, but bloody rawhide does not look like leather."

When Fara' finished speaking, Abtin's heart became hot for that girl. A sun of flame burned in his core, and modesty and wisdom were suddenly incinerated. His heart began leaping in his chest, and caution took flight from his heart.

He said to him, "O essence of righteousness, you torment me with these words. Why should I ask you to speak? You have revived ancient sorrows. Without yet having seen that face you painted, my heart drowns in a sea of love. If I have even the slightest chance to get a glimpse of her, that sight would be as if God, the exalted, crowned me king all over again."

Fara' said, "O king, have a happy heart and do not be troubled. 3400 I will put the garden of your affection in order and arrange things to suit your glory; if you follow my advice, you'll reap the fruit of the seed you sow.

Abtin said to him, "Advise me, what shall I command so that things turn out thus?"

"My advice is to confidently visit the king every day, and speak of wisdom, good conduct, and religion, for the world-king likes such things. When the king becomes aware of your knowledge, your heart will be freed of any misgivings. [207b] And then, when he tries to get closer with you, he will show you much kindness. He will treat you better than his own sons, as if you are a close relative.

"Then, give orders to your minister to comfort him with sweet words: 'I have come to the sovereign, keeping my distance from strangers and far from family. 3410 I take comfort with no one in the world but you, for you are kind and benevolent. Whatever goodness I believe in, I have found it in you, your majesty! I have one other hope from you, that my blood and veins become your own. If I join in a matrimonial alliance with the king, my fortune will be crowned by the heavens' sphere. Should the dear king grant me one daughter, he will make me a loyal servant to his honor.'

"In this request of yours, descendant of kings, make no mention of Fararang. For Tayhur will become suspicious of me and end my days in revenge. He will know that these secrets were given you by Fara'."

Abtin, upon hearing his words, kissed his face profusely and praised him. "When you have made my wish come true, I will make your honor shine brighter than the sun. 3420 When my days have become joyous on your account, I would not withhold anything from you. And if my crown returns to me, I will raise you up above all others. I'll have you in my sight always, and you'll have treasure and lands."

That night he gave him a robe and helmet, and went to bed drunk. His heart raced for love of Fararang, with no wits in his brain or sleep in his eyes. He was lost in a sea of thought all night, his spirit like a forest of worries.

The next day the curious king got up and went to the court as if he were lifeless. He said to Tayhur, "O beneficent king, I would enjoy playing some polo. If you see fit to play a game tomorrow, then let us play a little."

He answered, "Your wish is my command, I will do whatever makes you happy." 3430 When the bright stars were covered up from the world, he ordered his troops to stand ready. When the attendants awoke from their sleep, they went to the field and sprinkled water to settle the dust. The worldly-wise, pious Tayhur strutted onto the field with Abtin—and it was no field, but a vast and newly reordered world, the avenues and palace grounds spread out over it.

Abtin sat upon his saddle like a cypress springing from the ground, his reins fluttering like a partridge, the down of his face like ambergris, his earlobes like ivory, a ruby and turquoise crown on his head. From behind every curtain, women with covered faces took their places on the rooftops. Pointing with their fingers, they signaled to each other that this was the light of the world whose face made the field a rose garden, the stars illuminated by his eyes.

All of these girls, the veiled womenfolk of both the king and nobles, said 3440 "How lucky, whoever spends a night with Abtin—they'll be quite satisfied! Whoever has Abtin as her loving husband, the sun and moon surely kiss her head!"

When he went from the gate to the field, the happy king selected his team. On one side he stood with twelve boys and veterans he considered skillful. He picked whoever he wanted from the Tayhurians and one by one, they went to their team.

Then Abtin considered the situation, thinking that if he went with those Iranian riders and took the ball from those proud noblemen, they would be offended and vengeful.

He said to Tayhur, "O proudest of the proud, are not the rules of this fight different? God has not given talent to everyone who can sit astride a horse. One with plenty of weapons and tools, if lacking skill, is just extra weight for his horse. 3450 Of these worthies who are your sons, great men devoted to you, first send half to my side, for this would be a fair division, o king. When divisions are not fair, the result is flawed. Whoever has not the insight to be generous never gets what he deserves. I heard from the priest, 'Share generously, for men are drawn to radiance.'"

Tayhur followed this suggestion, finding it wise. He sent six of his descendants to Abtin's side, and they formed their teams. When they tossed the ball into the field, riders charged at it from all sides. Brave men were dismayed and the air filled with dust.

Abtin relaxed and waited for the Tayhurians to win one or two games and enjoy themselves. 3460 Then he began to show off, that peerless rider spurring his horse ahead. His mallet hit the ball with such speed that they could not see Abtin's face. The ball flew through the heavens, such that it seemed to be the moon's intimate companion. It had not even hit the ground when Abtin sent it into the sky again. He would charge and hit the ball from below so that it was still airborne as it passed through the goalposts.

He played in this way until he had hit the ball out of the court seven times. Everyone who saw his horsemanship bit their fingers in aston-ishment. The brave ones gave up reaching for the ball, as if the ground had bound the horses' hooves in place. Everyone said of this rider, "One could not play or fight against him. Any warrior that confronted him would be disgraced." 3470

Tayhur kissed his cheeks and was delighted by his feat. He said to him, "O proud sovereign, you show signs of the glory of Jamshid! May my heart never lack affection for you, for you are the crown jewel, the ornament of kingship. May the eyes of the malevolent stay away, and may the hearts of enemies be afflicted."

The great men of the mountain of Besila one by one fell to mutter-ing. "No one is the equal of this rider, no one has seen anyone like him!" They grew fond of him, and all returned from field to the king's court.

Delighted, Tayhur called for food and wine, and with the sword of wine he fought off pain. The day made him happy, and his kindness for Abtin grew. Tayhur went to such lengths feasting him, it was as if both his lifetime and the treasury were finished. 3480 They tied streamers from the trees, stretching from Tayhur's court to the throne, and sus-pended over them roses mixed together with narcissus.

For the next day and night, everyone was ebullient, ready for feast-ing and hunting. Everyone was so delighted with him that women cut off matrimonial ties with their husbands. Abtin threw two more feasts after that—the sun was lit up by them! The rose garden bloomed in springtime, in gold and cloth of gold. A throne was set up in the midst of the garden and the fortunate king spread out cloths. The lofty king came to that feast, the expensive cloth torn up under his horse's hooves. When he cast dinars under the hooves of his horse it was as if the heavens rained coins from a sieve. He was so generous, it was enough to fill up Tayhur's treasury. 3490 None of his children or retainers remained who was not showered with gold and gems.

ABTIN ASKS TAYHUR ABOUT SEEKING KNOWLEDGE

After that, Abtin sometimes visited the king without his army. When his spirit was deprived of wine, then he would begin to speak about the search for knowledge. Fara' the translator stood between the two kings, benevolent towards both.

The conversation turned to God and religion, and Abtin asked Tayhur, "What is the way to nearness with God? How are the wise to recognize it, o king?"

He replied, "God is one, there is no other creator of the earth, he is the almighty, who appoints creatures their days, they eat and sleep according to his command."

Abtin was pleased by this when he heard it, and said, "May wisdom accompany your pure soul! [208a] How do you know, your majesty, that there exists a creator, a maker?" 3500

"Our ancestors, kings of old, called themselves creator. Anyone who had sired a child by their mate said, in their callowness, 'I am a creator.' In that time, King Besila, after whom people also named the mountain, with wisdom exceeding that of his ancestors and better than our worthies and saints, built these cities upon this mountain, raising his head above the heavens.

"He had a child like the sun and moon. Besila loved him at once. He protected the child as best he could, but time was cruel to him. He died before he reached two years of age, and all of Besila's people took up mourning. Wailing erupted night and day, he trembled and grumbled in his suffering.

"One day he began to think that a knowing heart should contemplate suffering. 3510 'This child was a seed I planted and held dearer than my own life. Why did I create him imperfect and weak? Why did a flawed child come from me? Why is one born dead out of the womb, while others are buried in old age? If this creator is merely us, why can we not obtain what we want? Perhaps our creator is one to whose workings we have scarce access.'

"When day broke, the seeker of knowledge called an assembly of scholars. He showed them the key to this secret and enjoined them to devote themselves to justice. He said to them, 'I have not been able to sleep since last night. My heart was worn out from contemplation and I found no ease until dawn. Whoever among us bears an unblemished child calls himself a creator. 3520 Such a name does not suit us, these words seem unwise. Now I ask you a question, answer me briefly. If this creation comes from us, we must be able to create what satisfies us: hale and handsome, body unblemished, brave, wise, and warlike.

Their days should reach old age, as if they held the reins of the turning heavens and fate. One child is born to its mother and perishes immediately. Others last many years and then die, their soul never succumbing to evil days. Another suffers in old age, with a satisfied heart and meritorious soul. If this act of creation were ours, we would make all our children born hale and whole . . . You would create every one good and right, as if they were the branch of a mighty tree. 3530

"'One who loses their child, why should they still be called creator? The truth is that the same one created people who created the illuminated earth and the sky. He creates exactly as he wills, no more and no less. Bear witness before me now and cleave to wisdom, that our creator is one, abundance is from him, and from him, scarcity.'

"Great and small alike accepted these pleasing words and ceased fruitless discussion. The army of Besila from that day on turned to their peerless God. Our forefathers became goodly men, believers in the transcendent God. Now it has been four thousand years that we worship God, since those days."

Abtin said, "You spoke well, o king. What do you say about this water, wind, and earth, 3540 sunlight and radiant moon, the stars with their path across heaven's wheel?"

He answered, "They all are signs of God's existence. He drew the world's compass thus, so that our compass is the guiding judge. He has created months and years for us like a mother who looks after her child."

Abtin asked, "What do you say about matters of religion, about the worthy, chosen messengers?"

"Be certain, in case you doubted, that according to the books, they were sent from heaven."

"What can you show of hell, and of heaven? Of one's reward, of doing good and ill?"

He answered, "I have no knowledge of these matters. You, with your brilliant insight, tell me so that I learn more about matters of religion. Whatever I find pleasing I never tire of learning." 3550

Wise Abtin taught that pious man a portion of every form of knowledge. The king became so pleased by that knowledge that it was as if his soul were cleansed of sin. His heart became more and more delighted by Abtin, and he constantly showed him kindness. From what he learned of justice, that sober-hearted man became embarrassed of past days. All night he made apologies to the divine, praying to God constantly.

ABTIN GAZES AT THE STARS AND KNOWS THEIR SECRETS

At the new year, called Hormezd, the first day of the month of Farvardin, King Abtin gazed at the stars. This gave such knowledge of their secrets to the king, it was as if the moon were under his command. With such mastery over the works of the heavenly sphere, you'd think it had showed him its full face. His calculation was certain, and he kept it secret—that he could tell what would be and what would not be. The king examined the seven zodiac signs and the twelve stars to see what the years and months would bring. 3560 He saw greatness resulting from alliance with Tayhur—he would find what he hoped for there. The king saw that that seed would return the crown of greatness to him, and soon. He saw his kingdom in kinship with Tayhur's, and that sorrow and pain would stay far from his house. When he found the turning heavens favorable to him, he sought marriage alliance with Tayhur all the more urgently.

He sent Fara' and Kamdad, his minister, to deliver his message with appropriate courtesy. When the two of them came to the king to deliver the message, they kissed the ground and stood up, embellishing their speech with much praise. Tayhur looked at Kamdad, smiling, asking, "Why must you stand?"

He answered, "A message for the king. Abtin has a request, if the king would fulfill it. 3570 I will say it and then be seated, since my lord commands me to."

He smiled and called him close, seating him while swearing oaths, and said, "Now say what you want to say, what would you wish of me?"

Kamdad then began to speak concerning knowledge of many kinds. "That benevolent servant says, 'I am ashamed before the world's king. You have treated me with more respect than your own family, for when I had no shelter in all the world, I put my faith in the king. If you had not hosted me in Besila, the enemy would have taken me. So long as I am alive and secure, by God, I am thankful to that king. One wish remains, o king, and my fortune now follows this path: 3580 it is like a jewel hidden in a mine, shining brightly there.

"'If the lofty king would honor me and welcome me in this alliance, as part of his family, then bestow on me one of your daughters, and my head will rise to heights of greatness. I have seen in the stars, your majesty, that one will come from this seed who will be remembered. He will bring down Zahhak and banish magic and devilry.'"

When the man finished what he had to say, dust rose from the ocean of knowledge. If you seek satisfaction from satisfaction's storehouse, learn, so that fortune is your friend.

When pious Tayhur heard this, he surreptitiously bit his finger in sadness. He did not immediately answer, but remained in thought about the matter.

Kamdad quickly pulled him out of his reverie, saying, 3590 "Why does your majesty hesitate? Who on earth could there be like Abtin? In manliness, keenness of vision, cultivation, and insight, where else has God created his like? His grandfather a king, and himself, a king, and his father too, all proud crowned sovereigns. Many great men who rest in the dust were servants of my king. If his fortunes changed, the heavens' wheel was unjust to him. [208b] It is forever rising and falling, the world is constantly changing. There is no quarrel with the world's lord in this, and you will never be made ashamed by King Abtin. The lord of Iran is above that, he is a worthy king and capable."

He answered, "With regard to what is just, you are right, Kamdad. But to prevent shame and discord, the nobles never gave their daughter to a foreigner. 3600 The foreigner, though he be a king, is like a fish out of water. The foreigner's heart will invite grief on everyone."

Kamdad was angered by his words, and he said, "O just and capable king, what your majesty has said about strangers is correct, however this does not apply here. The way King Abtin rides a horse, how on earth could he be a source of disgrace? He is the grandson of the world-ruler, King Jamshid, all the kings of the world were crowned by him. If the turning heavens brought him a measure of suffering, greatness and prosperity will return to him. Don't see only the dry brambles and thorny rosebushes. Spring will come and the roses will bloom.

"You, o king, must know truly, that if Abtin seeks an alliance with you and this is your answer, that this would cause trouble. 3610 He will be suspicious of your majesty's friendship, and pack up and leave this city. The king would be commanding him to leave, he would not know how to handle this disgrace. He may kill himself and bury himself out of shame. What would they say? What would men of religion say? King Abtin sought an alliance with the king, and he did not see fit to ally with him, that he was not a fitting husband for his child. If you think he is lacking talent, what flaw have you seen, that the sovereign should reject him? What kind of heart does not melt for honor and pride? Not a heart, but a stone!"

The king raised his head upon hearing those words. His face showed sorrow. "She is young," he said, "Abtin is fully grown. He has distinguished himself in bravery and learning. But if I grant this hope of his, I fear he would become unfaithful. 3620 He would keep her for a while, then abandon her. My daughter would be hurt, and I would be terribly afflicted by her pain."

He said to him, "O just and faithful king, perhaps there is some way to avoid this trouble. If the king were to see all the daughters lined up side by side, if he chooses the one he loves, he will never relinquish that love. When he finds one suitable to him, he'll hold her as dear as his own eyes. If he has chosen her, how could he leave her? Since when does a faithful man commit such cruelty? Such a one is not called 'human,' but superficial or heartless."

Tayhur drew back, seeing no way out, and took a deep breath before answering. A man whose tongue is tied is stranded. A man falls silent when he is satisfied. 3630 He said to him, "Tell King Abtin, we will grant your wish."

They returned from that encounter happy. Fara' exactly repeated all that was said to Kamdad. Abtin's heart was overjoyed. He gave many gifts to him and Fara'—brocades and Arabian horses. They stood up in their glee and prepared a kingly feast.

While drunk, Abtin said to Fara', "Reveal a secret for me. What stratagem should I use to make that sweet-lipped woman mine? If I can have Fararang with me, I'll be king of all the world."

Fara' said, "O proud and noble king, do not speak Fararang's name to anyone. When Tayhur follows through, look at the daughters one by one. 3640 Listen and I will describe Fararang, for all of them are stars, and she the moon. Listen, I will tell you Tayhur's system, how he arranges the daughters.

"They are chosen in groups of ten from each house, adorned with gold and jewels. They select the loveliest, those worthy of the sovereigns of the world. They all reside in one home and they are not pledged to any of the nobles. They wear neither fine garments nor gold nor ornaments, and the least adorned will be Fararang. She will be taller and her face more beautiful than the others—more radiant than sun and moon. Between her two eyebrows is a black mole—o king, look for this mark. In breadth she's a ship, her stature a cypress, her face composed of snow and pheasants' blood. When you see her heart-stealing eyes, you will fall in love with her. 3650 She is dearest to Tayhur, and dotes on him."

He asked about the customs of courtship, how they make agreements and perform the ceremony.

"When they see each other's faces, if their hearts are drawn together in love, they need a tall stalk of a green herb that is not harmed by winter's cold. The same herb is used in spring and in autumn, in festivals all year round. They tie a bouquet of that herb to a golden citron, decorated with jewels. The noble groom takes it in his hand, and carries it before the bride's governess. If the bride does not want him then she refuses it, and sends it back to the man. And if she does want the man, she takes it, kisses it, and puts it down."

The king said to him, "Such a strange thing this is, that they see each other, then want to couple. 3660 I fear that Fararang would not take the citron from me, and I would be ashamed."

Fara' laughed at his words, and said to him, "O moon-faced sovereign, a fairy-faced girl will feel love for a king, do you fear the moon would scowl at you . . .?"

He sent Fara' before the king, asking when he should come over. "May the king fulfill my hopes and show his favor!"

He sent a response, "Whenever you wish to come, you are welcome. Let me know a week in advance, and then we can make arrangements."

The world-seeker looked to the turning heavens and selected a day. He sent Tayhur notice that he would come on the glorious first day of the month. He also ordered his minister to open the treasury. 3670 On Hormezd day Abtin stood ready, a citron and stalks of herbs in his hands. He placed on his head a precious crown whose memory was lost in the ancient past. He made his body, garments, and hair fragrant, placing a musk-pod in his hair. He mounted his horse in the morning. Fara' was with the king and Kamdad. Riding ahead into the palace, Tayhur approached him on foot. He alighted and sat on his throne—that happy, fortunate man, favored by the stars.

Tayhur took his hand, brought him to the harem and stood before him. He called to an old woman on the balcony, no strength left in her body, her head quaking and hair white from the years, for she had tasted many springs and summers. He sent Abtin to her, and said, "Remove the curtain from what is hidden. 3680 You must use heart and wits, as I told you."

The elderly woman immediately took Abtin and first showed him those two houses. They were decorated like paradise's garden, its full beauty showing in spring. Sitting there were twenty radiant beauties, the sun and moon ashamed before them. Their bodies were hidden by their adornments and makeup, the world was lit up by their faces. The lofty king made a round, and none of them were pleasing to him. He left, smiling, and said to the governess, "None of these girls is a match for me."

The governess said to him, "O worthy king, take a better look at these girls, they are the beauties of this mountain, most dear to the world-king. Each of these faces would brighten the face of sun and moon." 3690

He answered, "This is so, however the king has given me my choice. If you show me the others, I will be grateful to you."

She said to him, "These are ignoble and flighty, better as servants."

He laughed and said, "Did his majesty not tell you I was free to see them?" [209a]

The governess, stumped by Abtin, left and removed the curtain from the other house. Abtin strutted to that house, splendid like Nushan's palace in China. You'd think it was an idol-house, and Azar its mere servant, or else the like of heavens' dome, Jupiter, and the sun, with idols upon silvery pedestals, faces brighter than the sun, heart-bewitching and body-melting, eyes casting flirtatious glances.[14] 3700 No gold or ornaments for them, no garments and wealth.

Fararang sat alone in a corner, the whole house taking its color from her face, like a cypress whose fruit was raw honey and sugar, like a ship in the hands of a skilled mariner, a narcissus flower from which thousands upon thousands of ringlets tumbled over her ears. Upon her body, a garment as broad as an ox, the whole house rosy from its color. She'd thrown a broad garment over her body, like the sun through fog or the moon in the clouds.

14. Azar was Abraham's uncle.

When King Abtin then saw that mole, he felt his heart grow weak. From her loveliness, his brain lost its senses, his heart lost all strength. His eyes grew dark from the radiance of her face, her black mole made his wisdom frantic. He shook so, his heart full of fear, that his body lost its strength and his heart its caution. 3710

From the threshold, he went before the treasure and gave Fararang the golden citron. She kissed it and tossed it aside, and the citron landed between two pomegranates. Her fingertips caressed Abtin with the delicacy of Ramtin.[15] The world-seeker went away pleased and Besila began to talk about him. All the girls were ashamed, and cast the ornaments off their dresses. If a horse is Arabian, though it has no saddle, you'd still call it Arabian. Great men test the quality of a blade by its edge and disregard its ornamentation.

Fara' came before the king, who asked him, "Who did he choose?"

He said to him, "She who bears the mark befitting the nobles. Just as you said, she was the best, more radiant than the shining sun. 3720 May your lips ever taste wine, and the hearts of enemies be bereft of sense."

He distributed many gifts to the indigent and to Fara' as well.

When the governess came to King Tayhur, he awaited her anxiously. The king asked her, "Which one of the daughters did Abtin select?"

The governess said to him, "O distinguished king, what the world's judge does astounds us. Upon whoever has God as their guide, ruses and stratagems have no effect. When the lion came amidst the flock, he chose Fararang out of them all. As badly as I dressed her, God did not will what I wanted. He trembled as he stood when he saw her, his face turned the color of fenugreek. He gave her the citron of garnet and gold, radiating glory from head to foot. 3730 Fararang took it, kissed it warmly, and he turned and left with happy heart."

When Tayhur heard this he turned yellow again. He turned away, grieving. "If all my children had died today, it would not weigh on me more than this—that man who had nothing took her!"

He went into the palace. That brave man sat on his throne and wailed, wept, and cried very hard. He did not eat or sleep for three days and nights in his grief, not speaking to anyone. Mourning, he did

15. Ramtin was a famous harpist.

not accept any visitors out of grief for the loss of Fararang and his affection for her, who would soon no longer see his face.

When Fara' learned about his situation, he raced to the king's side. He kissed the ground and praised him. He said, "O king of the earth, 3740 you are a great king, your star has risen, you are wiser than the other kings of the earth. Unwise conduct does not suit you, none of the priests would approve of this. Since you have done nothing to cause yourself injury, why should you grieve like this? Since you are not aware of God's will, why burden your heart with so much pain? Do not be a tyrant to your own kingship. If you are God's servant, do not behave like you're God. May the king be pleased with whatever he does, always! Now, the house of Abtin and that of the king have become one, there is no distance between them. Fararang will be beside the king, more than in her husband's own house. Abtin cannot take her anywhere, he cannot leave this land. All that is destined will be, you can be sad about it or happy. 3750 Who knew that, out of thirty heart-melting idols, his heart would choose Fararang? It was written thus, o king, that when God enjoins, it cannot be undone." The words of that benevolent one settled, and he continued until the king was happy. He became delighted by Fara''s counsel, he left his palace and sat on his throne.

He ordered the minister to prepare to open up the treasury. He decorated everything properly and no one had seen such preparations or delight. Likewise, Abtin opened his treasury, preparing and entertaining guests for three weeks. He sent jewels to the king that amazed him and his army, an amber crown and a turquoise throne, both Roman thrones and Persian, one hundred or three hundred of every kind of garment 3760 and ten camels to bear them, and golden cradles, each loaded with a hundred gems. Each of the cradles was filled with ornaments, two chests full of rubies, garnets, and pearls, such as the sovereigns of the world had never seen—all these King Abtin brought before the sovereign. Neither had Jamshid had such gems, nor could anyone say that they had ever seen them. To the great men of the city he sent all kinds of things, and to the relatives too, and to all of Fararang's sisters, and to the army and civilians as well, he sent plenty of the most valuable gifts. Not a youth was left in Besila who did not get a cap or belt from the king.

KING ABTIN REACHES HIS BELOVED

When the day came in the month of April, the world blossomed heaven-like with tulips. Nightingales sung from rosebushes like Christian monks before a cross. 3770 Tayhur's garden took on the colors of a peacock. Myrtle and poplar intertwined like two longing lovers reunited. The branches of the rosebushes were full of nightingales, the world filled with their trilling. At the sweet wailing of the nightingales, the roses tore open their gowns of fluttering silk. The violets bent back their heads and stretched their tongues out from under their robes, and the tulips, breathlessly cantering in their fields, lit bonfires in the place of Abraham's illumination. Burgundy swayed upon young trees like rubies pulling down on idols' necks. The quality of spring is heaven-sent, that of autumn is from hell. They each leave their own mark upon the world, heavenly spring and infernal autumn.

Verdure and cool running water lightened wise men's spirits. 3780 The fish and fowl all sought companions, all paired in trilling and conversing. Abtin's heart, too, seeking its mate, hid the fire inside—he told no one. When the sun raised its head over the mountaintop, it tied shut its robe and burned musk underneath. Its warmth radiated and banished wisdom, and he rode toward Tayhur's palace.

When love's forces advance over men's hearts, shame cannot bear to show its face. Wisdom is drowned in love's ocean and shame grows weak. Shame, sleep, and wisdom remain far from the heart into which love drives its horns.

Proud, pious Tayhur called his nobles before him. They set the dowry according to the laws of their creed and then took King Abtin's hand. He took him from his palace to that of Fararang, and he granted him his daughter. [209b] 3790

When Abtin placed her hand in his, he was thunderstruck. He covertly kissed her hands, like stalks of silver woven together with cane. From there, they went to the royal palace, the nobles arriving to meet them. In that celebration they exuded such happiness, showering Abtin's head with coins. That gold and silver made the throne look like the heavenly sphere had hung its garments over it. The palace was so filled with musk and ambergris that footsteps fell upon nothing else.

The men and women of that city rose up and decked Besila in brocades. They rained saffron upon the bride, Fararang, from end to end. You'd think the heavens had been jostled out of their place from the songs of the musicians and the noise of flutes. All the streets and gardens twittered, all the mountains bloomed with roses. 3800 The spring breeze gathered roses from the gardens and cast them over her as bridal gifts. From the voices of harps, *robabs*, and singers, you'd think that Venus had descended.[16] Every corner of the rooftops was a party, the way the city was the battle-station of soldiers. The cry of flutes and sound of *robabs* drew the fish out of the water.

The women of Besila, like tall cypresses, danced in great rings, holding hands. Beauty and pomp in every corner, every street lit up by fire, the city spent a month in such celebration that the children could not sleep. In that mountain, that land, there was no one left who had not feasted from Abtin's banquet. Again and again, new delights and new feasts and banquets! Besila was emptied of cows and sheep, even horses were consumed. 3810 At the start of the new month, food became scarce.

He went to Fararang. She looked to him like a fairy from heaven, well built and pure of character. With the loveliness of a peacock and pleasant like life itself, her eyes two corals stealing life and love, her face a palace enthroned on her body, she blushed like an apple, her mouth like the letter *mim*, her face made the palace grounds Eram, her coquettish glances made hearts toil.[17] There were spots of musk upon her rosy cheeks and eagle-shaped pins in her hair. Her skirts were scented by her locks like long, black raven wings, her tunic like the treasure of Gayomard. Her sides were covered in pearls and she did not sleep, and by morning her un-pierced pearl was pierced.

That Manuchehr experienced such a union that his affection was doubled.[18] He gave up hunting and polo, and made no visits for several months. 3820 He remained happily beside Fararang, paying no mind to the king or his kingship. He did not leave her alone for a moment and never took his eyes off her face.

16. A *robab* is a lute-like musical instrument.

17. *Mim* is a letter of the alphabet, shaped like small circle. Eram was a legendary palace garden.

18. Abtin here is identified with Manuchehr, a legendary lover, like Romeo.

The commander of the mountain was upset by them, he summoned Fara' from among the company. He said to him, "See what that faithless Abtin has done to me. He was colorless before this union, now he's in full color![19] We've now been dismounted from two asses, you're the one who led us here."

Fara' went and sought an audience with King Abtin. When he came before him and praised him, he said to him, "O ruler of the land, King Tayhur is aggrieved by you, it has been too long he has not seen your face. It has now been more than forty days that your majesty has not paid him a visit. 3830 What pain would it cause you, o king, if every other day you see that world-illumining branch? One who wants the scent of rose petals does not drop the rose. Though your fetters be pleasing to you, it is unbecoming if you remain at home. When the creator created the world, he created it with the days and nights divided, so that you spend the days on wine and honor, and leave your nights for the bedroom.

"Tayhur said to me, 'King Abtin, why have you left us? Losing Fararang was bad enough, but to be deprived of your company too is a disaster!'"

Abtin was embarrassed by the king's message, and went to his palace, his face contorted in concern. He summoned Fararang with these words, "Look at how Tayhur has pulled the rug out from under us."

Fararang said, "O proud sovereign, don't hurt the king. 3840 Take good care of his heart and less care of ours. Visiting the king is most important. Spend more time with him, on the field and polo court, in feasting and hunting. At night, come back here, partake of day and night in their proper portions."

Abtin said to her, "O moon-faced one, has your heart had its fill of love, that you seek separation from me now—do you not want to see me anymore?"

She answered, "No heart is not overjoyed at the sight of you. May one who does not hold you dear never open their eyes upon the world. But you are knowing and wise—does twisted conduct befit you? What would the nobles say in their gatherings? All blame would fall on me,

19. "In full color" here is *fararang*—her name means "colorful." The meaning seems to be that Tayhur once had the companionship of both Abtin and Fararang and now has neither.

that the knowing and insightful King Abtin has, on a whim, chosen me over the king. 3850 The wise man must look to the future and hold people's tongues at bay."

He knew that she had spoken the truth, and only for the sake of his good name. When the day broke, he came before the king, and delivered an apology to his army. When a sinner produces an apology, it should be heard even if it is a lie. And if you do not accept it, evil is multiplied, and spite will debase you further. It will generate enmity, and who is safe then?

And for so many days he was with flute and harp, and when night fell, he was with Fararang. After that they carried on in that way, sometimes feasting, at other times playing polo, or else hunting. Sometimes at the home of the renowned Tayhur, at other times at that of fortunate Abtin. The years stretched on like this, and no sad day was brought by the turning heavens. 3860 When Zahhak had eighty years left, he'd overstayed his kingship and he reigned unjustly. His kingship had gone on more than nine hundred years, and all of that sorcery and trickery ended.

ABTIN DREAMS

One night, Abtin was sleeping happily and saw the world's king in a dream. Sovar, who had been killed by Kush's hand, came to him as a messenger angel. A stick was in his hand, all dry. Then it turned green and fragrant like musk. King Abtin planted it on the mountain, its roots dug down into the ground. After a while it became a tall tree. Its branches spread out and cast shade. It grew outwards until its top reached the heavens, and then grew even higher. It covered the whole world with its shade, nourishing it from its verdure and branches. Then a pleasant breeze blew, and leaves flew from its branches, 3870 circling the world like a lantern, every mountain and meadow lit up. The world was lit by that brilliance, and everyone said that sorrows had ended.

When he woke up in the morning, he ordered Kamdad brought before him. He revealed his secret to him, telling him the whole dream at once.

He replied, "O king, you who increase comfort, God has given us a path. He gave you in your sleep a blessed sign, that the world will not remain ensorcelled. The head and crown of injudicious Zahhak will soon be in the dust. The world will return to your descendant, and your family and allies will delight in him. That heavenly Sovar who gave you that dry stick, more fragrant than aloeswood and musk, will have a brother. Throne and crown will be his. 3880 Because the branch turned a strong green in your hand, fortune will rejuvenate your glory. As you planted it on the mountain, it will be lofty, your glory will grow and rise. Because it raised its head and its branches grew out, he will take this vast world by the sword. Because it cast its shadow across the world, great and small alike will be under your command. Those leaves that were spread out like a lamp upon countries, mountains, and meadows show that you will be joined by just kings, their hearts happy and hands generous. [210a] They will take the seven lands in their hand and exercise great judgment upon the world."

When Abtin heard the explanation from him, he praised his learning copiously. He said to him, "Keep this dream of mine a secret, do not tell it to strangers." He gave him generous gifts of all kinds, horses and other animals, and dinars too. 3890 He kept this secret for many years, as good and bad times passed.

KING ABTIN SEES JAMSHID IN A DREAM

One night, he fell into a frightening sleep. The spirit of the pure world-ruler Jamshid came to his pillow like a candle to kiss his world-seeing eyes. He handed him a sealed letter and said, "Now stay here a while. Return quickly to the land of Iran. Reveal nothing to strangers. It has now come to pass that you will take vengeance for your father against the unjust Zahhak."

When the king awoke, he sat with Kamdad and told him the dream. He answered, "O king, why remain any longer within these narrow borders? For the letter will surely be promulgated. A wise man could not ask for a better sign. That king proclaimed your kingship. You must prepare for the journey. 3900 The world will now please the noble ones and be purged of demons and the wayward. They have shown you this twice in your dreams, what excuse is there now? Hurry! This is the dream's meaning. Think carefully on this, your majesty."

The king said, "But what can we do about this? We do not know the sea routes. The only sea route we know is where the Tusked has stationed his men. We cannot pass that way secretly, nor can we fight him openly."

He said, "Many ships must be built, and God supports your cause. Let us be on board our ships at night, and travel across the water for a month."

Abtin was not satisfied by this view.

He said to him, "Then think of a different plan. You must share your secret with the king. Without him, no plan can be carried out."

3910

That night ended and the dawn passed, and he sent his minister before the king. The worldly-wise minister came and said, "May faith and friendship be ever with the king. Abtin says, 'Your majesty, all your beneficence has put me to shame. The king has shown such humanity to me here, which I cannot describe. Were I to try, I would not know the words to say . . . So long as I live, I will be grateful to the proud and humane king. Now the time has come, o honorable one, for God to satisfy our hearts. The world will be emptied of demonic men and all glory return to us. They have shown me these last few nights in my dreams that I must hasten to the borders of Iran. It was not a confused or superficial dream, but one of hope and promise. 3920 I request that the beneficent king treat his servant magnanimously: that he send me toward Iran, for I do not know the way to get there; that he guide me across the sea, that he give me a guide who can show the way and deliver me to dry land, so that people there do not recognize me. Whatever booty I have, I will deposit in the sovereign's treasury. Other than provisions for the sea journey, I will not take anything with me. When I reach a habitable place from the sea, God will provide me whatever I need."

When Tayhur heard his message, he lost his temper, shouting, "Abtin is careless and ignorant! Why does he leave this place that has no fear, fright, or worry, and walk right into a trap? 3930 Surely the evil eye has found him, that he has turned away from comfort. He does not know that in all the seven lands, no one names their son Abtin. If he speaks these words from a dream, it was Ahriman who showed him such a dream. Not all dreams have a pure source, this one is a tree that casts nothing but shadows."

When the minister saw his anger, he said, "Do not increase your sorrow. You know that King Abtin came into the world hidden from its people. In all the seven lands he had no place to plant his feet. He took refuge with his majesty and found peace, a period of ease and calm. That King Abtin then saw that he should go to Iran, does not diminish his prudence and judgment to follow the minister's advice ... 3940 When he was informed further in his dream, he consulted the stars. He saw all fulfillment for his family, and injury for the heart and fortune of the enemy. The heavens favor him so much, you'd think the heavenly sphere showed him its face.

"Since Jamshid, we have known no one in the world like him, o king. He can foretell all that can be, and it turns out no more or less than what he predicted. He has another sign, too, o king, that Jamshid once described. When I read his testament closely, I read that Zahhak's reign would last a thousand years, and no more. And then the world will be returned to us and emptied of demons and wayward men. A king will appear from us whose reign few on earth could resist. 3950 The world will be adorned by his glory, and the work of demons diminished. He will take revenge for his father against Zahhak, employing neither tricks nor alchemy. He will purge the earth from sorcery, religion will be empowered by his blade. Of Zahhak's sorcerous reign there remains no more than eighty years."

When the king heard Kamdad's words, he became lost in contemplation.

The eloquent man said to him, "O commanding king, if that person appears from your daughter, then he will avenge Jamshid. By the honor of the nobles, the support of the great and pillar of the knights, the hope of the world, only remainder of his line whose kingship will extend to all frontiers. As long as the world exists, your name will be refreshed and revived to your satisfaction." 3960

King Tayhur grew cheerful and he was quiet, then said to him, "Now, think about how this will be achieved without an army, for that would be necessary. Wherever the Tusked has stationed his men, that way is blocked. You would suffer the enemy's vengeance."

He answered, "King Abtin has thought on this. I suggested that we sneak past the enemy at night. But he was not convinced. He said, 'We must find another way.' He sent me to your majesty because you have people who know the way."

He said to him, "There is another way, however it is very long. It is a terrifying, dangerous path that reaches land after a year and a half. 3970 When the ship makes haste for many days and nights, they'll emerge from the water after a year and three months. You will see a place full of cities and gardens, tulips and verdant pastures. It is not one of the known regions, but another land, another country. From that frontier many merchants sometimes come to my land.

"In the time Abtin was here, no one came from that land. When you travel two days from those cities, you will find a route that is rocky. That difficult route goes straight towards Mount Qaf, those who are fortunate never see it. If they can travel that way for six months, their feet, veins, and spirits suffer. When you come to a fork in the road, the world spreads out before you. You will emerge in the land of the Slavs and Rome, and from there you can reach anywhere.[20] 3980

"My heart will ache for Fararang and Abtin, and the worthy Iranians, for [210b] how can you emerge from this gossamer green sea, when the *simorgh* cannot fly over it? I have navigators who would be willing to make the trip, but there is one time-worn elder, his straight back bent by his travails, whose mind has lost little to the passing of days, whose body is weakened. He has taken this route a lot, surely more than ten times. No one but him knows it. He can guide the king best. If God gives him strength or ability, he can take you."

Kamdad said to him, "By the glory of the fortunate king this difficult route will become easy to us. 3990 We will reach prosperous places quickly, we will reach the borders of our lord's country."

Kamdad took haste following him to bring the news, "The sovereign has granted your request."

The next day Abtin came before the king, and acclaimed him and praised him effusively. He said, "O brave king, my heart never tires of your company. However, I fear the passing days will turn against us. If we remain forever nameless, the world remains in the hands of the wicked. Our dynasty, our honor will be returned to the dust."

20. Mount Qaf will be depicted in lines 4060–4090 as adjacent to the lands of Gog and Magog. While some maps placed these lands in Southeast Asia, they were more commonly placed in Northeast Asia. If the reader wishes to picture this journey on the map, Iranshah's understanding of the geography of Asia seems to be that Mount Qaf and the lands of Gog and Magog occupy a large landmass north of Korea. Abtin must sail around it, northeast and then back west. After rounding the tip of this landmass, he must make landfall and proceed west to the land of the Slavs.

Abtin said this to the king, "Why should I walk into the pit of doom? Now I have cheer and safety, day and night in happiness and festivity. I am tangled in the crown's shadow, he has looked on me with humanity." 4000 He made many such apologies; apologetic speech is easy to hear.

Tayhur said to him, "O honorable one, fortune has turned away from me. My wish was such that so long as I was alive, you would never be parted from my sight. None of the priests ever tell us how long we'll be alive on the earth. You have given me gifts to which I cannot respond in kind. Take care in leaving, so that not even a vein of your own body finds out."

Then they called for that old mariner, who was all skin and bones, yellowed and dry like straw, his back bent over from age like a letter *dal*.[21] His hands and head trembled like a willow in the wind. one that had lost all hope of verdant spring, no power or facility, strength or vigor, no motion in his hands or speed in his feet. 4010 He could not tell Tayhur apart from Abtin and acclaimed them both.

When the king showed affection and he at last recognized him, he said to him, "O you who have reached old age twice over, you are the master of all navigators, and you must now undertake a new labor. Several people are here from the land of Iran, who are of our family, and most honored. They must return to Iran, by the route to Mount Qaf—a long way—because they cannot go by way of China, its lands full of enemy forces. Take this path—if nothing pains you, you'll see no treasure—no pain no gain! When you deliver these people to the mountain, it will raise your stature. I will make you lord of the sea, you'll have treasure and authority."

The tongue-tied elder said in response, "O champion, 4020 I have lived more than three hundred years. There is no blood left in my limbs. My abilities and wisdom have left me, how can I traverse a route like that? Knowledge can keep us straight along the path, whoever's knowledge is diminished gets lost. Old age and indigence, your majesty—there are no worse afflictions to visit one's days. I have suffered plenty from both of them, and have neither strength of limbs, nor gold or coins to gain husbands for my four daughters—like the moon and

---

21. The letter *dal* is shaped like a sideways *v*. The meaning of the comparison is that the man's back is very bent.

ambergris, their face and hair. Because of my indigence, o wise sovereign, no one will even look at them. If your majesty would resolve this
difficulty for me, give those daughters a dowry, then I will have no fear
of the sea or the day of resurrection, I'll take my revenge on this bottomless water and set out anew on the sea route. 4030 Difficulty with daughters, suffering and poverty, will make a man restless. It has been
more than a hundred years that I have not seen what that route is like.
But by the strength of God, exalted, and the royal glory, I shall without
fear or hesitation deliver the Iranians to dry land, and cross the rust-
green sea."

Tayhur smiled. "See what the man says! No one was ever so brave
in old age!" He said to him, "Arise, and have no sorrow, we will arrange
the affairs of your daughters." He ordered the minister to make the
arrangements, and collect those girls' dowries. When the lunar glory
shone upon their heads, suitors piled up at their doors. The nobles
each took a daughter, and he would have given more daughters if he
had them. The worldly-wise mariner was now at ease, like a young
man again with his new wealth. 4040 Coin straightens the crooked,
and performs many a feat.

Then he outfitted four ships, each one of them with a deck like a
fortress. Three ships were loaded with victuals, the fourth with dirhams
and dinars. He gave whatever else he had to Tayhur, and much affection on top of this. They added supplies and packed the cargo, sending
it immediately to the sea.

When Abtin left Besila, men and women wept tears of blood.
Youths wept bitterly from their hearts, women cried for Fararang. A
cry arose from alleys, streets, and fields, a great lament that rose to the
sky. All of Fararang's sisters, women's hands beating their rosebud
heads and narcissus eyes in mourning, proud Tayhur and his relations, and all of his descendants, 4050 came trembling to the seaside,
with eyes like spring rainclouds. Every one of them cried tears of
blood. And who can imagine how Tayhur himself cried?

Then he took the two of them in his embrace, kissed them profusely, and cried bitterly. He said, "I entrust you to God."

The aspiring world-conqueror praised the king, and Fararang
kissed the ground. They boarded the ship and the king returned, a
pleasant breeze accompanying them. Right then, the veteran mariner

set the ship in motion with all the craft of Mercury. All the sails were unfurled and they were gone from the island in a week.

They went on, and God looked after them, for they were not one day without wind. It was never still, nor was it violent—so it goes for one who has God at their back. 4060 The mariner went on for five months, never stopping to rest or deviating from the route. Mount Qaf appeared on their left side, reaching up as if level with the turning heavens. For four months they passed by the mountain, and so on until ten months had passed. They approached Gog now, who were a very numerous group on a broad mountain. They covered that mountaintop like ants, they saw the ship and made a great commotion. That clamor poured over mountain and sea like a spring gale through a garden.

They asked the mariner, "What is this commotion? What are this multitude, like ants?"

The old mariner answered, "We must pass this frontier of Gog swift as Mercury. These beasts hold the mountains and plains there. The world's creator has created no beast in the world more evil. 4070 If the water of the sea were not in front of them, full of fishes, they would bring calamity to the world, who knows how terrible. This world would be ruined in a day by these catastrophic and mad creatures. They are a hundred times more numerous than humankind, knowing no kindness or humanity. The greatest land of the seven lands did the creator give to these beasts. It lies a day from the sea and from Mount Qaf. The world's structure is no tall tale, your majesty."

He said these words, and they drove the ship swiftly, traveling for another two months. They saw not a field or mountaintop without them, their shouts rising beyond the sky. They passed them and then drove their ships across the deep sea for three months. I do not know the extent of the world, or the rainclouds it took to fill the sea. 4080 Whatever part of it you can find is but a little, for this is only one of the seven seas. Many wonders they saw in the water that would frighten you even if you saw them in your sleep. [211a]

They went on until the mountain divided the sea into two branches, and they alighted on a long stretch of seashore. When Abtin saw land, habitation and fields, he lowered his crowned head to the ground. With his face, he rubbed the black earth and praised God profusely.

He said, "O you higher than the sun, creator of earth and water, the water of the sea and the wind are under your command, you know the foundations of this creation. I give thanks to you, for we have crossed the sea and tall mountains without suffering harm."

He gave many gifts to the poor and to the ailing mariner and his men. All of the food he had left he gave the mariner, who returned to the ship and set sail. 4090

He sent a letter to King Tayhur, "We have crossed this deep road safely. From the sea, we happily reached land, thanks to the mariner, with no grief from the wind. My one wish came true, by the glory of the noble-natured world-ruler. I hope that my other wish will also come true by the glory of the crowned king."

When the king had let those men go, he halted there by the seaside. He set up his tent in that meadow, a plain like verdant spring, all green with streams of running water, a place fit for royalty. Blooming flowers and game abounded, its fields and valleys resembled a garden. People came from the nearby towns to admire the king. Whoever came near him complimented him, and he entertained them as guests according to his custom. 4100 He did so, and everyone did their buying and selling, their faces radiant with happiness.

Finding herbs and cool places, the king stayed there for four months. He sent fifty men to the mountain—brave men of Iran, leaders in battle—quietly, so that news of him would not escape and no one become aware of his secret. Of those, he sent three men to climb the mountain, brave and intrepid, lovers of knowledge, so that they would have knowledge of the route, of where the proud king should travel. They ran quickly upon Mount Qaf like a nightingale chick upon a rosebush branch.

They crossed the mountain with great toil and found a path to the plain. Night and day, staying back from the road and exploring over the mountain, plain, and everywhere else, those brave men made it out in a month, arriving in Bulgaria, which you know as . . . run, . . . 4110 which was along the border of the Slavs, its valleys and plains verdant and well watered. They continued through that frontier for a month, seeing cities, hollows, and highlands. The king's men reached the sea and saw no way ahead from there. Because people were at ease on that frontier, they have named that water Damandan.[22] They quickly returned to Abtin, and informed him about what lay in that direction.

Abtin was greatly pleased by this. He packed up as night was falling. He put away his kingly clothing, and dressed as a merchant. He moved swiftly every night, and by day he camped—that king, inspiration of soldiers. They kept strict discipline and soon passed the frontiers of the Slavs. They arrived near the deep sea. Autumn came and the mountains were covered with snow. 4120 When well-stocked merchants returned from the lands of the Slavs and Bulgaria, they carried all their cargo to the sea, close to that victorious king.

The world-seeker bought three ships from them, launched them, and continued on his way, traveling with that group and never tiring of the voyage. He made landfall on the Khazar frontier, but was unable to stay in that region. Once again he moved on, he reached the sea of Gilan and stayed there. He drove his ships three weeks more, and was near Amol when he made landfall.[23]

He entered the forest and remained hidden there—do you wonder what such a life profited him? If evil in the world may befall the excellent Abtin, then no one remains free from harm, not people of little consequence, not lofty kings. 4130 It is so hard on the soul and body of human beings, for toil and trouble are not scarce. One can only try to escape evil, for it's better to stay alive even if there are thousands of calamities. No one can stay in God's company, and ease is found in no other house.

22. The connection between this sea being a place of ease and the name Damandan is not clear. It may refer to the use of the term *daman*, literally "skirt," for a flat area that skirts a mountain, and thus a plain; the word also means an area thick with date palms. The suffix *-dan* means that which gives or yields something, hence, the name may be glossed as "the water which yields fertile plains." In later texts, *damandan* is used to mean hell.

23. On the significance of the forested region between the Caspian Sea and the Alborz mountains, see introduction.

Chapter 3

King Abtin remained in the forest, troubled by the turning heavens and time's ravages. One day he emerged onto the plain and a young man, on foot, came upon him. He brought him into the forest and courteously asked him about the toils of the road.

"What do you know about Zahhak's doings? What news is there of that shameless man?"

The youth said, "The world is at his fingertips, the seven lands all under his banner. The affairs of the religious guides are wrecked, you'd think there were none of them left. I see everyone acting without shame, no one who is not obedient to Zahhak. 4140 Except Salkot, that treasure of the passing days, who holds a fortress on Mount Damavand.[1] He is the only one who sympathizes with the Jamshidians and is not loyal to Zahhak. Zahhak sent armies against him several times, and they saw the face of the fortress from a league away. And twice they engaged in battle, but could not touch him. He has a place where the sun and wind cannot turn their anger on him. Zahhak has stationed armies around Amol, all battle-ready. Since then, none of the Iranians goes near Salkot."

Abtin said to him, "Do you know anything about the descendant of Jamshid and his men?

---

1. Mount Damavand is the most legendary mountain in Iran; Zahhak is imprisoned there by Faridun in *The Shahnameh*.

He said in response, "It has been years since we have asked the Iranians about this. A man reported that his descendant went to the bottomless sea. 4150 He disappeared into the peak of a great mountain, by the hand of the mighty, malevolent Kush."

Abtin smiled and responded, "O well-wisher, how is the road to Salkot?"

He said in response, "On horseback a man could reach the fortress in three days."

Abtin said, "Do you know the way from here, to Mount Damavand and that place?"

He said, "I know the route is rough, all forest and places for ambush."

Then Abtin asked, "Of whose people are you? Whose business are you on, tell me?"

He said, "You of pure intent, I am from a prosperous place called Nimruz.[2] I took a letter to King Zahhak, from the brave Garshasp, champion of the army. Now I am returning to Nimruz, to the gallant Garshasp."

The world-ruler gave him some dinars and swore him to silence. 4160 "Do not reveal my secret to anyone, do not tell anyone that you saw someone."

The youth said, "O happy lord, now that you have bound my tongue with an oath, perhaps you could reveal your secret to me. Will you tell me why you are here? What is your name? From whom is your ancestry and lineage?"

Abtin said, "I am one of the Iranians persecuted and forced to flee by Zahhak. I am hiding in this forest in case he leaves the world as our inheritance."

The youth said, "Many proud Iranians are in hiding, all around, that is no secret. How could it be that world's keeper fled from Kush by sea, without war or confrontation? What injury was it, o worthy one, that caused you to flee into the forest?"

. . .

The youth left and the king remained in the forest, spending his days in solitude. 4170

---

2. Nimruz is a place between Zabol and Qandahar.

ABTIN SEES SUNLIGHT IN HIS SLEEP

Full of worry, the sovereign was asleep one night and saw the world in a foggy pandemonium. The land turned dark like the pitch-black sea, with the moon, Saturn, and Mercury behind a curtain. The chaotic night, the frightening air, seized the whole world, water and soil. Men and women were terrified, pleading with each other. All raised their hands to the sky, their bodies weary, their hearts grieving. He saw himself, too, in a high place, his heart full of cheer and his soul brave. The world all turned their eyes to him. The sun shined from his face, each one of them soaking up its brightness. [211b] Darkness fled the world completely, agitation vanished from people's hearts. They all lowered their heads to the ground like idolators before King Abtin. 4180 When the dawn came, he described his dream to Kamdad in detail.

He said, "O king, you bring comfort! The world-revealing God will reveal that which King Jamshid promised as a hope and shelter for the world. No goodness remains among the people, there is only sorcery before them. In the coming days, they hope to find that loftiness and permanence that they turned to you for.

"One of your children will sit upon the throne so that the people may be free from grievous travail. Then the sunlight that you saw in your dream, that sunlight that radiated from your face, made all the fog disappear, its brightness reached everyone. From you, your majesty, and not long from now, a king will arise 4190 whose crown will radiate like the sun and whose wisdom will be as armor to the earth.

"The world will bring ruin upon the wicked, and through him, the good will find happy fates. Men of religion will be delighted by him and the malevolent will find sorrow and travail from him. That king will adorn the world with justice as in the days of joyous Jamshid. People of the world will all prosper, sorcery and demons will be ruined by him. The land will become fruitful by his glory, as he adorns the world with faith and justice."

Abtin was cheered by what he said and rejoiced in his heart. He consulted the stars and his situation, he saw that everything was in his favor: for the noble, increase, kingship, cheer, and treasure; and for the enemy, pain, sorrow, and toil.

He soon came to Fararang and her heart was cheered by the news. 4200 Night fell and they were together, they planted a seed that would bear happiness. Fararang became pregnant from the sovereign and the king rejoiced when he found out. Day and night he never left her alone, he held her life very dear. The fertile soil, when it sees a seed, must toil constantly to nourish it.

When nine months and a day had passed, that planted seed bore fruit. When Fararang's time came, they distributed coins to beggars. A child without blemish appeared like the moon, a moon that could brighten crown and palace. The tent turned red reflecting the color of his face, the mountains and stones were radiant with his glory. As tall as a one-year-old child when he was born, he had cheeks like snow streaked with blood.

They quickly brought the good news to Abtin, taking their share of the spreading cheer. 4210 The world-seeker put aside food and sleep, he drew out an astrolabe in the sun. That moment that he heard the good news, he examined the stars at the moment of birth. The sun was rising in Leo—not in grief, not in haste. He found Saturn in his enemy's house, his own soul and body far from its effects. Venus was in the desired house, injury was wiped away. Hope's banquet had guests, it was calm, without vengeance or judgment. He saw Mars' blade drawn, rending the soul and heart of his enemies.

Abtin was pleased by those stars, none of the kings before him had seen such things. Draco's tail doubled back on itself, pointing to the secrets of the two creations, heaven and earth. When he saw that tail rising, he grew sorrowful, that king of distinguished lineage. 4220

He said to himself discreetly, "Having to leave this world, it is better that I leave someone behind, who will be distinguished and renowned. My name will live on eternally and free the world from the injuries of the wicked."

The proud king went to his child and looked upon his face with delight. He saw his face like a shining sun, bearing the glory of Jamshid. He smiled and said, "Faridun," meaning "glory is here," "the world will flourish from this bliss."

From that horoscope, he was called Faridun, and men and women were cheered by his face. That same day, two women came from Iran, with shapely limbs and pure essences. 4230 They gave him milk for three years, and on the fourth year Faridun radiated bravery.

THE DESCRIPTION OF ABTIN'S
FOURTH DREAM

One night Abtin was sleeping happy and drunk when he sprung out of bed afraid. He called for Kamdad to come to him, and said, "Remember what I tell you. Tonight I saw in my sleep a ravishing garden with running streams. [212a] I sat within it, in royal fashion, a bejeweled crown on my head. The world was illuminated by my radiant crown, the whole world under my command. Suddenly, Jamshid, the sovereign, sat upon a horse in midair. He descended into that feasting-ground, and kept looking straight at my crown . . .[3]

"'When so much wonder abounds, must not the passing days bring evil too?' He said to me, 'Sit behind me.' I sat and the horse took off into the air, and flew into the sky. I disappeared from the world. Can you tell me from this dream what will come to pass?" 4240

Having been told that dream, the king's minister was left speechless and he stared at his shoes.

Abtin said to him, "My good man, why did my dream trouble you? This awareness came to me when I went to attend to my child. I want an interpretation from you, not grief, tell me what you know, no more, no less!"

The minister said to him, "Your majesty, do not let your heart grieve because of this. This world gives hope to no one, it is not the place of durability and permanence. Whoever comes into this benighted place must pass on to another abode. The world does not remain as it was, no matter that you are great, the lord in command of a country. Your majesty, if you saw a garden in your sleep, that is the world with all its toil and complications. Men have compared it to a garden, sometimes containing joy, sometimes pain. 4250

"When the world-ruler, Jamshid, came from the sky upon a horse like the blowing wind, when he removed the crown happily from the king's head, he placed a cup of wine there. Your crown was Faridun, your majesty, and the cup of wine was endless knowledge. All of your

---

3. Kamdad's interpretation of the dream in line 4250 below refers to Jamshid removing Abtin's crown and placing a cup of wine on his head in its place, and then, apparently, passing the wine and crown to someone else—presumably Abtin's son, Faridun. The absence of these actions from the description of the dream itself suggests that a number of couplets have been omitted.

knowledge King Jamshid gave to this worthy one, with throne and high station. When he sat down upon the throne, King Jamshid sent it from God to that royal court. It is better to place that crown he granted elsewhere.

"This you must do now—you must send him out of this forest. Send him to a very secure place to be safe from the ravages of time. It would be best if the king draws on his wisdom to take this worthy one to a place where there is a worthy lord, wise, enlightened, and kind. 4260 When we put our trust in his doings, know that God is our companion. What fear do we have of harm from Zahhak? Everyone will return beneath the dust. Our lord is not truly dead if his worthy descendant remains."

This filled Abtin's heart with worry: he knew that this was what the dream meant.

One day he ventured out of his camp and heard a cry for help. He mounted his black horse to see what was going on and went to where he heard the cry. He saw two men struggling with a young man whom they held. He asked the young man, "What harm was done to you that you cried out?"

His attacker said, "This ill-born one shows signs of being a spy. 4270 He's a companion of Salkot, no doubt, who holds a castle higher than the sky. He has rebelled against us—a sympathizer of Jamshid and Abtin. I want to drag him before the king so that he may be executed before the throne."

He was astonished, drew his blade from his belt, and separated their two heads from their bodies.

They quickly brought the youth from the forest. He asked, "What was all this quarreling about?"

The afflicted fellow said, "O lordly man, Ahura Mazda is delighted by your glory, now that you have freed me, why should I keep any secrets from you? Salkot sent me to this place, having given me many instructions. A man of the mountain brought him news that you are a rebellious Iranian with many companions hiding in the forest, having taken a difficult journey across the world. 4280 He said to me, 'Go, ask him what he is about, learn his character and plans, and get a look at him. If they are Iranians, be sure to send a rider straight back to us.' And so I have come on this business from the fortress, seeking brave men in the forest. [212b] I had not yet reached the forest when the king's men set upon me."

Abtin laughed and comforted him, and gave him a horse with trappings and a saddle. He asked him, "Who is Salkot, what kind of man is he? What is his fortress like, how is it situated?"

He answered, "He is a man among men, unmatched in honor and battle. He has a fortress there atop the mountain that God alone knows the way to reach. Like the king, he abides there alone. He does not consort with the Zahhakians."

"From here," he asked, "how long is the way to Mount Damavand and that abode?" 4290

The youth said to him, "You can reach it from here by horse in three days."

Abtin said, "If you mean us well, can you lead us there? I will give you some of my possessions, so that you be in good condition and well dressed."

The youth said, "O essence of humaneness, I've never seen a man like you on the earth. I have come down from the fortress on this business—otherwise, does a man tire of being alive?"

The world-seeker summoned his minister, and repeated to him all that had been said. He then said to him, "This afflicted man you must follow. Share his hard road. Go, approach Salkot on the mountain, see him and his companions. Look at his fortress, inquire a bit about his knowledge and judgment. If he is kind and God-fearing, wise, cautious, and fair-dealing, 4300 I will send the brave Faridun to him, if he would consent to guardianship. If he is heedful of his creator, I will give that brave one to him for protection. When Faridun's affairs are in order, then I will be free of worry. I traveled throughout the world, a vagrant. If you are in the open, or hidden, there is nothing but what God, the exalted, wants—nothing more or less."

THE MINISTER GOES FROM THE FOREST TO MOUNT DAMAVAND

The worthy minister along with the guide set out from the forest. They made for Mount Damavand stealthily, seeking out secret routes to that mountain fortress. He also taught him about Buyan. The Magians all lived upon Mount Damghan and called this place Buyan. The world-ruler, Jamshid, renewed it, raising his head to the heavens. 4310 In the time when Tahmuras, the demon-binder, became a lofty king upon the earth, his brother, Jamshid, raised a fortress there to the heavens. He dug a well down towards the bull and the fish, cutting a path through bare sulfur.[4] That castle was bustling all year, it was a place that many men and women enjoyed.

So it was, until the time of King Kavus, when Afrasiyab came to Rayy.[5] When Kavus fought against the heavens, his enemies feasted in his palace. Afrasiyab sat upon his throne the likes of which could scarcely be dreamed of. Do not be in your core like a leopard, year after year at war with your creator.

The king of Turan tried many stratagems against him, set many snakes loose among the people. With a hundred stratagems he gained entry to the mountain and fortress, and burned it down. 4320 He threw fire into the king's sulfur; its tongues rose to the lofty turning heavens. No one ever saw that castle flourish again, and the mountain range was consigned to the leopards.

He said to the guide, "O clever fellow, go ahead toward the fortress, give that honorable man notice of my arrival, my greetings on behalf of the king and the others."

The guide went from the plain toward the fortress and told them everything. "Zahhak's men called out that they had found me, they seized me in order to kill me. A worthy one raced from the forest, raised the sword of vengeance and separated the heads of those two from their bodies. That sword-wielding lion freed me. He has now sent me along with one of his elders, who wants to speak with you of many things. When he found out about you, he came to meet you and see your situation." 4330

The benevolent Salkot, leader of the righteous, was cheered by those grief-dispelling words and sent several of his closest companions to

---

4. This well digging references the ancient Mesopotamian myth that the world rests on the back of a bull, which rests upon a fish—the image is used here in a strictly metaphorical sense, that is, he dug down very deep.

5. King Kavus and Afrasiyab are figures from a much later time than the events narrated here, so this paragraph and the next should be understood as an aside by the author. The story of Afrasiyab's invasion is told in *The Shahnameh*.

accompany Kamdad and give him a warm welcome. He gave Kamdad the seat of honor. When the turning heaven hid its gleaming blade, plunging it into the dark fog, they slept and rested, and in the morning, Kamdad came before him. [213a]

He praised Salkot and said, "May humanity always accompany the righteous. You have adorned the tree of faithfulness and thus sought manliness and humaneness. You have watered it with purity and goodness, and shone chivalry and righteousness upon it. Now it has come to bear fruit, hope of faithfulness has been gathered. When its topmost branches rise up, its fruit is ease, its leaves affection. 4340 It uproots sorcery and devilry, it prepares the way for the world-sovereign."

Hearing this, Salkot became exuberant. He said to him, "O man of pure judgment, it is my hope that in time the tree of faithfulness will bear me fruit, so I may see with my eyes what I hold in my heart, and my soul not be ashamed before God. Now, if you uncover your secret, you'll find in me a willing coconspirator."

The world-seeking minister revealed the secret to him, and said, "O proud noble man, we have arrived from Iran with a company, traveling here through forests, there through mountains. Out of fear of the shameful, malevolent Zahhak, we could not expose ourselves in inhabited places. Know that we have an elder with us who serves the turning heavens. He sent me before you to illuminate your unlit path, 4350 to assess your knowledge, to test your liberality and boldness. I see that it can be secure with you, o honorable brave. If I find these qualities in you, and also in your minister, and if I receive a letter of response quickly, know that things will turn out as you wish.

"There is someone with us full of concern, his mind clouded with worry. He holds a secret of cheer, happiness, and tenderness for the world, the secret of leaders and support of valiant warriors, hope of the great, ruin of the wicked. He will give you this secret now, foremost of the righteous, sovereign of the age."

Salkot said to him, "O pathfinder, it would be fitting if you instruct us. Ask what you wish and hear the answers, for you surely increase our good cheer. 4360 If you hear an answer from me today in this gathering that is to your satisfaction, ask it again tomorrow, from our sage. Seek all knowledge and religion from him. He is an elderly man of keen insight, the passing of time has all but knocked him off his feet."[6]

Kamdad asked, "In a man's body, what demons are there that bring such sorrow, demons that find a way through everyone's heart? No one can long protect their body from this."

He answered, "There are ten demons in the body of a wayward man: desperation, greed, envy, and sloth, calumny, hypocrisy, anger, and haste. [213b] Also, shame, vengefulness, and ingratitude.[7] Know that all ten are the demons of the world."

"Of these ten, which is most hideous?"

He said, "Discontentment, paired with vengefulness."

"Which," he asked, "is most full of sorrow?"

"Desperation, that is always saddest." 4370

"Which of them is malevolent?"

He said, "Envy."

"Which spends its years in pain and tears, which one oppresses thus?"

He said, "Shame."

"Which begins strife, from spite? Which is it that causes fear?"

He said, "Vengefulness."

"Which has its horse saddled at all times, most harmful of all the demons—who?"

6. The dialogue that follows is a versified translation of a Pahlavi text, *The Testament of Bozorgmehr (Andarzname-ye Bozorgmehr)*. A different translation of *The Testament of Bozorgmehr* can be found in *The Shahnameh*, under the heading "Bozorgmehr Advises Anushirvan." Anushirvan was a Sassanian emperor, Bozorgmehr his minister. Both this version and that in *The Shahnameh* omit some contents of the extant Pahlavi version.

7. There are of course eleven qualities listed here as demons, not ten. There is no indication in the phrasing that two of the qualities should be grouped together to count as one demon. In the dialogue that follows, the names of the demons are altered— "desperation" becomes "discontentment"—and Kamdad asks about only eight of the demons, one of which is "forgetfulness," which was not mentioned in the original list. Given the discrepancies in the demons' names and their number, it seems that Iranshah took a somewhat cavalier approach to rendering the list of demons and evil qualities in this passage. It is therefore unclear whether a copyist omitted couplets containing Kamdad's questions about two of the demons, or whether Iranshah simply never wrote them.

"Forgetfulness, whose brain is empty."

"Which is most deceitful and wayward?"

"A demon," he said, "by the name of hypocrisy."

"Which," he asked, "is not grateful to anyone?"

"One who is barren and gives little thanks."

When the right answers were given by the man of religion, he sought to investigate him more critically. He said to him, "O elder of pure judgment, all of those answers were satisfactory. Another question has occurred to me. If you can find the answer, say so. What is given to a kingly man," he asked, "that would drive away these many demons?" 4380

He answered, "There are seven treasures, there is no eighth one. Know them to be wisdom, good nature, hope, and skill, religion itself, and contentment, also, the knowing insight of a pure creed, by which one can know through one's heart about what is to come.[8] When you have these seven things in your heart, those shameful demons will leave your body."

He asked, "What deeds does each of them perform in the heart of a temperate man?"

He answered, "Know the effect of wisdom is keeping oneself away from evil, it keeps grave sin away from oneself: not to speak frivolously, to strive not to let tribulations be fruitless, not to set one's heart on the world, always to tread righteously upon it and always know good from evil, to choose those deeds that are of the right path, for surely no one seeks a crooked path, 4390 to consider the causes and consequences of all things, to know a piece of pure gold from a fish scale . . . any deed that God would condemn, not to seek it in your heart that it not trouble your soul; not to have eyes for possessions of others—this is the creed and conduct of wisdom.

"Other works of a good nature are to preserve oneself from evil and embrace goodness; to maintain a man's body and adorn it with words and deeds; to withhold his body from desire, for desire is his greatest enemy.

"Next, let me tell you what hope is, for one must escape from hopelessness. If you have hope for the next world, then orient yourself toward

8. In Persian the seven treasures are *kherad, khim, omid, honar, din, khorsandi,* and *ray-e dana.*

good deeds. Your breaths are numbered, breath them in goodness, carry on righteously as long as your days allow. For a hopeless person does not see goodness, black and white are the same to them. 4400

"Consider the effect of contentment, o goodly man, that excess may not bring you pain. Whatever the world brings upon you, be content with it outwardly and inwardly. Turn away and avoid dishonorable deeds. Think! Never seek what is unattainable. Do not grieve for what is lost like the wind and the fog. What skill is better, o you of pure judgment, than to be content in God's garden? One who lacks contentment can never enjoy restful sleep. Never stray from contentment, o elder.

"Another work of religion is to keep your body on the narrow path, aware of death and sin. Be aware of what this dim body contains— whether it treads the path of the creator or of Ahriman. One must strive to do deeds that will yield both worlds, the seen and the unseen. Those who investigate both steer themselves away from self-indulgence. 4410 Avoid weakness day and night, do not move your lips the slightest bit to speak evil. Whoever has self-indulgence under control has reached paradise and escaped the fire. When a body becomes self-indulgent in deed, every demon finds its way into it. The self-indulgent man is a coarse demon, wisdom wants nothing to do with him."

The exalted minister said to him, "Which of these virtues grants most insight?"

"Wisdom," he said, "grants most insight of them all, wisdom is like a shepherd, the others the flock. From wisdom, gain greater awareness; no one can tell good from evil without it. Whoever has even a little wisdom, it grows every moment like a branch."

"Which is most righteous and whole?"

He said to him, "One with a good character endowed. Whoever is endowed with a good character, and righteous of heart, the demon seeks not his company." 4420

"Which one is steadfast, and enduring, too?"

He said, "Contentment is steadfast. When you are content with God's justice, both worlds are given to you. Life is happy for the content. Those who lack contentment, their hearts burn."

"Which is most gentle?"

He said, "Hope, which shrinks away from evil as a willow quivers in the wind. Grief and pain and difficulty in this dark place give way to hope in the other abode. The autumn passes with the scent of spring's arrival, it seeks the red rose and fears not the thorn. The foul dark night pleases not, and passes with great difficulty into hopeful day. So the priest said to the Lord of dawn, 'The world stands ready in hope.'"

"Which one of these various things suffers?"

"The soul is most aggrieved," he said.

"Which is most aware?"

"Alertness. Whoever has no alertness has no eyes or ears." 4430

"Which of these virtues is best for a man?"

He said to him, "Knowledge is better than gems. Whoever has the treasure of knowledge, his head is doubtless raised above the sky."

He said to him, "Which essence is the best, such that a man is best off with that best of essences?"

He said to him, "Goodness of heart is an essence whose kindness shines like a star. Eloquent, benevolent, and diplomatic, do not look for more than this in a man of good character."

He asked, "Of the names, which is best?"

"Do not consider any name better than honorable reputation. When you do good, without doubt, people will speak your name favorably behind your back."

"What is the soul's worst enemy," he asked, "that one must flee, in body and soul?"

He answered, "Evil deeds that no wise man would approve of."

When he heard these correct answers from Salkot, the minister's face was a blooming rose. 4440 He got up from his seat out of joy, went over and kissed his hands. He said, "O great, honorable man, you have done all due justice to our queries. The responses I received, o you of pure nature, were all I could hope for. I hope, too, that the minister may give me answers as well." He left the assembly in good cheer, and walked late through the night.

When the sun revealed its face from the curtain, the stars disappeared without fight or struggle. Salkot of the mountain arranged a gathering. He sent for the nobles of Iran and the scholar, and summoned his own minister, having him sit in the seat of honor. An old man of enlightened heart, an inspiring fellow, he soon sat him down. Strength had fled his body, alertness his mind. He sat holding his two knees above his ears. 4450 For a moment his head shook like a willow, comfort far from his body, his soul far from hope. Sad of heart with a hearth cold as ice, his knees were pillars made of string.

Salkot said to the gathering, "A learned man has come before me, he asked me some questions and heard the answers, and found no fault with them. He now wants to inquire from our minister in this gathering."

As soon as the commander of the mountain made this statement, Kamdad came through the door. He bowed down in obeisance, offered praise, and acclaimed him at length. The proud Salkot called him forward, asked after his health, spoke gentle words to him, and seated him beside himself.

When Kamdad saw Barmayon of pure creed, he began once again to compliment him. He said, "O man of pure learning, our heart has longed for you. 4460 I have come in order to see you, whom I deem most distinguished of heart and soul. I will pose some questions to your wisdom, that I may perhaps receive a bit from you. I know that our hope is fulfilled, we have received in full from these worthies. [214a]

"This protected one who is with us is the light of our hearts and our dark souls. We will entrust him to you, and show you a great deal of gratitude for this. For the fate of the great ones is in him, he shines more brightly upon the world than the sun. By that blossoming branch from the Kayanid garden, the Iranians will be illumined! All affairs would be improved by his light, by that face radiating the glory of greatness. The works of sorcery and demons will be brought to naught, he will renew the command of the world sovereign."

Barmayon said, "O man of justice, adorn this branch with knowledge, by your learning! 4470 As the clouds have blanketed the mountains with snow, now the red roses bloom. When my heart was young, it was without branches. With knowledge, there were many branches upon it. But then, let me answer your questions, to the extent that God has granted me knowledge. Ask what you wish and hear my replies, let this aged elder lead the way."

The experienced, high-born minister said, "O just and religious man, what is most fortunate in people? For comfort is in this fortune."

"It was once said, 'No one is more fortunate than he who has no sins.'"

He said, "Then who is most sinless? I would see his fame and honor with my own eyes."

"The sinless man," he said, "is he who obeys God's commands, avoids the ways and commands of the demon, and cleaves to the path of the world-sovereign." 4480

He said, "Tell me those two paths we must cleave to, where and what is the path of exalted God, and how to avoid the path of the demons."

"We know only the good path of God, there is a worse one leading to demons."

He asked him about the worse one and the good, which they call ignorance and knowledge.

"I'll tell you," he said, "if you'll hear, precious words in the Pahlavi tongue: goodness we call *humt, ahukht* and *hur,* corruption *dushmat, dush-hukht,* and *dush-hur.* All three of these are opposites of those three things, goodness and corruption are from them too."

He said to him, "I do not fully understand these—the distinction between them."

"Your heart says, 'If you know Pahlavi, then you'll gain what you should from this tale.' I will speak to you in clear and simple Persian. First I will speak of *humt.* 4490 *Humt* is surely the guarantee of one's character, its insight surpasses the heavens. It regards the good and evil of the world. It strives for that which makes one triumphant, and eschews that which makes one shameful and ignominious. It is dissatisfied with whatever makes the soul gravitate towards hell.

"If you ask of *ahukht,* it is courage, which brings you happiness all your years. It suffers not from troubles that come and go, the world's venoms are like nourishment to it. It satisfies: nothing is more beneficial to purity and goodness. As spirit and body are preserved from harm, it is doubtless of benefit to the fearful.

"As for *hur,* it is righteousness; wherever righteousness is, the enemy is weakened. With it, your soul will never fear, if you have avoided your soul's deception. 4500 If you deceive your soul in dishonesty, it is thus dim and without light.

"Those are the effects of these three, now let us describe their opposites. *Dusht* is that which we call profligacy, not expressing good and not doing good. In this world day and night are established, but it knows nothing about that. If it obtains any treasure, it seeks more, and becomes drunk on the deeds of the wicked. It races like a greedy wolf and is led, running, straight into hell.

"Then, *dushukht* is the way of rage, as overflowing rage surely burns everything up. It does not forgive, it does not overlook, it does not accept. Everything the world brings it is a tribulation. Whoever has material wealth and poverty of heart, free your heart from him at once. For one poor of heart is vile and flimsy, this fault is not in their lineage, but in their individual body. 4510 Their body is susceptible to physical harm, their soul is found wanting.

"The third is *dush-hur,* crooked and dishonest, taking delight from words and deeds. One thus deceives oneself, not tempering one's desires with patience; year after year of indulgence, sloth, and desire, a wicked heart in command of one's body. I know the lie to be that which pours from the mouth in words of all kinds."

Kamdad was pleased by what he said and praised him at length. After that, he asked, "In all the world, who is most praised among the great men?"

He answered, "That king who is victorious and a doer of good deeds."

He asked, "In the disordered world, who is footsore, debased, and miserable?"

Barmayon answered, "The ill-tempered wretch who strives for ill-considered ends." 4520

Kamdad asked him, "Who is the unfortunate one, who cries tears of blood at misfortune?"

Barmayon said to him, "The wise one who does no good works, who has accumulated bad deeds."

He asked, "Who in the world is pure, who has no fear of corruption?"

Barmayon answered, "One who worships God and takes little from the world. The one who has obtained their share of purity is the one Ahriman turns his face away from."

Kamdad asked, "Who in the world is steadfast?"

He said, "One who is most cautious in all his deeds."

"Who is the most cautious man?"

He said, "The youth who does not blame others."

He asked, "Who is hopeful?"

"The one," he said, "who exerts effort. If you do not bring effort to bear, what hope can you have for the next world? The priest-revering *dehqan* said, 'A day comes when effort pays off. 4530 But to seize that game, sometimes the dog catches and sometimes it has to chase.' When you scatter seed, you'll reap the harvest, for if you strive, you'll reach heaven. As others who came before you have said, 'Those who seek, find.' Not everyone who chases catches game, but whoever catches is the one who was swiftest."

"Who is most alert?"

"One who is knowledgeable, who has much experience."

Kamdad asked, "Who is most troubled?"

"The mighty one who has no sons."

"Who," he asked, "is intoxicated by the world, and always meets with new troubles?"

"The virtuous one," Barmayon said, "whenever the unvirtuous succeeds against him, it gnaws at his liver—that is, the heart of the good man, whom the bad man harms as a hawk would a partridge."

"Who among humanity is most fallen?"

"The honored one," Barmayon said, "who unexpectedly 4540 falls from great deeds, his days become difficult and coarse."

Kamdad asked, "What, in all the world, is most loved by all?"

He answered, "Until a man is healthy, he wishes for nothing but health. When a man has sickness in his body, he wants nothing more than good health."

He asked, "About whom should we have fearful thoughts—whom should we fear?"

He answered, "An evil king, and a deceitful and unwise friend, and an enemy more powerful than you, toward whom good conduct bears no fruit."

He asked, "What worldly things benefit us? What ought we be most bold with?"

He said to him, "The just sovereign, when he is in accord with you; and one should be bold with friends, for concord with friends is good indeed." 4550

"What time," he asked, "best distinguishes the great from the petty?"

"A time without war and strife," he said. "In such good times, night is like day. In times when hands refrain from grasping, and not times when everyone is a king."

He said to him, "Which is the better creed, the one that befits God's praise?"

He answered, "That creed in which reminders of God are abundant. In it they lay out a good creed and path, with generosity to the poor and indigent. When they extend their hands to do good deeds, know that they worship God."

He said, "Which is the commander, the great one, whose good name will be everlasting?"

Barmayon answered, "That sovereign you find to be generous and forgiving. He is kind to the small and the great, he is the same, inwardly and outwardly." 4560

"Who is most a friend to you?"

He said, "One who is with you in difficult times."

"Who is the greatest friend," he asked, "in the world?"

"One who is privately noble and ebullient, [214b] speaking sweet, gentle, and courteous words, more benevolent than others."

He said, "Who is the greatest enemy, whose enmity is grave?"

"The sour-faced one who speaks coarse words, who never turns his back to his enemy."

He said to him, "Then who is a perennial friend, whom we can live beside in comfort?"

He answered, "Good deeds—stay far from evil deeds!"

"Who is good, o wise one?"

He said, "He whose good deeds cannot be concealed."

He asked, "What is brightest in all the world?"

He answered, "Deeds are brightest. For the deeds of the knowing and enlightened of soul are bright like the flowing water of a garden." 4570

"What is most prolific in the world," he asked, "like the leaves on the branches?"

He answered, "Two noble hands are prolific, and let there be no covetousness."

He asked, "What is most fruitless and blameworthy?"

He said to him, "Doing good for an ingrate who never acknowledges favors. A clever man does not approve when good people consort with wicked."

"Who is most troubled?" he asked. "Of these folk, who always fears their own destruction?"

"The one who adores a king of evil nature," he said, "has no ease during the day and sleeps uneasily."

He said, "What is most troublesome before the king?"

He replied, "The conduct of sinful men."

He asked, "Who in the world is most shocking, such that whoever sees them wails?"

He said, "One who is ignorant but fortunate, and also a wise person who is malevolent and wicked." 4580

"Who is the greatest villain, o wise one?"

He said, "A tongue partnered with lies."

"Who is the most blameworthy in the world? What actions are blameworthy?"

He said, "Grotesque deeds from great men, women who are impudent and quarrelsome, as well as a king who is quick to anger, and noblemen who are impatient and violent. Also, a mean man who is haughty; ugly and unseemly conduct toward those of little means. Most blameworthy of all is the lie, which severs happiness from people."

He then asked him, "O great man, which deeds are good to do, and which are better not to do?"

He said, "Courtesy is good, whoever does not do this good has opened the possibility of war."

"What should be watched most closely?" he asked.

"The tongue, that no sin should come from it."

"What is best for you to restrain yourself from?"

He said, "Anger, which intoxicates you . . ." 4590

He asked, "What is the worst of all things, bound to hell?"

He said, "Sin is the worst, the gate to terrifying Hell."

When he answered with his learning, he showed a path, and Kamdad showered praises upon him. He said to Salkot, "O honorable man, you have satisfied us. I do not know whether the minister is more learned, or the exalted king.

"Now that I know well who you are, I am most pleased to meet you. I will open the door of secrets for the two of you—and what a secret!—its yield is cheer and delight! If you are pleased with me, I will speak openly to the whole gathering, and if not, give your command and this whole force will remove itself from this place. 4600 For the secret is great and pleasing, the world will take comfort in it."

When Salkot heard those words, he ordered the gathering to disperse discreetly.

Then he spoke to Kamdad, and the speaker of Iran unleashed his tongue. "Hear these good tidings from the world-king, take comfort in this news and raise your cup. For that worthy king, in faith and justice, has appeared—the issue of King Abtin. Such glory radiates from his face that the heavens turn faster from his light. Now he is past four years of age, he's like a moon to the eyes, his stature like a pillar. His majesty is preoccupied with his care, every moment attending to him.

"The king saw an astonishing vision, he fears Zahhak and his armies. What might the passing moments bring, who knows what times will come? 4610 Now the king has his hopes set on you, that he might entrust you with this worthy one. He wanted to know about your learning and insight, to see your face and your situation. He has sent me to see them and bring word to the sovereign. You will be exalted across the seven lands if you become the guardian of the king. If you are the guardian of Faridun, the sun will be your companion."

Salkot's heart burst with joy. He cried out and lost his senses. "In the dark night," he said, "I long wandered, now I have found all that I sought." Then he lowered his head to the ground and praised the creator. "I thank you for these tidings," he said, "and for not leaving me buried in the dust. By the heavens, I have attained my desire to see the king's radiant face!" 4620

ABTIN RECEIVES SALKOT

When crows' feathers covered the ground and the sun hid and lost its radiance, he entrusted the fortress and mountain to his companions and descended with a hundred riders. He rode to the forest of Abtin and presented himself before him. Kamdad informed Abtin of his learning and justice, and of his castle, wealth, and stability, of the good cheer that he witnessed from him.

When those good tidings reached his ears, he became restless, and he said to the king regarding Salkot, "Now he has come this way."

Abtin was cheered by those words and ordered his horse saddled. He went to receive him with his own riders, proud chosen men from among his companions. When the commander met the king, he bowed down humbly before him. Having brought himself down to the dust from his dun horse, he said, "Your exalted majesty, 4630 had someone given me news that the world had been emptied of Zahhak-ians, my heart would not be as pleased as it is at seeing the face of the sovereign of this age."

The world-seeker took his hands in his own, asked and ordered that he mount his horse. They trotted along down the path and dis-mounted, and he had him seated in his camp. His cook brought out a gold banquet cloth, dishes of partridge, hens, and cocks. When the meal was eaten, they requested winecups, and carried on a fitting feast. When the effects of the wine began to show, many gifts were brought for Salkot: Arabian horses and Chinese brocades, blades and fine coats of mail.

An admirer said, "Bring that branch of roses, that everyone's cups may be made joyous."

The sovereign's admirers moved excitedly, many of them taking Faridun's hands. 4640 Like a lion veiled in gauze curtains, that radiant face appeared. The land was illumined by his visage. The time of his appearance was a happy one. His guardian gently revealed him. The proud Salkot touched his face. He kissed that face like the new spring, and held him affectionately.

Abtin smiled, looking upon his face, and said to him, "O chosen worthy one, he is a tree, his fruit is illumination, he will uproot all that is Ahrimanic. He will be the ruin of the oppressive Zahhak and Kush. They will fall into his hands, be sure of it. Such a king he will be, that the moon and sun in heaven's sphere will adore him. I fear the passing days bringing him harm, for the turning heavens hold me in bondage. Keep him, for the sake of God, the exalted, and nurture his pure soul. 4650 Teach him whatever will be useful, for which his majesty be praised. How to ride and dress, justice and faith, so that his like is seen nowhere on earth."

Then, he entrusted Jamshid's testament and his father's papers to Salkot, that crown-worthy king. Of those fleet-footed sea horses, he gave four to him, along with kingly gems . . . and continued giving him gems. When he had arranged things for Faridun, proud Salkot went on his way. The world-seeker traveled with him for a day, then took him and the boy in his embrace. [215a] He kissed his two eyes and bade him farewell, his tears flowing rivers down his cheeks.

While Abtin grieved at the absence of his child, proud Salkot went to the mountain. He took gentle care of him for three years, and when he was seven, he was growing up strong. 4660 He entrusted him to the minister who was endowed with exceptional learning. He learned writing and reading first, his learning constantly increased.

He built a throne for him on the mountain, a precious throne traced with gold, its whole surface chased in kingly gems. Quite a few men of learning visited the mountain. A scholar went to that throne-room and recorded the turning heavens as they were. The sun and moon showed from that horoscope as if they had descended from the heavens. In it was the location of every star, it opened the gate of every kind of knowledge. Faridun ascended the throne gloriously, arduously seeking knowledge. Upon that throne he constantly sought and came to know the secrets of sun and moon. From the works of Mars to those of Jupiter, he became informed of tribulations and judgments. 4670 Through the turning heavens, he comprehended the world—as if he had created the heavens himself! In time, his learning grew such that nothing remained hidden from him.

One dark night, with the elders out on the field, he asked how much of the night had passed.

The learned one revealed to him the situation: "This throne and palace are a secret," he said. Their discourse was a secret between Faridun, that throne, and the mountain.

People say that he drank the milk of the cow, Barmayeh, but if you hear the story from ordinary people, you won't hear it told as it happened. That "milk" secretly signifies knowledge, and that throne they call "cow." Faridun gained knowledge upon that throne that Barmayon built of knowledge. Then, whoever obtains knowledge, it is said that they are seated on the throne of the sovereign. 4680 In knowledge, Faridun became such a champion that he reckoned people like cattle. He surpassed people in knowledge, and thus sat above cows and men. This is the discourse of this Pahlavi, it can be learned if you hear it.

KUSH RECEIVES WORD OF
ABTIN'S SEA VOYAGE

Now I return to the story of Kush, which will amaze you when you hear it. The learned one says that when Abtin left Besila for the land of Iran, neither Kush nor his army knew that he had set his sights on the sea route. So it was, and those ten years passed in which not one person came to Besila from China. Tayhur knew that part of the China-army had taken to the sea and blockaded him. He outfitted a ship with many men, and launched it into the sea. He sent it to the coast of China to get a look at that endless army. 4690

"If they are still at the seashore, say, 'Midsummer is upon us. If you are within your fortifications, you'll endure drawn-out suffering. We are unharmed by your actions, we only see you wasting your time. If your spite is against the Iranians, well, Abtin has crossed the sea and left.'"

The envoy crossed the sea like the wind, remembering Tayhur's words. When the ship drew near dry land, the Chinese general saw those brave men approach. He ordered that they draw up ranks, swords and spears in their hands.

From the ship, brave men raised a cry, "Things will not go easy for you, you are too late! King Tayhur has said that the barricade that you have set up by the sea won't give you any advantage over us, as it is limited to the land, and there are crossings by sea. 4700 If your quarrel is with King Abtin, he did not remain long in the city of Besila. It is more than ten years since he left by the route of Mount Qaf. The men who traveled with him like the wind have already returned to us victorious and happy. He emerged from the sea unharmed. And how long have you been sitting here?"

There was among the Iranians one companion who was ill at the time they left. He suffered in pain and grief on board the ship, saying to the ship's captain, "I do not wish to remain with you, if you release me I'll go and when I'm on land I'll figure out a way to end that siege for the sake of King Tayhur."

The commander laughed and praised him, telling him, "Go, then, if you can."

The sickly man made for the sea. He sought dry land and soldiers. 4710 They took him and a cry went up.

Kush's commander asked, "Who goes there?"

He answered, "I am an Iranian, bringing news for the king. I have a secret about the Iran-army, I will tell it to no one but the king."

When Kush's commander heard these words he chose ten people from his company, he entrusted this unwise man to them and they hurried off, taking him along.

When he came before Kush, that foolhardy man began to praise him with flattering words.

He asked, "Who is this man? What is he going on about?"

His riders said, "Your majesty, he came by sea and appeared on the shore. He said, 'Send me before the sovereign, that I have a secret to share with him.'"

Kush asked him, "What is this secret?" He said, "First tell me what you are about." 4720

He said "O victorious king, count me as one of Abtin's companions. Know that he took off over the sea, passing Mount Qaf, then he landed. He took a girl with him, men and women alike are astonished by her. Of the covered faces of King Tayhur, he wanted a daughter like unto the moon. Since the world-creator created the whole world, no one has seen her like. I meant to give you the news then, however I could not cross the sea to reach the triumphant king."

When Kush was informed about Abtin, color fled his face and wits his brain. He was astonished and said, "Just look at what has happened because of Abtin! Striving for years and months with my army, and I could not destroy one man. 4730 What will happen to us, and what I will have to endure because of him?"

Because of the grief that this man had brought him, he swung his sword and severed his head. How can the head answer for the tongue? Don't ask about the struggle between them! Consider this and think about what it means. When you know who wishes you ill, do not speak.

The heart of the Tusked ached with grief. He sent a simple letter to the sorcerous Zahhak. "That ill-born Abtin escaped from the mountain of Besila, not by way of China, but he departed to Bulgaria and the land of the Slavs by a route that passes Qaf. He took a daughter of Tayhur with him beside whom the sun seems dim. None but her befits the king, and he has her—what a pity that in all the seven lands, it should not come to pass—alas that she is with Abtin!" 4740

When he had sent the envoys, he sent other men by sea. He called his armies back from the sea, after they had been there all that time. When his letter reached the sorcerous Zahhak, he bit his lip in astonishment. To Bulgaria, the land of the Slavs and the gates of Rome he sent letters—to all lands and regions.

He said, "Patiently watch sea and mountain alike, so that you might catch Abtin." An army was sent by the Alhom River, they saw Abtin on its banks.

One day King Abtin came out of the forest with his fierce warriors. Suddenly, he was confronted with an army, raising a terrible hue and cry. They fought as well as they could, with many casualties on both sides. He struggled with manly might, but what good is manliness against the wounds of fate? 4750 In the battle, that worthy one was killed and fortune abandoned the Iranians. His two children, like moons beside him, were both killed.[9] [215b]

When they had cut the heads off all three of the bodies, they brought them to Zahhak's court. He took the brains out of the heads and shortly after prepared food for his snakes. Fararang was heartbroken and remained secluded for a while with a few of the Iranians. Faridun was unaware of what had happened, and he soon passed twenty years of age.

The wisest chanting *dehqan* heard this about the deeds of Kush: he badly mistreated the people after he departed the court of Zahhak. He took whatever he found, from whomever he wanted, and was quick to spill the blood of worthy people. He took women into his own bed, even children he took for himself. 4760 There was no recourse for distinguished men nor for anyone's women and children.

When injustice became excessive, the avenue of goodness became tangled. People went in secret by the thousands to the court of Zahhak the unwise. Everyone lamented the injustices of Kush, their wailing and shouting rose to the heavens. "Alas, o king who hears our cries, end that tyranny that is upon us—end it!"

When Zahhak became aware of Kush's behavior, which people were reporting just as it was, his heart was pleased by that conduct. He said, "If in every region there were an agent like him, even his lesser, I would have not an enemy in the world, openly or in secret."

The aggrieved said to the king, "Will you not come to our aid, then?" 4770

"I gave that territory to him, I sent him to be king. He may do what he wants, let him fear no one. This is all I have to say to you."

When the aggrieved returned hopeless, all of China was speaking about them. Kush found out about this group and he left Chang'an and went to the mountains. One by one he brought them up from the

9. This is the first time these two sons of Abtin are mentioned in the text. His other son, Sovar, was also introduced in the scene in which he dies (lines 1685–1700).

plain, and hung them from tree branches. The city was so shaken, as if by an earthquake, that no one dared complain. Oppression continued to grow worse, with all under his command in pain and sorrow. Never will you see worse times than under a king following every path of injustice.

The elder sage says of those days that no one followed the path of the creator. The whole world was an abyss, drunk and ignorant, as he blazed a trail to idolatry. 4780 When people all followed him down this path, it was all over. He summoned all the pious nobles, and at length advised them. "Henceforth, this is our creed and our religion, cherish it! Following me, you will maintain this path and creed, you shall sculpt my likeness from now on."

Do you not see what the son of Adam said, what came of our souls in secret? If you speak your own learning, you will not reach anyone. "Speak to them to the extent of their comprehension," so that you see no more evil.[10] Do you not recall what the leader of the Arabs said to you, when he revealed the hidden secret: not everywhere is the place to speak, not everyone can know the creator. One must hold one's tongue, it is not always safe to speak freely. 4790

When I reveal the secret of how things were, how good that two ears do not comprehend! What did the esteemed son of Adam say? "Men and women, maintain our faith and walk our path in secret, so that our religion be not lost to you."

But they built idols of stone, completing two human-like faces, one of Seth and the other of Adam—a story worthy of tears. They worshiped them for years, and infidelity was established among them. When those two departed the world, everyone's hearts went off-course. Having no one left in the world to guide them, they called those idols gods.

This was what Zahhak, of Arab lineage, wrought, as has been mentioned in books. If you ask the Arabs what his name is, they still call him Qays Lahbub. 4800 Another name of his in Pahlavi Persian is Biwarasb. His brother was named Hafran, this is what I know by way of men with lucid memories.

It is revealed in the *Epic of Kush* that he drew aside Nushan, his minister. Nushan had a daughter by the name of Negarin with a face like the moon, perfect in stature, the sun jealous of her appearance,

---

10. "Speak to people to the extent of their comprehension" is a *hadith*.

and wisdom obedient to her lovely face. Since the creator of souls spread out the Earth, such a face has never been seen on its surface. He entreated Nushan for her, a fire burned in his heart for union with her. He became so distracted when he saw her that his heart fluttered like a pigeon. He displayed his favor for her day and night and that fair-faced one was thus cheered. He courted her for a while, and from that time no harm came to anyone . . . 4810

At the new year it became clear he had a child, and no one had ever seen anyone so ugly. His teeth and ears resembled those of his father, but no one considered him human. His father gave him the name Kanʻan, his days and nights were spent in happiness at the sight of him. He was indeed father of Nimrod, and he had considered himself a god from the start.[11] May there never be such a lineage in the world that names itself gods!

Then, several years later, there was born to him a girl, most exquisite. Even more beautiful than her mother, in face and hair, she was the talk of the markets and streets. Kush called her Anushin, for her lips were nourishing and more pleasant than drink.[12] When her body emerged, Negarin died, and Kush's heart was consigned to grief.

When he was driven mad by the death of Negarin, his own heart estranged his wits. 4820 He spread out dirt and sat upon it, binding his waist in a girdle of Negarin's hair. He was wailing and bitterly moaning, tearing at his arms with his teeth. He did not eat or sleep, and spoke to no one, and for a while, even in dark of night he was sleepless from sorrow. His powerful body was upended into an ocean of death and ruin. The physicians tried their hand at cures, but who was ever cured of dying from a wicked creed?

His minister gave him advice as well. "Your exalted majesty, why do you still cling to Negarin? More than a thousand could take her place. You yourself are suffering in your grief, night and day in sorrow and a cold wind. Reach out for cheer, contentment, and satisfaction, for what is gone will never be regained. Your bedchamber is full of the beauties of China, choose one of them in place of Negarin. 4830 Every

---

11. The fact that Nimrod is Kanʻan's father of course means that he is also Kush's grandson.

12. The name Anushin resembles the verb meaning "to drink," *nushidan*.

time you enjoy the company of one of them, you'll see, Negarin is no different from them."

Kush's heart was sated by that advice. He ate, rested, and cheered up. Whenever he remembered his Negarin, his kingship all blew away. He cried and bled from his affection for her, and lived on in that agony.

From time to time, he called over his daughter, who looked just like her mother. He called her by no name other than "moon-faced," the moon and sun were ashamed before her radiance. Kush's heart was senseless before her beauty, his head once again boiling over.

When his heart became impatient for her love, he spoke to her and she was terrified. He opened the doors of his great treasury, presenting her many gifts and adornments, a bed covered in brocade and pleasant aromas. He said, "Do not rebel against me. 4840 Once you are with me I'll give you even more. I'll put the world in your hands."

"My heart does not want matrimony," she said, "no stranger is to see my face."

She did not show anger at his words, but took no pleasure in seeing him.

Every so often he would summon her before him, addressing her with sweet words. He put enough gold and ornaments before her, as if she could be convinced that way. He sent women, who also said that she was perturbed, and she did not accept anything. When Kush saw this, he decided that there was no recourse but silence.

He bid his time, until his daughter let her guard down. She fell deeply in love with Kanayash, who was always at Kush's side, a ravishing youth like the start of spring, his lineage not of China but of Qandahar. 4850 She called on him in secret and consorted with him, and gave him her love for more than three years. [216a] She bore him a moon-faced son in secret, keeping him hidden from the world.

This secret remained hidden for a long time, until the king found out what his daughter had done. Like an ocean he boiled over and then calmed again, wanting to bring him to an end. The king went in to his daughter, with deliberation, and saw no sign of this sin with her. He asked her thoroughly and entreated her, seating her beside him as a family member.

He said to her, "O glorious, beautiful moon, I was most impatient for your affection, now that passion is far from my heart, I will no longer say to you things that should not be said. My heart has now cooled off from that fire, and I remain hurt by those words. It would be just for you to reject me now; no one as ugly as me was born to any mother. 4860 I am ashamed at my own behavior and those unbecoming things I said. I would not be satisfied if you were perpetually feeling grief in your heart.

"But, moon-faced, God has directed the motion of the heavenly sphere such that a woman has security and honor with a husband, and if she is without a husband, that woman sins. When a woman who eschews sin is without a husband, whether she is a servant or a ruler, all that unmarried woman's seed is polluted with shame. Since having no husband dishonors you, find one from this gathering of worthies. Select a youth whose heart holds affection for you, one with the stature of a cypress and a face like the sun. Let me know, so I can make arrangements, and I will give you to that worthy one."

When the moon-faced one heard what he had said, she answered him with affection, 4870 "O king, I have no need for a husband, do not try to make this happen. For my husband's heart would not find justice from me, I would not be pleased by a strange man. But if this is your command and your judgment, that I have a lord over my head, I will not transgress the world-king's judgment. If a fire is lit upon my head, then, kind king, I cannot see one marcher-lord in China better than Kanayash. He is your friend, adorer of the king, who attends to you day and night. No one is cheered by the world-king as he is, there is no better groom than him today."

When the king heard this from his daughter, he took her words as a confession. He did not breathe a word to her. He left his daughter's room, saddened. He sent for Kanayash and split him open, and a stream of his blood flowed. 4880 His head, just like the head of a sheep, he severed before the lofty throne. He had it hung around the moon-faced one's neck and said, "Kiss these lips affectionately."

He swore many harsh oaths to that creator who laid the turning heavens' foundations. "If that head is ever taken off your neck, it will be when they find your dead body."

Her meals and sleep were with that corpse's head, a recompense for the evil that she had done. Have you not heard what the priest rightly said, that one finds no cure for what one has done to oneself?

The sage said that within the frontiers of China, there are three hundred and sixty great cities. All of these cities were prosperous, without exception, though in China there was suffering and injustice. In each city, a king from the court of Kush sits happily with drink and song: in Farkhar, Tibet, and Qandahar, full of beauties like the new spring. 4890 He sent a letter to each marcher-lord, and in his sorrow inscribed tyranny on silk paper. "You must take this task upon yourselves: each one must send me a beautiful girl, pleasing to the heart, virgin beauties with limbs like roses, silvery breasts, and hair of musk."

When those letters reached the marcher-lords, no one saw any way to evade his will. By royal command, three hundred idols and sixty moons appeared before him all at once. When he saw those ravishing beauties, his heart was content. He spent each day and night with a delightful one, and gave them ornaments of all kinds. When they arose from his royal bed, he adorned their bodies with jewelry. Then he would send them to his daughter, showing them off in those robes and jewelry of his.

The sight of those beauties made her anger burn brighter. Her anger over her own star grew more intense. 4900 Her heart was sorely wounded and she wept, as her misery lingered. His head hung from her neck, day and night in sorrow, her lips barricaded from speech.

If he wanted to satisfy himself with a woman, he never hesitated, no matter if he brought her to ruin, and if he saw a blade, he satisfied himself, never turning back without satisfaction. In one year, his round finished, he had seen those girls one by one. At the new year, three hundred and sixty companions had been brought by those marcher-lords.

Two years his daughter went on as she was, feeling grief every day. Afflicted, she died in that misery—she departed, and took the misery away with her. When Kush became aware of her death, he overflowed with weeping and wailing. He removed the head of that unworthy man, which was around her neck, restoring it to its owners. 4910 He looked upon that Negarin, her face and hair, and his two eyes bore two streams upon his cheeks.[13] He remembered his Negarin and he wept

13. The name Negarin means "painted" or "colorful," with a strong implication of beauty, so this sentence could also be translated as "He looked upon that painted beauty." But given that Negarin was the name of Anushin's mother, the use of the word *negarin* indicates that in Kush's eyes, Anushin has become her mother, or that they are interchangeable.

blood. How could such a tyrant cry like this? He washed her body and wrapped it in a shroud. He filled her ears and mouth with musk. He placed various garments over her and looked upon her once again. Her beauty was a hundred times greater than that of those beauties he had before.

Again, his love for her grew acute and his two eyes bore gems of sorrow. He became senseless like a drunkard, and he struck his head with both hands. Once again he was estranged from sleeping and eating, his heart wounded and his spirit in agony. His heart became impatient because of her whenever he remembered her face. When there was nothing else he could do, he ordered that, out of musk and raw aloeswood, 4920 they fashion an idol resembling her. He dressed and adorned her, an idol resembling his daughter. He had it standing night and day before the throne. The king was contented by looking at her.

When a long time had passed, he commanded the nobles of China again. Whoever they found to have a pleasing face, they should fashion a likeness of them, exactly as they were. The nobles, did whatever they could to bring idols before the king. They placed them before him in times of celebration, grasping feasting cups before their faces. Kush's idolatry became known throughout China and the land buzzed with turmoil. "Such infidelity for this moon-faced idol—as if the sun would return to you this way."

KAN'AN FLEES FROM KUSH
AND GOES TO ZAHHAK

Kan'an grew dejected when he saw the moon-faced one withdraw from the sun's radiance. 4930 He trembled in place like a willow and despaired of the malevolent Kush. In dark of night with a thousand riders, he fled toward the gate of the king. When he drew near the Temple of Jerusalem, word of his approach reached the sorcerous Zahhak. The king sent a detachment to receive him and was pleased to see him. He held him dear and flattered him, seating him in a seat of honor.

When a year and six months had passed, a letter arrived from the governor of China. "My faithless descendant has fled, leaving us in the dark of night. My heart is not content with separation from him, for I have no other child but him. Perhaps the king of kings can convince him to return, otherwise my heart will be filled with fire." He called him in and spoke at length on this matter, 4940 in hopes of reassuring him and persuading him to go back to the Tusked.

Kan'an said to him, "Your majesty, do not trouble your tongue with discourse. I will never again see the frontiers of China, I shudder when I so much as dream of that land. If the king sends for me again, I will kill myself here, for the dust beneath the hooves of the world-king's horse is better to me than rule over China. When a father is angry with his son, how can he get along with him? In all the world I had a sister, and nothing else. He killed her and no one came to her aid." [216b]

Zahhak was saddened and shocked. "They called him nothing but 'demon-born.' They all call him 'demon-born,' and they were right." He ordered a response written: "I have not seized Kan'an. 4950 I said much to him, kindly and harshly, and he quickly became upset. For he is most dear to me, a wise youth with a radiant face."

When this response reached the Tusked, hesitation appeared in his heart. He reached for wine and winecup, and became more oppressive, his senses intoxicated. He strayed further from justice and wisdom, never satisfied with wicked creed and evil deeds.

KUSH'S DEVIOUS LETTER TO TAYHUR

When Kush was informed that Abtin was taken care of, he sought a strategy against Tayhur. He wrote a letter filled with kind and just words. It opened with his own name.[14]

"From the lion-seizing king of the East, to the wise elder king of Besila. Know, o proud and brave king, that I have grown tired of fighting and strife. The reason for my war against you was that Abtin remained with you. 4960 I wanted that mighty one far gone, I did not wish you harm. Now our problem is solved, so the way is clear for us to make amends. The land will not be ravaged by him again, he will not appear again from the sea. Since he has fled Besila and taken to the sea, why should I hold a grudge?

"You may be as a father to me, and I as your child. Be an ally to me, as the kings of old worked together. Your forefathers were benevolent and never caused anyone any pain. The great men of Iran and kings of China had no spite for your forefathers. This is true of me and I know

14. That is, it opened with Kush's name instead of God's.

that no one has any ill will for Besila. You turned back my endless hosts with your wisdom and honor. 4970 But you know that if I were to send those armies that patrol the sea, Besila would suffer as it did before. Better that we be allies. Then if armies gathered from across the world marched on your gates, they would not dare attack. Let us make a new alliance, our hearts bound together. For we do not wish each other ill—though two bodies, our souls are as one. With our souls bound with oaths of the heart, both of us will be safe from harm. I will send plenty of manufactures and medicines from China, the sea will be like a Chinese market. Whatever goods we have will be made available to Besila. As soon as word reached China that Abtin has departed that country, I recalled my forces without hesitation, because I have no quarrel with you. 4980

"If you are satisfied with this, grace me with one daughter, I will be loyally under your command, you may count me as a young son. I will send you twice whatever you request in treasure, and if you ask for my life, I will not begrudge it. I will put all China under your command, and never deviate from my alliance with you. I will send you the standards of Machin; you may send your own men there. I will die if you tell me to die, if you grant me this wish."

When he had filled the letter with such words of humility, he sealed it with his signet ring. He summoned a proud man from among the nobles, an eloquent man and a sorcerer. He said to him, "Go to the sea and take this letter to King Tayhur. Make note of whatever he says, and answer him as much as you need to." 4990 The envoy traveled a month across the sea, and when the gatekeeper saw him at the gate, he came down and had his ship stopped, then sent a man ahead to ask about him.

He saw the mariner and asked, "Who is this man? What is his reason for approaching this border?"

The envoy answered him, "Do not be hostile, proud man, I am an envoy of China's king. We've taken an arduous journey across the sea."

The castellan sent a rider to Tayhur informing him of events. Tayhur was astonished. He said, "What is this? What more does he want with me? That envoy dares ask to see me? I have no worse enemy than Kush."

His minister said to him, "Your majesty, do not be so quick to humiliate the enemy. Invite the envoy in and speak with him, invite him to your table, 5000 for if your enemy is about to drown, he will cling to your hem with both hands. Wait until he is completely disgraced, then free your hem from his hands. Bring the king's envoy before you that you might see what that benighted man thinks."

The king listened to the minister's advice, and he sent a detachment to receive the envoy. By the time the envoy entered the city, he was feeling the rigor of the sea voyage. They entertained him hospitably for three days, and on the fourth brought him before the throne. He kissed the ground and gave the letter.

Tayhur recognized the seal and opened it. He read it all, from beginning to end, and was astonished by what was in it. He told the envoy to return to his quarters and rest for a week to recover.

Then he called for a translator, and said some words to him in private. 5010 He said, "Tonight go to the envoy with wine and song—don't hold back. See him and speak to him plenty, about the king and commander and others. Then ask him why it is that the king of China should seek peace. He was against us before, and now seeks concord with our king. What does the king of China hope for from him? How would this further his interests? When he gives an answer, remember all he says, do not be angered, do not trouble him, and be cheerful."

A while later, that benevolent translator brought wine, speaking as the king instructed. The envoy heard him out and listened to his questions.

He answered, "Listen to me, and when you've heard, keep this a secret. Now that Abtin is gone, the king of China is wary of Tayhur. 5020 Were Abtin to march his forces eastwards to China, King Tayhur would rise up and take advantage of the situation. Kush's fortunes would then be put down, Tayhur would devastate all of China and Machin. Having burned China and returned with booty, he would be untouchable. If he were to send an army to the sea to hold back Tayhur and guard the routes, they would need to number a hundred thousand strong, their salaries would drain the treasury in a month. And if a great man like King Abtin should rebel against China, it would cause the same kind of trouble. There are many benefits to reconciliation. Even dreaming of this reconciliation raises our king's spirits to the sun."

After the translator heard this speech, he went to King Tayhur. He told him all of it, and the king's face bloomed like a rose. 5030 He took in those ensorcelled words and was fooled like a drunkard. He summoned the envoy the next day and, treating him lavishly, had him seated before him.

He said, "Give my greetings to the king of China in the presence of the nobles. Tell him, 'A marriage alliance is not possible, but ask whatever else you want of me.' For, ever since Abtin took away my daughter, all manner of sorrows have found their way into my heart. We swore a strong oath, by the world-keeper and world-founder, that henceforth no other daughter should leave the country. However, there are many of my relations who are worthy of a commanding king. I shall send him one who pleases him, and by his marriage to her, we will be united. Now I will provide whatever you wish; I would give you all my treasure. 5040 I will send plenty of whatever goods are produced in this land, so you will not want for them. I am girded to obey your command, I will not break any agreement with you."

This was Tayhur's reply to him, and he also gave the envoy all manner of gifts. [217a] The envoy was delighted by these gifts and said, "May honor and renown be yours. The ruler of China said to me in private that if the king ends hostilities, if he abandons destruction for concord, have him swear an oath of alliance that he harbor no ill will for us. We want for him whatever he wants for us. He will no longer blockade the caravan routes or plunder merchants. He will not take anything that is his, and neither harbor nor tolerate ill will."

That king said to the minister, in his cheerful condition, "Kush must be very afraid of us, 5050 to so quickly seek a truce. He has become so friendly and cooperative."

Right then, he extended his hand to the envoy and had the envoy swear an oath. He sent with him a clever rider that he might get Kush's oath of allegiance in return.

When the envoy disembarked from his sea journey, he went to Kush immediately. He told him everything, and Kush's heart bloomed like a rose. He surreptitiously gave him many gifts, throwing open the gates of beneficence for him.

When day broke, that man who had born the toil of the journey was summoned from the emissaries of King Tayhur, brought in and placed on a golden seat. Kush spoke at length to him, eloquently. The envoy, terrified of his visage, his hideous appearance, did not acclaim and speak his praises, but seemed to have shriveled up before him. 5060

The king of China praised him at length, and when he no longer feared the king's wrath, he praised him back. Then he placed that letter before his throne, and when Nushan began to read the letter, all of it was gentility and kindness. His heart was cheered and his face shone. They treated him very well, never ceasing for a moment to feast him.

On the third day, he was called before the king. He spoke to him at great length. He said to him, "Listen to the king's command, then you may return. If the king is earnest, would he take my hand before the nobles of his realm and swear an oath as Tayhur did—let him find no fault with me."

The king gave the envoy his right hand and swore as he wanted. He thus returned cheerfully to proud Tayhur. 5070 When Tayhur's minister read the response, he was astonished by its gentility. He repeated his conversation with the envoy to Tayhur.

Tayhur's heart was pleased and he felt secure, freed from worry and calculation. He ordered his minister, "Prepare a celebratory gift for him, and have it sent. For there is no better gift than that God should hold the demon-born's evil at bay." He brought a throne from his treasury, the likes of which one could obtain only with greatest difficulty: a throne of emeralds, like a sheaf of green barley, the likes of which no king on earth had seen, and ten precious horses of water-horse stock, whose galloping outpaced the wind. He selected many precious, kingly gems and added them to these things. Those fruits which grew on the mountain, that were served in times of great celebration, 5080 he gave to his envoy, and said, "I wish that you should fly with the wind!"

The man so tasked traveled the sea, landed, and did not delay. He hurried to the city of Chang'an and word of his arrival reached Nushan. He went, bringing news to Kush, whose heart brimmed with joy.

Kush ordered that Nushan go with a detachment to receive him at a day's distance from the city. He received him well, presenting him wine and cup, and musicians. He rested a week after the travail of the journey, and on the eighth day the king summoned him. Praising him effusively, he had the envoy seated before him, treating him with much kindness.

Seeing the throne and so much treasure, Kush said, "He should not have done this! He is as a father to me, why should he go through so much trouble?" 5090

He hosted him for a month, and at the month's end had the envoy brought before him. The king brought forth a throne of turquoise, with gold upon it like the heavens and moon. No king had ever seen, nor had the world's creator created its like. Gold-embroidered Chinese garments that had never been touched, which the sage says were made of cotton. A thousand minks and ermines they counted in front of him, one by one. Fine squirrel pelts and black martens were brought before the king by the minister, and a thousand choice musk glands from Tibet. There was mail and a hundred fine, razor-sharp swords. There were several suits of Tibetan barding that would please great men. He sent a single piece of aloeswood weighing eighty *maund*s to the honorable king. His own envoy set out on the road with a caravan, and then set sail. 5100 In a month he reached the city of Besila and brought all of his cargo before the sovereign.

Kush's envoy delivered a letter. When the minister opened it, it read, "We received all of those memorable gifts from your majesty, and we are embarrassed by his gentility. Though it surely does not deplete his treasury, I would not be a man if I were not thankful to this benevolent world-knowing king. We have nothing suitable to give in return for what the king has done, except our own goodwill. What I have sent is like a lock of fragrant hair, only valuable if the sun-like king accepts it and does not close his heart to us. Such a scent is worth little now in Besila; but other days, it may be of value. If I live to see those days, I will show his majesty fitting solicitude. 5110 Henceforth, China and Machin are all yours, seek from it whatever you desire."

King Tayhur said to the envoy, "The king's treasury must be depleted, it is as if he did not mind cleaning it out to send us everything!"

The envoy answered, "By your glory, the ruler of China has great wealth in addition to these things. He asked me to apologize to the king, and indeed I'm ashamed that this is all we brought him. But first, he wanted me to make it clear that we seek nothing excessive from him."

He gave the envoy many gifts and sent him away happy with a letter. When Nushan read that letter to Kush, he summoned many merchants, and seeing one who was particularly well capitalized, ordered him to assemble a caravan. He set out upon the sea, upon that route that had not been traversed for months and years. 5120 They swarmed to Besila from Machin, day and night wending their way.

At the gate, their custom was once again such that when a caravan disembarked, a cry would arise from the gatekeepers, a dozen men rushing the caravan. They would search the caravan thoroughly, seizing any weapons or armor. Then the caravan would set out, toiling its way over the mountains. When it had crossed over to the other side, it would set up shop by the gatehouse on the mountainside. Young men rushed up the mountainside, taking whatever animals they could find. Youth of the market and men of the neighborhoods went from the city to the gatehouse and brought the caravan's goods toward the city. This was done for all caravans.

Kush set aside vengeance and war and bided his time. 5130 He paid no attention to the affairs of Besila, and Tayhur felt he was safe from him. He traveled several years with his men, as his throne was not threatened. A wealthy man with a great estate came to him from China, month after month, year after year. He had no one else from China to inform him, so he bound his tongue with an oath.

He said to him, "Reveal this secret to no one. Go now, set out with a caravan, go to Tayhur and seek an audience, give him many gifts. When he becomes cocky, flatter him, and always show him kindness. Bring him whatever he wants from Machin and China, and whatever grows in the land of Makran. Conduct yourself this way with this simple-hearted fellow, say you are a servant of that house. When you are sure you have gained his trust, come back and tell me all you have ascertained." 5140

He did as asked, the merchant took a caravan from China every season. When he had gained the king's acquaintance, he got along with him and came to accept him. [217b] Tayhur requested and bought all kinds of things, and he brought him whatever he saw. He flattered him—whenever he brought him a gift, he added additional things. The king had such confidence in him that he did not make him pay tariffs at the gatehouse. He tried to test him many times, but did not see any sign of deception. The gentleman became so close with the king that he was his companion, day and night. Whomever the turning heavens would bring to ruin, they first fetter their mind and wits. What good are alertness and learning to someone the turning heavens will make suffer? The merchant hurried back to Kush and recalled all of his conversations. 5150

He smiled and said, "O savvy fellow, you surely went through a lot of trouble. Since you have combined strategy with cunning and deceit, say to him, 'O proud king, why do you want all these goods from China? Do you not want any good weapons? China has many armorers making swords and breastplates that shine like the sun, and barding, helmets, and mail-coats whose links and chains are beyond number.' If he tells you, 'I don't want to trouble you for any of that, and Kush would object to you bringing breastplates and swords from his cities,' say, 'Far be it from him to object.' Say, 'How much would you like me to bring from China? That benevolent fellow is not monitoring us, and for months and years he has called you a father.' Take those things that he wants—barding and blades and axes. 5160 When you have brought three shipments of these things, let me know so we can make plans."

When the deceiver went before Tayhur, he tired himself out speaking. He piled on gifts, and personally showed much kindness. Among other things, he said to him, "I am surprised that of all the things your majesty wanted from China and Machin, he has not sought armor and swords. There is no place in all the seven lands of the earth with such life-stealing blades. Such armor, blades, and barding are not seen in all the world, by young or old."

He added, "It is as if you seek nothing but cordiality. Whenever my thoughts wander to all the things I want you to bring, I worry that Kush will bring you harm—this is my concern. 5170 He would not want to see armaments brought here, and you would suffer the consequences of his rage."

The deceitful merchant said, "The king would not think such things. O benevolent one, he has called you his father every time he opens his mouth, and there is nothing I bring you that he begrudges, so why should he begrudge maces and swords?"

Tayhur smiled and said, "So it is, this is exactly what I wish for."

Then the merchant brought implements of war, not delaying even one day at the caravan stations. So it was that he came and went three times, each time loaded with shining steel.

Kush was thus informed that he had done as ordered to do. The Tusked's heart was cheered and he praised him profusely. Then he spread news that the governor of Makran had rebelled, 5180 strayed from the path of justice and obedience, turning to face his judgment. And so, Kush selected a hundred heroes, brave men, alert and strong, who were renowned in his army and warlike, ready for battle. He gave each of them a horse and bestowed generous gifts on them. He sent a thousand dinars, gold-embroidered garments, and a pleasant-faced slave-boy, full of charm, to each noble man he dressed as a merchant. Indian sword-blades and suits of armor by the hundreds he added to the load, and bound them up. And breastplates and helmets by the hundreds too, he gave them—things of all kinds. The king thus disguised the brave men as merchants traveling that route. 5190 Valuable equipment and gifts of all kinds were loaded on.

They set out for Besila and he said, "You must travel as the wind! Pay close attention to the merchant, listen carefully to what he says. Whoever should disobey his orders will bring grievous harm upon himself."

He then said to the honored one, in secret, "These proud men and all of this materiel I have placed under your command. I have prepared them for that day."

Speaking to the merchants, he said, "When you reach the gatehouse, ten brave lions will come with you. They will bring you up to the mountaintop, and finally there will be no other soldiers in sight. When the night becomes dark you must, without delay, draw your blades for battle. When you cut off all their heads, by then I will have crossed the sea. 5200 When you have laid all those warriors under the dirt, light a fire. When I see it, I will set out and march on the gatekeepers. When the commotion arises on the mountainside, keep no more than fifty of your men there to hold the fort and guard the road. Depart there quickly like a lion chasing its prey, destroy those border guards with envenomed blades and spears. Soon the way will be cleared for me, I will approach the gate with the rest."

The caravan arrived, and three days later, Kush with his cavalry. When the merchant reached the gate, the gatekeepers let him through. They brought their cargo onto land and gave gifts to the gatekeepers. 5210 When he had taken all the cargo out and thanked them all, they quickly searched the cargo, which was all trappings and implements of war.

The commander of the storehouse said to the merchant, "This cargo is nothing but weapons and armor."

He said to him, "This is what your king requested, this is the wish that adorned his heart. You have already seen me bring three shipments like this, the same weapons and armor. He has accumulated a valuable store of these things, such that Besila is now more powerful than China."

Hearing this answer, he was satisfied and went from the ship to the gatehouse. He sent ten men with the caravan, some young, some old, from the gatehouse. They crossed the mountaintop, then those brave men all descended together. A young man raced from the city of Besila, seeing a large group of men approaching in the distance, 5220 in order to bring the caravan to the city without any further trouble.

KUSH'S VICTORY OVER THE
CITY OF BESILA

The turning heavens bound the earth in darkness, and the heroes donned their mail. They took hold of the hilts of their swords and cut the heads off all ten men. They amassed sticks and dry twigs and lit a fire that burned high. The light shined down from the mountaintop, turning the surface of the sea to liquid gold.

When Kush saw the bright fire in the water, he raced his horses like the wind. He emerged from the sea with that army, the brave men donning their helmets.

The brave men guarding the gate were asleep when the enemy attacked. The black night emerged from the sea like a demon's soul, with a stunning cry. The gatekeepers looked to see what the commotion was, preparing themselves to fight. 5230 Leaving the gate unprotected, they went towards the conflagration.

When that merchant saw that battle and commotion caused by Kush's attack, he sent ten men below, all veterans, young and brave. Covering their faces with mail and binding the armor over their waists, they drew their swords on those men, and soon the gatekeepers were no more.

They opened the gate and a cry rose up. Kush passed through the gate at dawn. He unfurled his banners over the mountaintops, leveling the fortifications there. They began a massacre, opening the way for many men to come from China. [218a] He sent scouts ahead toward the city, skillful warriors.

On the fifth day a man from among the king's heroes led a hundred men 5240 with animals to bring the caravan towards the city. That unlucky commander was slain. The scouts took him by surprise and raised dust putting him to the sword. Only three brave men escaped and raced toward the city, bewildered.

They alerted Tayhur to what had happened, and he sorrowfully descended from his great throne. He said to his minister, "This happened to us because of your conduct and judgment—otherwise, how would they have made it through the gate? This was the merchant's doing."

He marshaled his forces so that there was not a rider left on the island. His army was assembled in twenty days, proud hero-killing champion riders. He ordered them all to assemble in the city . . . 5250 a hundred and fifty thousand select brave swordsmen. When the men had amassed at the month's end, he marched his forces toward the mountains. He set up camp on the plain before the enemy, and none of the enemy made a move toward them. There was no way through the mountains, no battle, no commotion.

He was sorrowful and sent a message to Kush. "Allying with the wicked is unacceptable to wise men. One who is too familiar with the wicked cannot separate himself from wickedness. All of your tricks and deceit were your way to get your hands on Besila. In more than three thousand years, no such thing happened to my ancestors. So many kings who ruled China could not touch us. And you as well, no matter how you try, you are simply wasting your treasure. 5260

"What evil you inflicted on the one who raised and nurtured you, you mighty traitor! Abtin suffered so much because of you, he found no rest anywhere upon the earth. He was so afflicted by you that he became wasted and helpless. Who could ever expect loyalty from you, when your character is bad, your constitution cruel? I was aware of your deeds, of your foul, warped demonic visage. See what the wise man said—that to abjure you is always best. Who ever exchanged loyalty and kindness with a demon? Who ever befriended the demon-faced? However, we were not deprived of this advice. Since I've done this myself, how can I complain?" The envoy went toward the mountaintop and spoke all these words to them.

He said, "Tell that imbecile not to follow the path of injustice and crookedness. 5270 Whoever sought friendship with us found it. We seek vengeance against those who sought harm. You did not seek alliance with us, or kindness, you had kindness and warmth for the Iranians. Did you think that your dishonorable actions would never come to the attention of your enemies? Giving them a place beside you, giving them everything they wanted, giving them access to treasure, materiel, weapons, and laborers, and then they came and devastated China—what pain and injustice that land saw! You told me that vengeance was estranged from your heart. My heart sought alliance with Tayhur. I had Abtin right within my grasp, and you freed him from my hands. Otherwise, you would have seen me eradicate the Jamshidians. When I proposed an alliance with you, I wanted a sweet-lipped daughter. 5280 You did not seek an alliance with me, instead you sent a silvery-bodied girl to that fugitive.

"Struggle for your life, for you will find no quarter from Kush. I'm pointing a sword at your face now. Know that I'll soon do worse, as I did to the king of Machin, Behak—I destroyed him! You hardly measure up to him, and yet you have mistreated us, high and mighty in your redoubt on the mountain, not knowing how fortune turned its back, just as it can turn on an eagle that soars above the sun. You and your ancestors had such pride, and there were many struggles like this. The kings of China were unaware of the extent of the mountain or its location. They were content and calm, no one had knowledge of it, or designs 5290 to take this mountain from you and put an end to your rule. Now you have tangled with a man among men, get moving, for there is no turning back."

When the answer reached Tayhur, he was astonished and began to rage. He commanded his forces to stand ready and mounted up. They reached for their swords and spears. Pipes cried out and the drums roared, the mountain turned to ebony around them. Their iron made the air change color, the skirt of the mountain all grasped by men at arms. None of the men on the mountain or the Chinese leaders came forward to fight.

A rider cried out, "O demon-faced, you have come to do battle as if you were atop the sky. You'll never take Besila this way, as long as you sit on this mountaintop. Come down and show us a fight, show some manliness if you think you can face swords . . ." 5300

The reply came from the mountaintop, "The mountain does us no harm. Haste is yours and patience is ours, we will bring the battle when it is time. We will not be here all year, but patience in this situation would do us good. In matters of war, it is best to be cautious, haste is the way of corrupt demons. Never seek to make your house hasty, you will bring shame upon yourself. The pathfinding messenger said this: 'Haste comes from demons and patience from the Lord.'"

When the army heard this response from Kush, they settled down and their belligerence diminished. The two armies faced each other for three months, and not even a child from either side was harmed. With the army of Besila like a churning sea, Kush did not advance his forces across the divide. Day and night, new troops arrived from China, girded for battle and grim-faced. 5310 More than six hundred thousand men stood ready, armed with weapons of war. They brought all manner of fruits and victuals and whatever supplies they could bring.

Tayhur and that army faced off like that for three months. All of the cities were soundly secured, deep moats dug to surround them. The houses of Besila were so filled up storing supplies that there was scarcely room for the women. Whoever was poor and had no work, whoever had to struggle to procure food, since they had no way to provide for themselves, they were cast out of the city.

Having fortified the cities, his preparations were complete. The king departed at night and went into the city of Besila with his army. The tent and camp remained in place—only a few riders had remained there. 5320 He marshaled fifty thousand in the city, brave sword-wielding horsemen. The whole army flooded out of their position to the other cities. He ordered them to defend and be alert.

The next day, Kush mobilized his men, they came down from the mountain with a great cry. He saw no forces where the army had been, and his heart leapt with joy. He said, "A routed enemy is dead by its own hand."

He went to Tayhur's camp and dismounted, feeling relieved. He sent a substantial force after him, but they advanced until nightfall and found no one. A few sorry men were left behind on foot, without adequate provisions or gear. They captured and bound them, and brought them to the throne. 5330

The king asked them angrily, "When did Tayhur leave this area?"

None of them answered, and he said, "If the secret is uncovered, when I get a hold of your city, I'll send all its brave men into the dragon's mouth. But I'll do no harm to all of your homes, I have no quarrel with you. So make my work easy, inform me as I have requested, tell me the extent of the cities and fortifications hidden on this mountain.

How can I conquer Besila, what equipment and resources does it have?" [218b]

An experienced elder from among their number, who knew the lore of China and Machin, said to him, "Your brave majesty, God has made you master of this mountain, God has brought you here with this company, that they may know who is the true king of the mountain, 5340 for he has his servants upon the earth who count the mountains as nothing. This, in order that they stop boasting of their cities, wealth, mountain, and foothills, saying, 'No one in all the world could touch us!' This is his pride and his source of hope, in dark of night, in light of day. Thus the learned sage said, 'When the word comes down, God's will is done, whether in mountain or plain.'

"Know, o king, that seventy of the world's cities are upon this mountain, large, full, and very sturdy, filled with gardens and water and fruit trees. Of those, three cities are well armed, with walls of cut stone. The height of the walls exceeds a hundred spans and water fills their moats. You could cross their moats in a ship, and there is no other way to reach their land. 5350 Of these three strongholds, the city of Besila is one, few cities in the world compare. It is a refuge for Tayhur, with a great deal of men and treasure. The next city is Ghayr, the third is Ur, which stands out against the sky when seen from afar. He has a son, Karem, and those two cities are like portions of heaven allotted to him. The other cities you could conquer easily, though they are sturdy. There are twelve fortresses on the mountain's crest, a terrifying sight to the eyes. Filled with fruit, gardens, and running water, the sight of them would make an old man young. Two belong to his son, he does not fail to provide them anything. The others are decked with treasure—gems and valuables in every house."

When he heard these words from the old man, Kush strove even harder in his war-making efforts. 5360 He said to him, "I am not Kush's son if I fail to gird myself for this. Until such a time as I take hold of these cities by force of arms, no matter how long it takes, I will make its walls a flat meadow with my sword, and make the moats' water like blood. I will send the soil of this land to China, I'll make all the women widows and slaves. I have spared you, because of your old age, now go before us as our guide." He ordered them to hold him captive and never left him unguarded.

From there, he advanced his forces. When he saw the city of Besila, one of its towers reached the sky and it looked as if carved of a single piece of stone. The top of its towers was unreachable by scaling and too high for arrows to harm. An eagle could not reach its battlements, clouds could not brush the crown of its citadel. 5370 A deep sea flowed around it, an awe-inspiring sight. There was such a mass of men on the walls, greater than Magog on the mountain. Its walls were festooned with instruments of war, like a garden in spring with its colors. A cry rose up from every tower, a banner was hung from every side.

Kush's heart was suddenly constricted at the sight of that fortress and materiel, and those men of war. His army dismounted around him, setting up camp and putting up their tents. Banners rose high above every tent. Left and right the brave men established their abodes. He thought that the enemy would, without delay, launch an attack from the city.

Like wolves, Tayhur's riders roared, "Your majesty! Release us to take the fight to them, and submerge the heads of the Chinese in blood!" 5380

He answered, "This is not wise, we cannot stand toe to toe with that army. Hold until the enemy comes to attack, then launch arrows, javelins, and stones. We will show them our rage at the wall, we will burn the heart and soul of the king of China. Why should we let our army suffer death? God would be angered at the king for this. When he sees that we will not emerge, they will attack us head-on."

The king of China delayed for a month, and none of the Tayhurians emerged to attack. He was astonished, and he met with his elders on the field and circled Besila, that he might find a way in. He found none and it seemed that the world was closing in around him. Then, the roaring of the drums and the cry of the brave men seized the heart and wits of the wicked. Such a roar was emitted from mountain and plain that Mars itself was stunned by their war cry. 5390 From the rain of arrows and hail of stones, the ground was crowded with dead bodies. So many stones they threw from the fortress that they drove them away from the gates. It was as if the heavens rained so many stones that everyone needed to don steel helmets. In one attack, the stones of Besila brought down two times six thousand of them. None of the Tayhurians was wounded or killed, the battle was in Tayhur's hands.

Face downcast, the ruler of China turned back, and consulted his proud leading men. "I have walked the circumference of the city today, I see nothing but trouble here. The wall is high and very sturdy, we cannot breach it now. I see no place to attack other than the gate: it is narrow and there is very little space to go through. If we attack it every day, we will throw the heads of our proud men under the stones. 5400 No harm will come to the Tayhurians; the army will be devastated and suffer. There is no recourse here but to wait, and not attack the city. I am watching outside this city, I will send armies to the other cities. When the whole country is ruined, booty will reach our army's base. They will take women and children captive, slay young and old. They will light their leaders' houses on fire, and that will surely frighten others."

The nobles were well pleased by this, they withdrew straightaway from the battle. The next day Kush sent his forces of steel-clad riders in every direction. They took to plunder and killing, leveling many prosperous towns. They captured all the women and children. Dust from that country rose to the sky. 5410 The island saw ruination, and in two years nothing was left there. Only ten of those towns were left; as for the others, no one ever spoke their names again. They uprooted them and set them on fire—such verdant places they destroyed! After six years of Kush's reign of terror, the city of Besila was just as sound and well fed as before. There was no scarcity of bread or water, and no one could destroy its towers.

Then suddenly, a rider appeared bearing a letter that King Zahhak had given him. "Abtin was killed with his two sons, their three heads were sent to us from Iran."

Kush was so filled with cheer that he gave the envoy a robe of honor. He ordered that the army take up celebration, they went cheering to his threshold. Then they threw that letter before the door, and the drums raised a roar. 5420

A rider from among those noble champions emerged, took up the letter, and delivered it. The translator had it read for Tayhur, and sorrows drowned his heart. His two eyes were darkened with sorrow, and he was near to dying. His face turned the color of straw from that pain, but he tried not to let his sorrow show before the army.

He ordered a cry raised from the citadel, "O demon-born, of corrupted essence and blood, you thought that with this deceitful letter, full of lies, you'd make us grieve. Besila cannot be conquered with this letter. You still have to fight us."

Kush thus sat outside the city gate. His men were quiet. He was outside the city for twenty-two years, and food grew scarce in the city. So it was that no grain was left in the city, the army and beasts of burden had not two grains to rub together. 5430 Many wealthy people succumbed, groups of them collapsing in weakness. If you draw water out of the sea with a hair, it will eventually dry up if not replenished by a spring.

No cities but those three were left, they proved difficult for the armies of China. The other cities they ruined and razed, not a house left standing. He sent all his men back to China, ushering them like a shepherd would his flock, while he remained in Besila. When that army remained twenty-two years, many men in those cities succumbed. [219a]

KUSH LEARNS OF ZAHHAK'S CAPTURE BY FARIDUN

Tayhur became fearful and despondent, trembling day and night like a willow tree. He consulted with his elders, suggesting they give Kush treasure and daughters in marriage.

They said, "When people despair, the creator surely is generous to them. In the time it takes to gird yourself, times may change. 5440 And in the time it takes to remove your signet-ring, the world can be transformed."

When Tayhur despaired of the world, he told his proud men and nobles, "Whatever treasure I have stored I will bestow on this destructive enemy. I will send him all my daughters, that this vengeful one might turn away." Having said this, he passed the night without sleeping, until the sun revealed its face from concealment.

A ship arrived from the sea, three brave men disembarked and hurried to Kush. When they had a chance to speak to him in private, one of them said, "The king should take care to protect his person from the enemy, for Faridun has imprisoned King Zahhak and seated himself upon the great throne. He killed more than a thousand of his men; fortune has suddenly favored him." 5450

It was as if Kush's heart leapt out of his body; he trembled, but did not show his fear. When night fell, he fled across the sea to China with his closest companions. His equipment and supplies and army remained behind, both right and left wings.

Five or six of those slaves held upon the mountain, weary of captivity, escaped and raced to Tayhur, informing him, "The Tusked has taken flight, why sit here now in despair? God has brought an end to your suffering."

When Tayhur heard this from them, he said, "May this villain suffer! Would that an enemy turn against him and seize the throne of China and Machin from him! Or else, he will set a snare in the road and draw me onto the plain with my army." He quickly sent a force out in pursuit. 5460

"Seize the gatehouse," he said, "don't give in to hesitation! Whoever of his men you find, send them up in smoke!"

The army raced to the gatehouse, and whatever enemy they found they killed. A knight approached the Tayhurians, one of his proud, renowned companions. "The fleeing enemy has crossed the sea, their forces are scattered over hill and field."

Tayhur smeared his face with dust, supplicating God, the exalted. He called, just then, the commanders of his army and said, "The sorcerous Zahhak is gone now, the demon-born has fled in haste to the land of China."

He sent a rider to Karem, telling him, "Draw your sharp sword, whoever you find from the demon-born's army, burn them up and cast their ashes to the wind. 5470 God brought great tribulations, but now he has driven the dark night from this country. The baggage train remains there, along with all the booty; the camp and the tents are still standing."

Then the king opened the gates of the city, emerging with his army. He charged straight ahead, going to the gatehouse: whatever enemy he found he slew or captured. Anyone hiding along the escape route he ordered his men to put to the sword. The men holding the gatehouse faced Tayhur and he brought them all to an end. They killed three times five thousand brave men of China, wreaking their vengeance on them. A river of blood flowed from the dead and surged into the sea.

The king sent an army to the sea to stop the enemy from reaching it. The army went and brought many captives, young and old. 5480 They numbered more than ten thousand, riders and infantry, all worthy. He ordered that the army raise their blades and put them to the sword, one by one. Then he went to the camp of Kush and seized all of the booty.

There was not much treasure and supplies remaining, they had diminished over the years. The island became even more prosperous than before, full of gems and garments light as air. Besila once again amassed food, garments, and merchandise. The soldiers and civilians all received their shares and hastened back to the cities of Besila.

The king did not receive anyone for a week, and he supplicated the creator. He said, "O pure, exalted Lord, you give strength and display beneficence. All goodness and success are from you, the oppressed find strength and comfort in you. 5490 You are all-powerful, we are weak; you made impotent as great an enemy as this. Your power was enough to make this demon-faced foe flee in the night. Otherwise, no one would be more debased than me, you would have made dark smoke rise from my palace. I give you thanks, a thousand times a thousand times, that you brought ruin upon this wicked foe."

On the eighth day he distributed all of the goods to the soldiers; to the poor and indigent he gave money. When Karem came and appeared before his father, he said to him, "Do not take off your armor. Raise an army and build many ships, and race to the border of Machin. See what the turning heavens' sphere has wrought, as the demon-faced one has fled from here. Whoever he brought, in shame, from the island, and left with those border guards in Machin, see to it that you send them back to this mountain. Give equipment to whomever needs it." 5500 That same week they built ships, clearing the land of cedar trees.

Suddenly, on the new moon, an envoy came from the new king's mother, Fararang, who was the daughter of Tayhur, in exile from the throne for some time.

Her letter, in the scribe's hand, said, "O happy king, be at ease, for exalted royal glory belongs to my child, Faridun, may the king's benef-icence be auspicious! He is endowed by God with all virtues, and from the mountain, he hastened to war against the enemy. He felled Zahhak with one blow and bound his two hands and two feet in iron fetters. Damavand is now the place of his imprisonment, that terrible place is his abode. His neck is bound in a collar that none can open. He cannot work magic or sorcery. We thank God for this blessing. 5510 The world is freed from those who revere sorcery and the Zahhakians are nowhere to be found. All of his treasure was plundered, the king gave it to the deserving and to the army."

When the king read this message in the letter, venerable sorrows fled his soul. His heart and soul brimmed with joy and he let out a roar, and lost his wits. His attendants doused him with rosewater and he came to, but half-asleep. He ordered the minister read the letter out before the troops. The soldiers issued a roar that reached the sun, "All hail the new world-king!"

He gave the envoy many gifts, even though gifts were not expected. He distributed treasure to the deserving, to those who had suffered the most harm. That little treasure made the city prosperous, the people benefited greatly. 5520 The whole city feasted with singers and flutes to honor Faridun, the world-king.

Chapter 4

Such is the way of the turning world, sometimes one is healthy, sometimes in pain, sometimes in good cheer, and sometimes in sorrow, with only the briefest moment between them. When its sorrows and joys are passed, they seem to have been nothing more than a light breeze.

When you look deeply into its doings, my discourse upon it is lengthy. There is a gardener and a number of trees, one becomes weak while another grows strong. When he planted them, one grew and yielded fruit, one grew and after many years turned crooked. See how one bears fruit like musk, beside another whose branches turned dry, even as both have the same soil and water, and wind and sun. Why does a tree that receives these all in good measure become barren, yield nothing from its roots? 5530 One is in its old age straight as an arrow, while another is bent over like an old man. [219b]

Whatever the king obtained from this gardener, he saw the yields, straight and crooked. From the straight timbers, he builds a worthy palace and adorns it with brocades, it becomes splendid. From the crooked, he lit a tall fire, burning them one by one in front of his throne. What the guide reveals to us is that God will do the same thing. Take care that you do not turn your head away from righteousness, if you wish to remain unburnt. Fire does not burn the bodies of the righteous—this is the story passed down from antiquity. Demand uprightness from both body and soul, do not use the turns of fate's wheel as an excuse.

You'll never see one with an enlightened soul try to hide his doings from people. Muhammad, God-worshipping king of kings, demands uprightness from the faithful.[1] 5540 He recites the verse, "Go thou straight," whenever he discerns blameful conduct, and his charging horse overcomes it like the wind and the turning heavens witness it no more.[2] In this path, seek the creed that would cleanse the world of the impure of faith.

Word has also come to me that the branch of an old tree blossomed. The minister adorned the court with its fruit, and the happy king looked on kindly, the father giving his son the court and station—how lovely, the father's station given to the son! The ancient heavens' wheel has never seen, nor will see, a king like Muhammad, a minister like Ahmad. Malekshah and his distinguished minister would bring a smile to the philosopher's lips, were he alive. The justice he dealt was like a pearl possessing the essence of the sea, like a musk gland born from stone; his blade passes through stone as if it were water and his command could cover the face of the sun. 5550 By his blade, he draws destruction from the sea, his movements turn the spring garden into a flat plain. May the countenance of his fortune, by the one, and his throne, by the other, be ever radiant! May the enemy's heart be vexed, and the evil eye kept at bay for many years.

A king going to battle, you make the ground tremble with the hooves of your horse! By the sword of rage and the judgment of the upright, you have seized the world from the hands of the wicked. You take pride in the sword of generosity. Seize from me my penury! I suffered injury from the previous minister. Since he did me wrong, I saw how he reaped evil. He did not give to this servant what you ordered, your majesty, that unworthy minister. Whoever exalts manly honor sees nothing but harm from those of wicked essence. Whoever has no fragment of his generosity will never see any of his wishes granted by him. 5560

---

1. The reference is to Sultan Ghiyas al-Din Abu Shoja' Mohammad b. Malekshah, the ruler to whom the epic is dedicated.

2. Qur'an 11:112.

Now the works of wicked demons have returned, for his name is spoken throughout the world. You have your father's station and judgment; his honored descendant is worthy of his place. You saw nothing better than this judgment, that you give this most important position to him, for he is pure of faith and kind, his heart is guided by righteous convictions, and his tongue by his heart. May he remain before the lofty throne! Good cheer unto you, good cheer unto you, may you be far from harm!

[THE TALE CONTINUES]

Now that we have finished with Abtin and composed our discourse on Kush and Faridun, I heard from the sage who told me this ancient tale that Tayhur, when he had finished building ships and had raised his sails over the sea, ordered that the army assemble before him, and stood up from his royal throne. He offered fitting praise to God, making a thousand supplications. 5570

He then said to the people, "God brought an end to our sorrows! He is the all-powerful, all-knowing, and all-possessing, who inscribed the heavens' sphere and the earth. He brings good cheer to a servant such as myself. I will exalt him to the turning heavens! Whoever does not praise him as they should will not see such beneficence from their Lord, and whoever does not put him above themselves, the Lord revokes all abundance, treasure, and auspicious fortune from whoever sets foot on this path. If I learn from his doings, then I understand that all of that joy and contentment that I had obtained from him, all the good fortune he decreed and the many days we have been secure upon this mountain and sea, all depended on his creation of the mountain, and the gatehouse, and the sea, which have allowed our enemies no comfort.

"All of this must be seen as the Lord's doing, that we found this mountain and verdant place. 5580 He finally dealt us an enemy with no human face upon his cypress-tall body. He wrecked and leveled all of the towns, killing and wounding all of the proud people. Whatever women there were, young and old, he sent as captives to China. I have suffered such grief, difficulty, and helplessness from the enemy. And then, once again, the creator's generosity reached us, and he was vanquished. He did not cut him loose until he turned the night to day. He made my grandson happy, triumphant. He gave him aid against the sorcerous Zahhak, binding him where the mountain is shrouded in clouds, in fetters that will never be undone, his palace and treasure given over to plunder. Those evildoers have vanished from the earth. He shredded the hearts of the demon and sorcerer.

"With the help of the turning heavens, after all this time we now enjoy victory. 5590 Give thanks to God now, for he has driven sorrow from our hearts. After his anger, he has bestowed upon us kindness; he spared us, freed us from the demon-faced one. He drove that disaster away from our city and afflicted his Zahhak-loving heart.

"Act now with good judgment, do every good deed. Since things have changed, let us marshal a great army, set out upon the sea and cross it, and see all the lands of the Chinese. Those who were aggrieved and taken, humiliated, to China, let us find them and bring them back. Kush has no more bravery; defeat was at hand and he took flight. I will use the country of China to make Besila and the mountain better than they have ever been. 5600 I will bring so much treasure from that land, it will afflict the heart of the Tusked. I will seize from Machin and China taxes and tribute, I will make the land rich and verdant."

The army was cheered by his words and bared their necks in obedience. They grew brave by Faridun's glory. They had been like foxes and now were like lions. When the king finished his speech, those soldiers took to the sea. Hundreds of thousands crossed, all vengeful and seeking battle.

TAYHUR LEAVES THE ISLAND
OF BESILA AND CONQUERS

By sea, they rushed to the frontiers of Machin. They gave to whomever had been taken there from the island all manner of goods, and sent them back home. Three years within the borders of Machin and China, they took all treasure and goods from the land. To whomever they found from the line of Behak they gave gifts of all kinds, honoring them greatly. 5610 So much valuable treasure he sent that the sea strained under the burden. The island became even more prosperous than it had been before, its waters and gardens, farms and orchards.

When the noblemen of Machin saw justice done, they were cheered, most pleased with Tayhur. They all joined forces with him. Scarcely any remained loyal to Kush. From then on they no longer heeded his commands, they all rejected him. Whatever troops Kush tried to marshal denounced him as an oppressor and infidel. He had retreated with his armies to Chang'an, with enough troops to staff his court. Day and night, he bit his nails worrying about what his soldiers might do.

It carried on this way for seven years, until the sage and experienced Tayhur fell ill. He decided to return, and appointed someone to command that great army. 5620 The king returned from the country of Machin and remained in that condition for two months. And when the third month came, he died, and he entrusted everything to Karem.

Proud Karem ascended to his father's place, sat upon his throne and donned his crown. I have seen the ways and workings of the world, people do not remain here long. The end comes to this one and that, and another comes to take their place. [220a] The world always piles on death, I do not know to what end. After three, four, five years or more, one will soon depart this fleeting abode. You shall see that whatever is ceases to be, because the almighty created all that is. Though you may erect a palace, you cannot finish all its chambers. When the world-seeking Karem ascended the throne, he ruled justly, like his father. 5630 When a son remains standing in his father's glory, his mother was undoubtedly just.

He opened up his father's treasury and began building a new army. He emerged from the sea with an army, each of the soldiers like an army unto himself. The army followed him, as his father had bravely taken the lead in China. The world-seeker sat upon the throne of Machin, he opened his hands dealing justice and generosity. His generosity and justice were even greater than those of his father: they wrote his name with the epithet, "the Just." He made the whole country prosperous with his generosity, and cheered the hearts of all his subjects.

In those years, the glorious Faridun never rested. He pursued the grotesque Zahhakians and killed whomever of them they found. One by one, he eradicated them, and their days were surely numbered. 5640 Fifteen years he chased them across the plains and mountains. Only Kan'an, who fled to the plateau of Yemen, escaped, along with several companions. No lives were spared by his blade, as he destroyed countless Zahhakians. I heard that eighteen thousand men and women, unwarlike and unarmed, were gathered up and killed by Faridun as he avenged his ancestors with cruel blows.

When he could find no more of them, he returned and sat upon the great throne. He sent a speedy messenger bearing the good news, a letter telling Tayhur what had come to pass. When the good tidings reached the mountain of Besila, Tayhur was no more. The world-seeking Karem had taken his place on the throne, seated triumphantly, in good cheer. When he read out that letter to his troops, they all scattered gold upon it. 5650 Benevolent Karem was so generous to the envoy, he was embarrassed. He then knew a benevolent king had taken Tayhur's place.

He opened up his father's treasury, bringing out a great deal of treasure. The fortunate commander took out three thrones. The first was a turquoise throne, the one that ferocious Kush had sent to Tayhur. He selected another throne of topaz, the likes of which no one in the world had seen, and another, made of gold that shone like the sun, the likes of which no one in the world could obtain, adorned with garnets, turquoise, rubies, and coral.

He affixed to each throne a crown, and assembled ten more thrones, of ivory, and a thousand sheets of Chinese brocade, and a thousand swords, razor sharp. 5660 He also gathered a thousand coats of mail, not a kink or bind was to be found in them, and those thousand sheets of Chinese brocade, and besides, a thousand kingly steeds, a thousand Tibetan musk glands, a thousand deadly lances, a hundred garnets like spider webs that shone at night like lamps, and a hundred glistening pearls that kings could hardly dream of. He selected squirrel pelts and black sable and brought them to the royal treasury. Those pelts numbered ten thousand. A hundred Chinese and Tatar beauties, a hundred and twenty slave-girls of tree-like stature, all dancers and harp-players, who could seize hearts with a glance and whose faces could throw sturdy souls into turmoil.

The king chose a hundred Arabian horses of water-horse stock, with good and stable tempers. 5670 That horse's neighing startles the timid, and its stride reaches the farthest station. On the road, beneath a wise rider, it cuts through a hundred leagues in a day and a night. From the sea, a male horse, racing like a flash flood, like a bird on the wing, its silhouette like a mountain and solid as stone, hair like wild asses and with the color of a demon, its body like ebony, face like the crescent moon's silver, its hair, mane, and tail like the idols' curling locks, its movement like heaven's wheel and its leaping like an arrow, astounding to discerning people, its flight like the wind and its gallop like a tiger, its charge like a fire and its neighing like thunderclouds, its stride like the phoenix, awesome as a lion, racing across the field, brave and agile, coursing through the sea like a leviathan, flitting up the mountain faster than a leopard, its dark color like a black raven, racing with the wind to astound eagles, 5680 its warmth like fire, its luxuriant mane hanging over the ground like a proud peacock's tail. Behzad, the black steed of Siyavash, was one of these horses—this is no mere rumor.

FARIDUN RECEIVES A RESPONSE FROM KAREM

When Karem had produced these treasures, he called forth a sage scribe. He opened his letter of reply. "In the name of the creator, who created the sky and earth, who brought an end to the suffering and pain of his servants, author of seven heavens in the seven and five zodiac houses: satisfaction, abundance, rejoicing come from him, I give thanks and have my hopes set upon him. For in these days he has shown us the countenance of a glorious and victorious king, delivered us from the violent Zahhak, and renewed the world's religion, brought ruin upon the demon and sorcerer with a single blow of the bull-headed mace. Jamshid's soul rejoices and the brave warriors of China are cowed by his name. 5690 Our ancestors waited a thousand years in abasement in hope of this deliverance, not seeing it. Generations came and went, all carrying the hope of such a day. God made it appear in our time, praised be he who created the world!

"With this good news of the destruction of the snake-headed Zahhak, why should I fear giving up everything? May the world-sovereign be ever victorious, his night turn to day and his day be as the new year! It is thus my hope that by the king's glory, this benevolent one, too, will get his share of fortune. As Iran has been purged of sorcerers and all poisons turned to water and antidote, he will purge China of the wicked demon-born and eliminate his name and his lineage from the earth.

"His imperial majesty must know what tyranny the demon-born has visited on us. It has been more than seventy years that this blood-thirsty demon of foul creed 5700 has ruled the earth, tyrannizing his people. From China to the east he extracted treasure, effortlessly bringing it to Chang'an. The rich he made indigent, the hearts of the

faithful he made crooked. They worship idols instead of the Lord, o
you of benevolent judgment, who answers our pleas!

"No one could face him, but in you we find deliverance from his
undeterred bloodlust and pride, and anger like fire. Brave in war and
battle, no man compares to him. Perhaps the world-taking, world-
seizing ruler could be our recourse from his works. Deliver the lowly
from his evil, that he may obtain his recompense from God."

The envoy gathered up those gifts, assembling a whole caravan.
5710 He traveled until he reached the city of Amol, disembarked and
put up tents. The envoy to the king went before the king and told him
about the benevolent Karem. "When I hurried here from the mountain, Tayhur had departed. Proud Karem sat in his place, a wise youth
of pure judgment."

When he saw the name of the king in the letter, he kissed it and
praised him freely. His army scattered gems as they acclaimed the
name of the king. For more than two weeks, they drank strong wine in
honor of the new king. He brought out whatever treasure he had and
sent it without a second thought, [220b] and a thousand horses and
other gifts with it. No one had seen such extravagance since the kings
of old. 5720 The world-ruling king was cheered by this and sent some
of his forces to welcome him. The envoy of Karem arrived and kissed
the throne of the crowned king.

When Faridun saw those gifts and that throne from Karem, his
heart was mightily cheered. They placed that royal turquoise throne in
the golden palace.

When the king sat upon it, he said, smiling, to his army, "May I
reign triumphant over all of the seven lands from the turquoise
throne." He asked, "How did this turquoise-colored throne come to
Karem, and from where?"

The envoy answered, "This was given by the Tusked to Tayhur, when
he deceived him like a common fool and made him suffer greatly."

He made a wish upon the festive throne, "May I be victorious
here," 5730 placed it in the treasury, and hosted the envoy for two months.

Faridun called for a great, fierce army to advance on China and do
battle with Kush. There were not so many commanders at Faridun's
court now, so many brave and battle-ready champions, as before, for
every commander had taken his own forces on a campaign. General
Qaren had gone to Rome, advancing his forces on that region. Nar-

iman and Garshasp advanced on India with an army like a trumpeting elephant.[3] All of India was blood and spoils, for Garshasp was at war with Mehraj.

The king announced that he had chosen Nastuh son of Shiruy to lead, telling him, "Select a cavalry force, thirty thousand brave men and champions. Give them a wage that will cheer their hearts, use my treasury to make these brave men prosperous. 5740 Stake out a path towards the frontier of China, for I have given that country to you in its entirety. When you have reached there, strive valiantly to gain the upper hand over that vicious demon. Send him in fetters to this court, and let me get a look at the face of that sinner. Protect the army from that destructive one, and take care that you do not come to ruin at his hand. For he is a cunning and devious demon, proud and capable in time of war."

They gave Nastuh dominion over China, and Faridun bestowed on him the golden seal ring, a robe of honor fit for a king, sword, horse, cloak, and helmet. He then assembled gifts for Karem, all kinds of things fit for a king. He sent garments for his body, a helmet for his head, a crown and throne of gold, a Kavian banner and a gold-inlaid blade, a girdle set with gems, 5750 and a colossal elephant like fire in its attack, as ferocious as a lion, swift as an arrow, heavier than a mountain, and lighter than the wind, of terrifying disposition and built of death, its two arms and two legs like silvery columns, its tusks like tree trunks and its eyes like blood. The earth groaned under its weight, the air turned hellish from the smoke of its breath. Its size crushed the bull and fish, its color put the snowy mountaintops to shame. A rhinoceros would flee from its grasping trunk and death would hide from the sting of its tusks. At the time of battle, its attack equaled a hundred thousand riders. They draped that Indian elephant in rich brocades.

Machin, too, gave him gifts of all kinds. They sent a gold-chased palanquin for the elephant and a banner studded with kingly gems. 5760 Faridun gave all those valuables and that elephant and palanquin to Nastuh. He said, "When you arrive at that region, give my greetings to Karem. Send all of these gifts and those knights to him through his close companions."

3. Garshasp is the ancestor of the Sistani heroes; see introduction. He is mentioned only briefly in *The Shahnameh*, but is the title character of an epic romance. Nariman is his son, and is father of Sam, who is father of Zal, who is father of Rostam.

The king ordered a letter written to Karem. "In the name of the Lord of the sun and moon, who erected the sky supported by no pillar, author of clouds and blowing wind! Your envoy and letter arrived, and all of that gentility that you displayed. They arrived to us intact, we saw each one and they were pleasing. We are aware of your learning and judgment, as well as your enchanting treasures. You are a glorious grandfather to me, ruling in my place over Machin and the East.

"The lands of the East and Machin are yours, and we have given China to Nastuh, son of Shiruy. 5770 When he arrives, assist him with treasure, equipment, weapons, and laborers, so that the wicked demon-born is eradicated, his lineage annihilated, his subjects relieved of his oppression, and the world cleansed of the idolater's evil. You must keep sending emissaries of good character, so that I remain informed of that worthy and his grand court."

Then he summoned the envoy, seating him on the gold-chased seat, and brought many gifts for him and his companions too.

NASTUH TRAVELS WITH THE ARMY TO TRANSOXIANA

Faridun had Nastuh lead the army out of Amol and they began the journey. The army marched three days and three nights on the field, brave men's shouts reaching the lofty sky. On the fourth day a drum sounded at dawn, and the pipes exhaled their sound. 5780 From station to station they unfurled their banners, the sky turned ruby and violet. They hurried towards Transoxiana, toward the lands of Turan. When they reached a fork in the road, one way leading to China and the other to Machin, he entrusted what the king had sent for Karem to Karem's men, and they went ahead.

He added a letter from himself to go along with those valuable gifts. "His imperial majesty has entrusted to me China and war with the tyrannical Kush. When the sealed command of the king reaches you, come and meet me in this region. Gird yourself to battle the demon-faced, for he now poses little threat. When we join together, the Tusked one will suffer a grotesque fate. 5790 We will take Chang'an and ravage it for the emperor of Iran!"

The envoy traveled many days and nights to Machin, and approached Karem. When Karem was apprised of the traveler and all of what he had brought the king, he was beside himself with joy. He descended the throne and mounted a swift horse. He received him along with his noblemen, presenting him with wine, a banquet, and a place to rest. He also sent a thousand riders who, when they saw the sight of that worthy one, one by one dismounted their horses and approached him to give greetings. Karem asked about the exalted king and his lofty and lavish court.

The envoy said, "He basks eternally in your glory, o king, your benevolent sister as well. I bring abundant praises from them both, and other relatives, young and old." 5800

They returned so full of wine and song that dust of their footprints became drunk from the offerings they poured out. Consulting the stars, Karem chose an auspicious day aligned with rest and cheer. He donned the royal robe from glorious Faridun, and placed the helmet on his head. He wrapped that Kayanid belt around his waist and sat upon the mighty elephant. They scattered a great many gems over its head and anointed it with musk mixed with saffron.

The army and city thus heard the good news that Faridun's glory radiated upon that land. Nastuh's message was recited, Karem sent him whatever forces he had. He then liberally equipped a new force with all kinds of gear. On an auspicious day he marshaled his imperial army and they set out towards Nastuh. When they met face to face, they embraced each other. 5810 He asked him about the king and the toils of the trip.

"It is true," he said, "by your glory, by your magnanimity, my toil was lessened when I saw your face in such splendor."

They remained three days, rejoicing, sometimes with flute and harp, sometimes with falcon and cheetah. Proud Karem had a banquet set out, and gave many gifts to Nastuh and his brave men. [221a] Day and night their talk was about the deeds of Kush, thinking about the apparition of Kush and his works. They marched their forces from there to Chang'an and set up two camps when they arrived.

NASTUH SENDS A LETTER
TO KUSH THE TUSKED

He ordered a letter sent to Kush, decreeing his fate and challenging him. "I know you are aware of how things stand, how Zahhak has been captured by the sovereign, and what he did with the demonic ones. He extinguished their line! Those chains the serpentine one is bound in have freed the world from undying evil. 5820 Nothing remains of that seed but you, and death is closing in.

"The king has become aware of your creed, and of your oppression of the commoners and soldiers. He has sent me, that I may spare the people from your disasters. If you are obedient to the king now, then we will settle this quickly. Gird yourself and do not delay, come out with your riders. If you come out like that, appear before the king; say you will and I will give you passage to Iran, for the king's generosity is greater and he has many like you who are his servants. He will embrace you like the others, you will be a great man among the nobles. His imperial majesty is not Zahhak, he is not a shameless, bloodthirsty oppressor. If you seek absolution he will forgive you, so do what will not cause you harm. 5830 I will send a letter to the king of the earth saying that when we arrived in the land of China, Kush did not rebel against your command, he departed the city and headed for the court. His majesty will undoubtedly forgive you, for he is a generous, merciful king.

"And if you do not wish to present yourself to him because you are afraid for your life, you should escape stealthily and hide away in some corner of the world. Go, before these select troops close in on you. Then how could I, fearing the world's king, leave you a route of escape? You will not be able to wipe this away with apologies, nor will you find any recourse. Shame will do you no good, so it is best you accept this deal quickly."

When the scribe had completed it, a well-spoken and brave young man 5840 was chosen and given the letter. He said to him, "You must go fast as the wind." The quick-witted envoy left in haste and delivered the letter to Kush.

When the translator read those words to him he was astonished by what Nastuh said. Startled, he seized the letter, tore it up and swore. He said to the envoy, "Ill-born one, you've tossed your own head to the wind. Had I not wished that you deliver my answer to him, your head would surely have been separated from your body right here in front of everyone."

The envoy said, "O wise king, if you injured me, an innocent man, Faridun would not be frightened by this foul deed, nor would Nastuh be diverted from war."

KUSH'S LETTER OF RESPONSE TO NASTUH

He ordered a letter written in response, and said, "May people's brains be graced with wisdom. 5850 Speaking such empty words is not the way of wisdom, good conduct, or religion, and is incompatible with justice and righteousness. A wise person would not find this acceptable. This pointless letter from your king is not in accordance with wisdom. You have a solid position in the world, quite considerable before great and small. Though Faridun has fettered our king, he will not take me so easily. If it were Faridun himself in your place, by God, his conduct would be different. If you had seen these many years of toil and battle, eyes devoid of sleep or rejoicing, by God, if you were able, you would quickly turn back from your fate. If you come for me, you soon will see what violence Kush can do. I will roast the king's heart over you and make your army weep for you." 5860 When the scribe had sealed the letter he gave it to the envoy . . .

The general was angered by those words, astonished, his brow furrowed. That same day, he mobilized his forces. Drums roared and pipes cried out. The army traveled so far in a day that less than a mile was left before they reached the city. They set up camp and tightly encircled the city.

When Kush saw that army, its arms and equipment, he ordered ten thousand of his troops to sortie on armored mounts. He conscripted his subjects in the city, whoever was possessed of strength and manliness—young and old—and gave them shields, armor, blades, and arrows. He sent them into battle with the army. No one celebrated in Chang'an. Within the city, thirty thousand riders hid with him, prepared to make a move. 5870

"Be at ease, all of you," he said, "hidden from the enemy and concealed from the people, until the battle comes to us. Then it will be time to fight."

When his forces emerged from Chang'an, they drew up a battle line that was like a mountain. The two armies entangled as the earth was mixed with blood. The clashing of swords and the rain of arrows robbed young and old of their wits. Battle was joined like this for two months, with casualties on both sides.

The general, Nastuh, together with Karem, grew sorrowful from that fighting. He set up a deadly ballista outside the city and three more in different places, and many catapults and heavy crossbows that could shoot Saturn down from heaven's wheel. He girded himself and donned his armor, mounted a fleet-footed steed—5880 he and Karem and a thousand honorable brave men and armored knights.

When the battle grew fierce between the two armies, in the name of Faridun of auspicious fate he suddenly fell upon Kush's army, the head of his mace kissing their shoulders. The ranks of brave men collapsed on themselves and his mace smashed into them. They all fell upon the Chinese like a wolf amidst a flock of sheep. The edges of swords began cutting heads, the points of spears began stealing lives. They killed more than a thousand of them and the wounded disengaged from the battle. In pain, they threw themselves back into the city, lips dry with fear and faces yellow from struggle.

Near the gate, like a dragon lying in wait, Kush held his men at bay. Then he chose a moment and charged, all of them crying out his name. 5890 They engaged with that invading force that entered the city, and it suffered many casualties.

Having penetrated the city, Nastuh had brought his great tent out to the field nearby. Nastuh's force quickly gathered around its general. Kush turned back and secured the city's citadel, and did not engage the enemy in battle after that. He held the citadel day and night, their cries rising above the heavens.

Nastuh's general and the Iranians girded themselves to attack. They circled it day and night, occasionally hurling bolts and arrows. They smashed the top of its tower with a stone hurled by a catapult, its heart pierced like an arrow into its well. Forty days later the fighting had gone on so long that sleep and food became scarce for the brave men. 5900 Brave Nastuh thought, "Now that Kush has seen this show of force from me, although he may want very much to sortie, he will not do so, his army has been subdued."

Nastuh's forces dispersed throughout the lands of China, saddled up for plundering. The island's forces led the Iranian army and showed them the way. A wise man knows that when one feels secure against the enemy and lets his guard down, he quickly comes to ruin. When Kush saw Nastuh was without his army, his wits focused on the situation at hand. His riders and the youth of the city, whoever had the strength of heart, [221b] he invited them and showed them much courtesy, praising each one.

To them he said, "The Iran-army has dispersed from the battlefield. They have stretched out their hands to plunder the country, everyone's heart drunk on booty. 5910 The general scarcely has troops, my position relative to him is no longer the same. I have until now kept this army of mine hidden inside of the city for this purpose. Nastuh is undisciplined in his war-making, and there are few troops near the gate. Since his troops have become scattered, we will bury him with a nighttime raid.

"Now it is my plan to exact justice from the enemies. If the Iranians are defeated, no one will escape from my blade. If they could take wing like birds, I would not rest so long as they remain alive in Iran. Who is ready to race the whole route of five hundred leagues from China to Iran? If any harm comes toward us, it is but an arrow shot into the desert. We will escape like before, no toil for the horses and no harm to us. 5920 Now whoever is ready for battle, let them take up arms! We will show such bravery that our enemies' heads will be crushed under our feet. We will free ourselves from this great tribulation if the heavens' wheel augments our fortune."

The youth of the city and brave men of the king extended their necks in obedience to his command. Everyone said, "We put our lives at your disposal, o king!"

Kush was cheered by their words, by the city of steel-clad brave men. He selected fifty thousand young men and gave them shields and weapons.

KUSH'S NIGHTTIME SNEAK ATTACK AGAINST NASTUH

He opened the gate quickly at night and emerged with his forces like a plume of smoke. A hundred thousand and more riders came from inside, their commander mail-clad and battle-ready. At dawn he emerged and engaged the Iranians from all sides. 5930 They immediately raised a cry, soon echoed by the horsemen. In the night, dark like ebony, growling pipes and roaring drums quickly roused the Iranians from their sleep like the resurrection.

They leapt out and the brave Nastuh mounted, they drew their blades. One by one the army gathered around Nastuh, forming a mass around his tent. In that darkness they joined the melee, spilling each other's blood. With the clashing of blades, the exchange of blows, neither spear nor arrow was of any use. The Tusked spurred on his horse and it became the burning rage of Mehrab and Azorgoshasb. With each blow, the horse and rider like a mountain killed heroes of Iran in groups.

Nastuh bellowed, "O proud ones! Brave and haughty men of Iran! 5940 Be an obstacle like they've never seen! Do not be afraid, stand strong and fight! If we show reluctance in this battle, who will make it back to Iran?"

With those words, Faridun's army was by his side on that dark night. They fought with the Chinese until daybreak, when the world-illuminer raised its head over the mountains. Nastuh looked and saw no army, the whole field was scattered with limbs and heads. In his own camp, the enemy was picking through the tents and pavilions. He saw an army, arms at the ready, streams of blood splashing from their swords. There was no pavilion or tent left standing, none of his troops there, nor Karem.

When Karem saw their power, he immediately withdrew his forces to the sea. He returned to the mountain of Besila despondent, as if carried by the wind. 5950 Nastuh saw that his riders had escaped from the fight, but his infantry were killed in the battle. He was astonished and attacked with his elite troops, raising dust from the enemy with their lances. They killed a number of the Chinese, blood running across the fields of Chang'an. They cleared the field of them and inflicted pain, driving them away from their base.

When Kush saw this, he emerged like a drunk elephant, a javelin in his hand ready to fly. Rising up, he faced down his proud men, cursing and abusing his army. "With the enemy ruined, you have become weak in battle!? If we are weak and sluggish now, the enemy will gain the upper hand!"

He said this and called out to Nastuh, his weight making him a mountain in his stirrups. He hurled his javelin and it pierced the armor of Nastuh's horse but did not harm him. 5960 Nastuh pulled out the javelin, hurled it, and it traveled to its destination like the wind, striking Kush in the side, as if to avenge his warriors with that blow.

Kush showed no sign of exhaustion or pain, and he at once charged with his army. Throwing himself upon the Iranians, he drove them away with his sword. They killed, wounded, and captured many. Whoever fled before Kush saved his own life. At once, the Iranians turned and fled, humiliating their commander. Seeing the troops fleeing, he too quickly turned around, disappointed.

At just that moment, Kush fell from his horse, losing consciousness from all the blood he had lost. His officers and many of his troops remained by him, saddened. Someone who knew medicine drew the javelin from his body, washed him and applied a fresh ointment 5970 to the wound, and bound it tightly. He remained away from the battle and did not fight. He entered the city and slept in his home, not crying out or speaking to anyone for a month.

Of those thirty thousand riders from Iran, more than eighteen thousand were killed. When Faridun learned about them, his cheer was cut short and he grieved. He blamed their commander and said, "Sleeping like women in their beds, no wonder the enemy got the better of them! Most of my army has been wounded or killed."

One person from the surviving soldiers spoke, "O king, the fault is not with them, these few of us who returned only did so in the face of great hardship. By your glory, it was Nastuh who struggled, standing like a mountain before the enemy. Had he not wounded Kush, we would all have been cut down as we were routed. 5980 When he was wounded, his forces retreated, and nobody came after us. His army was three times our number, all hidden in places throughout the city. When we seemed secure, he staged a night raid. This is what happened, what good are words now?"

QOBAD, SON OF KAVEH, GOES TO WAR WITH KUSH

Faridun was astonished by the demon-born, and he ordered that Qobad be brought before him. "Assemble a strong army, make haste toward China to war with Kush. Take two years of supplies for them and build their confidence, protect them from worry. Take care not to be guileless like Nastuh and bring shame to our name. Do as your brother Qaren did, raising dust from Rome and the west.

The glorious Qobad answered, "I have taken to heart the king's command. I will do whatever you say and more, by the glory of his imperial majesty!" 5990

He reviewed all of the army that was ready and selected the most capable. To those brave men whose names he recorded in his book they gave salary and full equipment. On an auspicious day he packed his tent and prepared to leave. A cry arose from the city and from the court. The army set out into the desert at once. Faridun came and inspected the army, finding a well-chosen, elite force. He praised Qobad.

The commander kissed the ground before his feet, and mobilized the army, assembling provisions and following the road. The commander drove the army like the wind and alighted happily in Transoxiana.

Kush, who had dispensed with the Iranians and ungirded himself, little by little became aware of the situation, and his heart was bereft of calm or comfort. 6000 He summoned his army to assemble at dawn. Like ants and locusts they appeared before him, all of China and Machin appeared on the field, an army all of slaves and mercenaries. [222a] Kush emerged from his pavilion tent outside the city and saw numerous soldiers clad in steel. The scribe sat at court; it took a month to muster this army. Hundreds of thousands of riders appeared before him, heroes of the field, battle-hungry men.

Kush said, from his summit of command, "With this army, I shall conquer the world!" He selected three hundred thousand of them, worthy and fearsome knights. He opened the treasury and paid wages; they went from the city to face Qobad.

When Qobad reached the land of Tibet, he set up his pavilions and tents. He was apprised of Kush and his army, and no one wanted to advance to face them. 6010 The army held their position, waiting for the enemy to draw near. When Kush was within a two days' journey, the commander had the troops take positions. He prepared the wings and center, aligning the right with the left.

That same night, he sent out the advance guard and said, "From now on we must not sleep peacefully. We must remain alert day and night, for there is a fire-breathing dragon on the road ahead." He brought out a brave man from among the skilled warriors and sent him near the enemy, stealthily, in order to find out the number of the enemy.

The advance guard took him by surprise. They brought him before Kush, saying, "We captured this man on the road. He has certainly come from the Iran-army, which has marched on the king in rebellion."

Kush knew, when he saw that his face was yellow, that that man was a spy for the Iran-army, 6020 and he wanted to send him back to inform them about his army and its equipment. He spoke harshly to the advance guards, "You've taken some lowly man, what good is this?

Whoever gave these pointless orders, you have bothered an indigent man. A poor man who has been searching since morning for something to eat for dinner, what signs does he show of knowing what's going on? We cannot empty the land of people." He said to him, "Go wherever you want, nobody will bother you if you stay on the road."

The man's body was refreshed, he came to life, supplicated them, and left, running. He moved on to the army's camp and saw it, observing one by one the arms and troops. He observed expertly and quickly turned around. He told the commander what was there. He said, "The advance guard saw me on the road, they took me and brought me toward Kush. 6030 That proud one did not recognize me at all, he let me go and I ran right out! I went on, since I had escaped being killed, until my feet grew blisters. I examined his army and have understood all its weaknesses. It is a select army, more numerous than ants, with cutting blades and armored steeds. Most likely it has more than three hundred thousand riders, armored and wielding lances. I have not seen an army with such materiel, adornments, and tools in the king's court, except that which was sent with Qaren to war against Rome. It was of the same quality and equipment as the army that went with that proud fellow."

When the spy recounted this story, glorious Qobad knew right then that Kush had let the spy go in order to let him clearly see the army, 6040 see the equipment and adornments of the Chinese, and describe it to the Iranians, to break the spirit of the army with these words. The commander said to those assembled, "I know they are not as numerous as the army that Zahhak led against the king. See what glorious Faridun did with Zahhak, overcoming his whole army. Today, I will do that with this army. He will be ashamed to have shown his face! I will eradicate him, by the glory of Faridun and God's power! No one wishes to gird themselves for battle with the Iranians!"

Right then, he appointed several men, calling forth several champions from the army. He said to them, "This demon-born has marshaled an elite army from China against us. Let us right now, at twilight, make a trench before the army. 6050 The trench will cover all but several places, allowing passage for men and beasts. We have placed two sides, two armies on this battlefield, and we will place everyone in a hidden position. I have no doubt that this demon-born will stage a night raid on Qobad's army, as he did the last time with Nastuh, filling the king of Iran's heart with sorrow. He will approach confidently, leading his forces to attack in the night. They will all fall from the road into the trench, annihilated in our trap! The army, with blades drawn left and right, will emerge as I lead our ranks ahead. May the exalted judge, bringer of justice, grant me justice against that demon-born. I will now send an envoy, a clever and noble youth, to occupy them with conversation several days, so that the trench can be deep and tall. 6060 Keep a thorough watch on the road: their army must not become aware of this."

His nobles acclaimed him, and were cheered by his judgment and knowledge. That same night they took hold of both the road and the off-road routes, digging a trench before the troops. Its breadth and height were ten by forty spans, covered over with sticks and mud. They made many hidden places to cross that no stranger, only the troops, knew. The commander sent to Kush a rider who was eloquent and sharp-witted.

QOBAD, SON OF KAVEH, SENDS
A MESSAGE TO KUSH

He said, "O crooked one, of wicked lineage, no one as wicked as you was ever born to a mother. That evil that you did was not enough for you in the time of foul Zahhak. Now you add to that evil by not answering to the command of the king. You are surely not greater than Zahhak, see now what the heavens brought upon him. 6070 Your time is over: destiny favors Faridun. The king has been troubled by you greatly, by the harm you have caused to the army. You must understand this matter well: the king will not fail here. If he must set out upon the road himself and march against you with a few soldiers, he will come, rescue the land from you, and remove your destructiveness from China—unless, before this destruction arrives, you repent to the lofty king. And if you now beseech that court, they will, no doubt, forgive your sins. For the king is possessed of justice, magnanimity, and faith; he is not Zahhak the wayward sorcerer. If you approach with due reverence, the king will bestow upon you lands, he will give you the likes of what I have, and more. Thus have I advised you, know this now." 6080

When he heard the message from the commander of Iran, he smiled and bit his lip. He said, "It is as if the Iranians have seen great weakness from these Chinese. What power do they think they have, that they would send me a letter like this, telling me, with my kingship and lofty throne, to come and put on the fetters of servitude? Who ever chose servitude over kingship? This will not turn out well for them. Go and tell your elders that I said that this message means nothing to me. God has given me the throne of China just as he has given the throne of Iran to Faridun. I was king when you were not, Faridun did not grant me this crown and throne. Ask around, if you do not know: we have never bent our neck for anyone. We do not obey commands, we give commands. We are not of lowly lineage, we are the king of kings. 6090 There is nothing more for us to say, nothing for you but my mace and sword! We will see who destiny favors, who will have the heavens' aid."

When the envoy was leaving he sent one of his servants to go along with him. [222b] He said to him, "Observe that army in secret: what is its quality and how far away is it? How many scouts are patrolling it, guarding it during the day and at night?"

The spy went along with the man, acting like a sick man in pain, crying and bellyaching the whole way; he was dressed exactly like the Iranians. The envoy knew exactly what he was doing, but said nothing. When he came close to the army along the road, the man suddenly disappeared from his sight. The envoy came before Qobad, and repeated to him all that had been said. 6100

Then he said, "A man has come to our army in hiding, an informant, in order to become apprised of what we are doing, our men of war and materiel." The troops were ordered to gather by the riverside and sing and play fiddles. The soldiers began to open up the wine and their hullabaloo echoed through the valley. There was no advance guard and nobody on watch. The spy returned from the camp.

He said to Kush, "The Iran-army is not keeping watch over the road, they are reveling drunkenly, day and night, and they have no preparations against the enemy. It is a great army and well equipped, but their days and nights are given over to fiddles and winecups. Their great armaments and pride have made them overconfident. There is no trace of guards at night, and no one guards the route from our position." 6110 Kush was cheered by the report and became eager to mount a nighttime attack.

When Qobad became apprised that the spy from China had returned, he ordered that they watch the road, guarding it day and night. He thus sent two detachments across the trench, making haste like wind and smoke. One kept to the left, the other to the right, both sides equal, neither one greater or lesser than the other. He and his elite troops drew up ranks, on this side of the trench . . .

"Hold firm like this for three nights, so that seductive fortune favors us!"

KUSH DOES BATTLE WITH QOBAD,
AND QOBAD'S VICTORY

Kush selected a hundred thousand from his forces, veteran mail-clad riders, all with weapons and steeds of war, claws sharpened like diamonds. On the third night, he unfurled a great banner and ordered that army to charge ahead like a torrent. 6120 He sent a rider ahead to observe the fields and hills, and he saw no advance guard. No shouts of brave men, no cries of watchmen, as if they were all afraid of the dark—and a fearsome night it was. A darkness like the black smoke of hell veiled the moon's face.

The rider reported to Kush, and his face bloomed like a rose. His stirrups grew heavy, he struck his horse with his thighs, charging faster than Azorgoshasb's sacred fire. When the king closed in on the enemy, he ushered his whole force ahead. The troops then let out a roar and attacked like a demon. The breath of trumpets rose to the moon and the sky grew even darker from the army's dust; the galloping of the Arabian horses and their sharp cries were like the resurrection. The glint of the spearheads and blades of war cast light and color on the ground. 6130

Those in the lead fell right into the trench and were smashed to pieces. Those who went towards the right encountered Qobad's blade. The commander brought his mace down upon their necks in the name of the lofty and glorious Faridun.

A roar rose up from the troops and the sound of drums, raising dust so that the sky kissed the earth. When the troops' clamor rose from the battlefield, the two flanks sprung their ambush. Left and right, blades were spilling blood, sharp lances driving into the enemy. When the commander gained the upper hand over the Chinese, the ground drank its fill of brave men's blood, and all night until the pure day he gave the soil the color of coral.

Kush looked on from a corner, as if all his heart, judgment, and wits were with his army. When he saw that forces were advancing from the left and right, he was thrilled. 6140 The commander of China thought that it was his own troops that had staged those ambushes. They brought his heart cheer with their cries, the two forces charging at night with such rage. From the roaring drum and the pipes' cry, the army did not know its head from its feet. The clanging of blades terrified Mars. The galloping of riderless horses and heroes racing to fight, the torn bridles and broken arrows—the blood of brave men turned the plain horses piebald, and the piebald and white horses rusty red.

Folly overcame Kush's heart—he thought there was nothing left of the enemy that night. When dawn blazed over the mountain it was like a fire that burned his heart up. He looked around and saw his army all slain. Blood drenched the fields and valleys. The riders of Iran were all composed and ready, their blades and lances drawn for battle. 6150 One shot one man with an arrow, another took someone prisoner. A dark fog clouded his brain, as if he were no longer aware of this world. Just then he realized that Qobad had set a snare in his path and made a fool of him. Noticing the trench and the ambush, the governor of China trembled where he stood.

He said, when he finally opened his lips, "Surprise attacks at night are shameful. If I had not launched that earlier attack near the city, I would not have brought this fate on myself." Then Kush lashed out from his heart's pain and destroyed many steel-clad men.

When Qobad saw that violence from Kush, he charged toward him and said, "O wicked demon-born! You have marched your army into a trap, have you no shame or fear of God? Do you think you have even two hundred men left from this maneuver? 6160 Your throne shall remain emptied of you, you'll see no cheer or joy."

He said this, then charged with his elite troops, raising dust over the Chinese warriors. With heavy blows he unseated them, knocking them down with his attack. One group of riders took flight and another all rained down from their horses.

Kush tried to rally his men, but they did not follow him to their own destruction. They immediately took flight and when Kush saw this, he followed them.

The Iran-army left the field happy and victorious, showering praise on Qobad. Not long after, Qobad and his brave men—sword-swingers and launchers of darts and javelins . . .

And likewise, Kush and his men carried on back to the Chinese army's camp—how many were gone and how many captured! Of those hundred thousand select riders who were with Kush in that battle, 6170 no more than thirty thousand returned, with broken helmets and torn cloaks. A roar rose up from the troops, and they all threw their helmets to the ground. When Kush saw that turn of fate, he ordered the officers of the army all be killed. He saw the clamor of the army and heard grieving, he saw them all lamenting and mourning.

He rode around the field beside the troops, passing by every tent and pavilion. "If anyone in this army mourns, I'll quickly destroy them! I'll ruin the spirit of anyone who shows any sorrow for the dead."

No one dared weep for that tragedy, everyone held their breath in fear of him. Every night, he invited in the officers, the battle-riders and brave men.

With his conversation he raised their spirits, saying, "This ill-born one, Qobad, 6180 was deceitful and I was fooled; the army was destroyed by the trench. He did not face us honorably: using this trick, he cast a deceptive trap before us. I wanted to do to him what he did to us, but the azure dome turned a different way. A man may take comfort in this story, that there is a knowledge above all knowledge. If only I had been aware of the trench, I would have known better than to attack at night. But so it happened and the war has grown fierce.

"By God, until I take the throne and Qobad is killed or captive in my hands, his pavilion tent and throne lost, [223a] then have no doubt: it will be Qobad, me, the sword, and the battlefield. He has no more than fifty thousand riders; my army exceeds two hundred thousand. Qobad lacks the courage to march against us. 6190 And a larger army is needed. I will call for more troops from Tibet, which is not far from here. I'll summon troops from Chang'an and Makran. In a month I could marshal such an army that the dust it would raise in marching would block out the sun. When I end the threat of Qobad, my forces will descend on Iran like the wind. I will cast the throne and crown of Faridun into the dust, having no fear of anyone." The army was cheered and pleased by this, they took strength from the king's speech.

When the commander Qobad returned triumphantly, he took off his armor and sat upon the throne. He summoned his officers and sat down to eat, honoring the God-fearing Faridun. He drunkenly praised his brave men and distributed many gifts, and showed much kindness.

"You have shown bravery today," he said. "May God protect your lives. 6200 Because of this great struggle, now you feast on cheer and the enemy on grief. All of your labors surely pay off when you struggle: it yields throne and ornaments. The garnet is hidden in the stony mine, but with labor they get their hands on it. With labor, those great men of blessed lineage made medicines from plants. Faridun will give you the whole land and country of China as a reward. We now seek vengeance against this army of the Chinese, for Nastuh and the Iranians. It is my hope from the creator that he give assistance, that I may bring to ruin this one of demonic countenance, who holds China, that his name be effaced from the land."

QOBAD'S VICTORY-LETTER
TO KING FARIDUN

That same night he ordered a letter. "Exalted is the glorious king! When I marched on the land of Tibet, I set an ambush and dug a trench in the road. 6210 The field was covered with the enemy and I had insight into his intentions: he was going to launch a nighttime raid with his army and our worthy men would be ruined. They did exactly what I expected: the dark night came like a gale, I slung the mace of vengeance over my shoulder, and Kush's men fell into the trench. We put our blades and arrows into them, killing and taking captives. Now I have sent his banner to the king, may his armies forever be victorious. Now let us see the demon-born helpless before the faithful and just king."

Then those nobles and captives of China were mounted up; five hundred were chosen, bound up and sent before the king, and a thousand charging horses, dun and black, all worthy of being ridden by Faridun, that were taken at the time of the night raid. 6220 Whatever was left he distributed among the army, and was generous with his own property. Whoever the army held captive they ordered killed with blade and arrow. On the third day, he mobilized the troops and the trumpets let out a roar. They went on until they neared the enemy, and the troops drew up ranks.

When Kush saw them there, he said, "Qobad's confidence was inflated by that battle. He does not realize he cannot see what we're up to, just because some riders fell into a pit. He has become overconfident and charged ahead boldly. He does not know that I will now destroy him and his army in a single battle."

KUSH'S LETTER TO THE KING OF MAKRAN AND REQUEST FOR FORCES

Night fell and Kush sent out his advance guards, and called for a very clever scribe. He drafted a letter for the king of Makran, overflowing with uncouth words. 6230 "You have not hewn to the path of goodness, and you do not act as a vassal should. The brave men have once again girded themselves for battle and war against the Iranians. I wanted forces from you for the war, but not a single rider came from you. Now, once again, vengeful riders have come from Iran. We fought a battle and were pleased, Qobad's army suffered a loss. A spy has now informed me that the enemy has sent riders down the road. He has requested aid and I am certain that sooner or later, an army is coming. The troops are worried that his attack will make things very difficult.

"You must send whatever forces you have to me for this battle. If you hesitate at all in this matter, you will bring the world down on your head. 6240 When I have finished with the Iranians, by God, if I have a moment's rest, I will exact vengeful justice upon you with a fire that will burn you to the ground. Pull yourself together and marshal a force and send it to this battlefield. They are heading quickly for Chang'an. The two armies must join together in order to crush the invader's heart."

As the envoy set out on the road, Kush told him to tell the king of Makran, "If you show weakness in matters of war again, then you'd best prepare for my rage. For, to me, you'd be the greatest enemy, hidden or visible, in the world." The envoy picked up his lasso and mace, and took off charging on a swift horse.

When the sun raised its head over Taurus's station, the singing larks took wing. 6250 The two armies faced off on the field of combat and the warriors' shouts made the ground rumble. Kush and the king's commander deployed the left and right, the center and wings of their armies. Drums began to sound and the world turned ebony from the dust that army raised. He called the men of war to the battle with the sound of trumpet and pipe.

There was a loud roar from the melee, the clanging of javelins and the rain of arrows. Many were killed from both armies, the countryside was drenched by the great amounts of blood.

When Kush saw all of this he gathered a hundred riders, champions of China and brave warriors, and launched himself without fanfare at the Iran-army, leading them into the heart of the enemy force. They killed many of them, and whoever could, avoided them. Any of the Iranians who saw him fled like a deer from a wolf. 6260

When Qobad saw those troops fleeing, the haughty man was suddenly troubled. There was commotion among the warriors, fleeing in terror like asses from a lion. He was astonished and said, "What happened to you, that such an army is encountering trouble? No enemy's sword has made you flee like you're fleeing now. A fleeing army is helpless—they are no longer warriors. What is this retreat, now, have we no shame before the proud king?"

A fleeing rider called out, "The demon-born will smash us all. He has come here stealthily, in the middle of the army, leading a group of attackers. He has thrown this peerless army into turmoil and killed many of our companions. Kush made the hearts of the Chinese victorious, they've taken courage and they fight harder!" 6270

When the commander received this response, he said, "Grief unto the demon-spawn!"

Right then, he chose seventy men and threw on his battle armor. He threw himself upon the Chinese riders, blood turning the ground to a tulip-field. Faridun's army was emboldened by Qobad's blows and did justice with their counterattack. They engaged and became entangled with the enemy, the blood of brave men turning the ground to mud. The dirt all turned the color of tulips and the brave men found the ground crowded with corpses. With a blow, Kush killed a rider, and the charismatic Qobad fought on. Each blow that issued from his shoulder severed the limb of an enemy. The two armies collided in that manner, and the turning heavens were distraught by their blows. When the sun passed midday, suddenly horse and rider, [223b] 6280 Kush and Qobad, came face to face.

The commander charged at him like a gale, saying, "O ill-born tyrant, will you not die before resurrection day? Will the world never escape your misery? How long will you carry on, you drunken demon?

Today I will free the world from you, by the blows of the brave and the glory of the great ones!"

When Kush heard those words from Qobad, he was astonished and wheeled his night-black steed around. He became like the flame of Azorgoshasb, swung his blade and brought it down on the neck of Qobad's horse. The head of his mount was severed; the commander was in dire straits. He advanced on his enemy on foot and battled for a time with heavy mace.

Kush charged him once again, closing in, that he might strike him with his diamond-hued blade. The commander moved suddenly, throwing his mace at him with all his strength. 6290 The head of the mace went right into his shoulder, knocking him out of the saddle. His blade fell from his weakened arm, and the commander mounted up again. He paused and called him out again, then fought him for a long time.

Neither could gain the upper hand, and night was falling and making heads heavy with sleep. The two armies disengaged and the commander and king broke off their fight. The proud men all came before Kush, to the banquet, food and drink.

He said to them, "To my eyes, today's battle was a feast. The commander of Iran confronted us, and we raised dust over his soul. I killed his horse from under him, and that made him helpless. When those worthies retreated, they were spared from our blades. 6300 His companions all raced to him and the riders pulled away his mount. That troublemaker slipped out of my hands. If I see him again tomorrow, I will kill him with a single blow and make the hearts of his troops twist in pain."

He brought forth bright wine until midnight, opening their lips in play and relaxation. When their eyes grew heavy with wine and sleep, the brave men returned to their tents.

At dawn he prepared for battle and began to sound the drums. The hearts of the warriors leapt out of their chests from the cry of the trumpets and Indian bells. The brave men of China drew up ranks, foaming at the mouth in their rage.

Qobad said to his close companions, "This demon-born is coming hard at us today. In spite of what little strength they mustered yesterday, today they're coming fast. 6310 Hold on today and I will exact justice on the demon-born with my sword. All night I grieved bitterly. Had my mount not been slain by the sword, the Tusked would not have escaped me, even if he turned himself into a dragon. If I face him in battle today, I will fling his elephantine head into the dust."

The army was cheered by his speech and the roar of drums rose to the moon. The battle-riders grabbed their lances and drew swords that glittered like diamonds. One by one they charged at the lines, all lances and swords drawn for combat.

The king of China had laid a new trap, that he might be victorious. Whoever of that mighty force had distinguished themselves in manliness, whoever had been sent to battle the enemy armed with blades and javelins, he ordered: 6320 "Strive and show manliness, that the enemy be visited with misfortune. When the enemy witnesses this force with me at the center of my army—for they are all proud men of battle who grant unlimited strength to whatever army has them, each one surges like the sea and fights like a raging elephant—if that army engages in battle, the name of Iran will be reduced to shame. And then I will launch such a terrible attack that we will see the Iranians retreat. With one attack we will uproot them, break the hearts and backs of their commanders."

When the commander had them draw up ranks from his position, he called for a force of ten thousand brave men. He stayed with that force in the center, and another detachment made for the battlefield.

They fought a spread-out, running battle, brave men charging from every direction. 6330 Here the Chinese defeated them, there they brought the Chinese to ruin. Here the Iranians gained the upper hand, there they turned and fled from the Chinese. The air was dark like black night, the clashing of swords was bloodthirsty. The lances formed a reed-bed upon the field, and the blood made it a tulip-bed.

When the sun reached midday, Kush was overcoming the Iranians. When he saw his army gaining the upper hand, he launched an attack like a raging elephant. He was hidden, surrounded by his force, at the head of a vengeful company of men. When he had lit a fierce fire upon the Iranians, killing many with sword and lance, he struck at the heart of the army like a leopard upon a fawn, and charging right for the center.

When the commanding Qobad saw this, he charged out of the center 6340 with ten thousand worthy mail-clad knights upon armored steeds behind him. He launched himself at the Chinese, not a swordsman nor a lancer remaining in his path. Swords rained down upon him and his mount like a fierce hailstorm from the clouds.

When the broken-hearted men witnessed that brave man roaring with his Kabulian sword, they turned rapidly around, brandishing lances and battle-blades. Keen steel spilled out, heads falling from knights like leaves from trees. He launched his forces into the camp, tearing the enemy's shelter up from the root. The ground became like a blacksmiths' bazaar from the noise of heavy maces clashing. A river of blood ran over field and valley, corpses forming piles on the ground like Mount Bisotun. In that attack they killed more than four thousand veteran riders. 6350

Kush was wounded in two places in that battle, but in his manliness, remained on his feet. When he saw the enemy in his own camp, and saw cuts and wounds on his own body, he tilted his tusks like a boar, in his rage, attacking again, the brave men of China behind him like wind, roaring from their Arabian horses. The two forces mingled together so that sweat and blood spilled from their bodies. All the limbs, hands, and heads severed from necks and haunches, the blades and maces shattered, and the barding and links of mail covering field and valley, all shined like liquid silver. By the sword, the ruler of China and his forces drove the enemy out of their plundering-grounds.

Night fell and Kush said to the Chinese, "Today, the wind of your breath was a sweet zephyr ... Today, tomorrow, the battlefield! I'll blacken the world with wind and dust." 6360

He said this and entered his tent, worn down by time and toil. Then he summoned his nobles and heroes, and spoke at length about what had occurred. "Today what ruin befell us? What will the lofty heavens' turning wheel bring us? The cruel world is angered at us, I don't know what it wants with us. My army's morale was broken by the enemy, whatever pride they had is now ground into the mud. I know no solution, and I am astonished at my own good fortune. All I can see is that mountain, upon whose steep face rain turns to snow and whose peak is very high. I will soon take a position so it is behind me and delay them until reinforcements reach me. For that is a most secure place. On one side are the mountains, and in the direction of the Iranians' approach we will dig a trench in front of our forces. 6370 We will remain there until an army comes from China, the brave men of Machin and the land of Makran. Then all at once we will join the battle, and we will prevail completely. We will each show valiant effort, that fortune may again turn its face to us!"

The marcher-lords said, "This is the way, our proud guiding king!"

That same night those brave men and feisty heroes brought out their shovels and pickaxes. They dug a deep trench with one day and one night's labor.

He sent a message to Qobad: "The turning sphere has done you justice. I must rest for a few days for the army is exhausted and the horses worn down. When the army recovers from its wounds I will not turn back, I will turn to the battlefield."

Qobad was enraged by this message. He said, "That wicked-blooded man of evil lineage [224a] 6380 is frightened, trying to stall and seize his life from the leviathan's maw." He ordered a crafty and eloquent rider to deliver a response: "I have given you these three days and on the fourth, as the world-illumining sun shines, come quickly to the battlefield. When death has come, what good is a soft pillow?"

When the scout told this tale, Kush and his forces did not sleep three nights and three days. They dug many pits on the other side of the trench, each pit a trap for the enemy. They covered up the tops of the pits and no one in the world knew their secret. When the sun raised its head on the fourth day, Qobad the commander marshaled his forces. He had his army all clad in mail and made for Kush's camp.

The drums called the troops to battle, and Kush advanced with his forces. 6390 Emerging from behind the trench and pits, he joined battle with the enemy. When the army raised their hands to strike and their swords struck nothing but brains and helmets, the Chinese fled from Qobad's army like rose petals and tulips in a dust storm. He drew his army back from the field and no enemy came into their midst. They fled, humbled and wrecked, passing unharmed across those pits. Whichever of the Iranians went after them fell straight into those pits. A thousand men fell in, wounding the army's heart.

When Qobad became aware of his army's situation, they all immediately stepped down into the pits. They pulled them out of the pits, seeing them all grievously wounded. A great many with arms, legs, and heads broken, another group half-dead like drunkards. 6400

When brave Qobad saw this, he said "Woe upon the demon-spawn! He has deployed every trick and stratagem he knows, this is beyond description! What does he gain from this trench and these pitfalls when a razor-sharp blade is held at him?"

At daybreak he called forth his proud men and spoke at length about the enemy's deeds. "From this point on it would be better to fight them on foot than on horseback, crossing the field and passing the pits, filling them in when we find them. When a path is opened for us across the field, then I'll be safe from the trench and deep pits. We will march immediately to battle and make things dire for the malicious one."

He ordered that thirty thousand riders dismount and they quickly started off. All of the infantry took up shovels and filled up all the pits. 6410 He reached the edge of the trench and saw its breadth and looked into its depth and height. He could not lead his forces in that direction, lest they hear the cries of an army approaching.

THE ARMY FROM MAKRAN
APPROACHES KUSH

A month passed without battle or combat and the land found rest from heroes' blood. As the springtime returned to the lunar wheel, an army surged out of Makran. Chosen riders with horses and gear arrived upon the fields of Chang'an.

When Nushan saw this army and its materiel he departed Chang'an without delay. A hundred and thirty thousand brave champions from China were gathered under his command, all fully armed and armored and ready for battle. Two truculent armies marched boldly to battle and sought the king of China. He gave good news of the two forces from two stages' distance, and the king of China's heart was cheered. 6420 He called the officers of the army before him and expressed his joy.

Kush quickly had the two letters from Makran and Nushan read out together by the scribes. "Three hundred thousand warlike riders have I sent from Makran and China. I tell you this in confidence," they said, "this must not be known to everyone, lest the Iranians learn that an army has come and begin to move. We will approach the enemy then, and cut off their route of escape. We will surround them with our forces and bring ruin upon them, body and soul."

At night he sent a select force of ten thousand brave men and veteran riders to the two armies that Nushan had sent to the king. He ordered that that warlike company descend on them from behind the mountain. 6430

"Alert me to their arrival at night so that I am not in suspense. I will surely join the leaders of that army soon. We will turn our forces on the enemy and face them on the field."

That group raced ahead with that army and stealthily approached the mountain. Kush was alerted, and he mounted up, his head drunk with glee. He went from his camp toward the mountain, his forces racing ahead on foot. He asked the officers about the toil of their travel, then put that army in motion. He girded himself and pressed his lips together, driving them ahead without noise or commotion. No sounding of drums or striking of bells, no speech of men or sound of footsteps. At a distance of two miles from the Iranians, a world's worth of dust settled like an elephant, 6440 the Iranians unaware that a fierce lion crouched in the thicket.

When the sun cleansed the deep blue from the sky and scattered garnet across the field, a scout looked and saw an army and raced in panic toward the commander. He roared, "O worthy men of battle, the whole surface of the land is covered in soldiers, I do not know what enemy has approached, or if these are reinforcements sent by the king."

When the glorious Qobad heard those words, he raced to his horse. He came and saw that great army, so large that its center and wings were out of sight. He knew it was the enemy's army, the work of savage Kush. He said, "That evil-blooded scoundrel is not playing."

He listened to reports about that great army, how many were its riders in armor. 6450 "Now shall we be killed, our name tarnished, and the enemy cheered? Proud men, your task is before you, you must each show great bravery. For from where we are to the king is more than five hundred leagues' distance. If we show weakness in battle, the enemy will bring ruin upon us. There is now no quarter and no escape: the enemy will follow us with sharp blades drawn."

He decided to stand ahead of the army, racing with mace in hand. He saw no recourse but manhood and battle. First, he advanced to face this new army. "Let us see their number and condition," he said, "I will figure them out, understand their weaknesses."

He asked, "What is this great army? Who is its king and commander?"

Kush had them answer, "The governor of Makran has hurried to this battlefield 6460 and arrived ready for battle. An elite army from China has arrived accompanied by China's governor. They come with hearts full of fierce enthusiasm, riders numbering three hundred thousand, all renowned in battle. They have come at my request, because you have come to battle Kush."

The two armies faced each other in battle, a spectacle for the turning wheels of the sun and moon. Soon they became a pitch-colored cloud that rained arrows. The clashing of swords, maces, and lanceheads seized the reins from heroes' hands. Many troops were killed with a single blow and the rolling hills were choked with their bodies.

The brave men of Makran like ferocious lions fell upon the Iranians' center. They killed many and took captives, every lance and blade and arrow covered in blood. 6470 The riders of China crossed the trench, joining the battle as if it were a feast. When the Chinese sea came from left and right, waves of blood rose from the ground.

The Iranians remained in the middle, lacking heroes' force or Kayanid strength. There, with twelve thousand mail-clad knights on armored steeds, Qobad [224b] stood like a mountain over that incomparable force. Many riders were killed with a single blow, streams of their blood running across the meadow. They grotesquely smeared all of the Chinese. Thousands they wounded and thousands they killed.

When that war-like one concluded his attack, he found an enemy force reaching the center of his army, brave men of Makran surging like a raging lion, following Kush. All had drawn lances and blades of war, as blood turned the weeds the color of coral. 6480

Sorrow fell over them and he drew the heavy mace, calling the brave men up around him. Like a fire, he set upon the enemy, and the clanging of swords rang out. The heat and motion of their fighting was like a fog that settled on the land, their bloodstained blades like tongues of fire. As the riders crossed paths like the warp and weft of a net, the ground was a river of brave men's blood. In that charge, the commander had at once driven the center of the enemy force away from his own center. He killed several of the Makranians who had closed in like a fist clenching a blade. The two forces were joined in melee for a time, and the foxes turned to lion-tamers.

When the commanding Kush saw this, he said, "Why should I remain hidden now?" He charged out from the center of his force with six thousand commanding armored riders, throwing himself at

Qobad's army, brandished his mace and bared his chest. 6490 They had already killed many from that force, and no one could stand against him.

At nightfall, Kush caught sight of Qobad on that battlefield. The commander said to him, "Scoundrel, you have caused much confusion in this trench. You sought reinforcements from China and Makran, you have garrisoned the whole world with soldiers. Now, like a savage demon you entered the fray with your army!"

He said this and struck his head with his blade. His life remained intact in his head and helmet . . .[4]

Then he drew that mace that Qobad had held, baring his chest in rage. Qobad had held it during the battle with Kush, and now, Kush let it fly from his hand like a bewildered drunkard. It struck with great force upon the massive elephant's head, and he fell off his horse and lost his wits. His brain was so stunned by that rage that his eyes went dark. 6500 His companions seized him and pulled him away, taking him to his pavilion tent.

A rider went before Kush announcing, "The heavens once again turn in your favor. The commander now thinks it is night, bearing the weight of this army's travails. He says, 'Tomorrow, you and I must face off on this field of battle, in front of our armies.'"

When Kush heard this he returned, proud of his triumph. He summoned the nobles of Makran and China, seating them all to dine with him. While they were drinking, the king said, "Tomorrow at the break of day, we will be done with the Iranians. Everyone gird yourselves for battle."

Night fell and the commander did not regain consciousness and a cry rose up from the champions of Iran. The nobles sat in consultation, all of the renowned men gathered in that assembly. 6510 "What recourse do we have without a commander? We must all strive, so that we can spare our lives. When we all depart tonight, it must be as if we're throwing our lives at the king's threshold."

They all supported having the army leave that night and return home. A learned man brought out a pallet and had azure brocade stretched over it. They lifted the unconscious man's body and placed him on that golden bed. They packed up and quickly departed, escape

4. Lines are missing here. The next lines imply that Kush acquired Qobad's mace.

being preferable to death. The tents and pavilions remained in place, and the Kayanid banner and royal tent.

Though the army is courageous, it is a body and the commander its head. No matter how physically strong the body is, it cannot strive and struggle if ruin visits its head. It was a two-horse army, two columns, ten thousand mail-clad men armed for war. 6520 The commander remained still witless, befuddled. Not a vein of his body stirred. The army dared not stop anywhere or rest on their horses, but raced ahead helplessly, partaking of neither food nor sleep. They did not stop until dark night; the turning heavens passed and did not open their lips. They followed those who scouted ahead, the army traveling more than two stages each day.

Kush sought to battle with them when day broke, having scored a victory over his enemies the day before. They saw no army or commander, and quickly set to plundering. The mighty Kush said to his troops, "Everyone, great and small, hurry on, chase down the army! You must not tarry here."

He said much and they did not listen, and a war began to rage in the king's heart. 6530 He was astonished and went from there to his throne, when the army had finished looting. The next day he ordered thirty thousand of his men, sword-wielding riders, to hurry after the enemy, and they made haste for two days and two nights. They came near that brave army that had made it out of the battle.

When the Iranians saw the rising dust of the road, they hurriedly set up an ambush. They set up screens on two sides while a group readied their weapons. The riders of Makran and China, from out of the dust, launched their warhorses upon them. The experienced Iranians quickly gave ground, swords and lances in hand. When the horses passed the hiding places, they all turned around.

Their companions opened up the screens and their rain of arrows was thicker than rain. 6540 The two streams merged together such that they soon brought forth roses. They killed many men of Makran and China, taking their revenge on them all at once. Of that furious, vengeful army, not two bits made it back to Kush. The governor of China was disappointed by that force, and no one dared approach his throne.

When the commander Qobad regained his wits, he burst forth with harsh words for his army. "Why did you turn back? You should have left me to die! You strive and struggle for the sake of honor, that the blessed king be pleased with you. What excuse can I offer to the king now, when he asks why this army returned? Would that my wits had departed from my body altogether—what can I do, what can I say? For dying is better than leaving the king's task unfinished." 6550

The army said, "We did this in order to bring you back alive in case the king is willing to hear us—and if not, what does it matter? . . . each and every one of us would tell the king that you are not at fault for our retreat. When he shows his forgiveness, we will accept none, the blame will fall back on us. If the champion had not been borne by his riders until dawn, the army would not have escaped the swords of Kush: it would have been ground into the soil. Surely the king prefers that this army returns to him alive."

The commander was saddened by what they had said, and by their dishonorable actions, and by their retreat. The army reached them three days later. The brave men's hands were bathed in blood, and they had captured a herd of the enemy's horses. 6560 The most honorable riders in the saddle threw themselves upon the earth before him. One by one, they told him of what had come to pass on the field of battle with the army of China. He smiled and his heart was cheered, and the wilted rose bloomed.

When that army neared Amol, a detachment went ahead to the king. When the proud ruler looked upon them, he showered praises on each of them. He asked them, "What happened, that you returned so soon from that battlefield?"

The proud men answered, "A burning fire rained down upon us, an army from Makran and the land of China, an army that crowded the face of the earth, it numbered more than six hundred thousand, were you to count the riders one by one. We killed so many that the surface of the earth bloomed like roses from the Chinese riders' blood. 6570 Our commander confronted Kush, too, but he knocked him down with a blow and he lost consciousness." They told him the whole story, the deeds of Kush and actions of Qobad, and of that great army that appeared, how many champions of the great king were killed. [225a]

Faridun was downcast, hearing what they said of the disaster that had befallen his forces. The radiant king sat thinking about the battle against Kush and the events of the field. He asked about what had happened in detail, Kush's warfare and their deeds on the battlefield.

Then he said to him, "Benevolent fellow, the heavens do not always turn to our wishes. I am distraught by the deeds of this evil-natured one, than whom no one is more deserving of the gallows, yet whoever wages war against the demon-born pulls his own neck into the noose. If Qaren is here, he will go east, he is a moon over the army, the height of bravery. 6580 Nariman and Garshasp have led an army, of young and old, on the Hindus. I have no one better than him unless I were to go myself with my knights."

Nastuh said, "Your majesty, may the ravages of time be ever far from you. Since it is a year's journey from here to China, and your army scattered across the world, we can find no recourse against Kush, no one here can step forward. He has a son, a great man in Sham, who they call Kan'an. He has an army of Arabs, ten thousand. If your majesty were to give me an army, I could attack him by surprise, and reduce the number of wicked ones in the world."

NASTUH GOES TO WAR AGAINST KAN'AN, SON OF KUSH

Faridun was cheered by his words, his heart revivified and his face blossomed. He ordered an army marshaled for Nastuh, prepared for the attack. 6590 He gave them from his treasury what was available, weapons, magnificent steeds swift as smoke. The commander raced so fast from the court that the rushing wind could not keep up with his dust. The Arabs got word of this, and hurried to the side of Kan'an.

When Kan'an became aware of this, his face turned yellow as fenugreek flowers. He knew they were coming for him, that they had marshaled a vengeful army. He was wholly aware of his father's situation, how the king was greatly troubled by him, how he twice had defeated his armies and fate was astonished. Kan'an was terrified by this knowledge; he took to the desert, shedding his regal garments. He hurried to Hadramawt and the desert, and the commander came but did not find him. When he had turned everything upside down, the army and commander turned around. 6600

From there, they returned to the court, and the commander said secretly to the king, "Kan'an has fled into the desert, forsaking everything to go into hiding. In such a desert there is no water, no sleep for animals wild or tame. People cannot find a way through it, nor savage lion nor flying bird. Especially since he is not prepared for the trip, he will surely perish along the way.

Kan'an had a son by the name of Kush, who had reached the fullness of manhood. Another was born to him on the road and that ass, Kan'an, abandoned him, on a mountain wilderness higher than the clouds, a mountain with leopards and savage tigers. In those caves there was a rogue, bloodthirsty, fearless, and grim, who could pull a whale out of the sea by the teeth and take lions and leopards by the tail. 6610 Light-footed, fearless, and ambitious, he had been named Nemr by the Arabs. Nemr is a leopard that bathes his hands in blood, as leopards do.

He came across that lion-eating child and picked the poor thing up out of the dust. He gave that child, who cast a pall over the world, the name Nimrod. He kept him and raised him and showed him affection, and as he gained strength, he showed him kindness. When Nimrod grew older, he escaped from that rogue and became independent. He came to Syria and sought kingship, and from then on he turned away from God. He quarreled with the Lord in the heavens—hear this story, o judicious one!

There is another story I have read, from the discourse of the pure-hearted, righteous one. When the keeper of the world beheld him, he sent to him a leopard. 6620 Day and night, she nursed him, sometimes giving milk, sometimes meat from her prey. That baby passed three years of age, going out to explore like a leopard.

Then a hunter saw him sucking from the teats of a she-leopard. He killed that leopard brought him home, getting nothing from the kill but a small child. Because he was so small, they named him Nimrod, for the leopard was both his father and mother. When he gained strength from the sun, years, and fortune, he took hold of the throne and sat upon it. The whole world came to be under his command, every country under his command. He elevated himself and saw everything as his own work, "The world has me," he said, "as its creator."

Having taken over the whole world, he began a new war against the all-just. He sought to wage war on the heavens. His doom was a gnat, blind and lame. 6630 Such is the secret of the Lord, the exalted. He protected him from rain and dust, even making a leopard his nurse, making him reach manhood, kingship, and wealth, until he foolishly said, "Apart from me, who is the creator?" If you look into this a bit more deeply, take a look at the calf of Sameri.[5] Free your spirit from worry, and thus call out to honor God!

Listen, again, to this tale, look at the deeds and situation of Kush. The learned elder also said about the crafty Kush that when he inflicted a painful defeat on the Iran-army, he set out toward Transoxiana. When the king of Makran became aware of his approach, he became downcast and his joy was cut short. He received him with the leaders of his army, and brought him a lavish treasure, **6640** Arabian horses and Chinese brocades, throne and crown and helmet and signet ring, and a great quantity of food from the city, which provisioned his army for one month.

He passed through Makran without trouble, with his steel-clad riders. He traveled to the east and the dark dust-cloud took those regions by the sword. So it was until he reached the eastern river; he carried his pavilion tents to that frontier.

An informant who regularly traveled the river said to him, "There is a lovely place in these waters—do not veer away from it. There is an island with running streams, a resting-place fit for a king, filled with fruit and shade of willows and cypresses, its mountains full of game, pheasants and partridges. Spring and autumn, it is covered entirely in flowers, peacocks and warbling francolins, **6650** overflowing with verdure, scent, and color. Absent are terror of lion or fear of leopard."

When the twisted king heard about these places, his desires drew him there. He set out on the water and ascended mountains; the nobles of China all gathered, following him. Upon that mountain he found a turquoise mine, with gold that shone like fire.

He was pleased, sitting upon the mountain's vast height, and he laid out a mighty city there. They toiled thus for four months and its battlements rose above the moon. He erected a great marble marker, placing on it a likeness of his own face. His palms were spread open, and one or two people could sit upon them.

An inscription on it read: "This is the face of the proud Kush, who in time of battle is like an inferno, who seizes the crowns of kings by the mace, conqueror of the east by his glory and might." **6660**

There he wrote down his own deeds. In that city he founded, he settled thirty thousand men and women—farmers and merchants and

---

5. "The calf of Sameri" is the golden calf of the Israelites.

craftspeople. He brought them from their own country and put them in the city, endowing them with all manner of property. He gave food, cows, asses, and sheep to the merchants and cultivators. They named that city Kushan, founded by Kush, victory-seeker. The Chinese, they called it Faruneh, a city well-stocked with provisions and merchandise.[6] At the year's end he ordered that everyone gather as a flock before that mammoth of a man, bowing before his visage, praising his rule.

From there, he marched his army towards Makran. When word of his arrival reached Makran, [225b] the commander of Makran once again opened the treasury's doors and brought out everything. 6670 He accepted him and brought him all manner of Chinese brocades and coils of gold wire. Those victuals that he brought forth, he supplemented by his own stores. He hosted the king for one month, at the banquet, polo field, and hunting ground.

At the start of the new month the cry of pipes arose, and that devoted servant packed up his pavilion tent. The king of Makran was two stages along the way when the malevolent king seized him and killed him. He gave his palace and treasure over to plunder, with no shame before the Lord and no punishment. A fire was lit before him, and he had all his kin burned up. He gave his crown and throne to Nushan, transforming his fortunes all at once. He carried whatever pleased him from the tent—such was the reward he gave to that drunkard!

From there, he went toward the city of Chang'an, having met no one greater than himself. 6680 He called on a lion-hearted man to come before him, and spoke to him at length concerning Faridun. He said, "You must go to his threshold, I need someone to uncover his secrets. Go see his army—their number and condition—with your own eyes and by informants. See what is on Faridun's mind, what he has done with that humiliated army. If the king has plans for us, send me a message in secret." He gave him a good quantity of brocade and dinars, sending him on a swift steed.

The king sat confidently on the throne, his heart was relieved of worries. And every night he saw a beautiful girl, and married her the next day. Even if nothing about her pleased him, he had her shut in his bedchambers. Whoever was made pregnant by him, he would not

6. The term Faruneh may be a corruption of Farghaneh.

release without first killing her. 6690 Women, in fear of the malevolent king's blade, destroyed the children in their own wombs.

A sweet-lipped girl of the Makranians pleased him day and night. Her body like a rose, navel and breasts of silk, lips of sugar and locks of ambergris, her wink would bring ruin upon the king of sorcerers, the moon's heart bound in servitude to her face, with her heart more upright, her flirtatious glances, her stature like a boxwood, her skin like lilies, her eloquent speech and comportment like a peacock. The king called her Negarin.

Negarin was surely an adornment of the heart, and kin to none other than the king of Makran. His brother's daughter she was, and he kept her secret from the king. Whomever he saw of that seed, he killed, and that line suffered ill fortune. His love that he had before for Negarin still remained in his heart, a wound of grief.[7] 6700 He sat in his grief many days, his heart far from toil and injury far from his spirit. The king's heart was cheered by her, sometimes by her caressing, sometimes her kisses, sometimes her embrace.

He said to her, "O precious treasure, who has expressed no wish to us, have one wish and let your heart not veer away, for I never have any complaint of you."

Negarin thus answered him, saying, "May fortune ever accompany you. Your glory, o king, gives me cheer and greatness, benefit and peace. I have command over your harem, and I would willingly lay down my life for you. My wish is the king's happiness, that is all, and that wish is attainable."

He said to her, "Do not seek separation from me, without further ado, ask something of me."

She said to him, "O king, do not increase my troubles, I have whatever treasure I could want. 6710 A person who has wishes wants things that they cannot obtain. I indeed have no wants now, the treasure I have now is beyond description. If the king would permit it, I would not say anything, for I fear speaking importunately."

"If you wished for kingship," he said, "I'd not begrudge your request, my dear companion."

She said to him, "Now the king speaks this way to his faithful servant. I have no need of anything in the world, however I do have one

7. The reference here is to the first Negarin, his wife who died (lines 4803–30).

question. For many years, I have held these words in my heart, and my heart breaks."

The king said to her, "Do not worry, ask whatever you wish and do not let your heart be vexed."

Negarin said to him, "O benevolent one, tell me the story of when you marched your army from China, and were entrapped by the enemy, 6720 by the army of Faridun and great wounds, with a mountainside at your back. You used no stratagem against the enemy, you did not shoot at them. When you called on the king of Makran, you wrote this request in a letter. He sent an army equipped for battle that dealt with the enemy right away.

"While you traveled, as king, you traversed the land of Makran. He brought so much treasure before you that the elephants were burdened by carrying it. Your army was fed and provisioned for one month, such that food became scarce in the land. And after that, when you returned from the east, he received you with his nobles. Once again, he brought before you so much that none of his subjects had seen its like. He opened up the doors of his father's treasury, provisioned your army for forty days. 6730 When you prepared to come to China, he traveled two stages along the way with you, for he wanted to travel with you. The proud king cut him in half. When he made this his recompense, the world despaired of the king of China. Now I wish for the radiant king to show me, his servant, what sin he committed. For none of the kings of old ever treated their subjects in this way. No one ever rendered the kind of devotion for which the ruler of China killed him like an enemy. When it came time for his reward he got the sword, the tomb grieved for him."

Kush was suddenly astonished by this question, he said to her, "O impudent prideful one! What business do you have with such a story? Unwittingly supplicating the tail of a snake, you've become so careless with your affectations that you can ask just any kind of question! 6740 Time and toil would make my heart bleed, if even Faridun were to ask me this question! You'll be in a position to see what's what. Your blood led you to this question. If I should hold back in answering, I would be unwittingly confessing my guilt. First, I will give you a straight answer. I will grant you your heart's desire, first. Then I will give you your just desserts, for this wish has caused me to mistrust you.

"When Faridun killed the world's king, everything was soaked in the whale's maw. I fled the mountain of Besila, weeping as I sought refuge. The king of Makran was the first to rebel against my authority, the others all followed him. Everyone saw his actions and the nobles followed his example. Then, two times, an army came from Iran and I called on him for soldiers and materiel. 6750 He acted as though he'd never again see my face, he sent me neither assistance nor a response. And then, when I went to the king's threshold, an army came from the king of Besila.[8] So few soldiers were with Abtin, who brought ruination to the whole country of China!

"Would that he had charged in to attack him, marched his forces on him, China would have suffered no harm, nor would the deeds of the malevolent one have succeeded. Nushan would have overcome him and not worried about the situation. He was a horse to a shepherd, and the flock's leaders would have been able to deal with Abtin. But he did not act, and what he did in recent days, he did out of fear, that pathetic man! That was the answer, now this is the reward!" he said, and struck her head with the blade of vengeance. The bouquet of flowers was chopped in half by his blade, and he did not lament for that beautiful face. 6760

The world was split like locks of black hair, his brain became witless and fearless from wine. His heart filled with desire for Negarin, his hungover eyes sung her praises. He cried out and sought her for a long time, and no one dared tell him what had happened to her. Finally, as he remembered what he had done, he contorted and his joy was cut short. He became ashamed and began to weep, opening the gates of pain onto himself.

"This sin is entirely my own," he said. "I said, 'Ask me for something.' Now she has asked, and tasted my retribution." He drew a red veil of blood over his head.

The astute Nushan came to his side, saying, "Rise up from the dust and sit on your throne. [226a] This ill temper has become natural to you, it cannot simply be cast aside. One cannot escape from one's constitution and nature, from what God has fated us to have." 6770 He secretly sought out beautiful women, from the kings, warriors, and nobles. He sent proud men everywhere, to Khan and China and the

---

8. "When I went to the king's threshold" refers to his visit to Zahhak.

Eastern Lands.[9] He had them say, "I want one from each of you, send your most impressive virgins."

From every land and country, whatever nobles there were sent him virgins. A hundred and twenty of those elite moon-faced beauties arrived in the court of the ruler of China. He saw those idols, they did not please him. He discriminatingly passed them on to others.

They said to him, "Your majesty, there is a moon-faced beauty in Qandahar, of whose locks they weave armor and mail, and they illuminate the dark night with her face. Her seed is of a folk of noble race, of such beauty you'd say she was born to a houri. Traveling across the whole earth, you would find her like nowhere in the world. 6780 Her stature is like a cypress and eyes like a messenger angel, her gait like a peacock, her words sweet wine. If the king wants that girl, he would not find any mate but her."

He sent for that girl to come, brought her to him and seated her in luxury. He seized her and saw her one night, he was not pleased, and selected no one. No one took the place of Negarin, desire for her never left his head. Being untroubled and feeling secure, his spirit filled with thoughts of himself, he feared no one but the king of Iran, passing his time with nothing but wine and medicines.

The rider whom he had sent from China to Iran and instructed at length returned, appearing with word of the king and his champions and proud men. He said, "That lofty king has no desire for war or plans for attack. 6790 He has set his heart on justice and generosity, his forces scattered across the world. In Iran, he has made the whole country prosperous. He has filled the world with justice and generosity. He distributed his treasure in the land of Iran, emptied the treasury and reduced suffering. Night and day, his own heart set on manly work, he sorely broke the heart of hatred."

Kush's heart was cheered by this and he said, "May the stars favor you."

In that security, he took up the path of pleasure, wine, and relaxation, and added to his enjoyment. He said, "Whoever saw a king like me, with my glory and palace, with treasure and armies? Zahhak had so much magnificence and treasure that his people were oppressed.

9. "Khan" may have been changed from "Rum" or "Hend" by a copyist's error; the "Eastern Lands" are Khavarestan.

With my own hands, twice I defeated Faridun's army. He learned his lesson and has now left me alone."

Then in the land of China, wherever was ruined, 6800 the experienced one used his wealth to make it prosperous, and so he cheered the hearts of his subjects. But having cleaned out his treasury in this manner also burdened his heart. He took many valuable things from the people, from whoever had any wealth. Wherever in the land he found out about anyone with wealth, he left them with neither wealth nor peace. He made the world prosper from them and their treasure, until the people were oppressed by him. When the world saw this, it raised its head in rebellion, shrouded itself in mail, and drew its head away from the collar of servitude, its tongue lamenting uselessly.

To people who thought ill of him, he said, "I know no equal to myself. If I want, I'll make the world prosper, and if I were suddenly to bring ruin, its very life is in my hands, its death at the point of my blade and my bow. 6810 Because life and death come from me . . ."

Since the ignorant, from foolishness and the wise, from fear, acquiesced to the words of the accursed demon, he was blown up in his own mind, and began speaking of himself as creator.

No one living dared speak up to say, "You are a servant from among the servants!"

A learned master lamented of Kush, as did all who were wise and sharp-witted.

He asked him, "Who then am I? In this vast world, what am I about?"

"You," he said, "pay the salaries, you provide the food and other payments. And if a man says, 'You are the king,' you destroy him with Indian steel." Neither merchant, priest, nor road-guide dared call him anything but "God." For forty years, things carried on this way. He was well satisfied with what the days brought him. 6820

When Qaren had returned from the land of the Slavs and Rome, having conquered by force every land and country, he had reached the east and the west, Beja and Nubia all upended.[10] He had one of his nobles seated in every country, entrusted with veteran soldiers. He returned to his royal court victorious, having taken booty and tribute from every country. He took his repose beside the king for a year,

---

10. Beja, also written Bojjeh, is the region between the Nile and the Red Sea north of Eritrea, named after the Beja, a pastoral nomadic people.

the turning heavens a crown upon his head. He related all of the battles he'd fought to the king, who was pleased at his deeds and his report.

THE PEOPLE SEEK JUSTICE FROM KUSH, KING OF CHINA

So it happened that one day, from the land of China, fifty of the wisest sages came crying out to the king's threshold—oppressed people, seeking justice. "Alas, o king, answer our cries, for we have no one to answer our cries but you! You have purged the world of the Zahhakians, by the power of God and the glory of the great kings. 6830 India and Rome have prospered by your justice, not an inch of the country remains in ruin. You have made the earth prosper by your mace, you made everywhere radiate with greatness. By your blade, oppression shrinks away and by your justice, the wicked are driven into hiding. The world reposes—and we suffer, without children, estates, or treasure. A great pig sits on the throne of China, the whole land suffers at his hand. The wealthy of that land have become poor, oppressive, corrupt, and ill-tempered. He calls himself only 'God.' Do not let them continue like that, o king of unclouded judgment!"

The king was saddened by what they had said and felt himself personally responsible. He said, "O higher than the moon and sun, it is you who invest hearts with hatred or kindness. You gave him such a fate in which his belief in you is corrupted. 6840 He has suddenly become ungrateful to you, with no memory of death or difficulty."

He commanded the warlike Qaren to come quickly to his assembly. He called him forth, seated him, and praised him to the high heavens, and said, "My good companion, my brave rider and general, give me some insight, by your wit and judgment, that you may relieve me of Kush's torments. The world is filled with justice, content except for China, Makran, and those regions.

"The whole face of the world is in a slumber, except China, which is tormented by that cur. He has become so proud and prosperous from the suffering of his people and his long reign. Whoever says they are unique in all the world—let's see them create a living creature! If I let him remain as he is, I am maintaining his drunken ignorance. 6850 The all-powerful judge will ask me to account for the days of that demon's injustice. Twice I have sent armies at him, and they came running back to this court.

"Even if I made you suffer, weakened your limbs and your armor, I see no one else from among the Iranians who would gird themselves for this conflict. If you did not defeat Kush in battle . . .

"My army and treasure are all at your disposal! Coins, horses, garments, and helmets—distribute them, take with you as much as you need. If you diminish his oppression, he is the last of the seed of Zahhak, and the world will be purged of their oppression when that evil-natured one is eliminated. If you bring him back here in chains, your crown will reach as high as the heavens. 6860 I would like to get a look at the face of that monstrous demon who killed so many brave men of Iran. When you become victorious over the land of China, entrust that land to the lion-hearted Nastuh. Give him that country, its crown and throne, and return contented and victorious."

Qaren said to him, "I stake my life on fulfilling this request. I will do more than what I have been asked by the king, ruler of the world, in this worthy court." [226b]

He departed that lofty palace and sent his messengers searching in every direction. He called the king's nobles to the court, such that there was not a rider left in Iran. Of those elite, renowned riders, three hundred thousand arrived before him. Qaren vetted those brave men, having seen each of them in battle. Each of them a proud swordsman who could cut through enemy lines—ornament of armies, crushers of armies. 6870 Whoever failed to pass muster was immediately removed from the ranks, even if they had a horse. The indigent elderly, those without food, the weak—not one of these was listed in the registers. Having selected his army in this manner, he gave them arms and money, horses and saddles. He packed up his camp from Amol, carrying much materiel and new baggage.

Faridun came and saw that army with all its equipment. He was very much satisfied and he praised that good-hearted elite champion: "May you be victorious and sorrows stay far from you. Remain hale and whole and return in good cheer."

The army was set in motion at the start of the month of Mehr, the new month showing its face upon the heavens. As the advance guard crossed the first stage, it was a new army that now followed them. So they marched on, the main force a sea of champions, wave after wave of troops. 6880 It was as if the earth itself were in motion, hill and val-ley turned to iron. When they crossed into the land of Turan, they landed like fire in straw. They reached out to plunder and no one escaped from their swords unharmed.

A group of evil-doers holed up in a fortress. They did not spare any of them. The general showed mercy to whomever expressed support for Faridun . . . They prepared provisions and joined the champions, hearts wounded and weeping from Kush's torments.

When the mighty Kush found out that a massive army approached from Iran, he was full of worry and called on his troops. He invited his officers to appear at his court—from Machin and Makran and Tibet they came, racing like wind along the road. There were so many tents, great and small, the land of China was covered in brocade. 6890

He chose from among them seven times, counting a hundred thou-sand in his pay registers. Veterans all, and lion-hearted, their great numbers put the stars to shame. He bestowed a great reward of cash on them, and on the tenth day they departed Chang'an. Drums roared and banners unfurled, and the world turned violet-colored from the dust they kicked up. When the sun returned to the sky, in their camp their hearts were racing.

He called all the officers of the army before him, and told them many stories of their enemy. "The Iranians are always testing me; now a powerful army is advancing. For all of the good things I have done, instead of sending an army back against them—for twice I defeated their armies—not a single rider was sent in a counterattack. I never had designs on the land of Iran, never sent an army to attack them. 6900

"And so it was until their malevolence grew out of control—it grew and flourished. So I think that if I march an army on Iran and attack them, my armies will strip the fields bare and paint the countryside red with blood. I have made one corner of the world prosperous, the other side must now be ruined. Until I catch the thief, the thief will continue to rob me and leave me in dire straits.

"I long to avenge Zahhak, and I remain discontented about this. To that effect, I have sworn an oath, by the white-bright day and azure night, to bring ruination on my enemy's lands, and take vengeance for my own king. I will bring him down from his throne and hang him from the gallows, and not leave a single Iranian knight remaining. For an ignorant and foolish man counts silence as weakness. 6910 The nobles sing his praises and have called him the great king of the Turks and China."

The all answered, "By your might, the earth will quake under the head of your mace. You can say more—you can stake a claim on the throne of Faridun!" When the king sat back down on his turquoise throne, his army dispersed.

The officers of both groups slept for a while, until the morning light rose through the sky. The roar of drums rose up, and the song of pipes, and troops and general marched out. They went until they reached Qaren with his advance guard surrounding his camp.

At that moment, they collided. A melee broke out, a great scrum. The two groups engaged with such fury that a mountain would tremble from their blows. There were no more than a thousand of Faridun's forces and a hundred worthy men were killed. 6920 They retreated, wounded from the fight, they could not engage in battle more than a short time. A force of more than ten thousand came after them, mailclad with gleaming steel blades. They followed them more than three leagues, here and there launching arrows and spears.

They won the fight again, and told the king, who held his head high, "When we engaged the enemy, we mixed the dust they raised with blood. They killed some, and others fled in such haste that their armor fell off their bodies."

Kush's heart soared with joy and opened the gates of praise upon them.

The defeated troops marched back to their general. "We confronted their advance guard and were met with spearheads, swords, and daggers. We were not there more than a short time, there were ten of them for each one of us. 6930 When a hundred and two of our knights were killed, were had no choice but to turn back."

The general was saddened by this, and his brain churned with ancient hatred. He took it as a bad omen that the enemy was first to bathe its hands in brave men's blood.

He called Nastuh forward, and said to him, "Great man of pure faith, go and select six thousand of the troops, racers and battle riders, see what you can do to exact vengeance against the Chinese."

Nastuh girded himself and marched his troops, keeping fewer than half of them close to himself. The rest he put under the command of a nobleman, saying to him, "O renowned brave man, go and show your-

self so that the Chinese charge and draw near you, show weakness in
the fight, give ground and flee at the time of confrontation. 6940
When their vanguard comes charging after you, the time has come.
Pass by me and I will spring the ambush. Then, answer with your
swords and join the attack."

He said this and set up an ambush—a lion would not dare cross
that field. His forces reached their vanguard, which let out breath like
fire. A roar rose from the Turks and a melee ensued, blades glinted and
arrows rained down.[11]

When Faridun's forces saw mighty blows land, they at once turned
their backs, fleeing with the brave men of China in pursuit, until they
passed by where the ambush was set. Proud Nastuh and his forces
sprung their ambush and closed off the route. The fleeing detachment
turned back around and streams of blood flowed across that plain.
When they split open the astonished lions, here splitting open someone's chest, there a head, 6950 a mass of the dead piled up—you'd
think venom had fallen from the sky.

The brave men of Iran came upon the wolves like a dark night and
found them a shepherdless flock. They let loose against their enemies
like savage lions and drunk elephants. When they had killed a great
number with their blades, the rest sought an escape route. Nastuh
charged after those who were running, galloping fleet-footed steeds
giving their sweat and blood.

So it went on until they reached the Chinese camp; it was as if
blood spattered the Pleiades. More than three thousand brave men
were killed, the whole field covered with shining steel armor. He
returned to Qaren wreathed in victory and well satisfied. He kissed the
shoulders and chest of the champion, and cried out supplications, saying "O pure man who recognizes the good, I thank you for granting
my wish!" 6960

The next day the army set out, and the world was filled with the cry
of drums and pipes. Two forces came face to face, out of the thickets,
meadows, and rivers. The capable king of China sent knights to

11. Kush's troops are referred to as Turks here because early medieval Persian geographical knowledge closely associated China with the pastoralists who ruled Central
Asia and sometimes China itself, as in the period of the Tabghach Northern Wei Dynasty's rule over China's central plain—see introduction.

observe, [227a] as much as they could, the makeup of the enemy army and what commander had been sent.

One of the men-at-arms came, saw the army and horses, and raced back quick as the fire of Azorgoshasb. "It is an army," he said, "like the Sea of China, ready for battle and racing to attack. Under the weight and gear of the warriors, the earth shakes like the hearts of the wicked. Their horses' rumbling stirs up so much dust that it blocks out the moon. Their general is the benighted Qaren, brother of the one who, last time, you hit on the head with a mace, and routed his army." 6970

Kush said to him, "This worthless man will get worse than what his brother got."

Qaren did not send any messages to him, and Kush did not rest during that battle.

When dawn broke like a falcon's wings spreading the sun's glory across the field, a war cry rose up from both positions. A roar emitted from the drums and the cry of pipes. When the brave men's banners flew, General Qaren deployed his forces. He positioned Nastuh on the right with a world-conquering army, as he had requested. The brave Taliman he sent to the left with a well-prepared force. He positioned himself in the center, banners right behind him and Qobad in front of him.

And so, when Kush opened his eyes, he saw an army and the world in an uproar. He was astonished and he deployed his own forces— you'd think they had seized his brain. 6980 Korukhan, who was the king ruling over Qandahar, deployed his troops in a sturdy configuration. He gave him the right wing of his army and he went with his troops straying far from their base. The left wing he gave to Qara—he and no other king ruled the kingdom of Tibet. Kush placed himself in the center.

A thunderous roar issued from the two armies, as if Mars itself cried out, and the earth moaned to the heavens, and a great melee broke out between the two sides. Streams of blood ran across the field and all the armor of the fallen piled up in iron hillocks. From the blood-shedding swords and the striking of lances, the evildoers could not tell their reins from stirrups. The shower of spear-points and shuddering of bows stole their wits.

It went on like this until the brave and ambitious Nastuh launched an attack with the intensity of an inferno. 6990 He threw himself upon Qara like a mountain, circling behind him and breaking away from the brave men of his company.

Qara advanced with the Tibetan forces, a hundred and thirty thousand men and more on the march. Those two armies were engaged in battle; the world grieved from the mighty blows they struck. A wind blew and raised black dust that blocked and bewildered the sun.

Nastuh charged, mace in hand, and no living person he found escaped his reach. He went on until he reached the king of Tibet and roared like a lion when he saw him. He launched a sturdy javelin straight at him, its point went through him and stuck out of his back. When the Turks of Tibet saw that their king had fallen from his saddle into the black dust, slain, they turned right around—they were put to flight by that blow.

QAREN FIGHTS KUSH

When Qaren, from his position in the center, saw that defeat, he mounted a well-rested horse. 7000 He set upon the center of their army and attacked, smiting a knight with each of his blows.

Kush and his forces received him, each of them a one-man army. One by one, the knights and Turks of China shrunk away from Qaren. Every time a brave man charges into battle, he exposes his soul to injury. So it went, until many of the Turks were killed with heavy blows.

At that point the mighty Kush set upon the Iranians like a wolf with his mace. The mass of troops panicked like a flock of sheep whenever they saw him. The two armies so feared the Turks, you'd think the heavens grieved. When the sun's face paled and yellowed, the ground raced to drink up the blood.

The two warriors collided, Qaren and the haughty Kush. 7010 They engaged in battle with each other, their mouths dry and their breath heavy. General Qaren, when he recognized Kush, raged at him like a smoking inferno.

The ruler of China did not recognize him, but when he saw that brave and warlike man, said to himself, "Surely this is Qaren, an iron mountain in battle." He fought him with blade and lance, here striking at his head, there at his sides.

When Qaren saw such bravery from Kush, he was startled by his riding and his moves. Soon, Kush, like a drunken elephant, took a piercing javelin in his hand and struck, but the champion held up a shield, so it pierced only the shield. The general pulled out the javelin and struck, drawing blood from Kush's horse's chest. The javelin had pierced its liver and emerged through its thigh, and the charismatic warrior lost grip of his reins. 7020

He fell right off his horse, but sprang up from the ground, that ferocious king. On foot, he ran towards Qaren as if to tear up the earth. Qaren joined the battle with him on foot, roaring and leaping like a mad lion. The knights of China arrived like Azorgoshasb, bringing their horses close to him.

Kush raced to remount, astonishing the man-eating lion. He struck the horse's thigh and, like a soaring falcon, made straight for Qaren and joined the battle again.

When Qaren saw such ferocity from the ruler of China, he said, "May you vanish out of your saddle! In the whole world, I have never seen someone as absurd as you! The battlefield is like a game to you. Kingship and rank do not suit you, nor command, treasure, signet ring, and crown! Glorious Faridun is more deserving, he is like a divine messenger angel, and you are like a bull demon!" 7030

He said this and attacked him, scattering dust over the vast earth, the brave men of Iran behind him, roaring, forcing the Turks to turn their faces and flee. All at once they uprooted them and scattered them back into their camp. When the Iranians found strength, the army of Tibet was driven off. Fleeing, they left that chaos, and their flight was truly a victory.

Night fell and the cheered and victorious general praised God, granter of victory. He came to the camp and sat down to eat; they were all drunk on victory and wine. There were many dead bodies on that battlefield, thirty thousand Chinese and Makranians.

The emperor of China with his frustrated army dismounted from their warhorses. He saw that the officers of his army had all been killed, the Tibetan army had departed completely, 7040 and he noticed his own army's distress at so many dead and wounded from among their ranks, while the Iranian riders were so strong and brave that each one was like a savage lion. They saw no choice but to turn back, leaving their pavilions and tents where they stood. The army packed up and moved their baggage, marching back to the city of Chang'an like the wind.

When day broke and Qaren became aware that Kush had returned to his base, he sent after him thirty thousand elite riders of Iran. The army went and stopped on the battlefield. Qaren distributed the tents to those who were in the battle. Passing the pavilions and tents and pack animals left behind by the warriors of China, on the third day they came upon that army, taking many captives along the road.

They brought word of Kush to that devotee of the sovereign, saying that he had gone to the city of Chang'an and shut the gates. 7050 The general offered a prayer to the just and let go the captives of China. He ordered that one be killed, in revenge. All the others returned happily to China. On the fourth day the army occupied plains, valleys, and hills, where they took up positions within a league of Chang'an, taking over those thickets, plains, and streams.

When the king of China saw that the army had come, all the tents set up stretching a long way back from the road, he entrusted the gates to his officers. He gave them limitless ... He decked the fortress with brave, manly men, setting up a catapult on each tower.

So many mangonels and ballistas made the turning heavens shrink back in fear. Surrounding the city was a great moat that a mighty elephant could not cross. [227b] He cut a path from the city and it filled with water, and the troops and the city did not sleep. 7060

The next day, the general surrounded the city and saw that biting poison there. He was disappointed and thought hard about what to do, and then made for the great forests. He brought back a number of tall trees that elephants struggled to carry. He set up mangonels all around and let loose great boulders. Bows released arrows from both sides, the battle-hungry warrior dismounted and protected himself with a shield.

For two months, the battle carried on with casualties on both sides. Chang'an was not to be taken by assault, and the officers felt their situation growing more and more difficult.

The warriors joined the battle once again, taking casualties from stones and arrows. They fought twice a day, with stones and gleaming steel-headed arrows. Things carried on like this for another four months, and the fortress was not wrecked by arrows and stones. 7070 General Qaren had no options, and fervently supplicated the creator. Autumn came, and stormy days, leaving the brave men no recourse. Many were killed on both sides, wounded by stones and destroyed.

One day, Qaren was frustrated, and the earth was free of wind and rain. He went to the city gate with his forces, commanding that they alert the king. They brought word to Kush, and right then he sent an old man who knew the language of the Iranians. He honored well the ways and customs of the great kings. Approaching the champion and paying him his respects, he repeated his praises to him at length.

Qaren said to him, "My good fellow, you must swear a solemn oath, that whatever I say to you, you repeat to Kush in the presence of wise nobles." 7080

The envoy accepted, swearing this oath, "I will repeat your words precisely to the ruler of China in the presence of that company, for they are learned men of good judgment."

Qaren said to him, "Tell him, why do you angrily dishonor yourself? Do not think for a moment, o king of China, that I will return to the land of Iran without having bound your hands and feet and installed the brave Nastuh in your place, even if I must wait for years. By God, know that if I should return in shame while you rest in peace and comfort, God would not be pleased that we had given our troops over to slaughter in this way to crown our heads with greatness.

"If you would, for a brief while, venture out of the city, not alone, but with a few trusted companions, I will emerge from within the ranks of my army, and we can both meet on the battlefield. 7090 Let us see whose time the turning of the heavens will bring to an end. If I am destroyed at your hands, the commander is at your disposal and the army too. Do whatever pleases you, for he who is victor over the earth is king. And if I should overcome you, your rebellion will be put to rest. I will do with you whatever I see fit if my wish comes true."

The man departed and delivered Qaren's message before the nobles, not in private. Kush was embarrassed, the color left his face and his wits left his brain. He was troubled about what to do, nothing he could think of seemed free of shame. If he were to face the champion in battle he would consign his name to the dust.

First, he said, "If I turn him down, wouldn't fierce men of war say about me that 7100 the ruler of China did not face a warrior in combat, because his body was not able?" Second, he took faith in his own satanic strength, and third, he was ashamed before this assembly, and his heart was warm with rage against the Iranians.

He said to the envoy, "Go. Go back and tell him, 'You have issued a challenge of combat. If you were before me today, I would be able to face you in battle. In the morning when I awake, if I take too long to arrive, you may hold it against me.'"

The envoy delivered this reply to him, he repeated all of his words from start to finish. Qaren's heart fluttered with joy from the king of China's reply, and he praised the creator. In his joy, he could not sleep all night, his mind was anxious. Could it now be that that man of crooked creed would be captured for his injustice? 7110 When injustice from the king grows too great, time and fate will seize his crown. No unjust man ever walked the earth but the seeds of his injustice bore fruit.

When dawn's light soared across the heavens and opened the gates of brilliance upon the world, a man brought out the stores of combat gear and equipped Kush and returned. Right then, the ruler of China donned weapons he chose for the battle. He donned a gleaming coat of mail from Tibet and knotted its belt. Weapons never had any effect on it, neither swords nor armor-piercing arrows. He placed mail of Chinese make on his head, and wrapped a girdle around his waist and heart. He donned a red coat of mail over this and emerged with a force of brave men. A thousand riders followed behind him, and he held a blade of Indian steel in his hand. 7120 He crossed the moat and took his position on the battlefield.

He quickly sent a message to Qaren, as the sun appeared high in the sky. "Long have I waited for you to meet me on the battlefield."

Qaren laughed at his message as if he knew his fate. He said, "The world must be coming to an end for Kush to show such bravery. I have scared him with my boldness, calling him out on the battlefield in this way." He called for a girdle and the trappings of a brave champion and donned a coat of mail. He chose a thousand riders from among his forces and came out onto the battlefield.

General Qobad and Nastuh were behind him, a spear like a coiling serpent in his hand. The charismatic Qobad entreated him, "Allow me to go into battle instead, 7130 so I can get my revenge on him and satisfaction from the world."

Qaren said to him, "Do not say such words, you dishonor yourself before us. You cannot stand toe to toe with him when he comes out to fight, raging with his mace. Besides, we called this fight, do not resort to unfaithfulness. He did not seek a fight with you, and he would not stay on the field for long. He would use that as an excuse to return to his city, and we would be left with nothing but grief and suffering."

He said this and then hurried to the fight, racing toward the Chinese troops like smoke. Kush emerged from among his troops and came before Qaren ready to fight. They swore an oath that no one from among their troops would come near the contest.

Then they reached for their swords, two lions on the hunt, two raging elephants, 7140 attacking like wind and dust, the battlefield groaning beneath them. From the cries of those brave men and their sword-blows, their hearts pounded as if to leap out of their chests.

When their blades were cracked, they cast them aside and began to fight with lances. Their spear-points did not wound, their blows were ineffective. They resorted to every tactic and stratagem but could not wound each other with their lances. They were so worn out, suddenly, that they collapsed witless on their horses.

Then they both came to and charged at each other in a rage. They surged ahead, roaring like battling lions, and again they let loose on each other, heads hanging from heavy mace blows. It went on until the blood grew weak in their veins, no strength left in the men or speed in the horses. 7150 With that weakness, the king of China slackened, his spite-filled head drifting. He swung his mace.

Qaren held up his shield, he had more strength than his opponent. When the ruler of China circled around him, Qaren roared upon the flat field, raised up his mace and standing tall, as his opponent guarded his head and neck. He brought his heavy mace down on Kush's horse's head and it fell, trapping his thigh. [228a] The general landed another blow on Kush's fearsome head with his mace.

He collapsed and lost consciousness from that mighty blow. He was defeated. The general dismounted like the wind, cast aside his mace and fell upon him.

When the Chinese knights saw this from their side, they made an attack, in pain and rage. Thus Nastuh and the glorious Qobad spurred their horses on like the wind. 7160 They threw themselves at the Chinese, striking at their torsos and heads, until they killed seventy men at the edge of the moat. The dust of battle lifted. Qobad came and the two of them tied Kush's hands and threw him over their horse like a drunkard, lest the king try to fight back, deaf to fate's words.

When the commander of Iran came back victorious, a clear cry rose up from the Iran-army. "Victory to Faridun! His enemies' bodies are red as a tulip field!"

He quickly tied up Kush. Destiny had counseled his heart. They tied him up with a single piece of rope, impossible to untie. He set a thousand men to guard him, elite brave men of war selected from his troops.

Such is the final outcome of worldly things: sweet drink to outward appearances, poison inside. 7170 One is raised up from the pits by the heavens' turning wheel, and just so, it lowers him back beneath the dust. If you have taken your portion from it, it also gives you its poison. If it gives your heart satisfaction, know that one day it will leave you behind. If you are wise, don't set your heart on it, for its ways are corrupt and its effects ruinous.

The world-champion, king-capturing Qaren pleaded like Mercury, "O higher than the highest, the wind and mighty mountains at your command, you gave me strength and chance. You made me the victor. I shall not boast to anyone."

When he returned from his prayer, he brought brave and proud men from the army, and set up places of repose. He spoke and ate and gave gifts. In that cheer his night was turned to day, for God had fated him to be the victor. 7180

When that army returned to the city without a king, a cry rose up from the alleys and markets. The army and the city rushed together, one group out of happiness, the other in sorrow.

A cry rose up from Kush's pavilion, "Alas! Brave one! Steel-clad king!" His concubines all tore off their veils, lamenting the turn of fortune. A cry rose up across the city from the women, passing around fresh roses and musk and hyacinths.

The army and the city joined together, young and old all speaking their minds. "What shall we do now that the king of China is gone, shall our eyes and hearts fill with blood of grief?"

"No one can take the city from us, we must protect it every night and day."

"To die in the city because of our king is better than to live in the grasp of his enemy."

"We must fight and struggle as we can for the sake of our women and children, our lives and property." 7190

To that end, the men formed two groups to fight and to defend the city. They placed a group at the gates, an army and city prepared for battle. Groups of soldiers assembled at the gates like a mountain with their armor upon the top of the fortress. They appointed one man from the company for each gate, each leader unfurled a banner. The whole fortress was red and yellow and purple from the great variety of flying banners.

The next day, Qaren sent an envoy, a well-spoken noble youth, to the gate, and great and small raised their heads from the fortress. The speaker said, "O worthy brave men of China, men of stature, you who are old and who are young, I bring greetings from the tongue of the world-champion. That conquering lion says that it is the judgment of the world-king 7200 that this country be purged of Kush's tyranny."

A great cry rose up from the gate.

"There were fifty learned sages in China, and they came to King Faridun's court full of sorrow. A cry rose up from the young and the old, a great commotion at his threshold lasting more than a week. They spoke out about all of his injustices, piling dust upon his threshold. They donned clothes of dark blue and black.

"The glorious king became distraught from this. Faridun did not have the character of Zahhak, who could never hear the word *injustice*."

He said to them, "He sent us from Iran to protect China from his injustice. My quarrel was with this oppressor: he was a tyrant, and bloodthirsty. A tyrant deserves to be in fetters, so why must there be battle? I have no quarrel with any of you, nor have I any plan to set foot in the city. 7210 Now that I have alleviated Kush's injustice, I have one more desire: to remedy the wound that he inflicted, and make the hearts of the people of the city free from grief. Now, the troops one and all are like family to me. As they wish for us to keep them here, we will raise their heads higher than the heavens. Should any one of them come to serve King Faridun, I can be their guide to him. I would steward them before the throne until fortune shows them its face, so that city-dwellers and town gentry will not be reminded of the tyrant but of God and of my king, be they my enemies or well-wishers. You will one by one go about your business, your farms and your markets, for we will be watching over all, favoring all with justice and kindness.

7220 We will grant you more than other cities, and forge a remedy for the damage that was done."

When they had listened to the words of that well-spoken man from beginning to end, all about the city and markets, people began to voice support for Faridun.

The army decided to rebel; its only reply was blade, axe, and arrow.

The people of the city said to the soldiers, "The king was taken and left no one in his place. He has no legitimate son who could put on his father's crown. In whose name will we go to war and put ourselves in danger?"

They tried to persuade the troops, but their advice did no good. The merchants and city-dwellers could not prevail, the soldiers outnumbered them two to one. The army humiliated the envoy, paying him no heed. 7230 They chased him with stones and curses, the charismatic youth fled and did not return.

He went to Qaren and told what he had seen, and the champion's heart raced, hearing his report. Three months more they waited at the gate and food became scarce in the city.

They sent a secret envoy, who had many things to say. "If the champion continues hostilities, let him swear an oath before God, that he not oppress us in any way, that he forget about the war and never speak of it. We will deliver the city to him in dark of night, for fortune sent an opportunity our way." Immediately, Qaren gave him his hand, and swore to him his sword and his men, and that he would not look twice at the people of the city, except for those who fought him.

The envoy said, "O world-champion, now we can tell our secrets. 7240 We have in this city many gates, and each of those gates has one commander who has fifty thousand troops, brave knights of China. Up high is a hidden gate whose commander is one of ours. Come in dark of night with an attack force and we will open that gate. You will enter without trouble, and from there, you know how to fight man to man."

The champion's heart was cheered by that man's words; he secretly gave him garments and gold. He said to him, "When I enter the city I will give you a man's share out of the treasury."

The man sent a worthy fellow with him so that he could show him the way in. Night fell and he put on his armor and girded himself, along with a hundred thousand warriors. They went to that gate that the Chinese showed him, the Chinese opened the gate swift as smoke.

7250 The army entered and the cry of pipes rose up as if to dislodge Saturn. Drummers struck a beat whose roar overtook the clouds. A dark night of lances and blades and mail, brave men's cries reached the clouds.

When the army heard all of that noise, their hearts leapt from their chests, their wits from their brains. [228b] Men jumped up confused, knowing what fate had wrought. One group hid inside a house, another group charged into the bloodbath. When the sun painted the dust with its own color and imbued the turning heavens with its gravity, the world opened its eyes and saw an army like tulips wilted in a gale. They had all let go their blades and armor, and opened their mouths to make excuses. General Qaren pardoned them all and killed no more. 7260

And so he went to Kush's palace with steel-clad troops ahead and behind. They dismounted and registered the treasure and set watchmen over it, upright men. He stayed a month in that city and obtained all of the royal treasure there. He called for camels, twelve thousand of them, and loaded every one. All of the gold and gems were loaded up, Chinese garments and gold coins. Thrones, crowns, banners, and girdles he loaded onto another caravan. Four thousand Chinese beauties wearing earrings and bracelets departed Kush's portico, with hypnotic faces and lips out of a fairy tale. As well, ten thousand young male slaves, each one's good looks purloined from the sun. Chambermaids, all uproarious, he sent to Iran along with Kush, 7270 all entrusted to the high-born Taliman with a force of thirty thousand brave men.

He wrote a letter informing Faridun, light of the heavens, of everything that had happened. Taliman set off like dust in the wind. All Kush had amassed over a hundred years, Taliman took at once to the king. If a wise person were to take a lesson from this, it would be to not hoard treasure underground. If you have the means at your disposal to sit in good cheer and safety, you're better off than Kush and Faridun, and in this respect, your honor is greater, o goodly man, for contentment is a treasure that no enemy ever coveted.

He traveled across China with his forces, seizing the rebellious as he went, those by whom the people of that country were troubled. 7280 He sent them from the land of China to Iran, and likewise, women and children and property. Those who had done no injustice he did not bother—the people of the city and the merchants. Under

Qaren there was such justice and peace where Kush had earned infamy. He gave Kush's position to Nastuh, instructing him, "Do no ill, but strive for justice, for this was the recompense of the unjust man: to be cursed in both worlds."

He went toward Iran with his forces, his troops all having received rewards. When Taliman reached the king's court bearing Kush and all that treasure, the proud king was cheered by this, and he hurried to the temple.

He offered his praises to God, supplicating the giver of victory. 7290 "Thanks to you, I have obtained satisfaction, your will has bestowed honor upon me. I give thanks unto you for this blessing, you are my keeper and my guide."

When Taliman brought Kush before him, Faridun looked him over longer than was seemly. To those proud men he said, "You'd be astonished by this grotesque man if you've a good heart! For his appearance is a reflection of his character: he was a tyrant who sought out disaster."

They forged fetters for his feet and took him to Damavand to keep him there. They bound him with heavy bindings in the same manner as Zahhak and others. Whatever of his treasure was suitable was consigned to the world-king's treasury. Retainers brought it all at once to the treasury, one by one, placing the items in the vault of the kings. Whatever was left of the treasure after that, they gave to the poor and needy. 7300 The male slaves and beauties of Kush they gave to the fierce king's nobles. His night-chamber was given to the priests, both high-ranking and low.

Three years later, Qaren came back, having returned to see King Faridun. He kissed the ground and expressed praise and supplication. Faridun praised him at length, and said, "This is just what I expected from you. You have given me satisfaction, o champion, may your judgment be forever keen."

He sat that leader of leaders down to dine, feasting him and his long-suffering companions for forty days. He gave him his army and his lands, he went to his troops, his cheerful men. Faridun sat securely, having denied Ahriman access to the world. The tyrannical Kush remained imprisoned for forty years, his heart and body sore.

Chapter 5

7310 So it was, until a cry rose up from the west, as ruin befell the entirety of that country. The Black Hordes gave it all to plunder, raising dust from that land that blotted out the sun.[1] Those who escaped the blades of the hordes fled and gave each other aid. The hordes from Nubia and Beja at once made those lands go up in smoke. Little by little, they approached Egypt and threw all of the cities into chaos.

They sent an army against them and it returned wounded, distraught. The just king sent another army, but its travail bore no fruit. So many were killed by the Black Hordes' blades. It was driven out and returned, its morale crushed. The world-ruling king increased the size of his forces and they made short work of them. They returned defeated again, their banners torn and materiel lost. 7320 The victorious king was now at a loss, and summoned forces from every direction. From Iran, from Rome, from the Turks and China, the world-king mustered armies.

Nariman, son of Garshasp, and Qaren together marshaled their forces in the rainy season. When they drew up ranks facing the hordes, they covered their mouths with their hands like elephants. So many were killed on both sides, the flat plain turned to hills and hills to mountains. When their war had gone on for four months, the hordes were exhausted by their maces. They returned to Beja and Nubia, their hearts melted by the branding of those two champions.

---

1. See the introduction for a discussion of the term Black Hordes.

The forces of Nariman and Qaren together suffered greatly at the hands of the hordes. They thus returned to the court, and told the proud king of the injury that those fierce heroes had suffered at the hands of that hideous army. 7330 Their bravery and calm at the time of battle arrested the Black Hordes with sword-blows. "However much we suffered ourselves, we drove them back to their lands."

Faridun sung their praises. The world-king was pleased by this.

If you want the whole story of the battle with the Black Hordes, I will provide you its name. The land of Beja is the place the sages call Mazandaran. Seek out this story from Mas'udi, for he has taken pains to tell it.[2] Whoever recited the saga of the kings of Iran has told it.

Faridun then sent a man to whom he gave command of forces from Iran, so that they would protect that land from injustice and the blades of the shameful hordes. When the land became prosperous by his benevolence, all of the refugees returned home. 7340 Once again, the Nubians like ants and grasshoppers came and took all of the high mountaintops, and Faridun's forces fled, abandoning their things as they retreated. The hordes turned to plundering the whole country, subduing it at once. Once again, the western lands were in such a state that no garden or orchard remained.

As long as the wise Faridun was responsible for the affairs of those lands, he did not consider it fitting lordly conduct to let such lands stay barren. He considered himself at fault that men and women were driven out of their homes. Though he made them prosper by troops and treasure, they were ruined again by the hordes. In this way, they suffered great harm at the hands of the Nubians for many years.

Faridun was at a loss and said, "The sages must be capable of solving this." 7350 The worldly-wise man summoned them all and they spoke at length on the hordes and their doings, but regarding this demon-faced army, they were at a loss for a solution.

He said, "Each of you offers his own approach and gives a portion of his own knowledge." [229a]

The nobles bowed their heads to the ground. "O worthy king, just and faithful, you are wiser than us and the sages, and more capable.

2. The reference is to Mas'udi-ye Marvazi, not to the more famous Abu Hasan 'Ali al-Mas'udi.

You are king and we, before your throne, have girded ourselves to do whatever you order."

Faridun said to the nobles, "If I send a great army to that country, there are no resources left to support it, the land is now desolate. When a great army does not find food, it turns its head from war and struggle. If I send a smaller force, it will not be able to stand up to the hordes. 7360 What solution can we devise to banish this harm from these distraught people?"

A proud man of knightly lineage said, "O just and faithful king, if you want a proper solution to this, you must find a tyrannical man of fearless character, physically powerful, of sound constitution and noble birth, a mighty and fierce man of more fearsome visage than the worst of the demon-faced. Give him an army, materiel and garments of war, the same mace and keen-edged sword. Give him kingship over that land and country in order that he gird himself for kingship. He will make preparations day and night for kingship, fighting and planning against the hordes. He would deliver that land from the enemy and bring ruin to the shameful Black Hordes, erect his throne and sit upon it with his armies, and maintain his rule there. 7370 He is not like a nobleman who would, without ado, shrink from battle, from such trials."

The king was lost in thought for a while, then said to him, "O well-intentioned fellow, I do not know anyone that fits this description except the demon-born, vile and hideous. He is much worse than those demon-faced ones, brave and tyrannical and violent. It does seem acceptable now to free that demon from his bindings, bring him inside and dress him, soothe his heart and comfort him with praise, give him those lands in their entirety, troops, helmet, and girdle. He will struggle day and night against the enemy and eradicate those devils, make the land verdant and wealthy for its people, and relieve them of their suffering. No one would struggle for those lands but the demon-faced one, that fierce dragon." 7380

The nobles all expressed their acclaim for that just king of the earth. "Your judgment is loftier than the high heavens, you shelter the earth from harm. There is no other recourse against this enemy, no villain is more awful than Kush."

He ordered Qaren, man of good judgment, to ride there from Amol. He arrived at Damavand in one week, and reached that bound and injured prisoner. He freed his feet from their heavy bindings and brought him from that cramped place to Amol.

His face was blackened by his demonic deeds, his head, face, and neck all covered in hair. When they applied warm water to his body, he was like an almond removed from its shell. They sent him food and sweet drinks, bright wine, chicken and kebab. He donned a garment with Chinese designs, pleasant like the land in spring verdure. 7390 He spent a month with music and wine in order to soften his thick hide.

After that, Qaren said to him, "The king has forgiven you and pardoned you of your sins. See what harm you inflicted on the ancestors of the lofty king? Now that your recompense for this is forgiveness, you must not rebel against his authority. From now on, do as the king says, and you will remain at ease, and the king pleased. When you gird yourself to obey him and do as he commands, he will give you a measure of kingship, grant you independence and satisfaction; so long as his majesty is pleased with you, he will endeavor to serve you well."

Kush said to him, "O proud man, since his imperial majesty gave me life, I have not drunk dogs' milk or wolf meat. Why should I turn away from the great king? 7400 If I do not recognize his beneficence, then I of all people am deserving of death."

They thus took each other's hands and took to feasting, day and night at ease, wine in hand, with General Qaren in his own portico, having prepared ample accommodations for his guest, adorned like the garden of Eram, beautifully decorated all over. He returned his whole flock of chambermaids to him. Qaren took care of all his needs, giving him food and rest and suitable clothing. He had idol-like women wait on him and gave him whatever he wanted. In this manner he coddled him with wine, and with singing, lute strumming beauties. Not one day did his heart gather dust, nor cold wind strike his face.

When he had spent a year in the palace of Qaren, glorious Faridun summoned him. 7410 When his eyes fell upon the crown of the great kings, he saw its greatness and glory before him. He lowered his face into the ground and recited praise for the king.

The king smiled, looking at his face, and said, "Your fortune has revealed your face. From now on may you find only satisfaction, now that you have begun to realize your ultimate end."

When Kush heard these kind words from the king, he kissed the ground and raised his head. He said, "Your beneficent majesty, cultivator of wisdom and righteousness, forgiving, from now on I will be as a slave before you. I am ashamed of my deeds, my conduct. If the king would give me what I deserve for my conduct, what befits my deeds, my place would be on the gallows. Would that the king would grant me forgiveness!"

Faridun consoled him at length, "May your judgment be ever righteous." 7420 He let him go home in good shape, sending a number of nobles with him. He sent him all manner of gifts, gold dinars and spirited horses. When day broke, he hosted him lavishly, seating him on a golden throne. He set out a kingly banquet before him, they dined and then called for wine.

Intoxicated, he said to Kush, "Lofty king, prison is better than a high throne room! You suffered as you did because of your own bad character; you abandoned our ways. Now all of those travails have passed; good and ill pass as wind over the plain. From now on you will find your desires granted by us, provided you drive benighted character out of your brain."

Kush lowered his face to the ground and said to him, "O king, pure of thought, I am pleased by this kindness and good-heartedness, if you spare my life. 7430 It would be fair if I were to throw myself to be trampled under the hooves of the king's horse. Now that I have obtained forgiveness, I have seen what a sinner I am. Fetters and imprisonment befit this slave—not even prison, but a slicing blade! Know that no mighty servant would dare stray from the great king's command. But know, your majesty, that having seen myself to be a sinner, I dare not approach you, to kiss your head and king's crown. Now, if you punish me, it is your choice, and if you forgive me it is to your credit. Having seen the greatness and composure of the king, if you forgive my sins now, I will be a slave at your threshold, girded before the crowned king."

The king smiled at him and said, "Have no worry in your heart. 7440 I will forgive all of your sins and, by the heavens, bestow on you a crown."

As stars were revealed from behind the curtain, proud heads grew heavy from wine. As wits fled before the wine-goblet, the kings came home from their feast. And as the sun revealed its face from behind the curtain, the wine made brave men's minds race.

An envoy summoned Kush to appear before Faridun, and he seated him beside himself when he arrived. He had prepared a worthy place for him, and he addressed him with kind and abundant praises. When he returned and appeared before the king, a robe of honor was given him, and a precious throne and golden crown, beautiful chamber-maids with gold-embroidered sashes, Arabian horses and goods of all kinds, harp-playing and lute-strumming beauties, a thousand camel-loads of gifts, each one wrapped in brocades, 7450 a hundred of pure gold and a hundred kinds of perfume, a hundred garments and threads of various kinds. He also gave him implements of war and battle: mail and a Kabulian dagger, [229b] and a very precious banner with the image of a dragon.

Kush's eyes widened at the sight of those gifts and his spirit bubbled over with joy. No one has seen, nor has anyone remembered what the king granted to the demon-born.

As the ocean froths in the morning light, Kush dressed himself in the king's garments. He mounted a horse worthy of a world-king, tied a belt around his waist, and opened his hand. He went with the benevolent Qaren until he arrived at the court.

They had placed two chairs before the throne, and the two fortunate men sat down with the king. The just monarch gave him a regal turquoise belt from his own hands. 7460 He said to him, ominously, "May you be victorious and may your command be obeyed." He girded the waist of the mighty Kush, and by his right as the great king, smeared both of Kush's cheeks with ashes, adding supplications to his praise.

Faridun said to him, "There is a great difficulty, a headache that has arisen in the west. The Iranians have not felt themselves caught flat-footed and exposed like this for many years. The Black Hordes have again rebelled and are on the march, more numerous than fish in the sea. Because of them, the whole country has fallen into ruin, consigned to the lions and leopards. Over the distance of a six months' journey from Nubia, one cannot see through the dust. The whole country is deserted, some having fled to Rome, others to the east. I sent my forces there again and the whole west turned black with dead bodies. 7470 Once the land was prosperous again, the hordes returned, inflicting their violence. That land was plundered again—such was the decree of the creator.

"It seems to me then that if I make that land prosperous again, they'll return anew, like ants, and the west will again descend into war and upheaval. Dust will rise from those lands and the west will again become deserted. There is nobody up to the task but you, to turn the lives of the Nubians to dust. Select troops from the men of war, and take what you need from the treasury. Then march toward the west: I have given you those lands in their entirety. For upon the whole earth, you will find no better lands in Iran and China than these. Gold grows there in the manner of plants, and the plants all have alchemical properties. 7480 All of its mines and mountains are filled with gems; they are well-suited to you, and are yours to take.

"When you reach that place, make it prosperous. When you have made it prosper, dispense justice. For when your subjects receive justice from you, they will not wish to leave your shadow. People all flee from injustice, for all tyrants spill blood. Justice is what the world-creator finds acceptable, may there never be injustice in the world! Those places that are ruined and wrecked, forgive their taxes for three years. Distribute food and cows and donkeys and sheep, so that agriculture flourishes there. Be very mindful of internal conduct and watch yourself, for the Mazandaranis are all ill-born, with the strength of a lion and temper of a cur. If you observe the path of justice and wisdom, the snarling cur is better than a Mazandarani." 7490

When the king's speech ended, the experienced Kush showered praises on him. Having praised him, he said, "I will do so, and work Faridun's will upon the world."

He called for one of the priests to appear before the men of high station and young nobles, and in that court, advised Kush, and after advising him swore an oath. "Do not rebel against the king's command, never break our alliance and covenant."

They recorded this oath and Kush swore to it. The nobles of Iran all one by one bore witness in writing before each other. When the pact was made and the oath taken, the sovereign ordered that it be proclaimed to everyone. With this oath recorded, the just king stamped his seal on it.

Then they held a banquet, the nobles of Iran young and old 7500 sat to dine with the king, more than ten thousand wine-drinkers. When it was time for them to leave the feast, he gave him a Roman robe of honor and a golden helmet. Those same Arabian horses with golden bridles were feted in that party. Kush went to his quarters drunk and cheerful, hand in hand with Qaren.

When he had lost consciousness and then woke up, the renowned Kush went to the king. He kissed his throne and took his hand. He said to him, "O god-fearing king, the time has come for me to set out, and I must assemble my army."

Faridun was deep in thought for a long while, then said to him, "O brave and honorable fellow, you should depart on the day of Farvadin and assemble your forces then. For this day is called Farvadin, you will be satisfied and achieve victory. 7510 On the month of Farvadin and the day of Farvadin. March west in glory and faith!"[3]

He raised his head, his posture erect hearing those words, and took an omen for that month and day. "It was said to me it shall be both glory and faith, my head raised higher than the Pleiades."

The king went outside and called his troops; whoever appeared was showered with silver coins. The moon appeared, and then the day drew near, but the day was darkened by the troops' dust. Then the king emerged onto the field and took a brief tour around the great army he had assembled. He said to Kush, "Now select three hundred thousand knights from among your troops."

The proud Kush answered him, "O king, lend an ear to the words of your servant. You said that that land is not prosperous. To march a large force there would not be just. There is not enough food in the west to support a large army. 7520 When they forage, they'd find no food, for there are no orchards, no porticoes left or palaces. The people would suffer much injustice, just as the Black Hordes have done to them. The people will flee even further from us, and be even more oppressed by us. Would you send me, then, with an army, to ravage the country just like the Black Hordes? Must I not hold back the ruin inflicted on that country by the hordes, with my sword and treasure? Would those same troops that came from the land of China, who came with me to the land of Iran, be sufficient in the view of the king?"

He smiled and said, "There is no other way." He gave him forty thousand of the Iranians, proud armored knights. Those Chinese who had survived, whether imprisoned or free, numbered twelve thousand. The crowned king gave them to him. 7530

---

3. This is a pun: "*farr va din*" means "glory and faith."

THE KING SPEAKS ABOUT KUSH[4]

The experienced mystery-solving sage said, "This mystery is beyond compare: that Kush who marched west, he was not Kush the Tusked, but his son; for the first Kush died in prison, and left behind a small child, like his father in face and appearance; he has the mark of his father on his face. Faridun called him Kush as well—a savage wolf, and sharp-witted. When he grew up and reached his full height, he marched his armies to the west." However, the reality is that he was indeed Kush who had thrown the land of China into turmoil.

When it was time to depart, the king said to him, "Marching with such meager forces is displeasing to me, for I fear that the enemy will wreck them."

He answered him, "Your majesty, have no worries, 7540 the learned will one day record in their books what this vassal will do with this small force."

The king's heart was pleased by those words, and he changed his mind. He designated two years' payments from the treasury for those worthy, toiling men.

The army set out from Amol and went for one league with Kush, their king. From there, they took the road to Mosul, marching over desert, mountains, and inhabited areas. He sent fifty riders ahead with letters to the city of Mosul and its frontier garrisons, "We are passing through your lands, you must not fail to provide us what we need. [230a] Prepare whatever provisions you can, for this army is like a torrent. They must not encounter scarcity of provisions on the road, nor be delayed in this land."

When he reached Mosul he saw abundant materiel and those well-provisioned frontier garrisons. 7550 He stopped at those frontier garrisons and obtained kingly goods. From there he turned towards Egypt, his heart cheered, keeping a good pace.

He sent a rider ahead of his army, having written a letter, its message brief: "The great commanding king has sent us to make war on Mazandaran. Prepare two years' provisions for us to eat, present us with whatever is available. That country has been ruined, consigned to

4. It is not clear which king is intended here.

the leopards and lions. I must not let my army run short on provisions when I march beyond your prosperous lands."

He sent the message at the cock's crow, hurrying the message to Kiyus. For he resided in the city of Busir for many years in blissful ignorance. Before Fustat had been built, Busir flourished like April and springtime.[5] 7560

When the letter reached Nushan's son, he saw no choice but to comply. He gathered and presented what he could from the city, collecting a portion from the soldiers and civilians. He filled the whole field with food that he had gathered from the city and countryside.

Kush went on towards northern Mesopotamia with his steel-clad forces. When the roar of drums rose up from the road, Kiyus and his nobles welcomed him. When his eyes fell upon that warrior, he dismounted and praised him reverently. He was terrified of his fearsome visage and his sternness, his eyes like gems sparkling in mud. When Kush saw this, he reassured him, asked how he was, and bade him mount his horse again. They dismounted a league away from Busir; there were gardens on one side and a river on the other.

Kush called the proud Kiyus before him, and had him seated facing him 7570 and asked him, "What quantity of victuals and supplies have you provided?"

His answer was "O crowned one, notice of your arrival came late. There are victuals sufficient for one year, which will be granted to these honorable troops."

Kush's heart was cheered by this benevolent fellow, and he was freed from worry over his army. He said to him, "We too have a year's worth, with two years' worth I shall want for nothing. Nothing is abundant in that land but weeds, unless the whole land is enchanted with alchemy. Load up all of these provisions on the camels, set aside stores in your own lands. Then, whatever else you can obtain, send your men to bring it to us."

The worldly-wise Kiyus assented to this, and Kush praised him for his cooperation. He chose not to rest there, but set out immediately. 7580 He moved hurriedly to the city of Semab, he saw trees and vegetation, water and . . . This city is now called Barca [Cyrenaica], a

5. Fustat was the principle city of Egypt, an older city next to which the Fatimids built their capital, Cairo, in 969. Today it is part of Cairo.

frontier commander dwells happily there. Kush reckoned that city and its well-appointed king the frontier of the west.

Kush set up camp in the meadows, stationing men-at-arms all around. To whomever lacked civilized dwellings, he gave dirhams so that they could become householders. He sent everyone to his own city to be given treasure from his stores. For each area, he appointed an agent to go there, each agent bearing treasure. He ordered that whomever they found be sent back from their exile. He gave them valuables as was necessary, and released them of tax obligations for three years.

There were seven and five cities there that had suffered hardship from Beja and Nubia.[6] 7590 He founded a city there called Zowaylah that you'd think was a patch of paradise, as well as Yunos, Tarefah, and Kairouan, all three with gardens and running streams.[7] Aside from Boseyrah there were Bish and Nakur, which were constantly suffering from the Beja.[8] There was also Zawilah and Mahi, and sixteen other well-known regions, as well as Fez and –jang and Hum, all regions bordering the lands of Rome.[9] If you do not know Hum, it is also called the island of the Bani Zaghanna. Other cities are Tahart and Mobat—its water is nectar and its vegetation saffron.

All of these cities we have mentioned were destroyed by the Nubians. There was no verdant place left in this country, with no shelter left standing in any of them, except Cyrenaica, which was fine and prosperous, the place where the refugees sought shelter. 7600 Whoever had abandoned their homes went to Andalos empty-handed.[10] When

6. Beja and Nubia are regions south of Egypt—see chapter 3, note 24. The rest of the cities named here can for the most part be identified as cities located in North Africa, from Morocco to Libya.

7. For the first of these cities, the manuscript reads R-B-L-H. Given the spelling of other instances of the term, this appears to be a corruption of Zowaylah, a town adjacent to Mahdiyah, the first capital of the Fatimids, in Tunisia. Iranshah may have wished to avoid using the name Mahdiyah—see introduction. The name of the fourth city given here is unreadable; all we can say is that is ends with -jang.

8. Boseyrah, also known as Basra, is a coastal town in Morocco opposite Gibraltar.

9. The second appearance of the toponym Zawilah probably refers to a town in the Sahara, in present-day Libya. This may also be pronounced Zowaylah, as in the Bab al-Zuweila, a gate in the old city of Cairo.

10. The Arabic toponym al-Andalos refers to greater part of the Iberian Peninsula, including Portugal and southern and central Spain. Since the term is not equivalent to either Spain or Andalusia, Andalos has been used here.

Kush found out, he was cheered that he might find those people in Andalos. Cratus was king over that land, a proud youth with wealth and power at his disposal.[11] His armies were more numerous than tiny ants, than the uncountable stars.

KUSH'S LETTER TO CRATUS, KING OF ANDALOS

Kush sent a letter to Cratus, "We are world-rulers, glorious and wise." He quickly sent it to the west, and it was as if that land were suddenly going up in smoke. He sought to have whatever cities had suffered ruination and harm at once be made prosperous, and to gather people to return to their own cities. "When I arrived here, we investigated matters and heard the reports of our scouts. Those people belong to this country, and are still under our rule. 7610 Now if you in your regal palace should pay heed to my words, send those people back to their homes, for this is the will of our king. Women and children and property—whatever there is—return to those people. When you have done this, come before me and I will reward you generously. We will leave you your kingship and treasure. But if you turn aside in rebellion, you'll be pulling a burial shroud over yourself. You'll suffer blows from us heavier than a mountain—and a mountain would crumble under their damage. Steel arrows like hail with shafts of venom, tipped with death, will be your greeting from the Iranians, and from the king of Turan and his worthies."

He chose a reputable man and said, "May you travel in safety. 7620 Take this letter and bring me his response, answer whatever questions he has."

When he had crossed the sea, he sent the man to call on the court. It was located in a city called Córdoba, Cratus reigned happily there. He praised him and gave him the letter, which was given to the translator to read.

11. This name appears in the text as Q-R-A-T-U-S, pronounced either Qeratus or Qoratus provided one follows the Persian rule against initial consonant clusters. Since it was clearly intended to appear as a foreign, Greco-Roman name, "Cratus," to which the Persian spelling most closely corresponds, has been used here. Iranshah likely chose this name for its compatibility with the epic's meter.

When he understood Kush's words, he was taken aback, and narrowed his eyes in anger and disdain. He said to the envoy, an experienced elder, "Who is this man, of what lineage is he, to speak so tyrannically, to speak so unjustly?"

"He is the descendant of Kush, the king," he said, "of a lineage too proud to conceal. He is the son of the brother of King Zahhak, a most bloodthirsty and fearless king. The king of Makran and Machin and China, a fearsome and warlike man. 7630 After the courageous king imprisoned Zahhak and took him to Mount Damavand, he fought against the king for seventy years; no one had the fortitude to stand up to him. After he enjoyed a period of good fortune, he was taken captive by the general. He remained imprisoned by the world-king, and for forty years no one spoke his name.

"Now the king has freed him from prison and bestowed on him many precious gems. He gave him army and throne and golden crown, and granted him kingship over Samiran and the west. He is a proud man of great stature; in battle, a mountain of fire. If you would hear my advice, your majesty? You will not be able to stop him from getting what he wants. If you turn against him, you will guarantee your own enslavement. He'll accept no apology or excuses, and your courtesies will not make him ashamed." 7640

Cratus was at first very frightened by the words of that astute and fortunate man. He asked, "How large is his army, now that he is in this land?"

He said to him, "More than eighty thousand armored riders [230b] chosen from Iran and equipped, all eager for battle."

Cratus laughed at him and said, "A hot-headed fellow can't hide anything, as I have more than six hundred thousand—at least that many knights. One of them and ten of the enemy, the Iranians don't stand a chance! Times must be hard if he would go to war with such an army. For Zahhak, in his glory and magnificence, with his mighty army and his mace, sought no more than a 'hello' from us. Why is your king so lacking in judgment? 7650 All the Black Hordes of Mazandaran cannot cross this water."[12]

---

12. Cratus is comparing the army of Kush to that of Mazandaran, or even confusing them, presumably because Kush's army was to attack the Iberian Peninsula from North Africa, as the Umayyads, led by the Amazigh commander Tareq b. Ziyad had done.

The envoy said, "O proud king, consider the matter more closely. I have given bountiful advice, if you would hear an old man's counsel."

He ordered that the palace eunuchs arrange lodgings for the envoy. He was hosted well for three days, feasted the whole time. Cratus consulted with his people and considered every angle, the good and the bad. He could not figure out why he should send those people back to their homes. They had always been there with his army. His lands would be deserted.

He drafted a reply, saying, "The people's judgment is wise. Your words were delivered, I read them. I do not see the wisdom in your judgment. 7660 It does not seem fitting to us to show such generosity here. We will see on the battlefield whose speech is manly, whose is boasting. Besides, the people you asked for, you requested them with a letter. If these were subjects under your dominion before, dominion is mine now, for they are in my country. We did not extend you the courtesy of an invitation, and you did not seek one. We have not obeyed other kings before, you should not allow yourself to suggest such things."

When he had told all of this in his letter, he called forth Kush's envoy. He threw it in front of him for him to take back, and he soared along the road faster than a hawk.

When he reached Kush and gave him the letter, the translator read him its entire contents. He was taken aback and rubbed his hands together, then attached that letter to his own. 7670 He sent a camel back toward the king, carrying a letter saying, "To the throne: Cratus rebels, and it is appropriate that we go to battle against him. Having sent this letter to the king, the army now seeks to cross the ocean. I will then inform the king whether I encounter hardship or success."

The camels left and he began his departure, making full preparations to cross the sea. King Cratus never thought that that army would cross the ocean. He was completely heedless of that possibility; Kush did not seem a threat to him.

In two months, he had built forty ships and unfurled many sails over the sea. He did much business with the merchants, too, buying a great deal and leaving much with the people. First he crossed with thirty thousand from Iran and elite knights of China. 7680 On and on,

---

Cratus's reaction in the story is informed by this historical example as well as by the more recent conquest of al-Andalus by the Almoravids, also from North Africa.

the ships carried the troops, and they all crossed and landed near the king. He set up camp on a flat plain the sight of which would astonish the eyes. The water's edge met its margins and the army moved into its interior.

When Cratus became aware of his arrival, he said, "This man is surely not wise, but a rebellious devil, so sure of his manliness and his power. If he knew about my army he would not have crossed the wide sea." He ordered that the drums be brought out and set up their tents on the field. He summoned all of his troops, he offered dinars to increase their ranks. Of those worthy troops he selected three hundred and thirty thousand knights. He assisted them by decking them all out with horses and weapons. 7690 First he sent a scouting party to bring him reports of the enemy.

It went and sized up the enemy, and returned to inform Cratus. "The enemy is no more than fifty thousand, battle-riders and men of war."

He laughed and said, "Is this really so? Why did they even bother to cross the ocean?"

Kush was dishonored by crossing the water, not realizing that he would never dream again of Iran. He had dealt with the sea in order that Cratus would face him in battle. For Córdoba was a great city, and he knew he must not try to besiege it. He would feign weakness and delay, luring Cratus's army into battle.

Things played out as he expected and Cratus prepared to attack him. He traveled to within two leagues of Kush, his forces thirsty for action. 7700 His scouts came and informed him that everywhere was covered with tents.

He was pleased by this and said, "This is good, everyone did as they pleased. You, go and come back, do not confront the army; when their advance guards arrive feign weakness."

The night passed and the next day the battle was not joined, for he was carrying out this plan. Kush sent his advance guard and ordered them not to attack when they saw the enemy's vanguard. "When they attack, do not engage them for long, in order that the enemy grow bolder. Then, retreat towards the main army, show weakness whenever you engage them."

The advance guard approached the king and followed his instructions precisely. Cratus's advance guards were close, and made themselves visible. They saw them from afar and they grew excited, each and all roaring like thunder. 7710 When they were met with the heavy blows of those brave men, they fled like scoundrels. Those brave men cast aside their helmets and armor as they fled, and came near the king with unclothed bodies and bare heads. When the advance guards neared the army, they looked and saw that meager force.

They came back to Cratus and informed him of what had happened with the advance guards, their retreat: "Faridun's brain is lacking wisdom if he marshals men like these. He is proud of such a scanty force and musters such ignoble warriors. They had scarcely engaged with us when they turned and fled. The king should not be troubled by this meager band of scoundrels. Like a deer from a cheetah, they fled from us, o hero-besting king." 7720

Cratus was cheered by their words, as if his troubles were over. He decreed that at the cock's crow, they would sound the pipes and the drums.

The world was filled with commotion and action, making the ground quake. The neighing of the horses and the shouts of the brave men, the shining blades and armor, at once stole Mars's heart and wits and boiled the gall of living men.

Cratus had two brothers, who had armies, throne, and crown. He gave them command of his left and right wings, for they were both brave warriors. Each of them was given a hundred thousand brave and warlike knights. In the center, he took his place, banners aloft in front of him and behind.

On the other side, the world-seizing Kush again marshaled his own forces. 7730 He gave command of his forces to Mardan Khurreh, the Iranians' commander. He sent them to the right flank of his forces, equipping them well with blades and armor. He chose weapons for himself and a gave a warhorse to the commander's brother and put him in the center.

He said to him, "When the enemy attacks from their center, show weakness, make it so that they gain the upper hand and Cratus is tricked into overconfidence." He gave him another lightly armored force that would send him straight to Ahura Mazda. [231a]

The knight who considered himself a match for the warlike Qaren was right beside him, accompanying him, dearer to him than his son. He showed him his position on his left, went and arranged the force into two lines.

The king, when he had set to work commanding the army, became hidden amidst his troops. 7740 A great cry rose up and the battle was joined; waiting gave way to haste. The roar of drums and cry of brave men's maces made enemies' faces disappear, arrow shafts wounded their hearts and eyes, mighty lassos bound hands and necks, shining spearheads burned up their spirits, and blades sprouted from blood like tongues of flame. Brave men's blood flowed in a stream across the field, and the passing moments turned villains' heads into polo-balls. The seasoned warhorses had no place to plant their feet but upon heads and chests. Cratus's men gained the upper hand, then night fell and they all turned back.

The guards were posted and the commotion settled, and Kush asked the officers of his army, "What was the battle like today? How is the enemy in battle?"

The proud men answered, "The enemy is like a fire, 7750 brave of temper and physically strong. They inflicted much damage on us, since we were weak in this battle, as you had told us to be, your majesty. We do not know why you thought this was fitting, why you approve of weakness from your troops."

He answered them, "This was acceptable, everyone does as he sees fit. I wanted to deploy a stratagem against this enemy. Now that this stratagem has been put in play, see tomorrow what happens on this wide field. I will wage an attack on Cratus, take him and put him in a bad situation."

He called for the captives from that day, and asked them, "Tell me, truly, who is most impudent before Cratus, that I might ask him for information?"

They then showed him one old man, his face was saffron-colored beneath his heavy chains. 7760 "No one is closer to him than this man, the rest of us are lesser in authority."

He brought him and kept him by his side and set a watchman guarding the others. He said to him, "Tomorrow, if you can point out Cratus to me, I will give comfort to your body and soul, I will give you many kingly gems. When I have this city under my control, I will not trouble your people. I will give you a royal crown, I will give you lands and make you a lord."

The man was cheered by his words, and said to him, "I will show him to you during the battle. My life is dearer to me than king and city, than family, allies, children, and possessions. During a flood, does the clever woman not abandon her children?"

Kush said to Mardan Khurreh, "At night, go quietly, 7770 bring six thousand cavalry and infantry and block the enemy's path. When you see defeat draw near, you must look to the city gates. Block their entry to the city, and then we will have no trouble at all." He ordered the army to go, and the men left, being led to the city gate by its guide.

When the stars hid behind their curtain and the bright candle shone in the east, Cratus quickly roused his forces and positioned them as they had been the day before. He was there again in the center with his forces; they engaged and the dust they kicked up darkened the moon. A number of the Iranians were killed. The prisoner pointed his finger at him during the fighting.

When Kush identified him, he approached, as the day was darkened by the troops' dust. He attacked him with ten thousand lance-wielding knights of Iran. 7780 They turned back Cratus's army, killing many and forcing a retreat.

Kush spurred on his horse and surged ahead, roaring, "O dimwitted king! Why do you come grasping at real men when you're not man enough to fight?" He reached out and drew him out of the saddle, pulling him up and throwing him on the ground.

His men put their hands together in shock and he roared like a raging elephant. He drew his heavy mace from his mountainous saddle and set upon those men like an inferno. When they saw his power and his determination, their commander seized in his grasp, the troops fled in such terror that the sun lost its way in the darkness of their dust.

They headed back to the city piecemeal, having had their fill of battle and its tribulations. The defeat became apparent to Mardan Khurreh who drew up ranks before the city gate. 7790 When those vengeful troops approached, they suddenly turned back from the gate and charged at the scattering troops, attacking with arrows and blades. Not one of them entered the city, and only a few of the Iranians were killed. Kush charged toward the city, steel-clad troops ahead and behind, his heart full of worry, his mind troubled by how great and numerous the enemy was.

He said, "The Iranians must not be routed by this army!" When Mardan Khurreh arrived, the commanding Kush's face bloomed.

Mardan said to him, "O ambitious one, when the enemy saw you they turned their faces. We raised our spears and blades. We permitted no rider to enter the city. Those brave men are now all scattered, as wolves seeing the breath of day." 7800

Kush's heart was cheered by this, he said, "Mardan did not fail to show manliness!"

He showed kindness to that lion-hearted fellow and arrived quickly at the city gate. He sent a detachment to bring his baggage and his precious throne. He sent two thousand of the warlike Iranians to the barracks, so that the soldiers would be unable to plunder.

Next, he sent a message to the city. "Your king has done something very foolish. We sought the return of our subjects from him, and sent him a letter to this effect. He spoke imprudently to me and my king, without having considered my army. His error was immediately apparent; the world hid its face from the king's judgment. When I crossed the water, I waited, lest he veer off the path of war 7810 and send our subjects back home, but he had no intentions except conflict and confrontation. He marched his forces and drew up ranks against me, and then that happened which must happen.

"You are all under my protection, and under the protection of my army. If he was kind to you, have no doubt I will be kinder still. And if he was beneficent to you, if he was wise and not oppressive, the glorious Faridun is even less oppressive, wiser, and more beneficent. The army has not come to ruin, the king has commanded nothing but justice and generosity. We do not covet your possessions, so it would be best for you to open the gates for us now. You will see your share of suffering at our hands if we take the city by the sword."

The people were afraid, hearing his message, but eventually gave in. 7820 They opened the city and stood before him, everyone preparing gifts. They scattered many gems over his head, and offered many excuses and apologies. Kush made inquiries to them, and then, with his army, entered and approached the king's palace portico.

He found Cratus's palace full of treasure—the writer's hand was worn out describing it. He called for camels from the fields and capable men and ordered the camel-drivers to load up. In one week, he emptied King Cratus's treasury and acquired his throne and crown. On the eighth day he took all of this treasure to his camp and freed the afflicted people of the city.

He said to thirty thousand sword-wielding knights, along with troops of good reputation, "Without sealed orders from me, none of those troops should be allowed entry to the city."

He then sent several men bearing letters to Cratus's troops. 7830 "I have spared your lives, every man on foot and on horse. Take your tents back to the barracks, your lives secure against your enemies' blades. If anyone is unwelcoming to you, they will see their share of humiliation from us. For the intimates and allies of that dimwitted one who fought so hard against us, rebelling against the exalted king—see, what did they reap but ruin? [231b] They are wicked and corrupt, their just desserts were our blade."

Now that they were safe from Kush's blade, they hurried back to their barracks. The next day, the rebels and the troops brought many gifts to the king. Lowering their faces to the ground, they praised him profusely. After that, everyone said, "May the king forgive our sins this time! 7840 Cratus, his ancestors, and our ancestors were all under the king's rule. We had no evil designs, we were following the path of our ancestors. But then this servant rebelled against his majesty, and it was most unwise. Now that fate has turned its face, it took his throne and gave it to the king. We all are girded to serve him until time reaches its end before his throne. Henceforth, we will not set foot outside the radius of his glory, if only he forgives us now."

Kush's face was refreshed and he treated them most favorably, building many buildings for them. "Thus have I shown you my forgiveness on behalf of the king. If you rebel against my command again, you'll find no quarter from me, I will not be forgiving. 7850 Now, be cheerful again and conduct yourselves agreeably with these troops. You must not lay your hands on things that belong to others, as if you were drunk and senseless. Apart from those things that were your own property—be it even a bundle of bare stones—if you take anything, you'll be chained up even if you're a noble."

He cheered the troops and they went and returned, bringing him garments and gifts. Then the king said to the Iranians, "Now the enemy cooperates with you. You must not be stingy with them, show them beneficence and cooperation. Be of one heart with those troops. I want for no one to have any complaints."

Those two armies mingled and shared each other's sorrow and joy. He gave to them the enemy's pavilion tents, and whatever they had, showing them generosity. 7860 His womenfolk and children and the treasure of his bedchamber he had sent to him by ship.

He then sent criers from one end of that land to the other, calling to the king's court all the refugees from the western lands. When the cry rose up in the courts and alleys, they came one by one toward the court. Farmers and town gentry as well as merchants, all headed for the palace.

The king gave them whatever they needed, as much as he had at his disposal. The farmers were given cows, donkeys, and sheep to please their hearts. He exempted the gentry from taxes, as well—they would owe nothing for three years. To the merchants he gave gold and silver and sent them along to their cities. They returned across the sea and found all of that property and treasure waiting for them. 7870

That satisfied king made landfall in a city in the west by the name of Orileh [Orihuela]. Whatever men of renown were there loaded up booty for Faridun. From what I have heard, they loaded ten thousand camels: valuable garments, silver and gold, pure musk and fresh aloeswood, thrones with crowns and gold turban-cloths.

KUSH THE TUSKED'S LETTER TO FARIDUN

He sent a letter to the king, "When this servant arrived at this place, those people who fled, endangered, from the west, I found in Spain. I wrote a letter to the king, Cratus, who sat upon his throne in ease, asking that he return those people to their place, but he lacked the good judgment to take that advice. 7880 His response was shocked, he made a number of statements in his letter, which this servant all sent before the king and had read out in court. I set out upon the sea and waited so long we were running low on food . . . so that that dimwitted fellow might allow my subjects to return. He assembled an army and confronted me, outnumbering my forces ten to one.

"By your glory, when the breath of daylight rose, I snatched him like an eagle seizing a bone. I cut his banner in two with my blade and his forces took flight. He had a city so solid that its towers unfurled against the heavens, guarded with walls of solid stone, with lead in place of mortar. With the force of the world-king, I took it and wrecked its porticoes and palaces. 7890 I took my pick of whatever treasure was obtained from the king's treasury, and sent it along. The rest I distributed to these subjects who resided in his lands. We have entrusted them to these skillful men and taken them back to their cities.

"I will now stay here for a while, until prosperity returns to the west. It will all become prosperous, as it was before, to nourish wolf and mouse alike. To that end, I will lead my forces for a time and inform the king of what I do." Thus he wrote, and placed his seal upon the letter, and sent it in the hands of a man appointed to the task. It was given to him and a caravan was assembled, one leader at the head of ten caravans. Three thousand armored knights went along with him to the king. The rest of the booty he distributed to his men, be it horsemen, armored knights, or infantry. 7900

He set out over the sea again and traveled across the whole country. Whoever rebelled against his authority had a shroud of blood drawn over them. The mountain of Tareq—Gibraltar—which no one had conquered, he conquered with capable men.[13] The worldly-wise say those seven peaks are terrifying to behold. Its peak is above the enshrouding dark clouds, its slopes fetter the claws of tigers from its broad base all the way to its peak—thus was it created by the just. Flowing water runs down its slopes, and trees, morning glories, and redbuds. Crossing such places, passing through wilderness, they crossed fields and waters.

When he arrived on the plain of Orihuela, he set up his pavilion tents by the river. He found the west as he had never seen it, all gardens, orchards, fields, and groves, 7910 fruiting trees and flowing water, verdure fit for kings. All of the meadows were filled with sheep, all the streams lined with tall trees.

In that joyful place he held a feast, raising his crown over the heavens. He invited Cratus's people to that feast, and seated the officers of the army to dine. Cratus was sorrowfully bound, but content even in his bindings. Women and children, and his family and retainers, all were saddened and helpless at the sight of his captivity.

When Kush was drunk, he called him forth and said, "You of evil birth, of wicked creed, why did you rebel against our authority, why did you think you could face us in battle?"

Cratus did not answer him, in his frightening anger and rage, and dared not raise his eyes. The wine boiled over in Kush's head, he struck

13. In Arabic, Gibraltar is Jabal Tariq, named after Tariq b. Ziyad, the Amazigh Umayyad commander who led the conquest of the Iberian Peninsula.

him with his blade and cast his head off his shoulders. 7920 From that sword-blow, the feastgoers' hearts took flight, and they all got up and began to flee.

Everyone—people from both armies—said to each other, "May this demon be gone from his throne! Since that day when he obtained this army and treasure, which that mighty army strained to carry, no one has ever killed a captive in this way, O thou exalted judge, answerer of our cries!" Everyone who heard about Cratus and Kush's deed lost their wits. Fear of him spread throughout the world, among great and small alike.

From that position, Kush marshaled his forces and toured the whole west. He had only one request—that people provide him with garments and gifts. That land was so good and prosperous that it was said that no one had ever seen its like.

When the booty arrived in Iran, it was brought before the king of the courageous. 7930 They were excited to receive those gifts, loaded upon camels. [232a] Everyone said, "Among the great and among the small of the world . . ."

Faridun looked upon that booty and selected what he found most fitting. The rest he gave to his troops and brave men, whose faces shone at the sight of their reward. The king responded to Kush, "You have dealt justice, o you who are deserving of your throne. All of my wishes have been fulfilled. Your name is brightened as the sun. We offer our abundant praise to you and to those worthies of the land of Iran."

At the new year, the king received other news, that the malevolent Kush, during a feast, had torn apart the helpless Cratus and made the hearts of the people saddened with pain.

He was saddened, and in his sorrow ceased to smile, and said, "May that demon be buried in the dust! 7940 He is satanic and rebellious, he has the character of a leopard and the temperature of fire. There is no glory in killing a prisoner after struggle, killing, and battle. An evil character cannot be left as it is—may the Lord's wrath be always upon him!"

When the general, Qaren, saw him saddened, he spoke words that alleviated his grief. He said, "O king, cheer up! Do not let your heart grieve over this. Whoever rebels against your command, surely their head must be cut. Because Cratus rebelled, it was necessary that he be killed by the king's champions."

Faridun's face brightened with joy, he smiled kindly at Qaren.

As Kush spent five more years in the west, he traversed the whole country. He set out again for Andalos, crossed the sea and saw the land. 7950 He found it prosperous and verdant, more than China and even the land of Iran. This Andalos is a different land, surrounded by the deep sea—the Encompassing Sea, called the Tarbos, its coast is filled with cities and populous lands.[14] The sea and land offer two routes of travel, and even a demon would shy away from both. There is a quick sea-route to the lands of the Franks, sailed by many ships. Traveling inland leads to 'Ajalaskas [Jaca], surrounded by frontier-lands.[15] People come to the frontier-lands, wealthy and in search of profit and merchandise. Those borderlands, and all the land there, the knowledgeable consider to be part of Rome.

When he returned, having seen those borderlands, he had seen the whole country with his own eyes. On one side, Rome and another sea, all the cities there well apportioned, 7960 with pleasant air and waters like rosewater. The strength of the sun makes the climate cooler there. The faces of men and women are like blossoms, full of narcissus and white roses of the river. Its orchards and gardens full of pomegranates and apples and its enchanting women and babes pleased him. He made the wreckage prosperous, the whole country prospered and he was cheered.

When there was no part of the country he had not yet visited, he advanced his forces toward Gibraltar. He saw all of its peaks, which you'd think were pillars of the sky. Seven mountains rose up out of the sea that were terrifying to behold. Finally, a difficult and narrow path, on which a lion would find no ease nor a leopard place of rest, was made the abode of men. It had a great many springs, fruit, and verdure, though it took you higher up than a falcon could fly in the course of a day. 7970 The plateau was surrounded as if by the fingers of a hand with the thumb splayed out. Clouds passed over one half, and

14. Tarbos may be a corruption of Tagus, the largest river in the Iberian Peninsula, which roughly bisects the peninsula from east to west.

15. Jaca is given in the text as 'Ajalaskas, a corruption of al-Jasaqas, referring to a frontier principality established by Charlemagne that by Iranshah's time had grown into the kingdom of Aragon. Daniel König, *Arabic-Islamic Views of the Latin West: Tracing the Emergence of Medieval Europe* (Oxford: Oxford University Press, 2015), 132.

cranes made their nests in the peaks. Referring to its height, they call it the "Mountain of Cranes." In those mountains he found a lead mine, copper mines, and other things.

He said to himself, "Let us build an abode here and relieve people's worry. Why would we have to worry about children and treasure, if we bring them here? We'll have no fear of the world's dangers, of kings or fearsome armies."

He commanded that the priests bestow those seven peaks on the nobles and their families. The troops built their own dwellings there too, occupying them at the start of the seventh year. A city was built, neither broad nor narrow, its fortifications all lead and stone. 7980 He adorned it with a portico and a dome, and augmented it with gardens and rosebeds. He erected thirty gold-chased domes, with twenty gem-studded porticoes. On either side were two porticoes of shining crystal, adorned with the forms of lions and onagers made of gems. Its timber was all of sandalwood, adorned with figures in precious stones. Seven carpets made of Chinese cloth of gold—no great man possessed their like. He adorned it with these things, and the sleeping quarters had decorations hung in their porticoes. Women, children, and treasure he brought up the mountain; ministers and treasury and the king were housed there.

His troops brought their clothes and possessions up that steep mountain. He also brought tradesmen of every profession. He gave them equipment and all manner of gifts. The king filled the markets with people and opened the two gateways of the city. 7990 One faced the sea, one faced the inhabited country, and people passed through them day and night. He placed iron gates in both of them, the likes of which no one can recall seeing. Then he built several other large towns with great fortresses. Unto each town were three hundred and sixty villages—finer than the cities and more impressive. The mountains' peaks thus became more pleasant than their slopes, with villages upon villages and gardens upon gardens, filled with people and beasts of burden and flocks all gathered there without a watchman. When people were at ease there on that mountain, he named it the Oasis of the Crown.

Kush resided in that city for two years, content, at ease with wine and song. When it was time to hunt, he hunted game in the fields, taking a trip over the mountain and over the sea. Once he marched his forces toward the desert, another time toward the Lands of Darkness and the sea.[16] 8000 There was an astounding valley with rocky sides from which a great, wide river flowed from a land called Satira.[17] Rivers flow from all directions into this valley. Now, cities and villages, seas and mountains, can all be seen there. The Arab was so pleased by this that he named the city Bani Salem.[18]

For twenty years he labored there, bringing some of his womenfolk and children and treasure. Settling there, he was secure against the ravages of time and the king became informed of this. Of Faridun's reign, a hundred and twenty years had passed, and he was without equal. Learned ones have said, to the contrary, that in the time of the world-king Jamshid, Abraham came as a prophet, but this is incorrect. From him until the snake-summoning prophet Moses, there were four hundred and thirty-six years. 8010 Happy is he who knows that Moses came in the time of Manuchehr.

KUSH THE TUSKED GOES TO WAR AGAINST THE BLACK HORDES OF BEJA AND NUBIA

After the business in the west, the quarrelsome Black Hordes became informed that the west had returned to its former condition, with gold and silver and all manner of things, cattle, farmland, and trees, such as had never been there before. A detachment traveled there stealthily to see, and found it better than anyone in Nubia had heard of.

They brought back news of this discovery, their words making it seem even greater, "This land in its stunning condition we found without king or army. The fields are all full of animals, of herds, we saw no shepherd guarding the flocks." From Nubia and Beja, thousands upon thousands emerged, ready for war. One group of them, all most eager, headed towards Zowaylah. 8020 The other half charged down the road to Aswan, toward the land of Egypt—young and old. The Black

16. The Lands of Darkness (Zulmat in Arabic) are the regions near the Arctic Circle where the days remain dark in midwinter.

17. Satira may refer to Asturias, a province of Spain that remained beyond the limits of Umayyad rule.

18. Bani Salem literally means "Sons of the Secure," or "Tribe of the Secure."

men in the vanguard raised their arms and leveled cities to the ground. A wave of blood spread from the west, people fleeing in droves.

Riders raced to bring word to Kush that the Black Hordes had thrown the land into chaos. He smiled and descended from Gibraltar, with mariners and ships to cross sea and river. [232b] He sent letters to summon his troops to him, paid them silver dirhams and brought horses from all over. His force numbered more than six hundred thousand mail-clad armored knights. He crossed the sea and arrived on the field, the sky taken aback by the amount of armor. First he turned his attention to that force that had deprived Zowaylah of all color and scent.

The Black Hordes were dispersed and drunk, having given themselves over to looting and oppression. 8030 They were unaware of Kush and his great army and had not placed watchmen on the road, when a nighttime raid came from Kush—a great charge, roars of brave men, and the taking of vengeance.

They reached for their swords and daggers, and neither the sober nor the drunk escaped them. The black-faced men drew up ranks, showed their bravery and manliness. They were on foot, unclothed, and without horse or equipment, holding great wooden branches—a great pillar you know as a *farasb*, whose blows level man and horse alike. Once a blow is struck and a man taken down, then you do not see the dust of their charge. And if blade or arrow strikes their bodies, their skirts are covered in blood.

Not knowing the method or route of retreat, their hearts full of fear and their minds gripped by terror, two eyes bloodshot and faces the color of charcoal, bodies impressive in their strength and fearsome in war, 8040 with the force of an elephant and claws of a lion, mighty of body and brave of character, they never turn their faces away from men's blows until they are ground into the dust. They killed many men of the Iran-army, and many of the demon-faced ones were destroyed.

The troops said many importunate things to Kush, to which he replied, "O dim-witted troops, what kind of fighting is this? You took my words lightly. A group of Black men, without materiel or horses, armed with nothing but shepherd's staves, the enemy are not more than half our number. I am ashamed of you. How can I say to the mace-wielding king that we could not stand up to the blows of sticks? How could lances and sharp blades be thrown into pandemonium by the blows of sticks?"

He said this, and joined his troops, turning the dust and stones burgundy with blood. 8050 The army pressed on with blade and arrows, the ground turning into a sea of tar from the dead bodies. No one escaped the warriors and brave men, all were killed and cut down. When Nubia saw such sword-blows, they surreptitiously took flight. One by one, they vanished from the earth, as if no one had ever seen the face of Nubia.

When Kush was victorious and dismounted, in his joy he called for wine and stringed instruments. He ordered—with no embarrassment, no shame in his heart—that everyone take the corpse of a Black man, drenched in blood, and cook it and roast it up. They tore up many bodies and cooked them in those great cauldrons with all manner of things. They flayed the skin off of some of them, and no one had seen anything in the world like this. Some they cut in half, and others, they cut off their heads, hands, and feet. 8060

Everyone said to him, "Your majesty, this is unspeakable. No king ever did this to those he had slain, no one ever saw men roasted and cooked."

He laughed and said, "This is a new army—brave men of battle, champions! Those who are scattered across the land, looking for plunder and mayhem, whoever approaches the camp will be terrified and flee. When they see us doing this, they will not show up to fight again. They will think that we subsist on cooked human flesh. They will weep for their dead, and flee in fear of their own lives."

When he had blackened the ground with them, he turned toward that army again. He drove them to the mountainous country that today we call Hajat 8070 near Egypt, out of sight from sea or mountain. The sky deep blue, the earth raven-black from the color of steel-clawed Black men.

When they saw the army, they rose up and brandished their staves. Roaring like thunder, they drew up ranks, covering their lips with their hands like tigers. The world-seeking Kush and his intimidating army advanced two stages every day. They arrived, exhausted, and began to rest, playing flutes and strings to recover from the hardships of the road—so tired were the king and troops. The black-faced ones spread the word that the army was not ready for battle.

Kush said, "You are recovered from your travel, now you must do battle."

A roar rose up and the army was in motion. The plain turned black from their color. 8080 The advance guard charged toward Kush—you'd think he would be stunned witless with fear, for the army was now in such dire straits.

He cried out, "No room for hesitation!" The world-seeking Kush entered the fray on horseback and the army raged like the fire of Azorgoshasb.

He said to the troops, "O proud men! Headstrong brave men of Iran! First, fire a volley of arrows, then, a cavalry charge! Reach for your lances and blades—like fierce lions, like raging elephants! Whomever you take captive, whomever you take by the neck with your lasso, tear their body apart with your teeth! Destroy those warriors with your teeth! Let them believe that we are all man-eaters, 8090 be frightened, and flee from this battle, and never return to this place."

The troops did as their commander said, nocking their arrows. The bodies of the black-faced men became like the dawn from the shafts passing through them. They killed a great number in that volley of arrows, and more with javelins and mighty blows.

The demon-faced ones rained down blows on the army from all sides, with their heavy staves. Those heads struck by the ebony wood would never again see shining cap or crown. Horses that took blows from the staves suffered broken bones. Both armies suffered losses, as the black and white mingled in combat. Whomever the brave men of Iran got a hold of they quickly tore into with their teeth. They opened the hide off of their sides and backs. Each group of soldiers killed an enemy in this manner. 8100 The world-seeker had destroyed many of those demon-faced men. Those he struck near their middle, he cut in two, striking fear into those dark-faced ones. The enemy's unclothed bodies met Kush's blade and blood surged liked tears of sorrow.

The Black Hordes were enraged and vengeful against him, fury radiating from their eyes. Many such confrontations took place, and there was no room on the ground for the living. The Black men now arriving on the field saw what had happened to their companions. One was cooked from head to toe over stones, another was roasted in a pot. One was flayed and suspended, another had his feet and bones removed; one was set upon by dogs, who ate his entrails and cast aside his hindquarters. 8110

Whatever one could see on the battlefield was too much to take. People lost their heads to fear and took flight to their homeland. The army became aware that the battlefield was emptied of Black Hordes. Those soldiers, devouring the carnage, became a mighty army that killed all of the Nubians. They tore and devoured so many of them, none of those honorable men remained.

The Nubians were so taken aback when they realized this that their wits fled their minds. When the sun turned its face away from the dome, no Nubian was to be found on that battlefield. The troops mounted up and set off after them, killing or capturing whoever was left. Of those routed crow-faced men, not one out of three hundred remained. 8120

Kush traveled for a month into the desert, striving to make haste along with his army by way of Aswan, until he reached Tovveh, where he drew his blade in vengeance. Whomever of them he saw, he killed and burned, setting fire to that country. Again, he ordered a number of bodies to be cooked, so that the Nubians said, in secret, [233a] "These are ferocious leopards, to eat people raw and cooked!" Whatever country word of this spread to, they took flight.

After he had traveled a week in that land, he turned back toward Aswan. Along the way, he found gold that grew from the earth, shining from the gravel like lamps. They stopped and dismounted in that sandy desert that was hot enough to burn leather. 8130 Everyone looked around and took some of it, they loaded camels with it. He sent detachments, ten thousand of the Iranians, to seek out the errant gold.

He gave them a year's worth of bread and water, saying to them, "Do not return in a hurry. Spend a year searching this gravel desert to obtain the growing gold. At the end of the year I will send you beasts of burden, so stay where you are and don't worry."

He left and returned to the west, taking a treasure from that gold-mine. In whatever land he stopped, happily, enjoying wine and song the whole way, they put up festive decorations and showered gold, suspending saffron from the walls.

Then he said to a knowledgeable minister, in secret, "There is one thing I must do. I will build a fortress from stone, in case the Blacks wage war again, 8140 and surge out seeking to do battle. People will remain there, with their wives, children, and property, and they will be secure in that city."

He sent scouts out in that land, and they began searching it. They found a site in Tripoli and hurried to bring back the news. A city was built beside the sea, all of cut stone and lead. And so he built a fortress there, which grew tall as a mountain. He placed a sturdy iron gate that could never be opened by force, so solid that if the seven lands of the earth all went to war against it, it would be beyond their grasp—it need fear only the heavens. He placed abundant storehouses in it, more of their weapons and armor. 8150

He said to the people of that land, "If the demon-faced ones wage war, take refuge in this city with your women, children, and valuables. Do not let me hear news that people have been destroyed."

He looked over every side of that city and whoever was with him, and those who sought sanctuary there, he settled in that city, and then he turned back. That same fortress and other cities raised their head above the turning heavens—such as Nakur, Niru, and Kairouan—were built in its orbit, in the splendor that that commanding figure gave them, beauty upon beauty. Their people all appreciated them, jumping out of their skins in happiness. Since they were delivered from evil, the people, young and old alike, became his admirers. 8160 No longer did anyone hear any news of those demon-faced ones.

He gained control of two choice mines, from which precious gold poured out like stones. One mine was located beyond the city of Aswan, two weeks' journey across the sandy desert, through 'Aydhab and the land of Ethiopia—pure gems, like the sun! The route was such that one needed to plant posts to mark the route. No verdant place there, and no wells for water, all dry gravel boiled by the sun. Near Sijilmasa was another mine—you could not find purer gold than that. If you travel seven days from Zawilah, that world-illumining mine appears, and so on until the land of the crude Blacks. The gold flows—what a wonder! The eagle does not fly that route, because of the lack of water and rays of the sun. 8170 Treasure is always buried under toil, and all happiness is contained in treasure. In all that land you will not find a single thorny bush, not in all those sand dunes and dust storms. During spring and during autumn, all of that treasure sprouts from there. When he returned satisfied from the west, the whole world was talking about him.

[KUSH'S LETTER TO FARIDUN
AND HIS RESPONSE]

He sent a letter reporting all this to that great court. "We have cleared the land of the Nubians and raised dust from their cities. By the glory of the great king, this is what I wrought in the western lands. The dove and falcon rest peacefully together in one house and no harm is done."

Faridun was pleased by that letter and shortly wrote a response. "May you be ever cheered and victorious, for you have wrought honorable justice. 8180 No one had done to those demonic ones what you did, o lion-hearted warrior. May courage and cunning in battle be ever yours, and may you enjoy feasting and wine for many years."

Then the king's scribes and warriors who had gone with Kush to that theater of war sent word to everyone at that great throne and court of the Mountain of the Cranes and the deep sea, about those great and wide cities, and about that valuable treasure and gold mines, and his ferocious military maneuvers.

Faridun looked to Qaren and said, "Kush will be ungrateful. His heart will turn against us, away from righteousness."

Qaren said to him, "Until now he has not evaded the sovereign's authority. I don't know what will come next—let's hope he does not return to his old ways!" 8190

Faridun said to him, "This demon-born comes from a seed that should never have been a seed, a son who would kill his own father violently—kill him for worldly gain. His character is grotesque, his constitution evil, anyone with wisdom can foresee this. This snake will discover his own essence if you lay him down beside you. If you give rose oil to a fire, it will burn if you dip your finger in it. And if you nurture a wolf cub, it will revert to its own nature."

After Kush had come to see his own strength, in treasure and steel-clad men, that gold mine that God created, which no king on earth had seen, that mountain whose peak rose to the moon, and his steadfast and numerous army, he grew bold with his lands and position and treasure. Nothing gives more security than power and wealth. 8200

Day and night, he would tell himself, "In all the world there is no king like me. Why should I be subordinate to anyone, with this army, treasure, and abode? My lineage is greater and my men more numerous than the kings they have seen so far. For Faridun struggled so long against the Black Hordes of Mazandaran with his warriors—he is no greater than me in manliness, his treasure and army are no greater than mine. He would not be my match in wartime—I gave no second thought to these sorry fellows. I wrecked their country with blade and javelin of glistening steel."

When these thoughts stretched out in his brain, no more tribute or tax was sent to Iran. He sent letters only on occasion, nor did he send any gifts to the king.

Secretly, someone had the scribes write, "He has veered away from justice and righteousness." 8210 He entrusted it to people traveling to Iran, but Kush had secretly sent soldiers after him. If anyone wrote a letter to the king, saying that the commander had forsaken the righteous path and creed, that he now had no desire to serve him and had forsaken obedience, they would seize him and take him to the king with the letter, and Kush would remove his head from his body right there.

After that, if the king wanted any treasure, he would write a letter in response, saying, "How can I collect treasure to send from a ruined country and wrecked cities?"

When ten years had passed like this, the great king's upright scribe sent a man on foot in secret to the world-king. "This one of wicked nature has rebelled after being treated so well by you. The great treasure and armies went to his head, in his abode on the Mountain of Cranes. 8220 Whoever of the Zahhakians comes before him, his crown is raised above the heavens. Thousands upon thousands have come to him, mail-clad armored knights. Day and night he watches the roads to prevent me from conveying this message to the king. Several men traveling with letters he caught and killed in secret with cruel blows. [233b] If you do not discover his doings soon, it will turn into an unbearable tragedy. Things will not change if you wait, it will surely cause trouble for the king, for up to now he has been stalling the king with words, hoping it will be too late." When the messenger reached the sovereign, he quietly said what he had seen and heard.

He called for Qaren, the general of his army and all his troops, and said to him, "I told you before that he of such wicked creed would go astray. 8230 As soon as he obtained wealth and power, his own essence intoxicated him."

Qaren said to him, "The world-king does not know both what is manifest and what is hidden in him. He has committed no other sin that we have seen, and it took so long for word to reach us. That demonic one makes excuses, that he has taken over the western lands. If you wanted straight answers, he gave them: the whole west is like paradise. He has made it so prosperous that I have heard it has never been this verdant. Now that the king is worried, we must send a letter calling him to the court. If he rebels and does not appear, I will gird myself to battle him."

He called for the messenger to come before him, and he told everything to Qaren that he had heard from the sovereign's scribe. The champion bit his lips in worry. 8240

[FARIDUN'S LETTER TO KUSH, CALLING HIM TO FIGHT MEHRAJ AND THE RULER OF CHINA]

Then he said to him, "Your majesty, select a worthy man from Iran-army, write a letter stating your command, using kind words and all manner of courtesy. 'From the world-seizing king of lofty essence to the sovereign of the western lands: Because I am so pleased with you, o worthy one, the creator is also pleased with you. For you have built up the country so well, and delivered the land from the Black Hordes; none of the army-sheltering sovereigns was able to do what you did with that army.

"'Now that the country is prosperous and no enemy troops are left, a commander must be stationed there. Give him troops, so that we may have the pleasure of briefly seeing you, in your splendid condition. Bring whatever troops you need with you, for now things have changed. Mehraj, the ruler of India—may he disappear from that sorcerous land!—8250 has turned away from obedience to us and prepared to march on Iran. All of those garden palaces he has flattened with his men of war and raging elephants. He desires Kush's mace and must be met with piercing darts. You must be this court's affliction against that warlike force. Now, marshal your troops and assemble treasure, and labor to go to war against Mehraj. No one but you is man enough to undertake this labor—the world-champion himself is not up to the task.'"

Once the king had the letter sealed, he chose an experienced man from among his troops, and gave it to him to deliver: "Travel day and night, do not stall. Spread the word wherever you spend the night that Mehraj prepares for war against the king."

He thus got word to the king of China that they would eliminate all enmity . . .[19] 8260 The experienced rider wended his way and reached the court of Kush, seeking an audience. The court attendants brought him in quickly and received him with warmth and kindness. When the man saw the haughty Kush, he was startled and his face turned sallow. He kissed the ground and gave him the letter, offering praises before the throne and crown. He precisely conveyed the greetings from the king and Qaren, along with those of the nobles.

The clever Kush asked about the king, and about the steel-clad men of honor. He seated him graciously and showed him kindness.

The envoy offered many praises in return. "The world-conquering king continually speaks of you with his troops, praising you before them day and night, like a drunkard who won't stop talking. If you battle Mehraj and the governor of China, he will give that land to you. 8270 No one in all the world would be more honored than you, openly or in secret."

When the minister read Kush that letter, he saw what was going on and suppressed a smile. He knew what he had in mind, and the meaning of these sweet and lovely words. He bade the envoy be seated and said, "May you enjoy rest, music, and wine." He appointed royal scribes to watch him, in order that they not tell him the true state of affairs. No one was to go near him. They hosted him graciously for twenty days and no one knew who the visitor was.

KUSH'S LETTER RESPONDING
TO KING FARIDUN

He then wrote a letter to him, warm in tone, "The letter of the king, of sun-like visage, made my face bloom with happiness like a rose, and my heart and soul smile with joy. At the same time, my heart was stricken by the Indian Mehraj and the other Indians. 8280 The king called on me to deal with him and wishes that I face him in battle. The

19. The mention of China here is likely an error, as the text has made no mention up to this point of Mehraj being king of China, and in fact it states specifically that Qaren entrusted governorship of China to Nastuh, on Faridun's orders.

king in his sun-like glory knows that our troops are great in number. An army can be marshaled in two years here, and in two more years it would reach the king. Another year would be needed to assemble materiel. All of this time would pass, and who knows what fate would bring in the meantime! And besides, once the Black Hordes become aware that we have left and taken the troops, they will come and ruin this region, acting like lions and leopards. Our labor will be gone with the wind and our country ruined; the king would have consigned the people to suffering and injustice. I would thus not be so bold as to leave this place.

"Since the king, noble of spirit, has issued a command, I will send him as many troops as he needs, warlike and battle-hungry knights. 8290 I will send treasure worth three years of their daily expenses, and enchanting gifts. They will come to overthrow Mehraj and behead the Indians with their blades. We offer our praises to the king's life, the entire world under his command."

When the envoy was satisfied with this response from Kush, he raced back faster than smoke.

When the answer reached the court, the king's minister looked it over and read it out. Faridun sought to uncover whatever he could, and the envoy reported everything exactly as he saw it, of his crown and golden throne, of how he held court according to his own creed, of the solidity of his position, of the region and equipment and numbers of the army.

Faridun was taken aback by what he said, and turned his face to the champion, Qaren. He said, "Summon here those troops that went with Kush from this court." 8300

All uncertainty left the champion's heart, and the king's heart was troubled. "When they arrive I will marshal an army and take the life out of that demon's body. As I shake my steel spear, I shall do much worse to that demon-faced one than what I did when I knocked him off his horse during the battle in China."

The king remained in thought for a long time, and he then said, "O benevolent one, remember that the western lands have been barren. We reckoned that country still a ruin, still the stomping-ground of tigers and lions. As he has been sent there on royal orders, this judgment seems unfair. Otherwise I would call for more troops from him, if I thought it honorable!"

[FARIDUN'S LETTER TO KUSH AND HIS
SUMMONING OF THE IRANIANS]

He ordered the scribe to write, a scribe who wrote with great erudition. 8310 "I have read your letter, and what you said in the first place seems right to me. Be the guardian of those people. Be on guard against the enemy's interference. It would be fitting if you sent back to this court the troops that you took with you, so that they be ready to do battle against Mehraj, against this army that marches on us now. Let go those wise, alert men, send them all to us."

To those scribes and heroes he sent a letter with a translator, "Return immediately to the court, as you have undergone extended hardships. I will reward your travails—the sovereign is as the head, the army as the body."

When the letter reached the nobles, their faces bloomed with cheer. They took it and presented it to Kush. He was displeased by them and did not respond. [234a] 8320 Then he said, "This is fine. He is king and does as he pleases. He wrote me a letter saying these things, 'Send us those noblemen.' Now you must wait for a while and think on the honor of this matter."

The nobles left his court satisfied. Everyone had their hearts set on leaving. Kush's heart was worried by those letters. He set his mind to scheming. He never considered letting those proud men go back. He had gained such power, contentment, and peace in that land because of them—those brave, country-conquering, world-taking, battle-ready men of war.

A long time passed like this and the brave men saw no way to end this situation except to escape, and everyone made plans in secret. 8330 Kush learned about them. He sat upon his imperial throne. He called all of his nobles before him and spoke at length. He offered them manly praises, one by one, speaking kind and solicitous words to many. "We have our crown and throne because of you, when we left Iran to go to war. You have undergone great travail for us, as our allies and companions. I heard that you have a way to leave—such injustice must not come to pass. Whoever stays in this court, I will raise their crown to the heavens. I will keep them forever in seats of honor, dearer to me than my soul and body. Whoever does not wish to stay here, possessed of command and lands, if you wish to go to Khanireh, even though it means you will languish in obscurity, 8340 why go in secret?[20] We will send armies with them."

All of the nobles applauded, saying, "O your majesty, worthy king of the earth, may fortune ever be with you! May people not wag their tongues at you! You are our glorious Faridun, more splendid to us than the sovereign! We all came from Iran with nothing, when we came with our king whom we obey. Now we have wealth and means and treasure, though we suffered great travail with the king. Our grandfathers suffered as well and gained much from the kings of old, but not as much as we have, now that we followed the king. May the world-creator be pleased with you, and may your enemies' hearts fill with smoke.

"However, you know that forty years have passed since we uprooted our hearts 8350 from city, wives, and children, from hearth and home. How long will our hearts be full of worry? How many of our companions were killed, how many embraced by the soil? They have forgotten our names in Iran, they don't know who lives and who has died. We would by the king's order return once more to our places in Iran. At the new year, when the king sends a message calling us back, we will hurry back to this court."

The renowned king responded thus, "You may make your preparations, then. We will tell the high priest that you have promised to return."

The nobles left his presence—who could even know what happiness they felt!

Kush could not allow that army, so effective with its equipment and wealth, to depart from his camp and take everything back to Faridun. 8360 He planted a number of clever men secretly among those nobles. They still did not accept offers of lands, silver, and gold. They were not fooled.

There was a worthy man by the name of Mardan, at the peak of strength and manliness, a proud youth from the seed of Jamshid. The proud Salkot was his uncle. For years, he had been jealous of Qaren, shedding tears of spite night and day. Consider jealousy a demon black in color, night and day in battle with the divine. When he saw

---

20. Khanireh is a rendering of Khvaniras, the name used in Zoroastrian scripture for Iranzamin, the central region of the world, which includes Iran and Iraq.

Qaren receive high rank from the king in Iran for his heroism and leadership, his heart was wounded by that decision.

Qaren, too, was injured and spiteful, both in times of good cheer and those of battle, when the sovereign gave an army to Kush, because battle was his path and his creed. 8370 He said to him, "Take him out of Iran, send him with his army to the west."

Iranzamin was not called Iran; the priests called it Khanireh. When Iran was bestowed upon Iraj, Faridun gave it the name of Iran.[21]

When it was time to return from Kush's company, the steel-clad Mardan said to himself, "If I return to the country of Khanireh, I will be troubled by Qaren again. Being like a blacksmith, subordinate, I may as well be buried alive. And if I stay with the king, I'll be champion of the army like Qaren."

At night he sent his brother to Kush with a devious idea. "O king, you know no one girds themselves for manly deeds like I can. Since my lineage is from the seed of Iran, and such is my nature and my constitution, 8380 you should give me station above these nobles of Iran—a place beside yourself. I have a force of more than ten thousand, brave sword-wielding men of war. I can stay here, marshal my forces, and my life be the king's shield."

Kush raised his head in joy upon reading this letter. You'd think he'd boiled over with happiness. He gave the brother a horse with trappings, an Indian blade in a gold-chased scabbard, and sent a number of precious gifts, more decorated Arabian horses to the worthy men of his army, and many gifts of all kinds. Those brave men wanted for nothing in the world—all manner of gold and silver. As for the others, he contented his injured heart, imprisoning those who were able to write 8390 and putting them in dire straits, sending them warlike words: "From all this speaking and writing letters to the king, you have lost me my battle-ready army."

When the Iranians reached Iran safe and in good cheer with their treasure, the great king asked them about the conduct and deeds of the

---

21. In *The Shahnameh*, Faridun divides the world between his three sons, Iraj, Salm, and Tur, giving his youngest son Iraj the central land, called Iranzamin, because he finds him most worthy. Salm and Tur kill their younger brother out of jealousy. *Zamin* means "land," so Iranzamin and Iran are essentially the same name, and the name change here is from Khanireh to Iran(zamin).

mighty Kush. They all related to him what had transpired, what the heavens' turning wheel had brought them. They all spoke of the battle with the Black Hordes of Mazandaran, of the Mountain of Cranes and his labors there, of cities and seas, of his battles.

One said, "O king, glorious and just, he has put your scribes in fetters. He said, 'You made this most renowned army depart from this court, and caused trouble for me with the great king. Bit by bit you have put me in a bad place.' 8400 Mardan remains with him, pleasing his dark soul. Troops and men remain with him too, now endowed with all manner of wealth."

Faridun was disappointed by Mardan and said, "Evil cannot remain hidden. His ancestor was kin to my ancestors, and he has many grievances against me. Otherwise I would have destroyed him, brought ruin upon his retainers and family. For now, let us leave him alone—remove his name from the account books."

Thus the steel-clad men became the elite companions of the haughty Kush. His crown rose from the dust to the Pleiades and the whole army was under his command. After that, Kush sounded a call to head for the field and returned from the Maghreb to Andalos. He toured the land and purged the country of all injustice. 8410 He built three more cities, all of cut stone, that could not be breached by men of war. One of them he named Taltameh; he rested there for a while.[22] The second he named Torjaleh [Trujillo], another Shantarin [Santarém]. Then all the roads went by the sea. He found a great quantity of ambergris by the seaside and the troops all rushed to gather it. They found so much ambergris that they were inhaling its scent for years.

They saw a creature in the water, its two eyes shining like the sun. Its body was like a sharp-clawed cat, the hair all over its back was the color of the sun. With that hair, a skilled weaver could weave garments just like silk. If you were to throw it in the water and leave it for years, it would be dry when you took it out. [234b] Not one thread made of that hair would be wet—such a lovely and splendid garment it would be, 8420 showing ten colors at once, the sight of it cheers the heart! Whoever found thousands of those would find a treasury of gold dinars at their disposal! There remain so many of those animals in the sea, and that sweet-smelling, brilliant ambergris.

22. Taltameh is probably a corruption of Tulaytulah, that is, Toledo.

He worried for many years that he would suffer harm from Faridun. After years had passed, no army was sent by the Iranians. He was safe from the doings of Faridun, and he turned to the wine-cup, rest, and feasting. Whatever nobles remained in his army all gathered around his door, supplicating him. He ordered that they return, giving them silver dirhams, horses, and gifts of all kinds. His proud men he treated to polo and hunting and they spent those days enjoying themselves.

To the most knowledgeable Faridun he sent an experienced rider. 8430 He sent a letter with apologies and humility, without quarrelsome words. He advised the envoy to discretely become informed on all matters, both good and bad events. "See what he has planned, that foul king, how many steel-clad men he has."

The man rode like the wind and returned like smoke, he asked his questions and heard the responses. He said to Kush, "From today until many years from now, you'll suffer no harm by Faridun's hand. He has no hostile or violent intentions, he sits and feasts with his noblemen. You'd think his crown was the moon encircling his head as he stands. I asked about the markets and his troops. Faridun has no appetite for conflict."

Kush's heart was cheered when he learned this, and he gave many gifts to the envoy. He ordered that the king's innocent scribes be killed in prison. 8440 Because of that, he sat in good cheer, feasting and drunk on his treasure and security. He became so proud, and his character so benighted, that he desired nothing but blood and killing. He seized anyone he wanted to, women and lovely children, even those who were quick on their feet. He reverted to his own twisted nature, to his old ways. He showed no generosity to anyone, nor kindness, his conduct and visage becoming stranger and stranger.

Just as he had done in China, he commanded the priests of the land to build an idol in every house and paint them all. They crafted them in the likeness of the mighty Kush, idols of all sizes. When men and women rose from their beds, with a statue standing before them, they touched their heads to the floor before it and uttered many prayers to it. 8450

To the oppressed people, the benighted and unjust Kush said, "I am the world's creator, I make prosperous lands into ruins when I please. All life that exists is my doing; death is between my blade and my thumb. All good comes from me, and all evil and coarseness comes from me, and all wisdom. I make whomever I want powerful through my own power, using my own gold and jewels to bestow a crown. I bring harm to whomever I wish, casting them into the dust from their thrones."

When men and women heard his words, Satan became their companion. The people, whether they were strangers or his companions, accepted his creed. A number of people, out of ignorance and pride, turned to the path of darkness and evil, some out of fear, a few out of desire. 8460 It brought cheer to many people's hearts that he had made the world so prosperous. They all became idolaters at his command, and drunk demons by his wine-cup. Whomever he found did not have the idol, he of benighted creed cut their head from their body. Because of him, the whole west became idolatrous—I know of no one else who accomplished such a feat.

When news of this reached Faridun, it awakened old pains. He laughed and said, "This mighty, foul creature has suddenly turned his head away from the godly path, and even led the people astray. He has once again troubled my heart. May that wicked one receive no blessings. May the face of the earth be free of that demon!" Whoever learned about Kush, that he had strayed and rebelled against the king, Zahhakians and ill-born ones, flocked to him and formed a great host. 8470 A great army amassed under his command, a mountain upon the plains and fields of the west.

Chapter 6

AN OLD MAN TELLS THE STORY OF
THE LAND OF BEAUTIES

The storyteller passed down from the speech of the pure-of-heart that one day Kush sat feasting, filling the world with the warbling of pipes and wine. Many nobles sat with him, everyone was talking about the beauties of every land and country, of the Turks, of China, and of the land of Rome.

The conversation carried on until an old man in the gathering spoke. "I have traveled the whole earth, marking the whole earth with my footsteps. I never saw such beauty as I saw there—color, speech, stature, and hair as I saw in the land of women—so moon-faced and silvery! They're like cypresses, when the moon shines through a cypress tree, with hips like a wild ass and waists like reeds, 8480 limbs like flowers blooming in spring, white like snow and black like pitch, all ravishingly beautiful and sweet-tongued youths, with faces shining like the sun and lips like coral. Your heart cannot stay in your chest when you see them, their locks trample it under their feet. All black-haired with cheeks like the sun, jasmine-scented, with statures like cypresses."

When Kush heard that loquacious man's word's, his heart raced and he opened his ears. He said to him, "Tell me more of this heart-melting land—which country is it that the land be so verdant with beauties, and such beauties as this?"

The man who had spoken said, "This land is considered by the learned to be part of Rome. One must cross the sea first, then the road goes straight to Jaca. From that place, one must travel another month's journey through places both hospitable and hostile. 8490 By the month's end one reaches Bashkubosh [Basque Country], a pleasant land with agreeable people. From there, one must travel another twenty days, to arrive at a heart-pleasing land, adorned with fair-faced beauties and fleet-footed steeds, filled with valuable treasures."

Kush heard him out. He said, "We must travel to that land. We will bring ruin to their warriors and bring them under our command. We will see who the rulers are, how splendid those beauties are and what they're like."

Everyone became spiteful toward the man who spoke, and men and women alike cursed him: "This man has forced us to take to the road, where we will meet with fear and travail."

He marshaled some of his troops, six hundred thousand brave men of battle, warriors. He gave them a year's worth of provisions and treasure, those proud men and hardened riders. 8500 At the new year, an army like black dust hurried to the king's side. They crossed the sea and set foot on land. Spring came and the soil became like musk. The breeze passed over the plain, through roses and willows, and slowly rose above the heavens.

The world-seeking king reached Jaca, its king and his army unaware of him. The air was suddenly filled with soldiers' dust. Its fields and valleys' color turned suddenly. When the army was three days' journey away from his city, he learned of its approach and grieved. He was shocked by that news and his bright day darkened. He summoned those troops who were near him into the city, with none left outside. The city was fortified and solidly secured, guarded with brave armored men. He did not know what a disaster Kush and his army had in store for them, 8510 how many troops that battle-hungry warrior had marshaled. He was frightened and did not appear before anyone, as manliness and wisdom demand. He said to the honorable men of war, "For fame and honor, for the sake of your lives, your children, and treasure, your lineage and your families, strive and be men! Put your hearts into it! [235a] Strive, and with our men and our treasure, let us protect this land from harm!"

When Kush saw the tops of those towers and walls, fortresses all of solid stone, deep water running all around that city, and an imposing gate of iron, he commanded them to raise a loud cry—those brave men of war and courageous knights. Arrows rained down on the fortress and the battle was joined; it continued for a month. 8520 Many were killed on both sides, and the commanding Kush was afraid. He saw no prospect of taking the city, and was anxious, thoughts racing through his head. After that, he ordered his army to plunder all of the land. The whole countryside was burned—they despoiled that verdant land. They scattered its people whose homes and peace were destroyed. There was no prosperous place left in that country except the city and its lord's palace.

They cut a number of trees from the forest, for they were in a tight situation. They erected catapults all around, and the troops began digging a tunnel. One day, Kush put on his armor and shouted to his men. Everyone swiftly girded themselves for battle. The riders drew up even ranks. 8530 They covered their path with dirt and rocks as arrows rained down on the fortifications. The pope and bishops hid their heads from those mangonel and catapult stones. When the plain was struck more than a hundred times, the brave men showed courage with their blood. The dark night overtook the mountain's crest, and those courageous companies fought on. Kush, too, did not retreat from the edge of the moat, he did not sleep. The brave men swarmed around the moat, holding all the crossings.

When the turning heavens opened their veil, the sun's face made the ground radiant. He called for axes, shovels, and thick shields. He crossed the moat and advanced. When the commander stood before the fortress, the brave men picked up pickaxes. They began to cut through the rock, brave men and heroes with steel in hand. 8540 As they cut through, they set up pillars, building a colonnade greater than Bisotun. Then they set fire to the wood inside and, at once, the fortifications collapsed.

That weighty mountain tumbled down, and everyone who saw it was stunned and amazed. Those troops fell headfirst into the pit, in blood and dust. After they began spilling from the walls, the fortifications' garrison took flight. Kush hurled the army back into the city, raising commotion in every street and alley. He put the brave men to the sword, subduing every street and market.

Kush approached the royal palace, and restrained his troops from plundering. He cut the king's body through the middle with his blade, filling all kings' hearts with fear. 8550 He took captive the women of his night chambers, now languid, their hearts wounded. Then he lit a great fire that burned up the streets and markets and alleyways. No man or woman remained in that land, no king or commander.

Word of this reached Basque Country and every living creature fled. The commander of that country was terrified that this man lacked any humanity. Immediately, they and the men of the army and the city packed up their things, without a second thought. The land was emptied of people, who fled before Kush like flocks of sheep.

He raced to the city of Khalayeq, and told him of his terror of Kush. When Faruq heard this from him, how Kush in his wickedness turned everything upside down, he was astonished at his deeds and his injustice, became worried and called his army to him. 8560 He gave them horses, robes, and saddles, all kinds of blades and choice armor. He distributed coin and deployed his army on the plains; the ground disappeared under the horses' hooves.

He fortified himself in that worthy city and had a trench dug, deep and broad. First, he sent an investigator to spy on the enemy. He came and saw them from ten stages away, an army with such acumen and conviction. The king on his throne was so fearsome, so terrifying, that the envoy lost his way. You'd think those brave men were all lions, the officers and their men full of savagery. In shock, he returned and reported what he saw to Faruq, the king. Faruq was despondent and took in a breath. He dared not, with all his manliness, confront him.

[FARUQ] WRITES A LETTER FROM THE LAND OF THE BEAUTIES TO KUSH, OFFERING HIS OBEDIENCE

A short while later, he wrote a letter, offering all the supplication he thought would be useful. 8570 At the head of the letter, he said, "O world-seizing king, do not leave the world a shocking wasteland. If you take the wind captive, its dust will destroy you. Your ancestor, the warlike Zahhak—where is he? Waves of blood rose from his blade. Cleave to the creed of past kings, do not deviate from the kingly creed, for whatever king was there in the beginning, when he sought war with another king, he sent him a missive and warned him. This is the way of great kings. He then had a choice to satisfy his wishes, or else decide to go to war. No one ever saw the kings of old suffer what the commander of Jaca suffered at your hand. When the army approached

Jaca, it went straight into battle. You neither sent a message, nor warned him. Rain now falls upon his throne from the lofty clouds. 8580 When he retreated to his castle with his troops, you showed him no mercy, you killed him and burned his palace, lighting such a conflagration in his city. So many innocent women and children you destroyed by the sword of injustice! Two countries were turned into empty wildernesses, goodness and joy completely gone from them.

"If the king now has designs for us, and wishes to go to war with us, I do not know what sin I have committed that I should suffer at the glorious king's hands. If he seeks ruination and violence, the whole world lies before the king. No one turns on you without cause, except he whose time is near its end. If you wish to subordinate every sovereign, o world-worshiping king, tell us, that we may make it so, that we may give our lives over to you. 8590 Do not march your army on this country to ruin everything and destroy it. We are servants of the fortunate king, we would not transgress your judgment or your command. My eyes are now set on your response, may you receive many greetings from your friends."

The speedy and righteous envoy went before the commander of the fortress. They took him before the king and he saw his grandeur, his court. He lowered his clean face into the black dust and offered him much praise, and gave him the letter. When the letter was read out to the king, they had the envoy seated before him. He spoke frankly and delivered the message, and Kush's heart felt joy.

The king called for criers, who came quickly to his side. "Whoever of you is of this worthy army, do not go to the land of beautiful creatures. 8600 That soil must never see a rider, unless the king gives the order."

Then he called for a scribe to come before him, and dictated a lengthy response. He said, "I have received your envoy and had him seated. I asked him about your knowledge and judgment, and I see fit to leave you your throne. If you were not possessed of sober judgment, you would soon be ruined. But you strove to be wise from the beginning. So your crown and throne are yours. Why did that dim-witted tyrant not present himself before Kush? If he had come like you, as a servant before us, he would have found mercy. Whoever prepared for war with us in his cities, we tore away his palace without giving a second thought. He thought that that palace was the cosmos, now it has become flat like a plain. 8610 This was his just desserts, his reward. May you see things more clearly! [235b]

"Present yourself to me if you would like to retain your throne. If you have your mind set on war, you will lose it without delay. When the glorious new year begins, you will send tribute and taxes to our treasury, slave boys and slave girls, a thousand of each, with statures like cypresses and faces like the spring, befitting our place of rest. No one must be unaware of this command. In addition, whatever valuable treasure you have, send it to us, for we have undergone much travail. When you have done this, you will be free of my grasp, you will not see the point of my blade and my designs."

When the envoy reached Faruq, his helmet rose to Capella, the star, with joy. He quickly wrote a reply, "O proud and warlike king. 8620 I will do everything you asked, I will give my life to satisfy those wishes. To do other than bring myself before the king would ruin my heart with worry. May the king see that I would demand nothing, if he would look on me with eyes of magnanimity. Then I am girded to do whatever he says, as I have escaped the world-king's wrath."

When Kush witnessed his solicitousness, he showed him forgiveness and breathed easily. He said to the envoy, "O righteous fellow, tell him that it is unnecessary for him to come. Send us what we requested. We have prepared a letter with these demands."

When Kush was satisfied, Faruq said, "Now our treasure cannot be hidden from him." He selected a thousand of his frontier lords adorned with crowns and earrings. He ordered each of them, one by one, to bring him a slave-boy and a lovely girl, 8630 with faces like the moon and teeth like candy and glances that put all sorcery to shame. He brought a hundred racing horses too, a crown and throne and gifts of all kinds, a hundred camels all loaded with gold, and three hundred of those gold-embroidered garments. He had two sons, brave and young, two brothers of kingly lineage. He sent them with all of this treasure that adorned his troops.

His message read, "Your majesty, the passage of time has brought you success. It would do for you to return now and forgive this well-intentioned servant. That king of Basque Country is mine, fleeing from evil, he is my guest. He would not dare go near the king's throne, and has made me his protector. Would that the king were to leave him with me, lest a dark fate shine on him." 8640

When Faruq's sons and those gifts reached Kush, they were accepted by his officers and brave and warlike men of his army. Whoever saw Kush's visage was shaken and their heart became witless, and they dismounted and kissed the earth, reciting praises like one whose heart had departed. The king ordered them seated and they cheerfully went to their quarters. He then asked them about Faruq, as they found him possessed of intelligence and good judgment. He went on like this until they reached the pavilion tent, and places were given to those proud men. When day broke, he looked upon those gifts and each one of those beauties. His heart was cheered at the sight of each of them, and he gave generous gifts to those proud men. He ordered a covenant drawn up on silk, dedicated to the brave Faruqians. 8650 He gave them Basque Country and whatever lay therein, and added additional benefits. He said to him, "Make Jaca prosper, I have given it unto you, so dispense justice."

When it was time to send those brave men off, everyone was laden with precious gifts. When the troops were fully provisioned, they headed back to Andalos. He sat in good cheer and joy, drinking his wine, with no thought of Faridun the king. He took all of those girls, in their great beauty, in the span of a year. Each one of them that pleased him, they brought to his golden shrine. The rest he distributed among those nobles who were worthy and obedient. He did the same with those slave boys—those royal idols.

BRINGING ORDER TO THE REALM

Then, more of the same was received from Faruq each year thereafter—a full caravan. 8660 He made Jaca prosperous and emptied it of wine as he grew drunk. As the ambitious king's plans succeeded and he became renown for his conquests, he conquered all of Egypt as well and spread out a robe of honor. He took great treasure from that land. From Rome, too, he took half of its wealth by the blade, making dark clouds settle over the Romans.

Faridun felt a sadness when he heard, and considered going to war with the malevolent one. He ordered that Qaren come before him and said to him, "O companion of righteous creed, when we showed weakness with the demon-born, he raised his crown higher than the turning heavens. He has robbed every land and thrown the Land of

Beauties into turmoil. He has taken half of Rome as tribute and the world is like hot wax under his stamp. He has assembled troops under his command and paid them salaries, opened up the treasury and armory. 8670 When you do not attend to your affairs, they will slip out of your hands and things fall into ruin."

The general Qaren made preparations and opened the doors of the splendid treasury. He assembled the troops and paid them salaries, loosening the doors of the treasury and the sword of vengeance. When the king consulted the state of the heavens, the astrologer searched high and low. He saw all signs in favor of the malevolent Kush, his crowned head raised above the moon.

Since he saw no way to strike him, he said to Qaren, keen of judgment, "Whatever stars I see in the heavens revere the ill-starred Kush. So it is that for a hundred and eighty years, he will have no peer in all the world. He will suffer no harm from the celestial wheel."

He released Qaren from his martial task and the Iranians returned to their homes. 8680 And so, Kush continued his reign, sometimes engaged in battle, other times wine and song. He took the land of the Slavs and Rome by the sword; the earth became like soft wax under his seal.

When a hundred and eighty-one years had passed, he once again divined the heavens' will. The glorious Faridun had three sons, all held to his heart with bonds of love. He divided the earth into three parts for them, making each of their faces radiant with kingship. Brave Salm was given the region of Rome, all the countries of the west and their territories. Transoxiana, the Turks, and China, those lands went to brave Tur. Iran went to Iraj, for he merited the throne of Iran. From the River Jayhun to the Sea of Persia, Kufa shall be known as Iran's border. Then, all of Azerbaijan shall be known to everyone, sober or drunk, as part of Iran. 8690

When it was time for the mighty Salm to leave, the great king said to him, "When you have taken control of the country and frontiers, seek information about that shameful demon. Inform me about that oppressor, send a messenger on horseback. I will send the warlike Qaren from his place to you with an army. Deploy him immediately, before time runs out. If you leave one less Kush on the earth, you will immediately alleviate my heart's sorrow." The mighty Salm, like a sovereign, departed the court for Rome with a great army. The worthies and kings of Rome pressed their lips to the dust and kissed the earth. They all displayed obedience without fail, from the hills to the valleys.

When Faruq and the commander of the land of the Slavs gave nothing to the compelling Kush, 8700 he sent them each a message, saying, "What is your hidden agenda? Years and months have passed and you have not sent taxes and tribute."

Each of them answered, "You must immediately liberate us from Salm. When Faridun's Salm is upon the land, how can you ask for tribute from us?"

When the response reached that ferocious lion, he frothed and bit his lip. He loosened his tongue with an oath, "If the turning heavens grant me more days, my designs will be on verdant Iran, I will fill all the cities with woe. [236a] In vengeance for the world-keeper, king Zahhak, I will take King Faridun down from the throne." He summoned all the troops from his lands and all the proud, worthy men.

When Salm was well settled in that land, he wrote a letter to Faridun. 8710 "Rome has in all respects been put in order, according to the king of kings' wishes. I am expecting Qaren's arrival in order to go to war with Kush. Whether he comes or not, I have marshaled my forces for battle with that enemy."

Faridun was discomfited by that letter. The wise, experienced king knew that in battle with Kush, the brave Salm would be like a deer in a lion's claws. He ordered the renowned Qaren to select three hundred thousand men from the army. He also called for troops from the commanding Tur and equipped an army of Turks: along two routes, hundreds of thousands of battle-riders with bows and arrows.

When the armies arrived and assembled, he opened the doors to ancient treasures. He gave them two years' provisions, so that they would be ready to face death. 8720 He thus marshaled five hundred thousand from Iran and Turan—brave riders. General Qaren, when he arrived in Rome, found the countryside full of soldiers. Surrounding Salm's tent was an army that outnumbered the desert's sands. Salm received him and saw him, he embraced him as he should. He asked about his king and the brave men, and each of the heroes.

Qaren said to him, "They are well cared for by the king, he and the troops are well. The whole world is illuminated by you, evil hides inside its armor in fear of your blade."

They dismounted at a distance of five leagues; the world grew dark as the Nile from the dust the troops raised. Another army came from the land of the Slavs, from two directions, hundreds of thousands of worthy men. They all were given more than a month's provisions by the learned, expert scribes. 8730 The troops that were with the worthy Salm were added to those from the land of the Slavs and Iran, and he selected nine hundred thousand of them, all renowned for their feats in battle. He gave them arms and coin and made them prosperous, cheering each one's heart with his gifts. When the astrologer examined the days, he selected a day that was most encouraging.

SALM AND QAREN GO TO WAR WITH KUSH

At the start of May, they marshaled their forces to fight Kush. The worldly-wise say that the sun and moon never saw so many soldiers. Thousands upon thousands, four hundred thousand elite soldiers and lancers. The earth moaned under their weight and turned the color of tulips from their fires. Dust rose from the plain above the sun, obscuring both the sea and land. The whinnying of Arabian horses in their reins tore the wits from Mars and Saturn's hearts. 8740 The earth's soil was obscured beneath the horses' hooves, the air turned red and gold from their banners. Terror reached the fish and the bull, thick trees were flattened like a plain. The cry of trumpets and pipes was like a resurrection day to Satan. And so they headed towards Andalos, led by the warlike Qaren.

And the experienced Kush once again had marshaled an army. The heavens could not count his army, which outnumbered the stars. The registers held two million, counted by the wise scribes. So they were to cross the sea, Salm crossing first.

When he became aware of Salm and his army, he laughed and advanced confidently. He ordered that men of war all make their way again to Gibraltar. 8750 They brought all of their things there and secured them. Women and children and men and beasts—no one's roots remained in place. Women and children were safe from the conflict, along with farmers and village headmen and swordsmen. He sent a quantity of food to Gibraltar that would sustain them for years. Cows and flocks of sheep were driven up the mountain shepherdless.

After passing through the lands of the Franks, the mighty Salm reached the great sea of Rome. He launched a thousand ships on the sea, the worthy Qaren in the lead. He crossed the sea with that army that the king had given him from Iran and Turan. He sent ships to Salm as well, the warlike army boarded them.

When half the troops had crossed the sea, word was quickly sent to Kush. 8760 He sent a scout, swift as smoke, to quickly inform him, that he might know how much of the army had crossed and who had landed on this side.

They caught him and dragged him away, and the fear showed on his face. The champion said to him, "You of alert mind, what business are you doing for Kush?" He spoke, and the prisoner did not give up his secret.

He said, "Proud sovereign, I do not know who it is you refer to, I have no idea about this person you mention. I am just a wandering man going about his business, ask me about my business and leave me be!"

Qaren laughed and said to his face, "Go back to that corrupt fellow. We have not come to launch a sneak attack: we bring a razor-clawed army. Tell him, 'O dark and foul demon, may the turning heavens bring your ruin. 8770 In your situation, with all the favor the king showed you, why must you ruin it all? You were so sore wounded in your fetters, in prison, that any fool would cry for you. You were a wingless and featherless bird, and the king of kings endowed you with glory. That proud and noble king put the world at your fingertips. Now that fate has given you feathers, you harbor resentment against the king.

"'This time, if I find you still alive, I'll make you abandon kingship. I'll show what you're worth in front of the army and send you to the king, so that the other subjects do not rebel and make war on us. Once your situation becomes dire, you'll find no patience from the world, for from Iran, the Turkish and Arab warriors, from the land of the Slavs, Rome, and the Indians, 8780 all of the mace-wielders, ready to fight, turn against you. You'll see when we come face-to-face that I spoke rightly.'"

He ordered that that man then be let go, and he took flight. He hurried toward Kush, his soul having fled his body, his wits gone from his heart. With careful deliberation he repeated Qaren's message before the nobles, not in private.

Kush became ashamed before the nobles, guardians of the soldiers, and asked the traveler, "How much of his army has crossed the water? Is the army hesitating or hurrying?"

He said to him, "A part of it has crossed over, the whole field bears soldiers. Throughout the night, the troops have donned their battle dress, hearts prepared for death. Thus have they trembled before you, like a willow in an April wind. 8790 The army remains in two parts, all of the provisions are near the king."

Kush said to those worthy men, "Qaren is a knight possessed of glory and wits. Were it not so, he could be driven away like a flock of sheep, they would all have crossed the sea. I would have launched an attack on them tonight and brought ruin upon those brave men. But what can I do? That ill-born one is brave, of sound judgment, glorious and just." Immediately, he had an advance guard set up, for he was not safe from Qaren and his tricks.

In two months the army crossed the sea and at the new month the king landed. He selected some astute investigators who went and scouted out the army with care. They returned to Salm and said, "That army is very great, investigate them most carefully. You'd think that Kush had stirred up steel-clad men like dust from the earth. 8800 You'd think it was the same army that that vengeful one had before."

For his part, Mardan had gone ahead to watch the Iran-army from every direction. When he found them, he returned and said, "O king of exalted judgment, [236b] Your troops outnumber the enemy two to one. In this battle, the heavens' wheel turns in your favor."

Kush was cheered by this information; the roar of drums rose up, with clamor and shouts. He marched his forces to the edge of the sea. The seaside filled with black dust. When only two leagues remained between the two armies the world became like the black Nile in the dust. Sleep left their eyes and doubt left their hearts, a roar rose up and it was a time for roaring.

Two armies faced off on the battlefield. You'd have thought the face of the earth had constricted, as if a world of grief had boiled over, the stars echoing their shouts and commotion. 8810 Their advance guards clashed in a chaotic melee. With one assault, those men of war dislodged the Iranians from their position. Many were killed or taken captive, others wounded by blade and arrow.

Those warriors brought weapons and riders and war horses back to Kush. He was taken aback by the precocious success of his troops; all were cheered, and they gained strength. They beat the drums and began to advance, and that army moved forward one stage. They chose a difficult and narrow place. He dismounted and ordered the troops to hold their position.

The vanguards of both sides advanced with their two vengeful and proud commanders, Andiyan leading the brave Iranians like a lion. When he saw the army's dust in the distance, he reached with his hand and drew the sword of vengeance. 8820 With a single assault he drove them out of their position, sending them fleeing back to their camp.

Such a clamor arose among the troops that Kush raced toward the front lines like a storm. He asked them what all this roaring and strife and these loud cries were. One said, "Your majesty, o courageous one, it seems their army overcame our vanguard."

The ambitious king was wearing no armor or helmet, but the knots of his brow became rings of mail. He reached and drew his heavy mace, racing out from among his troops like a gale. He attacked Andiyan like a savage lion attacking a wounded onager. All at once, he drove the troops out of their position, trampling many of them under foot. That army was crushed beneath his blows and turned back toward their own side. He fought fiercely against Andiyan, trying to drive the Iranians back. 8830 No one dared confront that raging elephant—how many he killed, how many he wounded!

Andiyan charged at him vengefully, but when he saw his dark face he was terrified, cast off his armor and fled. And so Kush fought on, and so he slew men, until the sky darkened their faces. And so he turned back to his throne, his name raised to the heavens.

When they returned to Salm, Andiyan said, "O king of the Kayanids, when we engaged with their vanguard and raised black dust, we forced them back with a single attack, and they counterattacked vengefully. One rider rode out in front of the others like a raging lion amidst a flock of sheep. 8840 With such fear and terror, and such power, he is neither savage lion nor raging elephant but a demon to the core, his blade pointed to the heavens. When that leviathan made for the brave warriors, they could not even slow him down. I charged at him in a rage, and when I saw him, I cast off my armor. I fled before that snorting dragon, God spared me from him."

Salm was taken aback by his words and said, "Who ever heard of such a thing?"

Qaren said, "That was Kush, China was in turmoil for so many years because of him. Grandson of the world-conquering King Biwarasb, shelter of the brave and buttress of the army.[1] If he did not have such leonine ferocity, our king would have no vendetta against him. I have never seen his equal in manliness, with his might and stature and grandeur. 8850 I will cut him out of the saddle with my blade like a hawk seizes a *tayhu* bird."

When the dark night passed and day broke, the world's heart was illumined by the sun. A shout rose up from the brave men of Iran, you'd think the world had been covered in steel-clad men. On the right was the champion Qaren with an army like the waves of a deluge. Nastuh's son Shapur took the left, and Andiyan took up the advance guard. In the center was Salm with pipes and drums; they raised dust that made the world like ebony.

Kush's camp-commander brought word to him that the commander of Iran was on the move. He emerged from his tent, mace in hand, and ordered his forces to hold their positions. He gave Manush, king of Kairouan, command of the right wing and the banners and baggage. He sent Shammakh with his forces to the left of the most renowned king. 8860 The center of the advance guard was entrusted to Mardan, a capable brave man—fighting the Iran-army that stood before him was his creed. He took his place in the center, at the core, raising up his inspiring banner.

When the sound of drums and the cry of pipes rose up, both armies rose like clouds. A rain of arrows fell from both, then the roar of the melee, like thunder. You'd think it was truly the resurrection, for no one could escape but by salvation. By arrow, by mace, by blade and lasso, each side knocked down the other. Many were killed from both armies. The flowing blood blended the land and sea, and when the world's form and color changed, it dyed the Earth. Full of suffering, the two armies merged again, gear and swords drenched in blood. 8870

When the nobles came before Kush, the steel-clad king said to them, "The enemy came quick and fierce today, and they have us sized up. They know us, see us, and are experienced in war. My troops have

---

1. "King Biwarasb" refers to Zahhak.

seen much and their suffering has grown. When he faces us on the battlefield tomorrow, the troops must not show any weakness."

Qaren, too, returned in haste to Salm's tent. He said to him, "O king of lofty lineage, you have seen the demon-born's army. Think about what more we can do: it is better to think than to act right now. The army is more numerous than ants and locusts, covering deserts, seas, and mountaintops. You have seen what he has become—his sovereignty raised to such heights. I do not know what will be the outcome of this battle, I do not know what the turning of time has in store." 8880

He answered him, "O proud king, this is what occurred to me. We cannot take this demon-born: the enemy outnumbers us two to one. There are so many troops on the ground, the heavens' wheel has never seen so many in one place. Their position is fearfully strong, they have mounts and armored riders. Whatever you know of tricks and stratagems, use them now. Would that the peerless, just judge would relieve you of this malevolent one."

Qaren said to him, "Tomorrow at dawn, we must gird ourselves for battle, in order that the troops not lose morale and fear of the enemy undermine them. Tonight, order that the ships make haste and cross over from the other side of the water, so that the troops all know that we are not retreating from this battlefield. 8890 They will put heart and soul into the fight and be fierce as leopards."

At night he gave orders to an old mariner to have the ships cross over from the other side like arrows. All but two ships crossed the sea, then almost immediately turned back from the shore. At dawn, the warlike Qaren ordered that the army draw up ranks. With the roar of drums and cry of flutes, the army stirred like the sea from the seabed. He ordered that Qobad take his position as the commander of the right wing. He selected a thousand armored riders, brave battle-hardened swordsmen who drew up mountainous ranks in front of the center.

Then, the world-ruler, the clever Kush, arranged his army in the same formation as the day before. He gave his banner to Mardan Khurreh, who seemed to have returned from Iran, successful. 8900 He welcomed him in time of war and held him dear in time of feast. He had sent him to be king of Tangier and given him all of Sus al-Aqsa. [237a] The king came from the right side to the center, famous warriors following him.

A roar went up, then came keen sword-blows, commotion rising from every corner. Warlike and courageous men faced each other fiercely. They charged at each other with lances, here vengefully wielding a mace, there arrows. Like leaves from the trees, the riders fell from their saddles on that field of vengeance. Most of the army was deprived of head and hands, the black dust drunk on their blood. The heavens' turning wheel grew distraught from that battlefield, Venus's heart sunk away from celebration.

When the soil was warmed by the sun's breath, the warriors' heads were heated with haste. 8910 The Iranians were astonished. Kush looked out at them from among his troops. He threw himself upon Qobad's army, and Qobad bared his chest in bravery. He launched an attack, advanced toward him, and engaged with his famous warriors. Kush slew some of his knights, many of his renowned men and companions. The right flank was thrown into turmoil by the sword of that fiercely warlike king.

Then, Qaren from the center of the army threw himself at their center. Roaring and charging, foaming at the mouth, he raised his shoulders and tore through their line. They threw all of the enemy's center into turmoil, striking them here on their bodies, there on their heads.

When Mardan Khurreh saw this, he immediately raised a hew and cry and showed his bravery. He gave his brother his place and the banner. With his gold-shoed ranking men 8920 who were with him from among the knights of Iran—more than four thousand were girded for battle—he gripped his reins and came charging, drawing his blade against the champion. He pressed the Iranians fiercely and killed thousands of courageous men.

When the army's champion saw this, his troops being destroyed by Mardan, he roared and attacked those worthy men. He charged their ranks and slew, and went on until he reached Mardan, saying to him, "O foul demon-born, you have turned your back on the land of Iran and abandoned the king. You turned away from everything and became the agent of the demon-spawn. Finding such joy with that devil, you'll get your payment for this evil from me."

Mardan said to him, "How could a blacksmith become the general of such an army? 8930 We have always been noble leaders, I have had more than a thousand servants like you since the time of the Kayanid kings."

When Qaren heard this, he was taken aback and trembled like a tree branch. He let go a javelin with fierce rage; its head pierced the saddle through to the stomach, and the mighty rider toppled off his steed. The steed soon lost its life, and the commander rose up like a gale.

The brave men of Iran charged toward him brandishing lances and blades. Mardan had escaped him, but Qaren's heart was injured by the insult. They brought a high horse to him and the champion mounted it effortlessly. He was inflamed with rage and ferocity, rallying his troops like smoke. 8940 When he reached Mardan in the middle of the army, he reached and drew his heavy mace. He said to him, "You who have ashamed us all, what makes you think you'll escape me?"

Mardan Khurreh looked him over and turned to engage him in combat amidst the troops. They struck at each other with dagger blades and arrows, sometimes striking at each other's heads with steel maces. Finally, the champion struck him with his mace, and his brains flowed out his nose. When the champion had struck through him, he tumbled violently off his horse. They tied the fallen warrior to his horse and charged off with him like Azorgoshasb. The renowned warrior, descended from champions, gave up his dear life as they were moving.

Thus do the cruel heavens turn, doing all you do unto you anew. A harsh man will go under the dust, all he does will amount to dust. 8950 When Mardan fell, the brave men of Iran found strength, their spirits raised. They killed so many of the enemy that the field was filled with mounds and hills.

From the other side, the ferocious Kush threw the right wing into chaos. Qobad came and engaged with him and gave him a good fight. He struggled for a time, but it was of no avail, and a roaring charge drove him back. Whatever was left of the right flank was plundered.

When Salm saw this he made a show of manliness. He sent a hundred thousand Roman mounted warriors to assist them. The brave men fought fiercely and mingled in the melee. The clash went on until nightfall. The ground was full of blood and the heavens full of dust.

Night fell and the two armies separated, their hearts battered, full of grief and pain. 8960 More of Qobad's troops were killed, ten thousand twice over, under that brave worthy. Kush ungirded himself, came and sat down upon his golden throne. He gave booty to the officers of his army and called out the names of all who had fought in the battle.

When King Kush found out about Mardan, how Qaren had bested him, he was astonished and swore an oath in anger: "Tomorrow I will not relent from battle, that I might properly avenge Mardan and crush the heads of brave men under my foot."

He commanded that his brother be called forth and he gave him his banner and his troops. He praised him profusely, showed him warmth and kindness, and wrapped him in a robe of honor. Then he sat down to eat with the nobles. He brought in radiant wine and entertainers.

Qaren the champion went to Salm, with the great men and heroes. 8970 He said to him, "O honorable sovereign, today the battle went in your favor. We killed so many of the enemy that the plain was completely covered in blood and bodies. When Mardan Khurreh came charging, eyes bloodshot like a champion, he engaged me amidst our forces and I wrecked him with one blow. You'd think that it was not the same warrior knight who had come to the king's side from Iran. O king, he was twice as strong, and had been given a steel-clad steed. I charged in every direction and dispatched that brave man in the battle. If only I had been within sight of the demon-born! I could not see him and my rage grew and grew."

Qobad said to Qaren and Salm, "That corrupt, ferocious demon-born has fought with us day after day, reducing many brave men to dust. 8980 When we struggled against him, we were not up to the task, and fled. When his majesty saw this, he sent a detachment to our aid from the core of his forces. If dark night had not fallen, everything would have gone his way—he of dark creed. The right wing would have been defeated, undoubtedly, neither men nor officer would remain."

Qaren said to him, "See tomorrow how I draw his blood with the vengeful sword. If he escapes from my sword with his life, then I am no warrior!"

THE KINGS LINE UP FOR BATTLE

When the sun went to battle and the dawn turned against the night, the world once again filled with strife and commotion. Two armies, in vengeance, donned mail. Two sovereigns deployed their forces on the field. Shouts rose beyond the heavens. Qaren arrived. Kush girded himself, his head full of rage and his heart churning. 8990 He brought a translator with him and raced to appear before those who had gathered.

He cried out, "O brave men of the king! Tell the warrior, Qaren, come and try to drive me off! Let no one but the champion face me!"

A rider came and spoke to the champion, and he laughed. He said, "The wolf has fallen straight into the trap. I will win this battle today. I will erase his name from the world, fill his bedchamber with mourning." He donned his gear and weapons of war, mounted his horse and approached like a dust cloud.

When Qaren drew near, he said to him, "O demon-born, you have not given Faridun his due! [237b] May that mother who bore a corrupt and ill-fated child like you be cursed by fate! What did his imperial majesty do for you that his reward should be the blade and battle? 9000 He has imbibed your venom for a while now. Your heart has forgotten beneficence. If the world-king had not forgiven you, your body and soul would be at rest in prison, and you would not have returned to the battlefield with vengeful blade and mace today."

Kush said to him, "You sorry man, has blacksmithing made your brain proud? As long as there are justice and vengeance upon the earth, this has befallen many sovereigns. The turning heavens sometimes bring strife and other times amity. Such things have happened as long as the world has been here. Our ancestors and our excellent, exalted, world-ruler drove the Jamshidians clean off the face of the earth, and their cushions and beds were mudbricks. For so many thousands of years, no king, no commander arose from them. 9010 World-ruler Zahhak with his crown of gold girded himself for kingship with wisdom and glory. The Jamshidians' name was not seen on the earth, they found no rest in the mountains or the forest. If it was good that my feet be bound for a while, why not put your king in prison a while? A rose sees both wind and rain, and every injury afflicts kings too. A hunting lion is held in chains when they capture it from the forest and field. Was not Jamshid Zahhak's prisoner, sitting and sleeping on the dust? By hammer and anvil and bluster, you have reached a position like mine. And so your words ring true, you raise your head above the heavens. How warped is Faridun's character that he should want devotion from us? He is not satisfied with things as they are, that we withhold kingship from him. 9020 I have no designs on Iran, on those lands, but you have attacked Rome."

When Qaren heard this, he was astonished and said, "Vile curses upon your soul!" In his anger, Qaren reared his horse and roared, and charged into the fight. Steel mace, javelin, and blade brought no harm to his brain, head, or torso. Their blades and axes became notched, but neither could lay a hand on the other. The two commanders stood before hope and death, full of arrows, mail, blade, and helmet. They fought on until midday, as the world-illumining sun began its descent. No rest from battle, from war, here a blade and there an armor-piercing arrow, their fast-charging steeds became so exhausted that scarcely a vein stirred on their bodies. Blood and sweat left their exhausted bodies and made the dust into grime beneath their feet. 9030

Finally, Kush came in charging and released the steel of a javelin from his hand. The spear-point went into Qaren's thigh and the reins fell out of that commanding fellow's grip. It pierced leg, saddle, and belly, and Qaren fell down along with his mount.

The brave men of Iran charged out brandishing spears and blades, while from the other side the brave Kush's men made an attack like a lion. The Iranians arrived first and drew javelin, blade, and axe. Driving Kush back away from him, they drew the javelin from the warrior. They put him on a horse and rushed him away, a great commotion arising from among the Iranians. Everyone was frightened by that wound and they said, "This demon has the strength of an elephant!"

Kush made an attack on the Iranians, his troops following behind the steel-clad warrior. 9040 He struck with that peerless army and led them right into the center, killing and wounding many of them as he took the upper hand in the battle.

When Salm saw that terror and that damage, the broken morale of his troops, he came out of the center with a hundred thousand battle-riders and lancers. He engaged with Kush and his troops, sullying the watery luster of his blade. Their charge leveled what was high, and they made the earth drunk with the blood they spilled. He pressed against Kush with his army, and many on both sides were ruined. They fought on through the day, until the world turned raven-colored. The two groups parted from each other, bodies trembling from the ordeal, hearts ruined by grief.

Kush went to his throne with his nobles, called for wine and musicians. 9050 He said to them, "Today I struck the warrior Qaren with a javelin. His elephantine body went down into the dust, he fell along with his mount into the abyss. His riders delivered him from me, striking at me with blades and javelins. I don't know if he'll succumb to that wound, or if he will come at me with his troops again."

The nobles shouted their acclaim for him: "Long live the sovereign of the land! May the days turn in your favor, and may time bring ruin to the enemy! If Qaren was ruined by your wound, that army will not last long! We can crush them under our horses' hooves, neither great nor small will be left of them!"

And so, when Salm returned, he raced to the side of the champion. He found him decrepit and helpless from all of the blood that flowed from his wound. 9060 He spoke gentle words and his face paled with sympathy for his pain, his lips full of cold air, short of breath. Salm brought in some of the wise nobles of Rome, and some men from Iran and every land and region. The wise and loyal nobles set about seeking a remedy for the wound.

Salm said to him, "O world-champion, do not worry and do not let your spirit be in turmoil. The divine will relieve you of this pain and bring dread to your enemies' hearts. We are holding back from this battle for a while, until you can take to the saddle again. Without you, the battle would not turn out well. No drums or banners, no warlike army!"

Qaren said to him, "Your majesty, do not burden your tongue with these words. If the world ends for me, it is fine. The turning heavens are not under our command. I am but a conqueror from among the Iranians, what good could I do the turning heavens, and what harm? 9070 You and the king must remain in good cheer, remember me when you celebrate!"

Salm's heart was saddened by what had happened and he left, his face damp. He called the officers of the army one by one, and they arrived in response to his call. After he had done so, he said, "At dawn tomorrow, prepare to go to battle with the enemy. Fight them with conviction, so that they see you are men among men. For Qaren was not sent by the heavens, and even if they sent a fire-breathing dragon, Qaren now could not act as lions and heroes do."

He said this, lay down and slept. All of his nobles repeated this to the troops. The commanders of the army, having given him their hearts, now bared them for sacrifice. They prepared for the battle all night, and when day broke, they raised a shout. 9080

The roar of drums and pipes rose up and the troops marched like a surging sea. The brave men of Iran and Turan and Rome drew up ranks upon that field of shame. When a cry rose up from Salm's forces, Kush advanced his troops into the battle.

The radiance of spear-points reached the water and the soil was dampened with brave men's blood. Both armies struggled fiercely, and half of each side was destroyed. Mounds of the dead piled up on that battlefield, the earth became mountainous with injured bodies. Salm emerged from amidst the troops, the king's renowned men following him. He threw himself at the enemy and killed many brave swordsmen. Kush was burdened with exhaustion and stayed back from the battle. When night fell, both armies drew back and their advance guards came to the front. 9090

When a week of fighting had passed, a multitude of knights had perished on each side. The king of the Slavs came before Salm and said, "May your throne ever have supporters. Tomorrow, take a rest from this battle, and let me go ahead, o king of victorious fortune. If I do battle with Kush, I will surely crush his head into the dust."

Salm reclined and praised him, and said, "Go, and be alert." He went and prepared through the night, and when the sun ascended the heavens' wheel, Basuz came roaring out the gate and deliberately approached Kush. [238a]

He laughed and said, "Well look at this, look what Basuz has set out to do! The army of all the earth has thus come to do battle with us. They can never be satisfied with me, their skirts are red with blood. 9100 Now the king of the Slavs has arisen and asked permission from Salm to fight me. Let us see how he swings the blade of war, how he stands toe to toe with the leviathan."

He brought worthy men out of that army, a hundred thousand brave warriors, and ordered that the rest of his troops stand down. When he called out Basuz the Slav, his throne called him to be level with the earth. Dust rose to the clouds from both armies, each roared like a savage beast. The shining mail made the sky show upon the earth, the spears made the air into a reed-bed. The blades and javelins and rain of arrows left neither Mars nor Saturn nor Mercury unscathed. When the earth's dust took to the sky, the commander moved aside from his troops.

There were three thousand worthy men with him on the field, ready for battle. 9110 When the Slavs gained the upper hand, they spilled blood with enthusiasm. King Basuz charged from among them, banner fluttering behind him. He and his brave men launched an attack, raising dust from the plain to the heavens. The armies collided fiercely, so many killed and so many wounded. Those brave men were stirred from their places like steel drawn to a magnet. The arrows they fired into the center of the army dislodged the center from its position.

When Basuz saw Kush like that, he gripped his reins and charged at the brave warrior. He and his warriors launched such an attack that dust was raised from the bull and fish. Left and right, the troops swung their blades, spattering clouds of blood that covered everything like frost. The whole battlefield was covered in dead and wounded, the injured had no route of retreat. 9120

The warrior Basuz rose up to return to his position from the battlefield. The savage lion Kush reached him and said to him, "O vigorous warrior! Will you turn back without finishing the job? Stay a while on this battlefield, and reap the seed you've sown, do not turn away from the blows of brave men!"

Those two engaged each other in combat, like a massive elephant and a savage lion. Basuz fought on for a while, his body losing its endurance and his face its color. When he saw that he was losing his strength, he hastened to retreat. He fled with the raging elephant behind him holding a piercing javelin.

When the dart took flight from Kush's fingers, it pierced the steel of his armor and his back. The spearhead poked out through his chest and the crowned head fell into the dust. 9130 When the Slavs saw their king thus wounded by the malicious javelin they all at once turned around, shouting, taking blades and lances in hand and joining the battle as mud was stirred up from the brave men's blood.

Kush and his forces were amazed by the Slavs in that battle. If they had struggled and strove like this before, their commander would still have been alive upon the earth. Still they put up a fight, those unfortunate ones, battle-hungry and demonic. They fought until night fell upon the field, the two armies joined together. Three days those brave men made war, for the sake of honor. They killed so many to avenge their king—no mercy from that army!

On the fourth day the mighty world-seeking Salm brought a great force, 9140 and gave battle for ten days without rest or pause. There was no way around the many dead bodies, the severed limbs and heads, that covered the field. Not one of the troops remained uninjured; bodies grew deformed and armies grew weak.

The two kings then agreed that their armies would rest for a month, that men and beasts would retire, for they had drained the strength from the turning heavens. When the injured man's body recuperates, it launches a charge against weakness. He spends a month in good company, and the world is renewed. Then they'd put on coats and Roman helmets, and the two armies would continue the battle.

The champion, Qaren, smiled at this news and his spirit was refreshed. He said, "Let us back off—a truce—for a month, my spirit will be relieved of its exhaustion. 9150 Then I will take the saddle with the Lord's strength and drive off the twisted demon."

He then sent a message to Salm, "Thus has the king ordained for the world ... In the battles of the last several days the champion-slaying king has appeared before us. Order them to bring back the ships, provision the ships with everything they need." There and then, they had a ship brought in and prepared and provisioned.

SALM GOES TO BATTLE WITH KUSH, QAREN'S STRATAGEM, AND KUSH'S DEFEAT

At the new moon, men of war called for drums and pipes. At night Qaren said to Salm, "Do not tell anyone this secret. Call forth the troops and prepare for battle. Begin the battle by showing weakness, giving ground. Have a trench dug in front of the troops and spread the word that Qaren has fallen, that a blow passed through his steel, he died, and his troops are consumed in grief. 9160 If the demon-born thinks he is safe from me, he will no longer pay me any mind in the battle. So this idea occurred to me. Hopefully, that corrupt demon-born will become consumed with his own vices, caught up in his own business when things are going his way. By Faridun's glory, things will turn out to your satisfaction and your name ascend to the Pleiades. When you have fought on for several days, look for me, o champion-slaying king, when the sun rises high in the sky and the sea's water turns liquid gold."

He said this and took his peerless army upon the sea. Salm labored and struggled on, and gave ground in the battle. He then began digging a trench, tossing up the earth.

An evil thought came to Kush: Qaren was now clad in a burial shroud! 9170 His brave and warlike men took courage from this. They killed many men of the Iran-army, which was losing ground.

On the eighth day, an astonishing event! Good tidings turned the world a golden hue. From the sea came a leviathan borne upon a ship, its teeth and claws like diamonds. Behind Kush landed the army, and the world-champion warrior Qaren. With bull-headed mace in his hand, his mount leveled a mountain. His army scarcely hesitated, and soon Kush's men did not know reins from stirrups. Blood flowed from brave men's blades, and no one knew what was happening. A rider came at Kush like a gale, the enemy overran their camp. With the plains and mountains all covered by soldiers, the whole field was covered in severed heads. 9180

Kush was frightened and did not show his face, which was hidden like a crocus. He summoned a hundred thousand from among the troops, battle-hardened riders, to go and figure out was going on, what this army was doing and who was leading it. He said, "This is the work of the blacksmith! It's an ambush and he is leading them."

When the army emerged from their tents, they saw nowhere to go but into the swords and spears. Great and small tents and clean clothes caught fire, a terrifying blaze. The world's surface was filled with smoke and deserting seemed to all like the best course. He saw his troops in drunken disarray; they fled and abandoned each other.

Three hundred thousand who kept their wits about them during the battle remained with Kush. [238b] He saw the whole field on fire, tents and pavilions burning up, 9190 his troops killed and Qaren taking revenge, foes' blood running in streams. Their bedding, their encampments were wrecked, and their way of retreat was cut off.

In all that terror, he tried to rally his troops, saying, "Do not hide your bravery now! If we show any weakness, we'll be taken captive, humiliated in the hands of these wretches! Better we all be slain in battle than our necks bound in ropes!"

He said this and fought like a dragon to keep his dear sweet life free. By his sword, he kept enemies at bay, struggling at length in that battle. He cleared men out of his path as his fleeing soldiers were killed. He killed and wounded many brave men, and no one approached to confront him. He left everything that was there to be plundered, from horses to unsullied garments. 9200 All those coin bags, loot, and steeds, the warrior heroes carried off. It went on until dark night fell, and in the dark, the champions turned back.

When Faridun's army arrived, he gave his greetings to the champion, Qobad. He said to him, "Go with the army in pursuit of the demon-spawn. Choose a hundred thousand warriors and bring me the demon-visage head."

QOBAD GOES IN PURSUIT OF KUSH

The commanding Qobad assembled a force and stepped lightly, taking to the road in pursuit of Kush. Kush raced without stopping for six days, no strength left in his body or wits in his brain. On the seventh day a force reached him that you'd think had fully exerted itself.

King Jabolq had sent thirty thousand knights and hero-slayers, all armed for battle, to his aid.[2] When this army of his arrived, 9210 he showed its officers gentility and kindness.

Kush said, "I will intercept him en route with my forces. Qaren has departed by sea, leading his army to Andalos. If he takes the city by surprise, that would cause me a great deal of trouble. That ill-born vengeful one knows that I am fighting in the battle alongside my troops. I'll make a surprise attack on him and bring shame to his name. Give us well-rested horses and put your troops at my disposal for this battle; our horses are exhausted, they've borne all the toil of the battle. For honor! Draw up your ranks, if the enemy comes we will make war on them." 9220

They quickly went down to the field, and from the road to the riverbank. Kush quickly set a guard of a hundred men to watch that same road down which he had raced, and from which he knew an army would soon be coming—he kept a close watch. On the eighth day, the brave Qobad arrived. The guards saw the dust of his army and quickly brought word to Kush.

2. The name Jabolq here appears to be a variant of Jabolqa, which is a place referred to as part of a pair, Jabolqa and Jabolsa (or Jabarsa), as an island in an indeterminate distant region of the earth; it came to be associated with the Hidden Imam in Shi'i legends—see introduction. The legendary Jabolqa has no certain geographic location. Here, however, the domain of King Jabolq must be a region somewhere around northwest Africa or Western Europe.

Kush was pleased by the news—he was radiant and his cheeks turned rosy. He distributed the well-rested horses. He set an ambush with thirty thousand riders, and armed and positioned the rest of his force. He ordered that they draw up ranks.

Qobad came, he saw him and a shout rose up. The brave men drew blades of vengeance—you would have thought they'd cut the sky down to the earth. The commanding Kush waited so that his troops became even more eager to fight. Then he led his troops from the skirt of the mountain, and they all drew their blades. 9230

Qobad was very frightened by his ambush and called on the world-creator in his heart, for his horses were weak and tired, and it was as if fetters bound his hands and feet. They were so lagging in the fight that it was as if fate had tied them down. Borne on well-rested horses, brave Kush attacked like a lion.

The commanding Qobad struggled mightily, shaking in his rage like a tree branch. He killed and wounded many of the enemy, until finally the troops turned their backs on him. He mounted a well-rested horse and fled the enemy on that mountainous steed. Kush followed him down the road for ten leagues, searching for him but not finding him among his troops.

Then he said to his troops, "Whoever is noble, take them and hold them prisoner; having them captive will be to our advantage. 9240 Whoever among our heroes is taken prisoner, when they bring them here, young and old, we will stay our hands from them, for this is the way of war. Otherwise, whomever you find, this way or that, put them to the sword."

From Iran, from Rome, and from the Turks, ten thousand knights were taken captive. Others were wounded by arrow and blade, missing hands or feet or heads. Of that endless and worthy army, scarcely thirty thousand returned to Qaren.

From there, he marched his forces westwards. When he neared Gibraltar, he set up camp anew before the mountain. He rested there for a week with that group. He summoned the riders of Jabolq, and praised them all. He gave each of them gold dinars and sent them back to their king. 9250 He ordered that everyone send victuals and supplies to the mountain. He then returned to Gibraltar dejected, the nobles of his army along with him. There, on that mountaintop, were more than seventy thousand riders.

He said to everyone who came near him, "Send a portion of food here. The sorrow-worn Qobad is coming to our gate." He told them the whole story of what had happened, of the ambush and the rain of arrows, and those worthy men taken captive, and those many troops who perished on the field at the point of that vengeful one's blade.

Salm and Qaren's hearts were so crushed, you'd think they could not breathe. The young Salm said to Qaren, "Look upon the works of the turning heavens. If the passing days give us a measure of happiness, they'll bring twice as much grief and ruin." 9260

The champion said to him, "O prince, the works and constitution of the world are thus. The ancient heavens' wheel does not turn as we wish, it is at times like Sagittarius, at times like Mercury. The king's heart must not grieve because of this; whoever was born must die."

He ordered a cry go out to the army, and the criers said, "O brave men of the king! Whoever of the enemy you hold captive, whether young or whether old, keep them bound for now, until we see what is coming. With them we will purchase our own captives, those who are young and those who have seen sorrow." When they took count of their own captives, they numbered six thousand, young and old, nobles of Kush's brave army, steel-clad war-riders.

From there he marched his forces ahead until they reached the Mountain of Cranes. 9270 Ranks upon ranks of the army arrived and occupied plain, sea, and mountain.

When Salm saw that habitation, that mountain, and soldiers and men massed there, he knew that they would not be able to take it with a siege. He sent the champion at daybreak to the west with many troops.

Qaren crossed the sea and made landfall, passing prosperous and desolate lands. All of the nobles presented themselves before him, with open hearts and faces. He appointed a governor to each region and an overseer to each city. From there, he returned to Andalos, and the whole west sung his praises.

The astute Qaren devoted two years to these labors, and then returned to Salm. The whole west was under his command, and the king's heart was cheered and he laughed. 9280 He threw a robe fit for kings over him, and gave him throne, crown, horse, and gear. He gave many gifts to the Iranians and silver dirhams to the other troops, and to his brother's troops likewise he gave many things and acclaimed them. He sent him immediately to his king and everyone went before the throne. He sent them to him with much generosity, all cheered and faces refreshed. [239a]

With the armies of Rome, and men of war, he besieged the Mountain of Cranes. They watched it for eight years, they did not let even a bird fly off the mountain, but their food stores were not depleted and they saw not the least bit of suffering.

From time to time, Kush went to the front lines like a leviathan emerging from the sea. In one corner he stationed men, sometimes putting blades there, sometimes lighting fires. 9290 When troops had massed there, he went toward his own ship. He returned from the sea to the mountaintop, and the commanding Salm suffered much grief from Kush.

[TUR SENDS SALM A LETTER]

They had faced off in this way for eight years when a rider came racing from the field with a letter from Tur, whose mind was in turmoil: "How long will you be Kush's prisoner? Iraj asks for tribute from us, and says ridiculous things. Father seems to show us so much magnanimity, but gave us only subordination. He made him king over the Iranians and sent us packing. Our brother, who is younger than us both—why does our father favor him over us? If you are fine with this servitude, then leave him his crown and fortune. I have no such intentions, and I will not take any part in this. 9300 Otherwise, step lightly and come to my side, that we may come to an agreement. Let us clasp our hands in an oath that we shall never revere Iraj. Death would be preferable to such a life, for since when does one serve one's juniors?"

When the commanding Salm read that letter, he beat the drums and marched at dawn. The fortress was relieved of dearth and difficulty, and Kush came down from the mountain like a dragon. His troops, dispersed, now gathered around him and his armies blanketed the earth. He took all of Andalos and the lands of the west, and raised his head in victory. He made the desolate lands prosper again and cheered the people's hearts with his generosity. His might grew greater than it had been—the size of his army and treasure.

TUR AND SALM MAKE A PLAN

The ancient tale-teller said that this tale was passed down by the right-eous. 9310 When Tur and Salm concocted that evil and removed Iraj from the world, and he was slaughtered by Tur's hand, Faridun scarcely ate or slept.[3] The king's face shone yellow with pain.

Night and day he spent thinking up curses, saying "Give me justice, o creator, all-powerful, all-wise nurturer! From Iraj's line give me a worthy man who can gird himself for vengeance. For death took that innocent one unawares—heedless of his fate, he was murdered!"

Then, Salm said to the brave Tur, "What has come to pass cannot be hidden any more. We have gotten rid of one of our enemies, but planted seeds of evil. Now another enemy remains; we must gird our-selves to do battle with him. We will rid the land of the demon-spawn and relieve our hearts of grief." 9320

Tur said to him, "Brother, do not say this, for when you think on this further, you will see that if we pick this fight, we will throw our own heads under the boot. The demon-born will be on Faridun's side. We must never speak of this. He continues to hold Gibraltar, with many troops and a secure position. When he finds out we seek to con-front him, he will sort things out with Faridun. On one side Kush and on the other the king, our dominion will be wrecked. Better that we take the initiative.

"We should complain about the exalted king, seek to make amends with Kush and speak nothing but kind words, promise not to lay a hand on him and let him continue to rule over his realm, so that he makes a pact with us—and may he never break his pact. 9330 He will be secure against both us and the king, the king will not march another

3. This refers to a major episode in the Faridun cycle in *The Shahnameh*. Faridun has three sons: Tur, Salm, and the youngest, Iraj. While the three sons are traveling together, he turns himself into a dragon and confronts them, watching how each of them reacts—Salm demonstrates caution, Tur bravery, and Iraj wisdom. He then divides the world between them, with Salm being given Rum, meaning Rome and the west, Tur being given Turan, which includes the land of Turks and China, and Iraj being given Iranzamin. The two older brothers conspire to kill Iraj. Faridun grieves, but has a great-grandson by Iraj's daughter, named Manuchehr, whom he equips to lead armies and defeat Salm and Tur, restoring the rule of the rightful kings.

army against him. Besides, we and he are kinsmen, being Zahhakian on our mother's side.[4] If the king makes trouble for us, Kush can give us much assistance. And if he does not send troops to assist, then there is no quarrel between the Andalusian king and the king of Iran. He will not return or send reinforcements or support him."

Tur's suggestions seemed sensible, and the charismatic Tur had a letter written. The letter began, "From the mighty Tur and Salm to the great and worldly-wise Kush. Know, o renowned warrior king, that a conflict has arisen between the king and us. He treated us as he treated you, with dishonorable deeds and cold words. He has cast us out of those lands, sent one of us to the Turks and the other to Rome. 9340 To Iraj he then gave the throne and crown. The lucky fellow was pleased to accept them! And yet this evil was not enough for him: he then demanded tribute from both of us! How could he decide to make the youngest of his sons the greatest? When they show us the character of a leopard, we keep such shame far away from ourselves. We have rid the world of Iraj and made different arrangements. For our grandfather, Zahhak, in fetters, is bound by the leather of a lasso. You are our mother's kin, our uncle, and we would embrace you as kinsmen. We are of one mind in this matter, we want revenge against the malevolent king.

"When the mountain, plain, and cities are ours, we will divide the face of the Earth into three parts. The best part of the Earth will be yours, better than Iran, India, [the land of] Turk[s], and China. 9350 Keep whatever domains you have in the west, you will not obtain anything better than those.

"One partition will be Iran, China, and India, along with the land of Nimruz and Sind, which we will give to the commanding Salm. He will be their shepherd and the nobles his flock. The other partition includes the land of the Slavs and Rome, all the lands of the Turks, China, Taraz, the eastern lands, and Transoxiana too; this will be my portion of the world. The third part is Syria, Egypt, and Yemen, and all of the Arab lands to Aden. All of the west is yours.[5]

4. Up to this point, no mention has been made in the *Kushnameh* of Faridun's sons Tur and Salm having Zahhakian ancestry on their mother's side, however this is referred to again in line 9346.

5. Whereas in the *Shahnameh,* Tur and Salm took the eastern and western parts of the world, respectively, here Asia is divided between south (the first part) and north

"Do not think now that the young Salm has girded himself to wage war on you with his brave men. You suffered plenty on the field, but now those days have passed. We both had hearts bloodied with sorrow, we were all bound under Faridun. 9360 We had to follow his orders, but those days now have passed. Seize today, do not cling to the past, and accept our warm regards." They both placed their seals on the letter, and the envoy went to give Kush a portion of the earth.

When that speedy fellow reached Kush, he read out that letter. When he heard mention of those two sovereigns, you'd have thought his heart leapt with joy. He cheerfully called the envoy before him and gave him a seat of honor. First, he asked, "Are those honorable men in good cheer and in good health?"

The envoy said, "O world-seizing king, they are both amicable towards you." He then began to read out the letter.

A translation was read to the king. His face turned ruddy with joy and he called for cups and wine. 9370 They adorned the palace with fresh decorations and prepared quarters for the envoy. He spent a week with wine and song, to the satisfaction of the fortunate envoy.

On the eighth day he called for the scribe and seated him on his gold-chased seat. He prepared a good response, which opened with all manner of courtesies. "I am in agreement with what you have said, and I would not seek to trouble you any more. If the quarrel is with Faridun, I will aid you with treasure and troops. [239b] I would not begrudge you horses and equipment, nor proud men of war. So long as you keep my heart at ease, I will make all allowances for peace. Before my envoy . . . When your rule is secured, you shall not set any traps before me. 9380 You will partition the world in the manner you described, and ask nothing more of me."

He had these words written in musk and bore witness with his signature. "When you have done this, God is my witness that my soul, life, and treasure are yours." With that message he sent out his envoy, eloquent, learned, and clever. He gave those two inquirers gifts, and dirhams and dinars. They arrived before Salm and Tur where they ended their journey.

(the second part)—hence, China is mentioned twice—with southwest Asia and Africa, the third part, belonging to Kush.

Tur's envoy arrived before the throne and said to him, "O fortunate king, by your glory, we have performed our duty. Kush has answered to your satisfaction. He sent me back with a promise, that he may win your majesty's heart. He offers a righteous pact and agreement, for the wise do not seek a crooked pact." 9390

At those words, Salm and Tur's hearts were filled with worry that Kush would stray from comity. For he had suffered much from Salm, who had brought ruin to his army. He said, "I fear that something will happen with the king and trouble will arise."

They summoned Kush's envoy and seated him near the throne. Each of them asked him about the king, his heroes, his army, and his fortress. That most clever man conveyed to them the abundant praises spoken by Kush. When they read out the amicable words in the letter, you'd have thought they bloomed like fresh flowers. They prepared gifts for the envoy and raised his crown to the heavens. They swore a solemn oath before him, as the fortunate Kush had commanded. 9400 They added their signatures as well, and stamped their seals of gold upon it.

The lion-seizing king sent a scribe to go with the envoy, the wise and pure-witted scribe who had obtained the pact and oath from Kush. Those prisoners the king held, who had been taken on the battlefield, he sent back unharmed, giving them equipment and dun horses. When those noblemen came before Kush, he undid their heavy chains. His heart was pleased by Salm and Tur, and he celebrated his alliance with them for a week. He gave those prisoners many gifts, dinars and horses of Arabian stock. Those lands that they held were all returned to them.

When they had enjoyed wine for a week, Salm's envoy offered an oath. 9410 "Never wish them harm, and never think unacceptable thoughts. In times of difficulty, aid them, when they suffer humiliation, assist them. When they want, do not begrudge them your alliance, armies, treasure, and swords. And also, do not take the side of Faridun, give the enemy no assistance in any way."

They joined this covenant with their seals and the minister took the oaths of those haughty men. Then those nobles who were held captive he sent to Salm, young and old. The envoy returned from him, satisfied with the abundant garments and horses with golden trappings. When the prisoners reached Tur, they went from a dark dungeon into a celebration. Whatever nobles of Iran were among them, the mighty

Salm sent them to castles. To whoever was from Rome or the land of the Slavs, he showed great generosity. 9420

He returned happily from there to Rome and set to work dispensing justice and gifts. He now liberated the whole territory of Azerbaijan from his father. Tur went with his forces toward Salm and seized Khorasan from the king. The commanding Kush crossed the water and made all the lands of Syria and Egypt his own. He saw that this was the extent of his share, and took his share of booty from those lands.

Faridun became aware of this rebellion, he was contorted in worry and his joy cut short. He sent envoys calling troops from all directions, and spoke to Qaren and Nariman. The wise sovereign said to them, "I am most afflicted by my wicked sons. See what sorrows have fallen upon me! Old men would drink venom for my sake. I saw the dear head of the honorable Iraj severed and cast down. 9430 What could be worse than two bloodthirsty, wicked sons? Now, word has come from the priests that those evildoers have sided with Kush. They have divided the world into three parts, and my shepherds have scattered like flocks of sheep.

"If only you could place this burden upon yourselves, you'd make me grateful for your efforts. For if I, in my old age, were to don armor for battle, the priests would not approve. For days and nights I cry out before the creator, that he will allow Manuchehr to be unharmed, make him honored and raise up his throne, make his heart sharp and full of alchemy, and take revenge against those two for his father. Assemble troops so that the heavens' wheel is stained black from their dust. Give them whatever gifts there are, for they are our strength and our honor. 9440 Go find the worthless Tur and have him sawed in half."

Nariman and Qaren took off for Khorasan in the middle of the night. Tur was informed of their approach by all his runners; he had liberated Khorasan and was coming fast. He crossed the Oxus, and over smooth roads and rough roads, advanced toward Transoxiana. He called troops from Kush and the mighty Salm, and great armies came from all sides. Armies crossed plain, river, and mountain, all trampled flat by their horseshoes. He set up his tents on the field of Beykand, raising black dust higher than the moon. He set his eyes on the long road, for the commander of the Kayanid sovereign was coming.

Nariman and Qaren did not cross the Jayhun, waiting to see what the crowned sovereign would do and what his intentions were, what would come out of his commanding mind. 9450 A messenger was sent from the champion saying, "O king of alert and illumined spirit, when we rapidly advanced on Khorasan, we liberated it from Tur and his forces. We reached the Oxus and the enemy had crossed over to Beykand and camped there on an open plain. He has received armies from Kush and Salm, more numerous than the black gravel-stones. He has set up a camp on that field, their necks raised to the heavens' turning wheel. We await orders from our king. Shall we advance on him?"

The glorious Faridun saw it most fit to have Nariman take his place in that land. The vengeful swordsman, Qaren, should advance on Azerbaijan. When the response reached those honorable men, their hearts both accepted the sovereign's order. Qaren set off and left the champion there, his dust reached the turning heavens. 9460 The troops sent by the brave Salm were like wolves and lions in that land. When they caught the scent of a horse, they turned their heads like ravenous foxes. They cleared the land of the enemy completely, what few were left were put to the sword.

One marcher-lord with a great force was sent after Salm. From there, he went to Syria with his army, raising dust that hid the stars. In the same manner, he crossed the lands of the Arabs like a savage leopard chasing a deer. The plains and mountains were all under his command, and no one dared disobey that renowned man. He sent out a large detachment from the other side, a sharp-clawed dragon heading for Iran.

Then the steel-clawed Tur saw hesitation in Nariman. He knew that he had no heart for fighting, for he had nothing on his mind but rest and feasting. 9470 His troops were from the western lands, from Rome and other regions. He sent abundant horses and pack animals and garments and helmets along with his army, and led them from Beykand towards Bukhara, where he sat on his throne and chose to rest.

So it was until several years later, when Manuchehr raised up his neck like a cypress tree, taller than the moon. The king's heart was cheered by him. [240a] He girded himself to avenge the injury to Iraj, gathering his forces for many years. He opened up his grandfather's treasury and put gold in the laps of all his troops. A thousand thousands and three hundred thousand came to him, veteran riders. From Iran and India, from Nimruz and from the Arabs: a hero-slaying army.

On the day of the new year, he clad them one by one in steel. 9480 His troops were numerous like the clouds, like a fierce elephant, like a beast of war.

Tur received word, and Salm heard from him, that he was coming for revenge against both of them. Any thought of feasting now far from their hearts, sleep far from their heads, they left in haste. By the waters that I'd call hellfire, he would bring ruination to their happiness. They called out in all directions and rose up to call on Kush for assistance.

Kush sent them a number of troops that you'd have thought were racing upon the wind. The minister counted them, seven times a hundred thousand, young and old. The proud Kush sent a message with his steel-clad army: "You have set your hopes on me and I will fulfill them, now and in the future." Both of their hearts surged with cheer at the deeds and words of Kush. 9490

Both came to rest at the seaside, closing in on Manuchehr. A fierce cry rose up from both armies and the ground rumbled with the brave men's cries. Two armies, roaring on that bloody field, surely more numerous than the stars, they fought on for forty days as plain and valley were filled up with the dead and wounded. Manuchehr and Tur came face to face amidst that black dust. He raised his grandfather's mace over his neck and brought it down on the alchemical Tur's head. His elephantine body fell to the dust, his head and helmet and armor crushed.

Salm's heart was assailed by grief, he went wailing back to his tent. He spent all night consulting with his officers, gesturing at his feet with his fingertip, suggesting he retreat from the battle and take flight, that he might spare his life from the sword's edge. 9500

At the cock's crow, the roar of drums arose. The Tusked had come along with his army and sorrow fled Salm's heart at once. In happiness, his lips filled with a smile—you'd have thought the young Tur had come back to life. Because of Kush, he gained strength and his heart was cheered, and he went before that lion.

Kush asked, and he told him about the battle, that the renowned Tur was now one with the dust. Kush's heart sunk in grief for the brave Tur, and he thought long and hard. Then Salm's heart was cheered again.

Kush said to him, "O proud king, such is the nature of the turning heavens; it sometimes seeks fire, other times war; sometimes it gives a regal flame, and when it brings war it gives dust and humiliation. You must come to terms with that pain, and use wisdom to bind your sorrows. 9510 I want to avenge that honorable king and bring ruin to Iran."

Salm's heart was soothed and he collected himself. At dawn, the noise of trumpets and pipes rose up, and the armies engaged. They mixed the soil with brave men's blood. All day and all night, there was clashing of swords, the ground a bloody paste, the sky cleft asunder.

So it went on until the mighty Qaren let go his pride and joined the battle. For his pride had been his fortress, he raised his head from the sea to the sky. Qaren deployed a hundred stratagems—even a soaring vulture could not get past him.

Manuchehr was cheered at the sight of him, and explained to him what had come to pass. "With Tur's killing, the brave Salm became despondent and tired of battle, but he has regained much strength now that the demon-born has appeared." 9520

Qaren said to him, "O new king, he is grotesque and brave and fearless, a warrior. There is no man in the world with his strength, no one beneath the heavens is a match for him. I have fought him many times, and seen him in times of feasting. I defeated him and brought him in chains to the king, tied up like a sheep, over a pack animal. He is so humbled and aggrieved in your hands, like the notch of an arrow under your thumb."

Manuchehr said, "By the might of God, by the glory of the world-conqueror, pure of judgment, we will crush his head with our mace so that he will never see the Mountain of Cranes again.

When the day of battle came and they met on the field, he met that commanding leviathan. He knew that this was the haughty Kush, like fire in his attacks. Kush recognized Manuchehr, too—his garments and boots of gold. 9530

The two warriors engaged like a savage lion and furious elephant. They struck here with spear, there with blade, once on the head and other times on the torso. The laboring kings grew short of breath, the war-horses snorting fog. Then they took hold of their maces, and both were stunned by the heavy blows. The valiant Kush raised his heavy mace and struck the head and crown of the new king.

The weapon was heavy, and he struggled. When Kush drew away from him, he roared like the thunder of spring and struck him on the head with the bull-headed mace. The mighty Kush fell from his horse, springing away from it like a hungry wolf . . .[6]

Thus he raced toward his troops, taking the appearance of a ship's mast. The new commander was burning up, for now things had changed completely. 9540 Salm was thrown into confusion as the new king arrived, his troops following him. He was vexed by the shedding of his brother's blood, and having drawn blood, he had become bloodthirsty. The guide said to the king, "Those who are bloodthirsty will spill blood. Until you have spilled blood with your own hand, its odor is foul and its taste bitter as poison." By the seaside, he cut Salm in two, filling the Romans' hearts full of terror.

When the king had avenged Iraj, he took to the sea with his troops. He gave Qaren a mandate for Rome. All the eastern lands and territories, the lands of Turan, he gave to Shapur, showing him kindness and issuing him a mandate to rule. He and his proud men along with Nariman went to the land of Iran, free of worry.

The army in chaos, Kush charged ahead, his glory and wits lost to Manuchehr's blow. 9550 His bones were broken by the heavy mace, his heart and his fate in turmoil. His heart full of worry at King Manuchehr, he summoned his commanding army to his court. He went to the western lands and deployed stratagems, sometimes civility, other times war. He brought all the nobles under his command and ended their conflicts.

When Qaren learned about his situation, he raised an army and marched against him. The two armies faced off on the field, reaching for their blades and daggers. When they had fought for a while, Kush prevailed over the warlike Qaren.

Qaren retreated to Rome, his men without strength and horses without power. From then on, none of the kings within reach of Kush dared tangle with him. Qaren did not seek to fight him again, he had had enough of his violence and tricks. 9560

Kush's head grew drunk from a life of ease, and he turned his hands to injustice and ignorance. He had a daughter who was more radiant than sunlight. That daughter was born to a noblewoman the king of the Land of Beauties had given him. Limbs like flowers and a scent like

---

6. One or more lines may be missing here, as the topic abruptly shifts to Salm's battle with Manuchehr.

musk, her visage like jasmine, proud and impatient. Kush's heart was drawn to that face, without reservation, playing all manner of tricks.

Drunkenly one night he called her before him, and threw his sleeve around that beauty. The chaste woman declined to approach him. He grew despondent over his daughter and his wounded heart. Drunk, he cut off her head, cast it down, and said, "Since you do not come to us, may the dust be your companion!"

As his brain recovered from his drunken stupor, he was saddened by his own conduct. He wailed and lamented, and spoke of this matter to no one. 9570 Everyone fashioned an idol in her likeness—the west and Andalos in all these years never were known to be so idolatrous, all because of the twisted deeds of that drunken demon. He ruled in this manner until the reign of King Kavus, holding onto his throne.

The passage of time gave him such opportunities that he held the world in his grasp. [240b] Men and women accepted his rule. No minister or judge, nor anyone else in the world, knows to whom he was born, where his character and constitution came from. He never suffered a fever nor did his limbs suffer any pain, his hair did not turn white, nor did pain and longing take hold of him.

Then, from Beja and Nubia, a mighty man appeared, and his good fortune was ripped away. A brave man like an outraged, grieving elephant, his conduct all rebellion and tyranny: 9580 a youth who was a charismatic leader, with strength and cleverness and cultivation and judgment; that man sought to test his honor by seizing the commanding demon.

He raised an awesome army, appointing a number of officers. One was a champion by the name of Eridu, descendant of Noah, the prophet, through the line of Ham. He had a body like a camel and a white hide, his strength inspired fear and hope. The Nubians spoke much about him, they called him the White Demon. The men of that land had never seen anyone with such strength in times of battle and trials of honor. His upper body was like the branches of trees, his neck and shoulders like a savage elephant.

With the legendary White Demon, Arzhang and his sons, Ghandi and Bid, all champions, men of honor, rose up from Nubia in those days. 9590 An army gathered from plain and mountain—the heavens were astonished by it. An army of two million gathered for battle, each one of them like a tree in stature, all mighty, honorable men. In front of the center were Sanjah and Barbid, on the left and the right, Arzhang and the White Demon.

From Nubia they came, by way of Aswan, the horde surging like a flood. The hordes took over the west in its entirety, occupying the whole land. All of the marcher-lords packed their things and went to secure places. The Black Hordes crossed over the whole land, taking whatever they saw. They extended their hands in bloodshed and plunder, until they reached Raqqah.

When word reached the mighty Kush that such a great and mighty army had come, 9600 there was no worry in his heart, and he marshaled an army. He believed that their leaders were weak, like the others. He crossed the water with six hundred thousand men, veteran riders. He was not well informed about that peerless army covering the land like smoke.

Kush and his officers set up camp near the king of Mazandaran. When Sanjah saw this, he acted quickly; he sent a force toward them to block the way, and he marshaled his forces all over the field. When he formed a ring around Kush at night, no cry of drums, no commotion, he blocked every route of access, and ruin fell upon Kush's head from the sky. When the sky was effaced by blackness, the world was a torn garment of mourning. 9610 They engaged and fought for a while, mixing blood and dirt into grime. Left and right, front and back, officers took on the Black Hordes of Mazandaran.

Kush said, "My brave men, my honorable knights, my lions, this is no time for weakness, fight! Dress these foes in dirt!" The brave men took their lives in their hands, gripping tight their reins. The Black Hordes of Mazandaran unhorsed brave men with a single blow of their great staves. With all the hue and cry, the clashing of swords, Venus tore Mars asunder.

The White Demon engaged Kush in battle, behind him his sons and Ghandi and Bid, on foot, holding a wooden staff in both hands, striking down men and horses. No one made it out of the sharp claws of that fierce dragon alive. 9620 You'd think he had wrought sorcery, for iron had no effect on him. The commander, Kush, fought with him, his horse lacked the strength to stand up to him, and Kush had not the endurance. His men all turned away, leaving the commander helpless. The troops despaired of their commander—how could he escape the White Demon with his life?

When night fell, Kush returned with no strength left in his limbs. He departed with a body of troops, while others met their end. He went to Egypt and his army stayed there, and he granted several men domains there. He could not escape the terror of the Black Hordes, and his troubles increased.

He raced to King Kavus. They gave him entrance and showed him to the king. He kissed the foot of his throne and offered much praise to his fortunes. 9630 He praised his king and offered him prayers.

He said, "O exalted sovereign, there is no moon in the heavens like your face, no king on earth with your glory. I would guide you to a place that would increase your wealth and station. All its stone is emerald and gold grows from the soil instead of plants. Its warm season is not warm and its winter is not cold, people are protected from injury by its air."

He then took out emeralds and rubies by the hundreds and poured them out before his throne. "The kings and proud men have not seen even a marble's worth of those gems and wondrous things."

When King Kavus saw this he was taken aback, and his eyes narrowed before their brightness. He said to himself, "This country where gold grows like plants, and rocks are like this, I must see it with my own eyes, and rest my heart there for a while." 9640

He summoned both small companies and large, as greed and profligacy drew him toward that land. His army grew so massive that the surface of the earth was all steel, and mountainous. It numbered more than seven hundred thousand heroes and hero-killers. They set out on the path to Mazandaran, all of them perplexed. Kush went ahead of Kavus, his troops numerous and steel-clad.

From Iran to Egypt that Kayanid king traveled, and he spent a week in wine and song. There was a village some distance from the others, beside a river flowing between two mountains. People referred to it as Rif; its denizens were content and cheerful. The path crosses between two mountains whose slopes are of black rock. The length of that mountain is ten stages, all bare rock, with no dust or clay. 9650

He took King Kavus that way with those troops and renowned heroes, until he turned toward Aswan, seeking to seize those foes if he could. The army marched so hastily that a great part of his force was destroyed.

He breathed a tall tale to King Kavus and headed from Aswan towards Nubia. [241a] He ruined and razed those lands, obtaining much gold and gems. They killed many of the unfortunate ones who remained there without their menfolk—women and children. When Mazandaran's king became aware that Kush had marched there with that great army . . .

Those proud men remained helpless between two mountains, as if they'd lost their wits. The king and army saw such misery that they could not see the path, as if they were blind. The land of Iran fell into such turmoil because the White Demon had blinded that army. 9660 Everyone who had seen Kush or knew his reputation for vileness said, "He's a demon, how strange that King Kavus followed him, and marched his forces on Mazandaran. He is now blinded along with all his noblemen."

They remained until the crown-bestowing Rostam delivered them, arriving on his horse, Rakhsh. He came from Zavol, his heart full of pain, consigning the lives of the Black Hordes to the dust. Neither Sanjah remained, nor the White Demon, nor Arzhang nor Ghandi nor Barbid. Of that proud, peerless army, scarcely anyone returned home.

Know that the ancient tale-teller spoke many ciphers in this story. He said that the blood of the White Demon restored the king's hope of daylight. When that witless man was killed, the king was freed from the darkness. 9670 A wise man, when he considers what others have said, accepts it if it is not foolishness.

When Kush released those pillar-tumbling men, King Kavus emerged. Kush gave him many gems that could not be dug up by a gargantuan elephant.

Epilogue

Kush went to Andalos when he heard the news, now mighty and content. Soldiers turned to him from all directions, a mighty army gathered before him . . . His lands were under the direction of his minister, along with his servants and army. Sometimes for twenty years, other times for more or for less, that king of twisted creed disappeared.[1] And so it was that however long he was gone, no one transgressed his commands.

One day the king sat upon his throne and said, "O commanders of the army, I do not want anyone to call me king anymore: they shall only call me creator. 9680 The world has thus become manifest to me. Who would dare raise their head above my canopy? As long as the world is, I am its god, and if I wish, I can throw it under my feet. The apex of the turning heavens is my seat, all death and sustenance are my doing. When I am far from my lofty throne, do not say that I have met ruin. I have gone to another land that I would know its beauties from its evils. I guide those who have gone astray, I seize all who show enmity. When worldly events all reach their end, I shall sit in good cheer upon my great throne."

The nobles all spoke his praises and called him lord of the world. Many years passed like this, and no one transgressed his customs or

---

1. The implication here is that his rule was so unquestioned, his ministers could manage his affairs while he was absent and no one would consider disobeying them. This resembles the legend of Solomon: his subjects, including *jinn*s, did not know he was dead until a worm ate through his staff.

his commands. People all called him "god," the world was subject to his judgment and stratagems. 9690 May his mouth be filled with dust, he who does not recognize his own essence! He remained intoxicated in this way for many years, as long as hope remained immortal in his heart.

In his intemperance, he purged his heart of all kindness, more oppressive now than he was at first. Day and night, he secluded himself from human company, and spilled much innocent blood.

If anyone had any requests of him, they were never able to get an answer. "Do not bring this request to me, I do not grant your requests."

Whatever they said, he did not approve it, and his deeds were nothing but tyranny. He took whatever he wanted and made everyone suffer. He continued doing many such deeds for many years. The people hurt and suffered.

KUSH WISHES TO GO HUNTING

One day, Kush wished to go hunting and went out with his steel-clad riders. 9700 When the sun went down over the mountain, with cheetahs, dogs, falcons, eagle, and bow, his devoted and renowned soldiers brought in a lot of game.

A beast resembling a massive wild ass appeared before him, racing like a wolf. Its head like that of a steel-clawed lion, striped from head to foot with various colors.[2] When that fleet-footed gazelle with the gait of a cheetah, a falcon, a racing dog, became his game, you'd have thought Kush's heart had been marked with its stamp. Fleet-footed, he raced after it.

Upon one of those water-stock horses with legs of wind that the proud Tayhur had given him, all day and night he raced, leaping and dancing, but caught no sight of the wild ass's dust. The experienced Kush, in hot pursuit of the beast, raced through the wood like a gale. The ass slipped out of his sight, and let me tell you what wonders he saw. 9710

He wandered in the forest for a while, that he might find his way again. He became confused, the path did not appear again, for now the divine secret must be heard. Over the days he grew so thirsty, hunting

---

2. The beast thus described resembles a *qilin,* a fantastical creature from Chinese myth.

game at night; he lit campfires using arrow shafts and sticks of the forest. He made kebab from the legs of his game, he ate and slept when it was time for sleep. The felt of his saddle he used as warm bedding, putting soft vegetation under his head. So it went, for a great while— see that you do not cross fate! Everything is bound to its secrets, it is vast like a mine full of ruin.

Kush raced around that forest for forty days. He ran out of strength and endurance. Then one day, unexpectedly, he reached a hill and pulled on his reins to race towards it. 9720 He saw a beautiful palace upon it, rising above the black rock. The worldly-wise Kush announced himself at the door, "You must open the door for me!"

An elderly man with wit and stature came out, and looked upon the head and face and appearance of Kush. He said to him, "O Ahriman-faced man, who led you to my dwelling? What is your business? Where did you come from? Why did you enter this forest?"

"I am the creator who sustains all," Kush said. "The world's venom and sustenance all come from me."

The wise man laughed at what he said, and his unseemly appearance. He said, "O witless man, then what are you doing here?"

He said, "It has been more than forty days that I have been alone, separated from my army and company, having lost my way in this wood, apart from my throne and country." 9730

The man laughed at him again and Kush said to him, with pained heart, "Why do you laugh at me? Why this displeasing laughter?"

He said, "At your face and your appearance. Your words, too, are laughable. One moment you say, 'I am the lord,' the next moment you ask me for directions. Why does the creator who sustains the lives of men seek a path concealed from people? He shows the wayward ones the way, brings forth the night and day and sun and moon."

He said to him, "O elder of little wisdom, it has been more than seven hundred years that I, creator, have given sustenance. I am aware of all the world's doings."

The old man said to him, "Do not say such nonsense while you are still in this place. Who gives sustenance to those people? Who gives them goodness and happiness?" 9740

He answered, "There are a minister, many scribes, and a treasury, from which people's salaries are distributed; they dwell in splendid palaces because of my treasury."

The wise man said, "They should give you a portion of that food then, for here without your army or men, you have suffered much from not eating. Your strength has left you, left your ugly face and character. Now tell me, clearly, in those days when you were absent, o sustaining lord of men, who was there, you who believe evil things?"

He answered, "There were others, lords with crown and throne."

The elder said to him, "Where did they come from, why did they come to this dark world?"

He answered, "They were born unto men and women, each and every body." 9750

The elder said to him, "You who deserve evil, do not speak that which is unwise. It would not do for he who created the world to have appeared from a tight and narrow place. For, if he were like me and you—can you take the sky in your hands?"

Kush said to him, "O man of many words, you have disturbed my brain. If I do not give sustenance, what am I? If I am not lord of the world, what am I?"

"A slave," he said, "self-satisfied and vile, ungrateful to the core and far from paradise, a sinner, wayward, under command of a demon, heart straying from the path of the Lord of the world, beholden to the anger of the exalted Lord. Your place is in terrifying hell."

Kush said to him, "What are these things you say that would make whoever hears them cry?"

He answered, "O unfortunate one, we'll give you what you deserve all right. 9760 He created the world and us who created the peerless sky, placed there the moon and sun and uncountable stars. He made the earth and placed mountains upon it, gave it trees and flowing water. He made you king and commander upon the earth, gave you greatness, command, an army. He gave you such a life upon the world—and not just life but youth, so that you guide the servants of the Lord to his path. Whatever God gave you, o Ahriman, you take credit for, yourself. You have been ungrateful for these blessings. Alas, ingrate servant of the demon! If you got a fever, o speaker of nonsense, it would enter you like a narrow hair. [241b] You would find no one more wretched than yourself, more helpless or sorrier. 9770 In such a helpless, impotent state, do you think that all of a sudden you'd be able to play god?"

He said to him, "O foolish old man, I have lived a thousand years, and no fever ever afflicted my body, I have not suffered in pain even one night. If I am a slave like others, would my body not have suffered pain?"

The old man said to him, "O foolish man, who blessed you thus? You have lived in ease and thus grown intoxicated, that you say, 'I am the creator of the world.' Now, if you are the lord, go, return home, I have had my fill of stale words."

Kush was troubled, embarrassed by his words, he spurred on his horse and left ashamed and humbled. When he had traveled a while through the wood, he began to worry, his befuddled mind filled with anxiety. "If there were any inhabited place here, this old man would not speak these outrageous words. 9780 Surely he has been here a long time, laboring away. He must know the way to civilization. I have no guide. If I return to him like this, it will not trouble him. It would not do if I were unable to find this house again, unable to find this route again! If I were to perish in this forest, what would this man care about my disappearance? I have no way to leave this place, there is nothing for me to do here but run around. I will do whatever it takes to get this old man to deliver me from evil."

He turned around and went to the door of the mansion. He presented himself before the learned elder, and when he called for him, the elder appeared on the roof and said, "O callow man, benighted of heart, what happened to you that you turned around, that you did not go back to your throne?" 9790

He said to him, "O man of pure judgment, do me a good turn and show me the way. What would it trouble you to help me, to let me out of this forest?"

He said to him, "This is not something that can be heard, I do not know how to show the way to the lord. If I were to show you the way out of this bewilderment, I would be lord and you my follower. If you are the lord, o dimwitted one, why do you not remove your tusks and ears? You ought not have been constituted this way, but since you created them, you must be able to cut them off! With such a face and such tusks and ears, you look like a devil, o dimwitted one!"

He said to him, "Listen carefully—such nonsense you speak! Since my fundamental nature is this, how could I not follow a foul creed? I would be satisfied if I had no treasure and my heart did not suffer from this ugliness!" 9800

The elder said to him, "O destitute lord! Now that you put aside your nonsense words, I will obliterate this ugliness from your face, if you spend some time here with me. As the rust is cleansed from your heart, I will scour it until you learn righteousness. I will show you your guide, the world-creator, your Lord."

Kush was at a loss to respond to the old man's words. His speech soothed his heart. He said to him, "O comforting fellow, your words bring life to my heart. If you obliterate foulness from my heart, I shall be eternally subservient to you. I do not wish to be lord of the world. I will worship, openly and in private."

He answered, "Without a doubt, when I am freed from time's grasp, I will make the evil marks on your face harmless, in a way far different from what you have accepted. 9810 I will illumine your heart and soul and make wisdom the armor for your body. When you open both organs of sight from your heart, I'll show you your creator. Then I will send you on your way home, if evil fate does not intervene."

Kush was cheered by his words and quickly dismounted his horse.

The elder came down from the roof quickly, opened the door of his house and came outside. He received Kush warmly, praised him, and said, "May wisdom be your pure soul's companion, you must not worry about anything, for I have granted your request. But do what I demand, that I may scour the rust from your heart."

He set aside his weapons and tied up his horse, and applied the medicine to his face. He gave him nothing but fruits to eat. This nourishment deprived him of his strength. 9820 Kush's body grew emaciated, like one intoxicated. He fell ill, became humbled and despondent. You would think that hope had departed his soul, and his body trembled like a willow in the breeze.

The elder said to him, "O head of the company, how can you recognize yourself? Where now is your presumption of godhood, your pride, your grandeur, honor, and willfulness? Where now is your greatness and treasure and army, your high-starred crown and throne? Now they have left you all at once and your body has been humbled and strained."

He answered, "O honorable one, I see no one more lowly than myself. Without strength, ability, and power of body I see no one in the world like myself."

He said, "Then are you a slave, if you are the lord? Are you a seeker if you are the guide?"

He said, "There is no lowlier slave than me, there is no one as lowly and disgraced as me. 9830 I understand now that I do not yet know the world-creator."

Then, that learned elder, by means of his judgment and skill, worked his remedy upon him. He fashioned his two teeth and two ears anew, using medicine and a file to make them the right size. He gave him food and his body gained strength, his face took on a bright new coloring. After that, he set out upon the path of knowledge and his heart brightened with his learning.

He studied for ten years and the elder illumined his soul through writing. At once, he knew medicine and the lofty heavens' secrets—he knew all as it was. Strategy and talismans and other sorceries, he became skilled in them all. He showed him the many paths to God the exalted, and filled his heart with fear of the inferno.

He said to the learned man, "O exalted fellow, your knowledge and kindness have brought me life. 9840 What I saw was not game but a messenger angel sent from beyond the creator's veil. He brought me here in darkness, to drive confusion from my heart. Until I have learned everything from you, I shall not leave this place."

He spent forty-five years there, suffering great travail. When no knowledge remained hidden from him, the worldly-wise elder addressed him.

He said to him, "Now you wish to leave me, to leave this gathering, for if you have life left to live, you will not die without making a name and leaving behind descendants."

He said, "I wish, if you would approve, that you do me this kindness. For this, I am most grateful to you, for it was you who made me pure, a worshiper of God."

He replied, "Now you have the seven treasures—and I do not know an eighth. 9850 You have learned from me from the start that each one is truly an overflowing treasure. If you put these seven lessons into practice, you will receive the blessings of both worlds. Now that you are endowed from this abode, you will also find the Lord's paradise."

Kush said, "By your glorious command, who would dare depart from your message? I will practice everything you tell me. I will not transgress your command or your judgment."

The elder said to him, "First, now, you must practice this correctly: since you and I have a creator, he is our Lord in every respect. Since there is a Lord, we are his servants—we are all servants of the creator. Be in bondage to his command, observing the path of devotion. Render unto him thanks, not ill character, for he has bestowed upon you these blessings. 9860 For he created being from nothingness, and brought life to it. He gave you two eyes, ears, and a tongue, a soul to watch over your physical form. Better, then, that you render thanks for these blessings. Know truth in your heart."

Kush heard the words of the learned man and was pleased by them, and heeded them immediately. "I will forsake my old ways, I am ashamed of the terrible things I said. That hot air is gone from my brain, I shall now seek servitude."

The learned elder said, "Now know that men do not last eternally. This is how the world must be, know that your end will come. [242a] There is a narrow path ahead, when you tread it there is another world beyond. The creator rewards every good and ugly deed with verdant paradise or raging fire. 9870 When you manifest ugliness you receive its recompense, you get back whatever you did. Better, then, to carry those worthy seven treasures into this world and the next, that you enter the next as well. For people of this essence are human, otherwise they are lacking in humanity. If one is lacking humanity, they have not the essence of manhood.

"Know wisdom, for wisdom's crown is loftier than the sun that adorns the lands. Wisdom is the watchman over soul and body and would not suffer being fooled by wicked demons, for it knows the creator measures out the recompense for your life's deeds, to body and soul. It eschews foul deeds and conduct and delivers the spirit unto verdant paradise.

"The second precious jewel is learning, whose companion is comfort. Learning is the route to wisdom, which would not suffer being fooled by wicked demons, 9880 for it recognizes the sum of all learning and fears retribution. The deceitful demon does not lead to knowledge, nor does he who harbors ill will for the Lord of the earth.

"The third is cleverness, from which wisdom is begotten; it becomes apprised of all matters good and bad. When it is apprised of the measure, the shortcomings of any thing, it knows their causes.

"The fourth jewel is righteousness most good, for righteousness is more precious than a jewel. When your words are righteous, and your deeds too, your path will be straight, as will your speech. Your spirit will be satisfied by that righteousness, and people's hearts be at ease.

"I will now speak of the fifth, purity, which keeps contamination away from a person.

"The sixth is kindness. Whoever is kind opens his mouth in pleasantness and goodness. One with a good heart always wants for others what he wants for himself, lest he be embarrassed. 9890 He begrudges no kindness to anyone and is reluctant to wound a dog with his blade.

"The seventh is justice and nobility, by these two qualities the land sees prosperity.[3] Of these two, it is by nobility that you can travel any road you wish. Whoever does not practice all of these, it is as if there is a fissure in the wall of their castle. Their humanity is lacking, and people's hearts are not pleased by them. When you return from the forest and my domains, hold onto my words, my advice." In addition to this knowledge, he gave him several tomes. Kush was cheered by his books and his learning.

When the world turned the color of smoke, he showed him a bright star. He said to him, "Follow this star, camp during the day and travel by night. Struggle through the forest for a week, and it will not be twenty-five days 9900 before you reach prosperous lands—you'll be with throne and crown again. Do not give yourself over to the demons, for the divine does not depend on us."

Kush said to him, "O most righteous, we have an affair left to settle. Tell me why you came here, from whom is your lineage, where did you come from?"

---

3. These seven jewels may be contrasted with the seven treasures listed in the dialogue between Salkot and Kamdad, line 4380: wisdom *(kherad)*, good nature *(khim)*, hope *(omid)*, skill *(honar)*, religion itself *(din)*, contentment *(khorsandi)*, and a pure creed *(ray-e dana)*. Here, on the other hand, we have: wisdom *(kherad)*, learning *(danesh)*, cleverness *(hush)*, righteousness *(rasti)*, purity *(paki)*, kindness *(mehr)*, and justice and nobility *(dad, azadegi)*. The discrepancies are far too great to be transcription errors. Two possible explanations, which are not mutually exclusive, are that Iranshah was drawing on two different sources that contradicted each other, and that he did not consider the exact content or wording of the virtues to be critical—contrary to the insistence in both statements that there are exactly seven treasures and no eighth one—and even wanted to draw attention to the unreliability of ancient texts. That the final, "seventh" treasure in the second list is both justice *and* nobility supports the second explanation. See introduction for further discussion.

The learned elder answered, "My story you will not find pleasing. My ancestry is from the lineage of Jamshid, for his eldest son advised me, 'Do not set your heart on this fleeting abode, its drink is poison, its fruit rotten.[4] Labor for knowledge, it is better wherever knowledge's fruit obtains. Your labor is for that eternal world, this one is but a fleeting abode. If you desire a woman, seek a woman from an honorable lineage, o clever one. 9910 When a child is born, soon they must be made to let go their mother's skirts, gird themselves before the exalted divine, and be reverent with hope and fear. He who has no desire for wife and children strays far from people and company, takes up a corner of the world for himself and venerates the divine all his life.'

"I am one who has gone even farther, my body has melted away as you see. From what city? It is called mourning. I came and made this place my abode. I strayed far from my companions and city, that my wisdom might overcome my discontent. From here to that city is a ten-day journey, all deep forest and running water and greenery. For so many years, my companions, people of pure creed, come to me and ask for me to share my learning. My business, my secret, is only this." 9920

Kush then kissed the sage's hand, kissed his two cheeks, shoulders, and ears. Night fell, he mounted his dun horse and set his eyes on the star. He raced like the leopards in the nighttime, and when day came he went to sleep.

When twenty-five days had passed, he left his troubles behind in the city of Havareh. It had been six and forty years since he had left; you'd have thought the world was asleep and taking a respite from his terror. The nobles of those lands, the lands of the west, the land of the Slavs, and Rome, had no rest from fear of the blade of that warmonger. His treasury had collected tribute and his minister had labored for him over the years.

He struggled along the road to Havareh and made for Qorbit, which he had founded. He summoned the nobles of that city and explained everything to them. 9930 "I am truly your sovereign, kinder now than I was before. I went and reached a man of God, and learned

---

4. The hermit is thus the descendant of Jamshid's son, Farak, as was Mahanesh, the sage on the mountain encountered by Alexander in the second frame tale—see lines 740–860 for the story of Farak's exile.

soul-enlightening knowledge. It gave me dominion over the whole world, including the western lands. That colorful chase yielded me no wild ass. It was a divine messenger come from the creator. He called me to him, that I became an intimate of the threshold of that sovereign. He removed the ugliness from my face and illumined my heart with knowledge."

He spoke much, and people did not believe him. They turned to Qobta, who was the minister governing his lands, his armies under his command. When Qobta came, he looked on him with kindness. No longer was his conduct that of the demon-faced.

He was astonished and said, "O warrior knight, if you are Kush, that renowned sovereign, 9940 there are many secrets of the ways of the world between me and Kush. I will ask and if you answer correctly, you will wear the crown as king."

He asked him about a number of secrets, and he answered them one by one. He told him about all those things that were kept unknown to him. Then he told him about what he had experienced, the secrets of the exalted sage.

Qobta pressed his face to the ground and the troops all cried out his praises. They placed the encircling honor on his head, and the sovereign went toward Gibraltar. Envoys went to every land with a letter for every high noble. He called them all from where they were, they came and presented themselves before him. So much treasure came to him that there was no room left in his great palace. 9950

Then he refashioned those idols just as the learned elder had refashioned him. He then said before his courtiers, "Our subjects, men and women, you must first and foremost supplicate God. Supplicate him first, only then supplicate us, for he is the creator and I his viceroy. It is to him that you, and I, answer." Those lands all became God-worshiping, and the world was delivered from the grasp of twisted demons. The kings and the men of the army all accepted that letter obediently.

And so King Jabolq, to whom he sent the letter, said, "I am delighted that the king of the world has come to God and seen him in his heart. Now that he has understood God's decree, all of his deeds are good, and he is beneficent to the people—far from him, crookedness and ill will! 9960 I have in my heart a request of the beneficence of the king of the world. If, firstly, he would demonstrate his celestial knowledge, so that I can know for certain, then I and my descendants would praise that proud one, as long as they remain on Earth!

"Could he comfort that worthy subject whose domain is in the west? For they are in fear of the ants! They are ensnared by suffering and catastrophe! Know, o proud and rightful king, that there, where the sun hides beneath the earth, all the lands suffer from the ants. [242b] They come like racing cheetahs, bulky and bigger than dogs! They tear into man, woman, child, and livestock, then return whence they came. Were the king to remove this source of injury, the ants, were he to apply his labor, schemes, and strength, 9970 much land would immediately become verdant and forever a tribute to the king."

When the experienced Kush read the letter, he immediately led his army to the border. He saw a country that was like a whole world of plentiful trees and flowing water, all given over to the ants, its soil torn up by those animals. It was turned into a hell. And so from Rome and from the eastern lands, the wise one brought men of renown. He brought people who would work their schemes, and secured provisions for them from the surrounding lands. They answered his call and found a way there from all over, finally giving the king the means to do something.

He brought men from city and countryside. One man cut a trench to where the ants were, he dug thirty leagues to the water of the sea. The diggers undertook the digging quickly, they dug it a hundred spans wide, drawing water from the sea. 9980 Upon it, for the scheming king, they built a bridge, long and wide, of stone and lead, so that no harm would come to it from wind and rain. Another horseman, whose face looked like the shining sun, filled the middle with sulfur and black oil.

The king, who knew mineralogy, waited until the time was auspicious, until the opportune moment. He carried out his scheme, lining up horsemen across the path. It was as if there was no longer a way for even one man to cross the bridge. If one were to rub one's hand over that rampart, if a spark shot from it, a fire would light with such fury that it would burn up even a mountain.

Nearby, the sovereign, fearing its harm, brought a very long torch 9990 and placed ten brave men there. When they were in position, he ordered the army to draw up ranks.

When the ferocious ants became hungry again and returned, their bellies empty and rumbling, they came charging at that commander like lions and wolves. When they reached the trench, there was only one way to cross! The edge of the trench was black with ants. They sought a way across and found the bridge, hurrying right over it. They approached the horses and riders, thinking they had found their prey.

One by one they threw themselves at the men, like wolves, their jaws wide open. As the sulfur and oil received them, it was as if the whole world caught fire and went up in smoke. When the fire overcame the ants with its power, then what power could the ants have? In twisting tongues of flame they burned up by the thousands and thousands. 10000 The bridge became inky black and its stink spread for leagues. Some of them were taken by the deep water and the ones that returned died along the way.

The king thus removed the ants from that land and returned after two months. The land was lush and verdant, and the king was forever honored there. When King Jabolq became aware of this, he gathered up treasure and raced off. He came to Kush with his army and, softly, rubbed his face upon the warm earth.

He said, "This is surely knowledge divine, to turn away from it would be unwise!" He took some food back to the army and the king was his guest for a month.

This wondrous talisman remains in place, uncorrupted by springs and autumns in the place where Aries's mansion is veiled in wondrous color by the sun: 10010 the worldly-wise say that near here you can see a river running across the land that you can cut across in a ship—who ever saw such wonders from water? Saturday nights that water rises up in its place, not an inch over the top. When Sunday comes it returns—thus is the behavior of that channel of water.

When the king and troops were preparing to return, King Jabolq kissed the ground. He said to him, "O king of noble character, everything is done here, but I have one wish. There is a lovely countryside in my lands, its people are like lions. Every year, they suffer from lack of water. They receive no water but rainfall. Would that by the glory of the knowledge-seeking commander, a water source could be found by the mountain. The lands would grow prosperous and I would be cheered. The people's hearts would be relieved of grief. 10020 This is my heartfelt request. Your name would remain on earth for eternity.

When the proud Kush heard this, he marched his troops in that direction. He saw a village like a mirage, its plains and valleys and hillsides all dry. In every part there were six villages twice over; the people in each village were all impressive. Each of those villages was like a city with markets, districts, and streets. That was the place that was short on water, without the shade of gardens and canals.

He made a flood of reservoirs, from which young and old have drunk for many years. Near them was a steep mountain upon which snow was never seen. Its peak climbed above the black clouds and paths climbed up there from the countryside.

He built a solid, round, brazen box and erected a wondrous fountain as well. 10030 He placed a steel lock upon it that no one could open by any means. When Kush had finished doing that, he then dug a canal to each village. He then had a place prepared for that deep box upon the black mountain. It remained there until the sun crossed Aries. He then took an astrolabe and said, "In the name of the Lord, without peer or companion!" That triumphant king fixed the box firmly there with his own hands.

After a while, water shot out of that box toward the sky, and the obedient king was pleased. It spilled into the canal and flowed toward the villages, pleasing the king, officers, and nobles. Two mills were driven by the water, devices of that alchemical king. 10040 He then had that deep well in the mountain tightly shut—he had placed it where it was completely unreachable.

The king then allocated the water to flow for one night and one day to each village. They set watchmen over the box to protect it from men and demons, lest the lord of that land be of wicked creed. People flock to all of those villages in droves like shepherdless herds.

One by one, the reservoirs all fill, making water race through the fountain. They shake its lock three times, in the name of the peerless Lord. The lord of the village is most pleased by whoever mentions its water. Having placed the box, he set off with his troops, saying nothing but God's name all night and day. 1050

Traveling through the desert, he reached a place where he saw standing water. People who approached it were bewitched and grew weak. With helpless hearts and bodies unsound, they fell into fits of laughter and plunged into the water, falling unconscious like corpses. When Kush found out about this, he hurried to see the water and quickly pulled people out.

A crier called out to the army, telling them, "Take care around this water. Do not ever drink this water, to drink it is to pull a burial shroud over your head."

He ordered that they pull the dead out of the water quickly, and when the north wind blew on them, they came to—who has ever seen such a thing? Whoever had grown heavy became light again, their color and form better than before. 10060 All weakness and pain left them, people who were close to death became like revelers in a party.

He ordered that anyone in Andalos weak of body, bewitched, or missing a hand or foot be taken to that water, so that they would wash their bodies with it and be quickly restored. He inscribed his name over those pools. Only he and heaven could create such things!

Solomon passed by one day and saw all those peerless pools. He ordered that his vizier, Asef Barkhiya, who knew alchemy, [243a] build a city there, with much toil, and place all his treasure in it. He built its walls around the water, its battlements rising above the clouds. It was built with such technique that no one knew how to open its door. Anyone who climbs over its wall falls into fits of laughter, 10070 and they tumble headfirst into the city. No one knows how or why this happens. They are never seen again on earth, and no one knows the secret of this. Whoever passes through its door, their head is stunned by the barking of dogs.

Kush set out from that place and took a tour of his kingdom. He reached the city of Zorosh [Torrox] at the seaside, he found it a prosperous and verdant city. He built a dome there, eighty yards across, of cut stone, with no wood or plaster. He built a crystalline idol there with his own face, placed in that dome by his greatness. He made a chandelier of crystal and by a certain device gave it a small amount of oil. When they suspended it from the ceiling of the dome and poured oil into it, a fire ignited on the ground and burned like a lit candle. 10080 When the sun crossed the arc of Aries, it would suddenly light up the place of rest. And so it went, until the world was filled with gardens, and the sun shone through Cancer.

Alexander reached that idol and broke it, but did not lay a hand on that chandelier. The chandelier and the dome remain, autumn and spring have brought them no harm.

Another city is of pure silver, in the likeness of an eagle, its head in the clouds. Its measure cannot be taken, it is a great talisman and an astonishing place. A fine *simorgh* is situated there, built upon it.[5] Whoever would reach that city from any direction must travel ten days across desert sands. It is called Eram, and no one has seen anything like it. It is located somewhere between here and Andalos, neither friend sees it nor foe. 10090 Its trees are all of gold and their fruit rubies, their leaves all shining emeralds. Its ground is covered in bricks of gold and silver, its blossoms coral and pearls. Wine and milk flow in streams, and honey, too—who could build such a thing besides the world-creator?

He also founded a city beside the deep sea with an astounding marketplace. One must travel eight hundred leagues from Chang'an to reach it. Its founder gave it the name Maruq, its people are all in good cheer, all their roofs have a bony covering resembling the scales of fish. Any king who sought that city with the intent of oppression and plunder found his life cut short—this is what people with great magic built.

A four-columned chamber near the city provides antidotes for that city's poisons. 10100 Its walls are built of pure gold, no wood or stone or brick or shell. It has four gates of gold. Two face east and west. The third faces south and another north. Three doors they have kept shut since those times. The fourth door is the one that its ruler, Arshuy, kept open over the years. He placed a number of men to stand watch there, for fear of harm and ruin.

When they want cool wind and air, they slightly open the gate to the east. When the watchmen open it, wind and cold air blow from it quickly. In the season of fruits, the warmest time of year, the country has this at its disposal and receives a gentle breeze. They then open the door to the west, and fruit and victuals come through. In the spring rainy season, the door is available that brings radiant sunlight. 10110 The skies open up and rain upon everyone frequently. The sage says that Mahang, ruler of China, founded it. Others say that the former Kush built it, but no one remembers those days. No one knows but he who is possessed of secret knowledge; he knows the secret and no one else.

---

5. The *simorgh* is a wondrous, mythic bird—the king of birds. This evidently refers to a statue.

There are two mountains in Africa, too, one with a low peak and another high. He ordered that between the two mountains, a learned master be brought. The wise Kush built another talisman—drink up these stories, learn them! On two sides, with two high minarets, it rises to the lofty stars. One is higher than one hundred and sixty yards. One is thirty yards shorter. From those towers, obedient water shoots forty yards into the sky like an arch. 10120 From the other minaret water spills rapidly out below. Thirty villages he founded around that water, each of them like a city—greater, even. A number of people from Efriqiyeh remember these as having been built by Efriqos.[6]

And so, the mighty, worldly-wise Kush abandoned his wicked ways, his wolf-like temper. When he turned to this manner of kingship, every mountain and plain was under his command. Tax and tribute came from every land, he received a treasure hoard every month. He returned to Córdoba from the west and sat in peace and good company. He did not lay a hand on others' things, nor get mixed up with women and children. If any of his subjects sought justice, he dispensed justice between the two individuals. He stayed far from malevolent evil for all those years, and his subjects were happy.

6. The deeds of Kush, including the fountains and talismans he created after his repentance and transformation, are similar to wonders listed in works such as Qazwini's *Wonders of Creation* (*'Aja'eb al-makhluqat)*—except of course that here Kush is credited with creating them.

INDEX

Abaqa, 15

Abbasid, 8–9, 12–13, 15, 22–23

Abraha, 55

Abraham, 172 n, 14, 175, 327

Abtin, 6, 12–13, 17–18, 20–22, 26, 29, 73, 78–86, 88, 90–95, 98, 102–4, 106–9, 111–16, 119–28, 130–31, 133–36, 138, 140, 147–49, 151–57, 161–85, 187–94, 207–12, 219–22, 229–30, 234, 241, 282

Adam, 64–65, 129, 213

Aden, 374

affection, 97, 99, 101, 107, 110, 137–38, 161–62, 165, 174, 176, 183–84, 196, 208, 215–16, 277

Afghanistan, 9–10, 13, 15, 22n53

Afrasiyab, 43 n. 7, 195

aggrieved, 177, 200, 212, 242, 380

agreement, 53, 102–3, 171, 222, 372, 375–76

Ahmad-e Tabrizi, 3

Ahriman, 37, 105, 146, 180, 199, 203, 208, 301, 389

ahukht, 202

Ahura Mazda, 193, 317

'Ajalaskas. *See* Jaca

Aries, 38, 399

Al-Biruni, 4–5

Alborz. *See under* mountain

alchemy, 104, 181, 308, 311, 377, 379, 401

Alexander the Great, 1, 7, 10, 16–17, 19–21, 26, 42, 59 n. 13, 61–64, 66, 73–74, 78n, 396n, 401; romances, 1, 3, 7, 10, 14, 18, 20n, 59n13, 61, 247

Alhom, 211

'Ali b. Abu Taleb, 8

'Alids, 24–25

alley, 129, 153, 161, 184, 297, 322, 346–47

alliance, 163, 168–70, 220, 222, 229–30, 308, 376

Amazigh, 24, 314n, 323n

ambergris, 126, 128, 164, 175, 184, 280, 341

ambush, 86, 90, 133, 189, 260–61, 263, 274, 289, 368, 370–71

Amir Khosrow of Delhi, 1–2

Amol, 29, 187–88, 246, 248, 275, 286, 304–5, 310

ancestor, 6, 11, 13, 22, 42n5, 49, 67n7, 73, 117, 127, 134, 166–67, 219, 229–30, 243, 245, 247n, 305, 321, 341, 347, 362

Andalos, 17, 21, 312, 312n10, 313, 325, 341, 350, 353, 369, 371–72, 382, 387, 401–2

Andarzname-ye Bozorgmehr. *See* Testament of Bozorgmehr

Andiyan, 356–57

Andreas, 56–58

angel, messenger, 119, 159, 178, 283, 292, 393